FALLEN REALM

SKIES OF CYRNA BOOK 2

MORGAN K. BELL

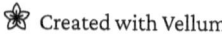

For families, those we're born to and those we choose.

PREVIOUSLY, ON SKIES OF CYRNA...

No one on the crew of the skyship *Phoenix* could figure out why Captain Xander hired Dorian Valmont. Awkward, clumsy, and woefully out of shape, the young scholar seemed poorly suited to the rigors of life in the sky. But Dorian Valmont had a secret. As son of the renowned adventurer Cyrus Valmont, and bonded host to the demon Hematite, Dorian had access to the research Cyrus hid from the rest of the world — dangerous arcane lore that could save the world's faltering magic, or destroy it once and for all.

Dorian's ambitious stepfather Janus Callahan would stop at nothing to get his hands on those spells. Forced to flee for his life, Dorian took his chances on a life in the open skies on the skyship *Phoenix*, with his father's old friend Xander Kane at the helm.

Dorian's first flight on the skyship was an unmitigated disaster. When Callahan and his soldiers attacked them riding dragons, a feat not seen in over a millennium, Dorian's own lack of flying skill was nearly their downfall. Worst of all, Callahan's pursuit meant that Dorian's problems were now the rest of the crew's problems, too. Despite all that, however, Dorian slowly began to form friendships with the rest of the crew, particularly with prickly-but-hard-working Tai, a winged Orith from beneath the underclouds.

To seek help evading their enemies, Captain Xander took the crew to visit his old friend, an archaeologist working in a crumbling old fortress in the deserts of Thlarknia. There, Dorian met someone he didn't expect — the dragon Solaris, with whom he unknowingly formed a bond.

Solaris narrowly escaped an attack on her dragon clan, during which her friends and family were taken into slavery by Callahan's forces. Solaris knew the only way to rescue her kinfolk was to form a spirit bond of her own. Unfortunately, she wound up with Dorian, who was as clueless as he was incompetent.

Dorian had to get stronger if he wanted to have a chance at stopping Callahan and saving the dragons. After enlisting Tai to help him get in shape and teach him how to fight, he began to train in earnest, and over time, he learned the art of sword fighting as well as improving his flying skills. Eventually, he even managed to free several of the enemy's dragons.

Dorian soon reunited with his estranged half-brother Bradford Callahan, who led a rebellion against his power-hungry father. Together, they managed to capture another of the enemy dragonauts. Unfortunately, their captive carried a hidden signal beacon, which led the enemy forces straight to their doorstep.

Bradford and Captain Xander believed they could find help and refuge with the Order of the Silver Dragon, a secret organization. Before they could escape, however, an enemy dragonaut set their main aether sail on fire. The demon Hematite sacrificed his own life to create a clear path through the clouds, allowing the *Phoenix* to make a rough but survivable landing in the forests of Toreen, on the planet's surface. The *Phoenix* itself was damaged beyond repair, but all crew save for Hematite survived.

Dusting themselves off as best they could, the crew of the *Phoenix* and Bradford's surviving rebels made the trek to Cloudfire

Mountain, where they would meet with the Order of the Silver Dragon and begin the next chapter in their fight against Callahan.

CHAPTER ONE
CLOUDFIRE

After two days' uphill slog through the rain, the last thing Tai Lunstrum wanted to see was a thrice-cursed angry mob.

The bedraggled crew of the skyship *Phoenix* stumbled up to the gates of Cloudfire Castle, wanting nothing more than a bath and a hot meal. Instead, what they found was an unruly crowd of winged Orith and wingless Aerish, buzzing like a swarm of angry wasps. Tai heard distinct cries of "Waited for days!" and "You can't do this."

"Looks like trouble," her former captain, Xander Kane, said with a frown.

Zachary Falgar grinned and rubbed his hands together. "Thank the Ancients for that. Things were getting way too peaceful and boring."

"Falgar." Their other former crew-mate, Jakob Sullivan, rolled his eyes. But he smiled, too, and took Falgar's hand in his.

"We traveled all this way from Westveil," complained one of the Orith in the crowd. "Let us pay our respects!"

The gate guard, a pinch-faced, harried-looking young Aerishman, crossed his arms. "As I have said, you are free to pay your respects at the temple. But Cloudfire Castle is closed to visitors."

"Never mind them, it's us who deserve to be let in," came a familiar, bullish voice.

Tai and the others exchanged excited glances.

"That's Graigor Beckett's voice," Dorian said. He sounded equal parts relieved and apprehensive — he and Graigor had never especially gotten along.

But if one member of Lord Bradford's rebellion had survived, then that meant there might be others. Tai scanned the crowd, and with delight and relief noted several faces she recognized. However, just as many were conspicuously absent.

"Thank the Gods you're safe." Lord Bradford Callahan rushed to the front of the crowd. Tai had to hand it to the man. The pampered nobleman had struggled more than most on the two-day hike, but even exhausted and mud-splattered, he put on a regal bearing. "What's happening here?"

"It's been days, and this man still won't let us in." Graigor crossed his burly arms and jutted out his chin.

"The Lady of Cloudfire said that there are to be no visitors," the guard repeated.

"Believe me, sir, Lady Sylvia will want to see *us*." Bradford puffed out his chest with all the lordly arrogance he could muster. "I am Viscount Bradford Tiruvian Callahan, Lord of Frostvale and son of—"

"I know whose bloody son you are." The guard massaged his temple. "Bloody void. I think you might understand why I'm reluctant to allow Janus Callahan's whelp into our hallowed halls."

"Now wait just a thrice cursed minute." This time, it was Xander's turn to elbow his way forward. "Jameson? Jameson Russel?"

The guard raised his eyebrows in surprise, but his expression quickly gave way to smugness. "Xander Kane. By all the gods and Ancients. You got old."

"You ... didn't." Captain Xander frowned.

Xander was right. The guard, Jameson, didn't look any older than his mid twenties. She eyed him curiously, noting his jaded demeanor in contrast to his youthful appearance. He dressed immaculately in a uniform of white and gold, unmarred by the dusty city streets. And around his neck he wore a familiar looking pendant — a silver dragon clutching a pearl-white stone.

"You're a dragonaut," Tai blurted without thinking.

Jameson recoiled as if he'd just bit down on something sour. "And what makes you suggest such an outlandish thing, little girl?"

Tai bristled, feathers flaring. She was twenty-one years old. Hardly a little girl.

"You've got a dragonstone." She gestured at the necklace.

Jameson made a sound like a boiling tea kettle. "Do not be ridiculous. This is a symbol of my office as one of the Stewards of Cloudfire. Outside of Emperor Callahan's abominations, there are no dragonauts. Everyone knows that."

"You're wrong." This time Dorian stepped forward. He clutched his own dragonstone, identical to Jameson's except in color — red and gold rather than Jameson's silver and white. Somewhere high above them, his dragon Solaris circled on the lookout for danger.

"You!" Jameson drew an ornate silver sword with its hilt wrought in the shape of a dragon.

Not a dragonaut, eh?

Dorian carried a similar blade on his belt. It was a gift from Solaris, a symbol of the strength of their bond.

Jameson relaxed slightly, sheathing the blade once more, but not letting go of the dragon-shaped hilt. "You're not one of Callahan's."

"Indeed not," Xander said with no small amount of pride. More quietly, so only Jameson and those standing nearest could hear, he said, "This is Dorian Valmont, rogue dragonaut, and the most promising young aeronaut since Cyrus Valmont himself."

"*Captain.*" Dorian blushed.

Jameson looked like he'd swallowed a poisonous toadstool.

"So if you please, Jameson," Xander said, "We have news for the

Order, and I believe the Dragonmar will be most annoyed if you continue to delay."

Jameson looked like he was about to suffer an aneurysm. "Not. Here." He looked around as if afraid Callahan's forces might emerge out of nowhere. "You three." He pointed at Xander, Dorian, and Bradford. "Come into the castle with me. The rest... the rest of you will just have to wait."

Tai's wing twitched. *The rest of you will just have to wait.* She ought to be used to this kind of thing by now. Tai wasn't a member of the nobility, or a dragonaut, or scion to a prestigious secret order. She was nobody. Of course, she would have to wait. Wasn't that always the way of it?

"Now, just one moment." Graigor Beckett crossed his arms. "If they are going in, I demand to be let in as well."

"And the rest of the crew, too," Dorian put in.

"And just what makes you so much more important?" an Orith pilgrim demanded. "This is *our* sacred site. *We* deserve to enter first."

Jameson shook his head rapidly, as if trying to frighten away a gadfly. "It will be you three, or nobody. Make your choice."

Tai sighed. She hated being excluded, but as always, practicality won out. They'd get nowhere if they stood there arguing all day. "It's okay." She put her hand gently on Dorian's forearm. "You should hear what this Order has to say. The rest of us can fend for ourselves."

"I expect you to put in a good word for us, mind," Falgar said.

Dorian smiled, but he still looked to Xander for the final say.

"I'll do everything I can to get the rest of you admitted." The former captain's face was etched with deep concern. "Tai, you're in charge until I get back."

"Aye sir." Tai smiled, even though Xander wasn't the captain anymore, and didn't have the authority to put her in charge of anything.

Graigor let out a frustrated "Hmph" and spat onto the dusty ground.

Tai, however, gave her former captain one last salute, and with no small amount of uneasiness, watched them depart.

Dorian stood in front of an ornate vanity mirror, examining his borrowed woolen frock coat. "What do you think?"

«It is fabric,» Solaris said, utterly deadpan. The dragon never understood why humans cared about clothing. «It was always Hematite who liked fabric.»

Dorian nodded sadly at the thought of his bonded demon, who had given his life to bring the *Phoenix* through the underclouds. "Yeah," he said, "Hematite would have liked this 'fabric.'"

The past hour had been a chaotic blur. Dorian, Bradford, and Captain Xander had been poked, prodded, and scrubbed within an inch of their lives. An elderly Healer named Estevan hummed and tutted over the size of Dorian's biceps as he fixed their various injuries. Dorian felt like a show gryphon on display. His arm worked again, though, so he thanked Zekador for the small miracles.

After getting cleaned up and Healed, he was then ushered into the most luxurious guest room he'd ever seen, handed a bundle of clothes, and told to get changed. The borrowed clothing fit awkwardly, but it wouldn't do to meet this much-vaunted Dragonmar wearing the tattered old rags he'd arrived in. He supposed he ought to be thankful they had anything on hand that came even close to fitting.

But would it be enough? He thought back to his adolescence in Callahan Manor, back when his stepfather always seemed to find a snide comment about what Dorian was wearing or how he presented himself. Dorian used to spend hours agonizing over this tunic or that doublet, until he eventually realized that Janus Callahan would never be pleased with anything, at which point he stopped bothering. Now, though, there was a whole new castle of people for him to disappoint.

«It is quite becoming on you, as fabric goes,» Solaris said. «But what of the arms? Are they not too tight?»

Dorian winced as he moved his upper arms experimentally and reached for the ornate dragon-hilt sword at his hip. "Let's hope Bradford's right and these Order people are friendly, because I'm hopeless if a fight breaks out."

Not auspicious words to start the evening. Still, when Dorian inspected himself in the gilded vanity mirror, he found to he didn't *entirely* hate what he saw.

The bulging muscles in his arms and shoulders were certainly new. No wonder his borrowed clothing was so restrictive. Unfamiliar, too, was the sharpened definition in his jawline. He was still soft around the middle — a newfound love for flying and sword fighting did not replace a long-standing love for cider and pie. But his paunch was, he thought, perhaps less pronounced than it had once been. A quiet, vain part of Dorian dared to wonder if some people might find him handsome now. If Tai Lunstrum, in particular, would find him handsome.

A knock at the door shook him out of his thoughts. Caught in his self-indulgent moment of vanity, Dorian flushed scarlet.

"Come in!" He scrambled to ensure he was fully covered.

The door to his guest quarters opened to reveal a familiar auburn-haired woman.

"Hildegard!" he blurted in surprise and relief. He'd feared the worst when he hadn't seen the arcane archaeologist among the rest of the survivors from the Dragon's Fangs. "What are you doing here?"

"I work here," she said with a sardonic half-smile. "I've been part of the Order for Cycles, remember?"

"You mean you've been working as a 'Steward of Cloudfire.'" Dorian returned her smile. One of the first things they'd been told was that they were *not* to mention the Order outside the castle walls.

As far as the people of Cloudfire city were aware, the denizens of Cloudfire Castle were just ordinary, if eccentric, rich people.

"Not just that," Hildegard said. She thumbed a gold chain around her neck, and there at the end, Dorian noted a dragon pendant matching his own, hers clutching an amber colored sphere.

"You're a dragonaut! But... since when?"

"Since the whole time." Hildegard's sheepish smile seemed apologetic, at least.

"So... so there's two of you?"

"Three, actually. You'll meet Dax in just a moment. I'm here to show you to dinner."

"Dinner. Right." Dorian's stomach gave a traitorous growl, reminding him it had been far too long since his last meal.

It stung, somewhat, to have secrets kept from him. How much easier would the past year have been if he'd known he wasn't alone in his bond with Solaris? That sting, however, couldn't fully dampen his excitement. There were *other dragonauts* here! Finally, here were people who could help him, who could teach him what it meant to bond a dragon. But with that excitement came the familiar fear of his own inadequacy. *What if I'm not good enough?*

If nothing else, Cloudfire Castle was impressive. Walking past ornately woven tapestries and marble busts of famous dead dragonauts, Dorian could almost feel like he, too, was one of the Ancients. He smiled sadly at the memory of a young boy pretending a twig was a sword, in a much different Ancient castle, so many years ago. Gods, but he wished Hematite were here to see this.

«I miss him too,» Solaris said. «But if not for his sacrifice, none of us would be here.»

"Well," said Hildegard, "Here we are."

Dorian thought Hematite would have liked the dining room too — it was even more ostentatious than the rest of the castle. A crystal chandelier hung suspended above a long mahogany table lined with a silk brocade table runner. Jameson was seated already, next to a snowy-winged Orith man Dorian had never met. From the shimmering blue dragonstone at his throat, Dorian assumed this must be the third remaining dragonaut. He wore a traditional Toreenish robe, pale blue silk open in the back to make room for his wings, with complicated silver embroidery on the hems and the collars.

"Just how rich is this place?" Dorian wondered.

"It is backed by the full might and wealth of my grandmother's house Ferran," Xander said, joining them. "Granted, wealth spent here is wealth not spent maintaining our province back in Vatea, but what do I know?"

Dorian blinked. He hadn't even been aware that Xander was Vatean nobility, which, after knowing the man for more than a year, felt like a gross oversight.

"A lot of finery for something that's supposed to be a secret," Dorian observed.

"The Queen of Toreen gifted my grandparents this castle as thanks for getting rid of some kind of crime cartel." Xander sounded uncomfortable with the topic. "That was before my time, of course."

The Orith man nodded. "Representatives of the Ferran family have worked alongside the local government to run the city for close to fifty years now. Of course," he added with a sigh, "Not everyone approves. Ah, but I'm getting ahead of myself. I am Dax Vesper, bonded dragonaut to the lovely Tempest, and youngest dragonaut in the Order. At least... youngest for now." He eyed Dorian with curiosity.

"A pleasure," Dorian said, shaking Dax's proffered hand. He worried over his grip strength, and hoped his palms weren't too sweaty.

With everyone dressed in their Valgrensday best, Dorian felt scruffy and out of place, even in the fine borrowed suit. Xander, clean-shaven for the first time Dorian had ever seen, looked every inch the nobleman in green and gold silk. Dorian was not a noble, as his stepfather always used to remind him. Would this Dragonmar and the others immediately know him for a fraud?

«You are not a fraud, you are a dragonaut,» Solaris said.

"So." Dorian valiantly tried to make friendly conversation. "How long have you and your dragons been bonded?"

Jameson, the dragonaut from the gate, stared down his nose at Dorian. "About twenty-five years."

"Twenty... twenty-five *years*?" Jameson didn't look a day over twenty-four. "Did you bond when you were a child?"

Jameson snorted. "Hardly. I was twenty-three."

"So that makes you... makes you..."

"Forty-eight, yes." Jameson sounded as though he doubted Dorian's ability to do basic math.

"But you're... but you're not..."

Taking pity on him, Hildegard laughed. "Something about the dragon bond slows down the aging process. I'm forty-three, myself."

Dorian clutched the edge of the dining table, stunned at the information. "So..." he swallowed. "Does that mean that I — that Solaris and me—"

"We're not immortal, if that's what you're asking," the Orith dragonaut, Dax, provided. "And if it makes you feel any better, I'm only twenty-six. But yes, it appears we do age slower than ordinary folks. They say the dragonauts of old could live up to three hundred. Path willing, we'll find out if that number's exaggerated or not."

"Three... hundred." Dorian suddenly wished he had some water.

«Ah, yes, that.» Solaris's mindvoice was sheepish. «Our Chronicler, Nocturne, might have mentioned it once or twice. But you must understand, for a dragon, there is not a terribly appreciable difference between one century and three.» Pensively, she added, «Even bonded humans are... depressingly short-lived.»

«Compared to a dragon, maybe.» Dorian didn't know what to think. He certainly wasn't about to *complain* about a few more Cycles of youthful vigor, but what about his friends? The idea of Falgar and Sullivan and Tai growing old without him left him feeling hollow.

"What I want to know is," Xander cut in, "How you've managed to keep actual legitimate real life dragons secret for all these years."

He didn't say *even from me,* but the accusation hung in the air so plainly that even Dorian could feel it.

"Quite simply, Illusion," Hildegard said.

Xander nodded. "My sister always did like her Illusions. But even so. Three giant dragons are bound to be difficult to hide."

"There is a sophisticated Illusion cloaking the outside of the castle, which allows us to fly nearby without being seen," Hildegard explained. "But even when we are spotted, we can pass that off as Illusion too."

"Oh?" Xander raised his eyebrows.

"This castle once belonged to the famed Orith dragonmage Rivka Sevarin," The Orith dragonaut Dax explained. "Every festival since before I was born, the House Ferran mages put on a show of Illusory dragons in her honor. If we're occasionally caught 'practicing' our Illusions, and if the dragons happened to have become more realistic these past few Cycles, well. That's easier for most folks to accept than actual bonded dragons returning for the first time in a thousand years."

Bradford laughed. "Fair point. But my father has dragonauts of his own, now. You won't be able to keep it secret forever."

"Perhaps not," Jameson allowed. "But don't underestimate the Lady Dragonmar. She is excellent at what she does."

Xander cleared his throat. "Where is my dear sister, anyway?"

"The Dragonmar will be along," Jameson said. "She's a very busy woman, and cannot drop everything just for—"

"That's right," came a feminine voice. "Busy Dragonmar, coming through. Now, Flight Leader Jameson, do you care to explain to me why it was so urgent that I needed to—" she cut off with a sharp intake of breath as her gaze shifted from Dorian, to Bradford, to Xander, and back to Dorian.

Dorian's first thought was that he knew this woman. He was absolutely certain that they had met before. The only problem was, he couldn't for the life of him remember when or where. From the way her blue eyes widened, and her startled hand rose to her mouth, he guessed she recognized him, too.

Xander's mouth twisted into a delighted grin. "You didn't tell her who we were. My gods, Jameson, I didn't know you had it in you. Have to say I'm impressed."

"Are you all right, Lady Dragonmar?" Hildegard was clearly torn between amusement and apprehension. "You look as though you've seen a ghost."

"For a moment I thought I had." Sylvia shook herself and straightened her posture, suddenly the picture of poise and composure. "Forgive me, Mr. Valmont. Your father was a very dear friend of mine, and you look so much like him, I almost thought he was back from the dead."

"Ah." Dorian scratched his neck. Usually, people were eager to tell him how much he *wasn't* like his famous father. "Ah, no, just me, I'm afraid."

"Just you," Sylvia said quietly, "Is more than good enough." She turned her attention to Bradford and said, "Thank the Ancients you're safe. When I heard that the Dragon's Fangs had fallen, I... feared the worst." Her composure cracked again, there, just for a moment, but she recovered so quickly that Dorian was sure he must have imagined it.

"Takes more than my Void-cursed father to kill me," Bradford said.

Xander cleared his throat. "Nice to see you again, Syl."

Sylvia turned to her brother, her mouth drawn into an amused smirk. "Alexander. I confess I'm surprised to find you here after all this time."

Xander looked about to argue, but then he just shook his head. "Void Eternal, Syl. You must think me such a pig-headed fool."

"You are my brother always," Sylvia said. "Of course I think you're a pig-headed fool." But she smiled, and Xander visibly relaxed. Sylvia dusted her hands together. "Right, then, to business.

Tell me, Mr. Valmont. Are the rumors true? Have you bonded a dragon?"

"Ah, yes." He thumbed his dragonstone. "I'm, ah, Solaris's rider, yes."

"Remarkable." She looked like the Mystictide Festivals had never ended. "You are, of course, just a boy, so you'll need training. But with four of you now, we are all the closer to forming a full flight of seven."

"Now wait just a minute," Jameson said. "How in the Void did he get a dragonstone? For all we know, he enthralled that dragon, just like Emperor Callahan."

"He has a dragonaut's sword, Jameson," Hildegard said. "You and I both know you can't simply Coerce one of *those* into existence."

"That man Kadmin Crowley conned *his* captive dragon into giving him a sword." Jameson crossed his arms.

"I believe," Captain Xander interjected, "That the boy can speak for himself."

Dorian swallowed nervously. "Right. Okay."

To the best of his ability, Dorian told the entire story, starting with Hematite the demon, and his father's research, and his accidental bond with Solaris. He talked about his time on the skyship *Phoenix*, and their work with Bradford and his rebels. Dorian glossed over some things, like his relationship with Empress Saedra, and how incompetent he'd been in the beginning. He didn't want to varnish the truth, but there was no need to make these people think any less of him.

Jameson regarded Dorian with an air of skepticism, then turned to Captain Xander. "And you back up this version of events, do you?"

"Of course."

"Be that as it may." Jameson wrinkled his nose. "The means by which Valmont bonded Solaris are unconventional, to say the least. The rest of us had to *earn* our dragonstones. This boy has done none of that, and yet, you expect us to believe he is on the same level as us?"

Dorian slumped down in his chair. At the moment, he didn't feel on the level with any of them.

"If the rumors are any sign," Sylvia said, "The rogue dragonaut has considerable skill at flying."

"He's one of the best I've seen," Xander put in. "Dorian will be better than Cyrus one day if he sticks with it. He's already better than me."

"Captain!" Dorian felt his face turn scarlet.

Jameson continued to look unimpressed. "A brick with wings is a better aeronaut than you, Xander."

Xander seemed to take Jameson's insult in stride. "A lot better than me, then."

Dorian was used to being underestimated, but Jameson's obvious disdain still stung. No small part of him wondered if Jameson was right. *If you're so good at flying,* he thought, *Why did Hematite have to die for you?*

"How are you with the sword?" Jameson asked.

"I'm... not bad," Dorian hedged.

«You have improved more in a single year than I had any right to hope for,» Solaris said.

Dorian smiled at the dragon's words, but the smile was short-lived. He *had* improved in a year, but it was still only a year.

"Why don't we just run some training exercises tomorrow morning and see what the boy can do, instead of talking in circles for the next hour?" Hildegard threw out her arms in annoyance. "Void take it. I'm getting hungry."

Dorian felt a rush of affection for Hildegard.

Xander cleared his throat. "Instead of talking like joining the Order is a given, let's discuss what we came here for."

"And that is?" Jameson asked snidely.

"What do you think?" Xander's annoyance was evident. "Janus Callahan's fledgling empire, and his son's upstart rebellion. His Lordship here seemed to think that you'd help."

"That's true, m... m'lady Dragonmar." Bradford straightened

himself and brushed imaginary dust off his sleeves. "I know the Order is secretive. But my father wants to end all magic. Surely if you were waiting for an emergency, there can be none more dire than that."

"And what good would we do?" Jameson protested. "Emperor Callahan has six dragonauts, we only have three."

Sylvia cut him off with a wave of her hand. "If Dorian and Solaris join us, we will have four. And as you well know, Emperor Callahan is down to only three captive dragons, largely thanks to Dorian here."

"Yes well... that is... He's just a boy." This felt extremely odd coming from Jameson, who didn't look more than a year or two older than Dorian. "Anyway, there's more to war than just dragons. Janus has the full might of the Kasani Sky Navy at his disposal. We have three, maybe four dragons."

"That's true," Sylvia admitted, "But we may yet recruit more dragons still."

Everyone, even Jameson, looked at her in surprise.

"My contact in Kasanarae received a delegation," Sylvia said, "From the dragons Meridian, Borealis, and Northstar."

«My rescued clan-mates?» Solaris's mindvoice was surprised, but also hopeful.

"They wish to help us," Sylvia said. "By forming new human bonds. This time, ones they choose for themselves."

For a brief glorious moment, Dorian imagined the dragons choosing Tai, Falgar, and Sullivan, and all of them living out the centuries in glory as dragonauts together.

"We have three more dragonstones," Hildegard said. "With those, and Valmont here, we'd be able to form a full Flight."

"The dragonauts of old always flew in groups of seven," Dorian provided, happy to at least have some knowledge to contribute.

"Indeed," Sylvia said. "With a full flight of seven, we might begin to consider taking direct action against Janus Callahan."

"How will the dragons choose?" Xander wondered. "A few of the old standing favorites, I imagine. Vale, for certain, probably Anders too. Perhaps Toric?"

"Anders is dead," Jameson said.

Xander's face fell. "I'm sorry. I didn't know."

"Maybe you would have, if you—" Jameson began, but Sylvia shook her head warningly, and he left the sentence unfinished.

"The festival of the Retreating Void is in two weeks time," Sylvia said.

Hildegard's eyes widened. "The Trials! You can't be serious."

Sylvia actually looked like she was enjoying herself. "It makes the perfect cover."

"Sorry," Dorian said, "But I have no idea what you're talking about."

"The Trials, Dorian," Bradford said with an air of exasperation. "I know you wanted nothing to do with them save for the food stalls, but surely you haven't forgotten they existed." Sylvia shot Bradford a pointed glance, and the lordling almost seemed to wither in her presence. "Sorry."

Dorian smiled and shrugged, not particularly offended. "I remember, I remember. You won the thrice-cursed Retreating Void Trials three years running, which meant I never got to stop hearing about it."

"Would've been four years running, too, if I hadn't twisted my ankle during that melee." Bradford gave a wistful sigh. "You should enter this year, little brother. Hard as you've been training, you might stand a chance at winning."

Dorian flushed. The compliment meant more than he cared to admit. But then he shook his head. "Do they even celebrate Retreating Void in Toreen? And anyway, I'm sorry, but I still don't understand what any of this has to do with dragons."

"To answer your first question, Cloudfire is as near much an Aerish city as it is an Orith one."

"That's debatable," Dax interjected. "But we do celebrate

Retreating Void here, yes. Our contests test the intellectual and the magical as well as the physical. I believe it's different in Adenthul."

Bradford nodded. "Just flying and the sword, in Adenthul. Goodness, imagine if I'd had to do math."

Sylvia snorted. "You'd've done fine, I'm certain. The dragonauts of old were supposed to be elite scholars and magi as well as warriors, so this makes for the perfect opportunity. For the rest of the city, the Trials shall be nothing other than what they always have been. A magical games and sports competition to herald the coming of spring. But for those of us in the Order, they'll serve another purpose. Their original purpose, set by the Ancients."

"I see," Jameson said. "So those Order members who perform best in the Trials will earn the dragonstones. But Dragonmar, are we sure this is wise? That's only two weeks away, so we don't have much time to prepare."

Sylvia looked wholly undeterred. "I suggest we get started."

CHAPTER TWO
SIBLINGS ESTRANGED

Evening fell, and bitter winter rain blanketed the streets of Cloudfire. Tai shook the water droplets out of her wings and moved closer to the makeshift campfire. They might be above the underclouds, but it seemed like she would never get out of the perpetual overcast.

"I wonder what Captain Xander and the others are up to now," she mused as she took a sip of watery mushroom stew. At least the food was warm. But after three days foraging in the woods, if she never saw another mushroom again, it would be too soon.

"By which," Falgar said with a knowing smirk, "You mean you wonder what *Dorian* is doing."

Tai twitched her wing, scattering rainwater. "I did not say that." But she hadn't needed to. She'd known Falgar for years, and he always could figure out what she was really thinking.

"Anyone with eyes can see the way you look at each other," Falgar said. "The longer you put off admitting it, the more agonizing it's going to be for the rest of us.."

She flung more raindrops towards him, and said, "You deserved that."

Falgar took her attitude in stride. "All I'm saying is that sometimes you just need to tell people how you feel. It worked for me and Sullivan."

Tai smiled despite herself. Typical Falgar. He finally had some modicum of romantic success and suddenly he fancied himself an expert.

"You two are officially together, then?"

Falgar nodded, grinning ear to ear. "Can't believe I got so lucky."

She patted him on the shoulder. "I'm happy for you both. Really. But ... it's different with Dorian and I."

"I don't see how."

Tai sighed, thinking back to Dorian's earliest days on the ship. He'd been so hopelessly naïve, and a bit helpless, but he'd always tried his best at everything, and his determination had been infectious. She just regretted she hadn't recognized her feelings for what they were. Not that it mattered, she supposed. She had a longstanding policy of not getting involved with crew-members.

Now, though. Dorian wasn't a crew-member anymore. No. He was more than that. He was a legend, a hero, a *dragonaut*. Tai was an unemployed aeronaut sitting here in the rain because she wasn't important enough to be invited to the castle. Tai didn't want to live in Dorian's shadow. She didn't want to live in anyone's shadow ever again.

"You're thinking about what happened in Kasanarae," Falgar guessed.

"That's not true," Tai lied. Curse that man. He surely had telepathic powers.

"Look." Falgar sighed. "I just know two things. First, I can't think of two people more radically different than Dorian and Kadmin. Second, when Valmont showed up, you started acting like yourself again. That's got to be worth something."

"Had no idea you were so invested in my love life."

"Hey now, I wouldn't say that. I'm just utterly besotted with a lover of my own, and wish for everyone to experience that kind of joy."

She playfully shoved him on the shoulder. "You are despicable, you know that?"

Her smile faltered, however, when she heard the flutter of wing-beats and watched one of the Orith porters flying past.

"Speaking of me and all my good advice," Falgar said, noting her changed expression. "Have you spoken to your brother?"

Tai sighed. "No."

She spared a guilty glance towards the second campfire the rest of the winged Orith sat hunched over their own bowls of soup. Tai told herself that it was the language barrier that kept the two groups apart, but she knew the rift was deeper than that. After so many years, she ought to be thrilled to see her brother again. She *was* thrilled. And yet...

"We didn't... depart on the best of terms," Tai admitted.

"I never had the impression that Valmont and that Bradford lordling used to much along, either, but they supported each other up that mountain just fine."

"That's Dorian and Bradford," Tai said.

"All right, then." Falgar changed tack. "But don't you think you'll regret it if you don't talk to him?"

Tai opened her mouth for a rebuttal, then closed it again. Falgar was right, Void curse him.

"Fine," she said, "You win."

Tai set down her soup bowl and strode to the other fire with a determined gait, lest she lose her nerve. Several of the porters looked at her, none of them friendly. *There's the traitor,* their eyes seem to say. She twitched her own stunted wings and wondered if this had been a mistake. But then there was Tanis, and he automatically moved over on the blanket and motioned for her to join him. That was a good sign, wasn't it? He met her gaze, his sharp brown eyes so much like her own, and his expression was carefully neutral, not friendly, but not outwardly hostile, either. It was a start.

"You've grown up," she blurted. "How old are you now? Fifteen?"

"Sixteen," he said, and his expression darkened.

"Right." Tai ran a nervous hand through her chin-length hair. He'd been eight when she left, and that had been eight years ago, which would make him sixteen. She'd been absent for half his life. *Void Eternal.* "How's Mother? And Roan?"

Tanis's hands balled into fists. There was nothing neutral about his expression now. The teenage boy's brown eyes flashed with long-suppressed resentment. "You'd know that, wouldn't you, if you'd ever bothered to come visit."

Tai winced at this well-deserved outburst. She'd once harbored similar resentment towards her own father. Then she'd turned around and done the same thing.

"I sent letters." She knew how weak that sounded.

Tanis snorted. "Not enough of them."

Tai lowered her wings. "I know. I'm sorry."

"And then." Tanis was well and truly angry now. "The Path, for some reason, conspired to literally drop you on top of us, and all you can do is whine about how much you want to go back to your precious sky. Savior's Wings, Tai, why are you so desperate to abandon your own people? Why do you want so badly to be one of *them?*"

"I don't ... I never wanted to abandon anyone." Tai felt rudderless, like a broken skyship in a Voidstorm. "But you know as well as I that I couldn't stay forever. I didn't fit in."

"And you fit in so well up there, do you?" Tanis jerked his thumb towards the sky. "I'm sure nobody ever stares at your wings, or excludes you, or treats you like a freak."

Tai ruffled her wings and remembered all the indignities large and small she'd endured over the years. But she shook her head and said, "I may have been an outsider, but at least I could contribute. I was a skyship mage. I was even pretty good at it." She smiled, allowing herself a bit of self-indulgent pride. "I could *fly*, Tanis. Down below, Mother just wanted to shut me up in a corner like the family embarrassment I was." Years of bitterness and resentment rose like bile in her throat. *Stop it.* She tried to shove down the bothersome emotions.

"Mother's gone," Tanis blurted, and it was not anger, but pain she saw reflected in his eyes.

Tai felt as if the ground had fallen out beneath her. Suddenly, her petty complaints seemed insignificant. "...Gone? She... died?"

It *couldn't* be. Tai ought to have written more letters. That was a fact. But it wasn't like she'd *never* been in contact. Surely Tai would *know* if her mother had died. Reora Lunstrum was too Void-cursed *stubborn* to die.

Tanis shook his head, gazing up at the wrought iron castle gates. "I don't know. She's just... gone." He ran his hand through his ebony ponytail, a gesture so reminiscent of herself that it made her heart ache. "She... got demon possessed. Citrine, the creature called herself. Mother was doing what she thought she needed to do to help Everwood."

"A demon? But how?" Tai knew, from her interactions with Hematite, that demons weren't *always* as bad as the border guards made them out to be. But why had her mother thought a demon would help their town? Why were there demons in Everwood at all? Last she'd heard, the border guards kept them well away.

"Thing is, though, Mother's not as young as she used to be. The demon Citrine got too powerful, and, well, she went into fugue."

Tai's breath caught in her throat. Demonic fugues were the stuff of Autumntide scare tales. They were the reason demons were so feared and mistrusted.

"But you said she's alive. Alive and just ... missing?" Tai tried desperately to find some mooring in the storm of her thoughts.

"Oh, she recovered," Tanis confirmed. "But, well, you know Mother. Possession is one thing, but a fugue? No, no, that's something negligent people do. '*What will the neighbors think?*'" He affected such an accurate impression of their mother that Tai might have laughed, had the situation not been so serious. "And then she just… left. Honestly, I thought she'd gone looking for you. But here you are. And here Mother isn't." Tanis cast her another glare.

"Fallen, Tanis, I didn't know. I'm so sorry."

Tanis shook his head. "Like I said. It's not like I have any right to blame you. Truth is, I don't really know you."

Tai squirmed. She supposed she deserved that.

A few moments later, a stocky dark-haired Aerishman strode up to the camp and cleared his throat. "I am Ser Toric Verity, Knight of House Ferran."

Tai raised her eyebrows. "Knight of who now?"

Tanis rolled his eyes. "You know, the Aerish family who've been squatting in the castle for fifty Void-cursed years? I know you've been gone, but I figured you at least knew that much."

Ser Toric Verity wrinkled his nose. "The Lady of Cloudfire has declared that the surviving members of Bradford's militia shall be welcomed into the castle as our honored guests. If you will please come with me, we want to do this as efficiently as possible."

"That's great news!" Tai said. "But what about the Orith porters? And the people on pilgrimage?"

The knight tugged on his shirt lace. "I'm afraid I was only asked to invite Bradford's militia."

"I—" she began. She couldn't just abandon Tanis out here.

"Go," Tanis said. "At least one of us should be warm and dry." His stony expression indicated he wasn't up for more conversation, anyway.

Tai wavered, but ultimately relented. Perhaps she was selfish, but she didn't see how continuing to let the rain soak her would solve anything. Somehow, though, going inside felt even worse than waiting outside.

Lady Sylvia Kane, granddaughter of Frederica Ferran, Countess of Skyhaven and Dragonmar of Cloudfire, flopped unceremoniously onto the divan. *Unladylike*, the voice of her alter ego intoned in her head. The curly-haired figment of Sylvia's imagination waggled her finger in disapproval, but Sylvia batted the mental image aside with an irritable slap of her hand.

Sylvia spent most of her life in one disguise or another. Sometimes, not even she knew for certain who she really was. But here, in her personal study, alone at the end of the day, was when she felt closest to her authentic self.

Curse Hildegard and Jameson. Hildegard had always been a prankster, but Jameson ought to know better. To send her into that meeting without the slightest preparation? Sylvia had never handled surprises well, not even pleasant ones, like her thrice-cursed *brother* showing up on her doorstep with Bradford and Dorian, of all people.

Sylvia retrieved a crystal decanter and tumbler from the mahogany cabinet. If there was ever a time to drink, it was now. Xander, Bradford, and Dorian. All here, all together. And Dorian was, of all things, the fabled rogue dragonaut. The fabled rogue dragonaut was Dorian. When had that happened? Why hadn't she known?

She'd just raised the glass to her lips when there was a knock on the door. *Curse it all.* She set down the tumbler and schooled her face into a professionally neutral expression. All-important Duty was not finished with her yet.

"Enter." She hoped her voice didn't convey her exhaustion.

The door opened to reveal Xander, looking uncomfortable in his borrowed suit with his hair tied back in an awkward tail. She let her expression relax slightly, both relieved and disappointed that it wasn't Dorian. She knew she'd have to speak to the boy, eventually. But not yet. Not today. He'd only just arrived.

Xander, though. Xander was little better. What did one say to a sibling after twenty-two years of estrangement?

"Hello, Xander," seemed a good place to start.

Xander's gaze flickered to the decanter and tumbler on the table, and his eyebrows raised just a fraction. "Drinking alone?"

Sylvia's mouth twitched. "I won't be, if you join me."

"I never turn down free booze." Xander fetched a matching tumbler and poured himself a generous amount.

"I don't suppose," Sylvia said with an air of mingled patience and exhaustion, "You're about to tell me why you're here."

"I'd thought we went over that in the meeting just now." Xander examined the amber liquid before taking a swig.

Sylvia gave him the stare she usually reserved for novice recruits. "You know that's not what I meant. How did you get wrapped up in all this? You made it perfectly clear when you left that you wanted nothing more to do with the Order *or* this family."

Xander ran his hand through his hair, partially undoing the slick-back ponytail. "As to that... Well. Seems the Valmont boy landed himself in a spot of trouble. Bradford wrote asking if I could take him in, and I mean to say, what was I supposed to do? Leave him there?"

Sylvia's indignation popped and dissipated like a soap bubble. "No. No, I am glad you did not."

Her mind returned to two hours prior, to the way Dorian had looked at her, recognition mingling with confusion in his wide blue eyes. Did he know her for who she truly was? Surely he could not. Sylvia was the most gifted Illusionist of her generation. She'd fooled Janus Bloody Callahan while working in his household for a bloody Cycle and a half. Surely she'd fooled Dorian, too.

He'd been just a boy when she lost her position as the nurse, Rowena Selene. He'd not even hit puberty when she took her new job as his tutor and governess, Tahlia Weatherbee. Never once had he given the slightest hint that he knew his old nurse and his new tutor were one and the same.

But here, displaying her actual face without the benefit of Illusion, he recognized her. Meanwhile, she, Sylvia Kane, master of disguise, greatest Illusionist of her generation, couldn't prevent herself from gawping like a startled gryphlet.

One year ago, to her shame and regret, she left behind a nervous and awkward boy. And now, here Dorian was, a man in truth, who carried himself with purpose and determination. The spitting image of his bloody father.

"You saved his life," Sylvia said.

Xander evidently gave up trying to fix his ponytail and massaged his neck instead. "Yes, well. As I said. Wasn't about to leave him to Callahan's whims, was I?"

There was a glint of accusation in his hazel-brown eyes. The suggestion that she *did* abandon him to Callahan's whims. Which, she supposed, she had. Oh, gods, she had.

"You're still a right bastard, springing all this on me without warning." She took another long swig of whiskey.

Xander's expression was all infuriating innocence. "Bastard? Now, now, Syl, you know our parents were happily married. Unless Leanore was my mother. I always did wonder."

She let out a puff of indignation. "Leanore was not your mother. Anyway. You could have at least sent a letter."

"And miss the look on your face?" He placed his hand on his chest. "Never. I'm surprised Jameson or Hildegard didn't ruin the surprise, though."

"They probably wanted to see the look on my face, too." *Insubordination at every turn.*

"He's a good kid," Xander said. "A hard worker, and he cares about others. The other boy, Bradford, I don't know him as well, but he seems to have a decent head on his shoulders. As their *tutor*," he added with just the slightest hint of a smirk, "You should be proud."

Sylvia exhaled sharply. They were fine boys, to be sure, but she could not help but thinking it was in *spite* of, not *because* of, her clumsy attempts at raising them.

"You're going to tell them the truth, aren't you?" This time, there was no denying the reproach in Xander's tone.

"Bradford already knows everything," A coward's non-answer, gods curse it all.

"And Dorian?"

"I'm surprised *you* haven't told him by now." *Coward, coward.*

"I keep your Void-cursed secrets, Syl. I always have. But the boy needs to know. The longer you wait to tell him, the harder it's going to be when he finds out. And he *will* find out. He's not a complete fool."

Sylvia stifled a scowl. Easy for Xander to sit there, smugly casting judgement, when he'd been out of their lives for more than twenty years. But he was right, gods curse him. He was right.

"I will tell him." She set her tumbler down. "When the time is right."

Xander's lips pursed. "See that you do."

"And what about you?" she asked, eager to change the subject. "Are you back in the fold?"

"Suppose I have to be." He took a swig from his own glass. "The *Phoenix* was destroyed, after all."

Sylvia was not above enjoying the look on Xander's face when she said, "Tomorrow morning, speak with Ser Vale. He'll get you situated as a squire."

"Squire?" Xander sputtered. "But — that is — you can't be serious."

Sylvia raised her eyebrows and turned the whiskey tumbler casually in her hand. "You think you deserve special treatment because you're my brother?"

"That's not — I don't — Void Eternal, Sylvia. I'm forty-two years old, not some raw teenage recruit. I was almost Dragonmar, for the Ancients' sakes."

This time, Sylvia didn't bother to hide her scowl. "*Almost* Dragonmar. And I seem to recall when you didn't get what you wanted, you stormed away like a toddler, for *three bloody Cycles.* You're lucky I'm even letting you start from squire."

Xander's hands balled into fists. "I *left*," he said, "Because I was tired of all the lies and deception. I know you've never uttered an honest statement in your life, but some of us—" Xander sighed, downed the rest of his drink, and shook his head. "It doesn't matter. Void Eternal. Five minutes into our reunion and we're already bickering like children. I'll start over as a bloody squire, if that's what you want."

Sylvia shook her head. "I will not make you start over from squire. I was only trying to get a rise out of you, as I ever have." She smiled ruefully. "But you need to understand my reluctance to let you back in the inner circle. How do I know you won't run off again?"

"You don't," he admitted. But then, more firmly, he added, "I won't."

"I'll take your word for now."

"Since I've got your ear," Xander said, "Would it really kill you to let those Orith pilgrims into the castle? Not the whole thing," he added quickly, "Just the main halls and the temple. They were pretty upset, I gather, when the rebels were let in but they were not."

Sylvia massaged her temples. She'd closed the castle off to visitors after Janus Callahan rose to power. It had seemed like a good idea at the time — Strangers in the castle were a security risk she just couldn't countenance. But unfortunately, her brother also had a point. Her family had use of this castle by the grace of the Toreenish government. Closing it off to visitors had already soured her reputation with the locals, and things would only get worse the longer she tarried. Throwing up some extra Illusions to protect the inner sanctum was far easier than finding new headquarters altogether.

"Very well," she sighed, "I will see what can be done."

With just a touch of the smile she remembered, Xander asked, "You really think we can do it? Form a full flight of seven?"

Sylvia nodded and reached into her desk drawer, removing a mahogany lockbox. She opened it to reveal three spherical gray stones inside. Dragonstones, the rarest and most precious artifacts of Ancient times. There were few left in the world, too few. But these were, for now, enough.

"We have the dragonstones, and we have the dragons. Now all we need are three more riders."

"Zekador's poorly fitting pants." Xander let out a low whistle. "Seems like I returned right on time."

"Will you enter the Trials?"

Xander snorted. "Me? A bit old, don't you think?"

"Not at all. In the Ancient times, plenty of riders bonded in their forties."

Xander shook his head. "You know I've never been much one for bonding. I'm just here for the food."

Sylvia smiled and rolled her eyes. "I'm still furious with you for leaving. But you brought Dorian and Bradford back, and a dragon, besides. I suppose I owe you for that."

Xander chuckled. "And I'll never let you forget it."

"I can drink to that." She poured herself more whiskey.

They clinked their glasses together, and for a moment, Sylvia allowed herself to simply enjoy sharing a drink with her estranged brother. But the mistakes of the past were never far from the forefront of her mind. It seemed all her debts were coming due at once, and much sooner than she would have liked.

CHAPTER THREE
THE TRIALS

Not since her earliest days in the skies of Aeris had Tai had so much trouble reading a book. Even the simplest runes and sigils seemed to swim around on the page, leaving her brain as quickly as they entered. "The greater rune of Kassoria, connected to the Zekadorite rune of transformation... oh, Fallen take it, I'm never going to get this right."

Dorian put a comforting hand on her shoulder, and then, seeming to realize that was inappropriate, quickly snatched it away. A pity, really. She'd've liked for him to keep his hand there a bit longer.

"Maybe we should take a break," he said. "I mean. When was the last time you actually slept?"

"I can't sleep." Tai rubbed her exhausted eyes. "The Trials are in less than a week."

"Yes, but the judges will hardly be impressed if you collapse in front of them."

Tai grunted. "Easy for you to say. You already have a dragon bond."

Dorian's face fell. "Yes. And already half the Order's speculating whether I deserve her or not. I overheard Jameson complaining to Sylvia that she only let me join the Order because of my family connections."

Tai flushed slightly in sudden shame. She'd argued much the same thing to Captain Xander when Dorian joined the Phoenix crew more than a year ago. "Jameson just doesn't know you yet," she said. "He'll come around."

"Here's hoping." Dorian grimaced. "It seems half the people here resent me because of who my father was, and the other half expect me to be him, which, I'm afraid to say, they're going to be disappointed. But anyway, this isn't about me. If anyone deserves to be here, it's you. It's just, you'll never get the chance to show it if you burn yourself out before the Trials even get here."

Tai buried her head in her arms. He was right, gods curse him. But the looming specter of the Trials made something as trite as *relaxation* seem impossible.

"I feel like I'm getting worse," she complained. "None of these spell circles make any Void-cursed sense. And don't get me started on physical training. This morning's workout was abysmal. Since when can you bench press more than me, anyway?"

"I'm quite a bit bigger than you," Dorian pointed out evenly.

Tai, however, would not be reassured. "Everyone's going to immediately know I didn't grow up in Aeris. If I don't catch up... if I don't do *something*..."

"All right," Dorian dusted off his hands. "How about this. We look at one more book, then *you* are going to go straight to your quarters and take a nap."

"Fine, fine." Tai closed the volume she'd been perusing and pulled another at random from the shelf. Despite her frazzled exhaustion, she smiled at the familiar red leather binding. "We hauled this book out of Greystone, remember?"

Dorian chuckled. "Rings a bell. Didn't we fall into an underground chamber and find out I'd bonded a dragon by accident?"

"Seems like yesterday," Tai said, "And yet also like Cycles ago."

"I was so overwhelmed," Dorian said wistfully. "I felt so weak and helpless, and I had no idea how I was going to help Solaris."

"But look at you now." Tai grinned and elbowed him in the side. "Able to bench press more than me. If Dragonmar Sylvia doesn't figure out your worth, more the fool is she."

"It's really more Flight Leader Jameson who doesn't like me." Dorian scratched his neck. "The Dragonmar seems pretty nice, all things considered. Just wish I knew why she looks so familiar."

Shrugging it off, Dorian flipped the book open to a random page. Tai leaned across the table to see. Last time she'd opened this book, it had appeared like a dusty old accounting ledger. But the *Phoenix's* fateful trip through the underclouds had dispelled the book's powerful Illusion, revealing the treasure inside.

"A recipe for fish sauce," Dorian observed.

Tai nodded solemnly. "I can see why it was so important to keep hidden."

"Maybe it was really *good* fish sauce."

Tai didn't know why the recipe was there, but chances were it was a recent addition. Who knew how many times the book had changed hands over the centuries? This recipe called for undersea salt mackerel, and as far as Tai knew there was no way to travel beneath the underclouds before Orith sank.

The next page was written in High Kasani, the language of the Ancients, and although it allegedly shared many similarities with the modern Kasani trade tongue, Tai couldn't read a word of it. She had no trouble recognizing the wood-cut printed illustration on the page, however, and she shuddered at what it depicted. Several demons cloaked in flame darted back and forth around a massive creature of ash and smoke.

"What is that?" Dorian's face scrunched up into a puzzled expression. "It looks like a dragon, except... twisted somehow. And wrong."

"You mean you don't know?" Tai was honestly surprised. Her friend was usually so knowledgeable about this kind of thing.

This time, however, Dorian shook his head.

"Voidwraith," she explained in a hushed whisper, as if simply naming the creature might summon it.

Dorian's eyes widened, but he still looked more confused than scared, giving the situation nowhere near the gravity she thought it warranted. "Like from the War of the Magi?"

This time it was Tai's turn to feel ignorant. She'd lived among the Aerish for more than a Cycle, but her knowledge of their history was still spotty. "Sure," she lied. "Something like that."

"But they're not *real*, are they? I mean, they say Archmage Roark summoned one, but I think it was probably just like a really big fireball or something."

Tai had no idea who Archmage Roark was, but she figured now wasn't a good time to mention that. "They're real. I've met one."

Now Dorian had the good sense to look afraid. "You've *met* one?"

Tai nodded. "During a Voidstorm. On my old ship, before the *Phoenix*."

Tai tried and failed to banish the image of Captain Brielle's broken neck and lifeless gaze from her memory. She didn't feel ready to talk about that, not yet, not even to Dorian. "It was a Voidwraith the Ancients summoned to sink Orith."

Dorian's mouth fell open. "I thought the Ancients sacrificed their dragons to sink Orith."

"Yes," Tai said. "By summoning Voidwraiths."

Dorian swallowed. "Oh."

"Yes," Tai agreed, "Oh."

Well, it was just an illustration, and unlikely to jump out of the page and attack her. So, feeling rather embarrassed by her outburst, she turned the page.

The next few pages proved much less exciting, mainly depicting tide tables and moon phases, so dry and lifeless that Tai found her attention beginning to drift once more. "Void take me, this book was more interesting when it was an accounting ledger."

She yawned and turned the page, expecting more dull miscellany. What greeted her on the page was something else entirely.

"What," she breathed, "Have we here?"

A magnificent spell circle covered the pages, more complicated than any she'd ever seen. But unlike the other spells she'd studied that morning, this one seemed to shine like a beacon, almost begging to be deciphered.

Tai didn't recognize any of the runes or sigils. She traced her finger along a squiggly sort of symbol that reminded her of waves in the undersea. Runes didn't have any particular power of their own. They existed as a conduit for the spell caster's focus and intent. Tai could perform the spell letter-perfect and it wouldn't do a thing, because she didn't understand the context behind it. But was it possible, perhaps, to "translate" the spell for modern times?

"Is that a rune of displacement?" Dorian's eyes were wide with fascination.

"It... might be," Tai agreed.

That symbol in the middle looked a bit like a Greater Sigil of Kassoria. And that one there *could* represent position. *Void Eternal,* she could tell just by looking that the power requirement was incredible. That meant the spell must be powerful, too.

If Dorian was right and that *was* displacement, and that funny little spiral probably meant travel of some sort... Tai felt her feathers stand on end. If she didn't know better... *No.* She would *not* get her hopes up. But she also absolutely *had* to know more. Somewhere in this library there must be a book of Ancient runes symbols, and Tai was determined to find it.

"Sorry, Dorian," she said. "That nap is going to have to wait."

The morning of the Festival of the Retreating Void dawned bright and clear. It was cold still, but Tai could tell winter was finally loosening its grip on Cloudfire Mountain. Enchanted flickering orbs floated like fireflies in the castle's great hall, decked out in white and gold. The effect gave the alabaster walls a sparkling ambiance.

Tai wished she could enjoy it. But as she poked listlessly at her waffles, all she could think about was the tournament ahead.

Overall, she believed she was prepared. Probably. Maybe.

She was competent in the three categories — combat, magic, and flight. But a dragonaut had to be better than merely competent.

"You've got to eat breakfast, Tai." Dorian looked at her untouched plate with consternation. "You need your strength."

"I know." She sighed and forced down a mouthful waffles and fruit preserves. But she wasn't sure how much good it would do. Her stomach writhed in protest. Everything tasted like dust.

"If it's any consolation, I know how you feel," said Lord Bradford, who was seated across from them.

"Are you entering this year?" Tai was slightly curious if Bradford's alleged skill with the sword was all talk or not. If he was even half as competent as he claimed, he'd be tough competition.

Bradford, however, shook his head. "I'm afraid not. Never did have much interest in all this business with dragons and Ancient lore. Dreadfully tedious. If I enter and wow the dragons with my brilliance, they'll only be resentful they cannot have me. It's not fair to the rest of you." He flashed his cocky grin. "But don't feel so alone, Miss Lunstrum. My first Trials, I was so nervous I couldn't eat a Void-cursed thing."

"But you won, though, right?" Tai asked.

"No, actually. That year I placed third. But I did win the next year, and the year after that, and the year after that. Would've won a fourth time if I hadn't turned my ankle. And each of those times, I had a full, hearty breakfast."

Tai grunted. Chances were, there wouldn't be more dragonstones next year. It was either today, or not at all.

"Hey," Dorian said, "You'll do great. You've prepared for weeks. Nobody's more deserving."

His smile looked so hopeful and genuine that she really wanted to smile in return, but the best she could manage was a nervous little grimace.

She couldn't stop thinking about all the things she should have done differently. Should have trained harder, should have studied different topics. Should've spent more time focused on *this* instead of that mysterious Ancient spell circle she'd found in the old red-covered volume. *Should have, should have, should have.*

These nervous thoughts followed her as she left the dining hall and moved out to the banner-bedecked competition fields. Falgar and Sullivan were there already, doing stretches and practicing foot-work. *Void,* Tai thought. She should've arrived early, too.

"Ready to show these land-bound fops how it's done?" Falgar flexed his wiry biceps.

"Our competition are not land-bound fops," Sullivan said. But then he added, "That doesn't, however, mean I'm averse to some showing off."

Tai forced a smile. Her friends seemed so calm and confident. Why couldn't *she* be calm and confident, too?

They said their farewells to Dorian and Bradford, then made their way to the waiting area. Tai's meager breakfast was a leaden weight in her stomach, and she marched forward with the air of someone summoned to a tribunal.

"Excuse me." An unfamiliar voice caught her off guard.

"Eh?" Tai spun around to find Dax Vesper, the Orith dragonaut.

"You're Tai Lunstrum, right?"

"Ah, yes." She wondered how he knew her name. Perhaps Dorian or Xander had mentioned her. She stood straighter, smoothing her short dark hair and preening her black feathers. Her wings felt so small compared to his massive snowy ones.

Like the rest of the dragonauts, Dax dressed formally for the occasion. In his case this meant a traditional robe of aquamarine silk to match the scales of his dragon, Tempest. Plenty of embroidery, of course. Whoever Dax was, he'd advanced far on the Path.

"For what it's worth, I'm glad you're competing," Dax said. "As a judge, I must remain impartial, but as an Orith, I hope you do well. We need more of us among our ranks."

She thanked him politely and hurried to catch up with Falgar and Sullivan. She supposed she ought to be relieved that one judge seemed to be on her side, but it also made her uncomfortable that even a fellow Orith saw her wings before he saw the rest of her. Flightless as she was, she doubted Dax would treat her with the same kinship if they were down beneath the clouds.

For the rest of that morning and well into the afternoon, Tai and her friends performed like dancing gryphlets in front of the entire Void-cursed city. By the time the winter sun crested the horizon, Tai had fought with swords and staves, run a short foot race, stood on one foot blindfolded while reciting the Sanorian Epics, and cast an array of increasingly strange and arbitrary magical spells. By late afternoon, she felt wrung out like a dishrag, but there was still the most important contest left to go: the flying demonstrations.

The good news was, she and her friends had made an admirable showing thus far. Despite her earlier frustration, Tai's hours in the library paid off, and she did exceptionally well in the magic competition. Falgar, who'd always been good with a blade, handily won the melee, and Sullivan made a strong showing all around. Tai almost dared to hope that all three of them might come away with dragonstones.

"Completely unfair," complained Graigor Beckett, who was tied with Tai for third place. "The judges favor you three, because *you* used to work for the Dragonmar's brother."

Falgar smirked and crossed his arms. "Come off it, dung-for-brains. First of all, half these judges don't even know what a Dragonmar is. Second, you're just jealous because you're not as *marvelously skilled* as we are. You've had your pampered rich boy life, but there's nothing like honest labor on a skyship to toughen you up."

"We'll see." Graigor glowered at the rest of them. "I've been flying ornithopters since I was seven."

"Instead of arguing, perhaps pay attention," said Sullivan, ever the peace keeper. "They're about to draw lots to see who goes first."

The audience grew quiet as the Mayor of Cloudfire, a thin and unassuming Orith man with wispy brown hair, drew names out of a polished copper bowl. With his voice magically magnified, he announced, "The flight demonstrations shall occur in the following order: Rorach Felding, Anise Trebon, Toric Verity, Zachary Falgar, Graigor Beckett, Vale Garamond, Jakob Sullivan, Tai Lunstrum."

The audience erupted into applause, and Tai just nodded and swallowed. *Last.* Tai would fly last. On one hand, it meant she could analyze the competition, but it also gave her plenty of time to stew in her anxiety.

Anise Trebon performed quite well, and Rorach Felding quite poorly, but as both of them were part of the ordinary competition and not in the running for a dragonstone, Tai only half paid attention. To her delight, Falgar gave an excellent performance, with lots of loops and turns and exciting flourishes. It was obvious he had Academy training, even if his time there had been unfairly cut short.

Graigor, unfortunately, hadn't been lying about his skill either. He, too, put on an impressive show, though to her relief, he scored a few points behind Falgar. Vale's flight was nothing to write home about, and Toric lost control of the ornithopter half way through, landing roughly and kicking up a cloud of dirt. This got quite an excited reaction from the audience, but the judges were far from impressed.

"Not even a graceful landing," she overheard Dax tutting. "He'd've gotten some extra points for style."

Finally came Sullivan's turn, and while he lacked any of Falgar's showy flourishes, he tackled it with the same clean precision with which he did everything else. Tai waited with bated breath while the judges tallied up his scores.

In the end, Sullivan scored just above Graigor, slightly behind Falgar. Tai breathed a sigh of relief and cheered with the rest of the audience. With only one more contestant to go, Falgar and Sullivan had already secured spots in the top three.

"I can't believe it!" Falgar threw his arms around Sullivan and kissed him passionately.

"Get a room, you two," Tai said, but she smiled, too. "But also, congratulations."

"Just your turn left now," Falgar said, once he and Sullivan had disentangled themselves. "All you have to do is fly better than Graigor, which shouldn't be hard. Then we'll be flying in formation together, just like in the old days."

Tai forced a grin. She wanted that more than she knew how to say. But the possibility of failure made her sick to her stomach. She would not impress the judges if she vomited all over the training field.

The compact single-person vessel reminded Tai of a dragonfly, a long shaft of wood and metal with gossamer aether wings jutting out from either side. Built for agility rather than endurance, Ornithopters couldn't travel very far, but they were swift, light, and maneuverable.

Because it was so small, she didn't have to Link with the Ornithopter to fly it. A pity, really. She loved the sensation of swimming through the air under her own power. It almost made her forget her wings didn't work.

On the Ornithopter, she never forgot she was flying a vehicle, with the aether engine thrumming beneath her. Still, it was delightful to feel the wind in her short black hair and to put the lightweight flying machine through its paces.

Tai did a few graceful loop-de-loops over the stadium, earning some pleased applause from the crowd. She grinned. *I can do this,* she thought. *I can definitely do this!*

She had just taken the ornithopter into what she thought would be an impressive barrel roll when it gave a spasmodic jerk.

"What in the Void—"

Tai kicked the throttle and forced the ornithopter under control. She came out of the roll a little gracelessly and hoped that nobody noticed. She could almost feel Dax Vesper and his dragon Tempest's eyes on her, watchful, as though she carried the hopes of all of Orithkind.

The ornithopter lurched again, this time more violently. She heard nothing over the roar of the wind, but somehow, she could feel the crowd gasp in consternation.

Panic rose inside her and she forcibly tamped it down. If she could figure out what was wrong in midair, she might have a chance of fixing it. She was a skilled skyship mechanic. Everyone said so. Fixing a broken Ornithopter mid-flight was bound to impress the judges, wasn't it?

Something rattled near the back of the vehicle. A loose connection to the aether crystal? Carefully, more carefully than she'd ever done anything, she turned around in her saddle. The Ornithopter shuddered, but didn't lose elevation, at least not yet. She could see the startled faces of the crowd, but forced herself to ignore them. Holding the wooden hilt of her athame between her teeth, she partially unfastened her harness, then crawled away from the saddle and onto the wooden chassis. *Careful now... just a little further...*

The ornithopter lurched again and Tai dropped her spell knife.

"No!"

She watched with dismay as it turned end over end before landing point first in the field below. In the meantime, the aether engine sputtered and died.

Well isn't that just wonderful.

As the flying machine plummeted, she released the rest of her safety harness and leapt free of the failing vehicle. With only air surrounding her, she felt once more like the thirteen year old girl who tried in vain to fly.

Don't panic, she desperately chastised herself. If she made a graceful enough landing, that might still score her points. *Enough points?* She wasn't sure. She couldn't think about that now. She just needed to — with a sudden and unexpected *whumph* she landed on something rough and scaly.

"What the—" Tai struggled to right herself and found she was on Solaris's back, right behind Dorian Valmont.

"You're okay." Dorian's voice shook. "It's okay. I've got you."

"But—" Roaring cheers and applause drowned out her feeble protest. The audience had gotten a good show, all right. But it wasn't because of anything Tai had done. They cheered for Dorian and his heroics, yet again.

The next hour passed in a blur. Someone, perhaps her friends, perhaps anonymous Order members, whisked her off to the infirmary, where the wizened Healer Estevan asked her a series of questions. Tai barely registered them. She answered in flat monosyllables.

Meanwhile, the same word played in her head, over and over and over. *Failure. Failure. Failure.*

"I suppose it won't hurt you to have visitors," the wispy-haired Healer said at length. "Gods know your friend Mr. Valmont has been waiting anxiously outside the door this entire time. Though he perhaps should spend a little bit more time helping cover the mess caused by swooping in with a Void-cursed dragon in front of everyone." The elderly Healer's nostrils flared. "Thankfully, the Lady of the castle has played it off as some kind of spectacular Illusion. All part of the show, as it were. So. Your friend would like to see you, if you're ready."

"Dorian. I... yes. Of course." Part of her wanted to see him very much. The other part couldn't bear to look at him.

The Healer didn't seem to care what Tai wanted. He gestured for her friend to enter.

Dorian tumbled into the room, looking like he hadn't slept in a moon. Several emotions paraded through her mind. Irritated that he looked so disheveled after what only could have been an hour or two. Flattered, just a bit, that he was so worried on her behalf. And no small part of her was simply glad to see him, curse everything.

Tai didn't know what to say to him, so she blurted the first thing that came to mind. "What were you *thinking* compromising the Order's security like that?" This wasn't about the Order's security, of course. But it was something to cling to, something far less thorny and more straightforward than confronting her actual feelings on the matter.

"I... wasn't thinking." Dorian's face was even paler than usual. "I was so scared... When you fell off that ornithopter... gods, Tai. I thought you were going to die."

"Well." Her voice sounded hollow, like it came from the other end of a long tunnel, "I didn't."

He blinked at her brusqueness, his expression confused and maybe a little hurt. She was being unfair. She knew she was. Dorian thought he was saving her life. He'd done it because he cared about her. She ought to be more grateful. But all she could think about was how she might have just edged ahead of Graigor in the rankings if he had allowed her to make the landing on her own.

Falgar joined them in the infirmary, with his shining new dragonstone already looped around his neck. "Dorian, I love you, mate, but you're a Void-cursed fool."

"Eh?" Dorian looked, if possible, even more crestfallen.

"She's Orith, remember? Orith can take a fall. She didn't need you to swoop in and act like a hero."

Dorian's face became, if possible, even paler. "I... I forgot... I... sorry." He nervously fiddled with the chain of his own dragonstone.

Falgar put a hand on Dorian's shoulder. "She's had a long day. I think we should give her some space, yeah? It's still Retreating Void out there. Hildegard says we've got to try the octopus balls."

"Octopus balls?"

"Not actually their balls, regrettably. I'm not even sure if octopus anatomy works like that. But whatever it is, it's a Toreenish delicacy."

Dorian looked tempted, but then he shook his head and looked towards Tai, his face still awash with concern. "I'm not sure..."

The cheerful sound of light-hearted explosions and the colorful blossom of fireworks outside the infirmary window reminded Tai that it was, in fact, still a festival day. Tai didn't feel festive, but there was no point ruining it for everyone else.

"Go enjoy the celebrations," Tai said. "Try the octopus balls. I'll be fine."

As soon as her friends left, however, Tai wished they were still there. It was like that first night all over again. Dorian got to go to the castle, Tai was stuck in the rain. At least back then, she'd had Falgar and Sullivan to commiserate with. Now they, too, were moving up and on, leaving her behind. And Tai wondered if she'd ever catch up.

CHAPTER FOUR
FLIGHTLESS

EIGHT YEARS AGO

Tai sat perched on a branch in the dappled light of the silverleaves, gazing down at the ground below. The river wound like a ribbon of light, reflecting the silver of the trees and the gray of the perpetual overcast. She took several deep breaths.

"I can do this."

This time, she would fly. She *had* to.

She leapt from the branch.

For a long moment it was just her and the chill evening air. *Come on, come on...* The wind picked up, and for a brief, glorious moment, her stunted black wings caught the breeze. *Yes! I can do this!*

Plop. The wind died down, and Tai landed on the loamy ground all the grace of a sack of potatoes.

"Savior's hairless backside," she grumbled as she dusted herself off. Her mood soured further still when she realized the sound of clapping didn't come from her wiping dirt off of her robes.

"Oh, very good, very good!" Lucynde Vaughn sat perched on a

nearby branch, surrounded by her group of cronies as if holding court. She never went anywhere without her entourage. Jessamine Finbock, Larimar Vergus, and — her heart did an uncomfortable little flip flop — Jace Farnham.

Tai's face burned. The only thing worse than failing to fly was failing to fly *in front of an audience.*

"Can you believe it?" Lucynde turned to her friends with a look of imperious condescension. "The stunt-winged little runt actually believed she would take flight."

The others laughed, save for Jace, who looked uncomfortable. Her heart warmed just a bit at that. He was always nicer to her than the rest of Lucynde's cronies.

It was easy to see why Lucynde Vaughn held such sway over the others. Although only in her early teens like Tai, she already had the smooth curves of adulthood, as well as full-grown wings with luxurious golden feathers.

"Poor dear," Lucynde said with a voice like honeyed poison. "When will you learn that enough is enough? The longer you keep trying, the more embarrassing it will be." She shook her head in mock sympathy. "Your poor mother. Imagine the shame of birthing a flightless whelp."

"Come on, give the poor girl a break," Jace said. "She'll get it in her own time. I seem to remember *you* fell in the dirt four or five times before you achieved flight."

Lucynde flushed, but she recovered quickly. Lifting her face towards the shining silverleaf, she ran her hand down her embroidered robe sleeve. "Yes, well," she said. "I was only ten then, wasn't I? Tai here is thirteen. It's not natural to go that long without flying."

Jace cast her a sympathetic smile — a real one, it seemed, not a mockery like the one from Lucynde. A small mercy on this awful evening.

Tai saw no point in trying to fly again tonight, not with everyone else watching. So she said her glum farewells and began the tedious climb back up to the high branches where her family lived.

That was the worst part of being flightless. All the Savior-cursed ladders. Ladders were for small children, and those older folks who could still climb but couldn't fly around anymore. Everyone else used their wings.

Tai's family home was a modest sized spherical structure of wood and clay, nestled high in the silverwood branches. Tai's mother once explained that the dwellings were designed after the nests of their avian ancestors, but Tai thought it looked more like a wasp's nest than a bird's nest. And just as likely to sting her if she didn't conform.

She slipped off her sandals and opened the door as quietly as possible, hoping she could make herself presentable before anyone noticed her disheveled state.

No such luck.

"Where in the Depths have you been?" Her mother, Reora Lunstrum, demanded as soon as Tai crossed the threshold. Reora's nostrils flared. "And why are you covered in dirt?"

"I... fell," Tai admitted, shamefaced.

"Well, don't just stand there spreading dirt on my clean floor. Go get changed, and then help me with supper. Savior's Wings. Couldn't have landed somewhere clean, could you?"

"It's the ground," Tai said flatly, "None of it is clean."

Tai climbed up to her sleeping alcove and removed her filthy robes. She rummaged through her trunk, but found a depressing dearth of things to wear. Nothing but plain, gray, and unadorned clothing meant for a child. She'd had another growth spurt recently and almost everything was too short. She was *supposed* to have moved on to the robes of the First Waypost by now, with colorful accents on the collar and embroidery on the cuffs. But she couldn't advance on the Path until she'd taken her first flight, and she was becoming increasingly sure that would never happen.

She sighed and put on the most acceptable robe she could find, even though it was several handspans too short and stained with soot and linseed oil from one of her experiments. A clockwork mouse fell out of the robe's pocket and shattered on the floor, spreading cogs and springs across the woven grass floor mat.

"Bother." Tai gathered up the pieces and laid them out neatly on the shelf set into the wall. "Mr. Squeakers suffered an ill fate, but he may yet live another day." For as long as she could remember, she'd spent the bulk of her allowance on market days buying whatever strange cogs and gizmos the merchants had on sale. She loved to tinker, and *sometimes* her experiments even worked. Poor, lamented Mr. Squeakers used to so delight her younger brother Tanis. Of course, Tanis considered himself above such frivolities now, even though he was still only eight.

She set the remains of Mr. Squeakers down next to her latest project. This one, she thought, would be sure to impress even a jaded eight-year-old. If she could just get it to work.

The clockwork dragon's wings moved up and down well enough when she pushed on its head, and it only *sometimes* tripped on its own legs when she wound up the clockwork. But with just a bit more tinkering, Tai was confident she could make the automaton fly. And that, surely, would be praiseworthy even for her family's impossible standards.

Tai picked up her prized pair of magnets and idly stuck them and unstuck them. They'd cost the better part of her spending money for the season, but if her experiments worked, it would be worth it. She turned the stones over and marveled at how one way, they attached together, and the other way, they slid apart, repelled by some unseen force. Aerish magic didn't work here beneath the clouds, but surely this was a magic all its own.

"Do try and hurry along, or it'll be Autumntide before dinner is ready," came her mother's exasperated voice from below.

Sighing, Tai set the clockwork dragon down and jumped back into the living area. If Tai could fly, and therefore advance on the Sacred Path, her gadgets would be more than enough to earn her an apprenticeship with the Artificers Guild. But since she couldn't, her family regarded them as an idle pastime that distracted from more important business.

"Took you long enough," Reora said. "Here. Start peeling these tubers, won't you?"

Tai's face wrinkled, but she set to work without complaint.

"Honestly," Reora said. "Coming home as late as you please, all covered in dirt. What will the neighbors think?" *What will the neighbors think* was a constant refrain in Reora Lunstrum's household.

Reora's rant cut off, however, when the front door swung open once again. In marched Roan, Tai's stepfather, with her eight-year-old half-brother Tanis in tow. They, too, were in a state of disarray. Tanis's robe was torn and he had a bit of twig sticking out of his sleek black hair. Roan, for his part, was flush-faced and wind-swept, but looked to be in good spirits.

Reora greeted them both with considerably more affection than she'd given Tai. Tai noted she didn't complain about *their* effect on her clean floors.

Tanis bounded eagerly across the room, getting more dirt everywhere. Irritably, Tai covered the wooden bowl where she kept the peeled tubers.

"My," Reora laughed. "Someone's had a good day."

"I did it!" Tanis exclaimed. "I flew!"

Tai narrowly avoided dropping the bowl. "You... you what?"

"Oh! How wonderful!" Reora clasped her hands together and hurried over to embrace her youngest child.

Tai's face burned as she continued peeling tubers. Tanis could fly? *Tanis?* He was just a little kid, rambunctious and always underfoot. How was it possible that *he* had his first flight before she did?

"*Tai,*" Reora said, in a tone of obvious reprimand.

Tai plunged her knife into the tuber with a touch too much vehemence, sending its skin flying. "Right, right. Congratulations, Tanis."

"I'm sure you can summon more enthusiasm than that." Reora's nostrils flared.

Tai tried hard to force a better smile, but mostly she wanted to throw up. She couldn't fly at age thirteen. She'd just humiliated herself while everyone was watching. Yet her brother — *her baby brother, five years her junior* — just took flight with no fuss? It wasn't right. It wasn't *fair*.

"There will have to be a coming of age party, of course," Reora continued, ignoring Tai now that there was nothing to criticize. "Perhaps you could catch a giant crab, Roan, and I'll do the crab bake. And I suppose Tai can do the embroidery."

Tai dropped the paring knife, causing it to hit the floor with a clatter. "I'll do what now?"

"Well, naturally, everyone in the family must do our part," Reora said. "Honestly, you're not a bad hand with the needle, you could be one of the greats if you didn't insist on fiddling with those gizmos all day."

Tai's hand shook. "So I'm not permitted to even *wear* embroidery, but I'm expected to *provide it* for everyone else?"

"It's your wings that don't work, not your hands." Reora pursed her lips. "Honestly, Tai, when did you become so selfish? And *why* have you stopped peeling the tubers?"

It was too much. It was all too much. Tai shoved the bowl aside in anger. "Perhaps perfect Tanis can peel the Savior-cursed tubers himself from now on. He's a big fancy grown-up man, after all."

With all the petulance a thirteen year old could muster, Tai flared her stunted wings, and disappeared angrily back into her alcove.

CHAPTER FIVE
ANCIENT MAGIC

PRESENT DAY

Dorian uncomfortably shifted his weight between his feet as he listened to Jameson's angry tirade. The rant seemed to go on forever, with phrases like *disgraceful* and *grossly incompetent* spat out at regular intervals.

"The dragonauts of old were the shining exemplars of what humanity had to offer," Jameson spat. "If this is the best you can do, then you don't deserve to mop the floors in Cloudfire Castle, much less have the honor of being one of our dragonauts."

Years ago, in a fit of pique over one of Dorian's many shortcomings — he could scarcely remember which — Janus Callahan had snapped and said, *"Pathetic. If your best effort is going to consistently look like everyone else's bare minimum, you may as well stop trying."* Dorian couldn't afford to stop trying, not with Solaris's companions still in captivity. But it had been a long time since he felt his stepfather's words as keenly as he felt them during his first few weeks with the Order of the Silver Dragon.

And Jameson wasn't even done. "Members of an elite fighting

force," he said, "Should at least be able to avoid collapsing during hill sprints."

There it was. Dorian buried his face in his hands.

Dorian had thought he'd done fairly well for himself, improving his physical fitness over the past year. He'd gone from a soft and out-of-shape boy who'd never picked up a sword, to a competent aeronaut who'd managed to free no less than three of the enemy's captive dragons. He'd been proud of that, *Void curse it.* Proud enough to think that he might prove himself equal to the rest of the Order dragonauts.

Less than a week of training in Cloudfire was enough to disavow him of that notion. He wasn't just behind the others. He was woefully, humiliatingly, *laughably* behind. He lost every sparring match he participated in, he could only do about half the amount of push-ups as the others, and he could just *forget* about pull-ups. But that was nothing compared to the hill sprints.

Whoever invented hill sprints, Dorian thought, ought to be thrown the dungeons. Though perhaps they already *worked* in the dungeons, because they were obviously skilled in the art of torture. Defensively, Dorian thought he wasn't *entirely* to blame. In the past year living on a relatively small skyship, there was simply no easy way to emulate the act of running uphill. But that didn't seem to be a problem for Falgar and Sullivan, who ran up and down the Void-cursed hills just fine, sometimes stopping to sympathetically pat Dorian on the shoulder while he collapsed to his knees heaving for breath, or worse, vomiting into the grass.

«Just when I was starting to feel so pleased with myself,» he confided in Solaris ruefully.

«You were out of your depths before, and rose to the occasion. I have no doubt you will do so again. There's a free hour after this one. Why not do some extra training? I heard the sparring dummies are enchanted to fight back. And that hill is not going anywhere.»

No, the hill Void-cursed wasn't.

Dorian had hoped to spend his free hour in his quarters reading the same adventure novel he'd read half a dozen times already. Anything to turn his brain off. But he had a long road ahead of him — a long hill to sprint, as it were — if he wanted to catch up with the others. «I suppose you're right,» Dorian said with a real sigh to match his telepathic one. «Extra training it is.»

To his embarrassment, Dorian realized that during his conversation with Solaris, he'd utterly missed the end of Jameson's tirade. The flight leader finally finished with a snide, "Any questions?"

"Yeah," Falgar said. "I've got a question."

Sullivan groaned and covered his face with his hand.

"Very well." Jameson's jaw twitched. "Ask it."

"What in the Void are we doing here?"

More jaw twitching. "I'm certain I don't know what you mean."

Falgar folded his wiry arms. "I mean, what's the point of all this? We're training like some kind of secret army, but are we ever going to see any actual action?"

Jameson's nostrils flared. "Surely you don't think after today's display that you're ready for real action."

"Perhaps not yet." Sullivan came to Falgar's defense. "But we'd probably do a lot better in training if we knew what we were training *for*. What's the end game here? Do we really intend to just keep flying formation drills under cover of Illusion forever? *Why are we doing this?*"

Jameson seemed to consider and discard many responses before finally speaking. "The problem with secrets is, once they're out, there's no making them secret again. Janus Callahan leaves us alone because last time he was part of the Order, we were nothing more than a bunch of rich arseholes pontificating about a better world."

"Aren't we?" Dorian wasn't aware he'd made the decision to speak before the words were out of his mouth.

Jameson turned his sharp hawklike gaze towards Dorian. "Aren't we what?"

Dorian swallowed, mouth dry. "All due respect, ah flight leader, sir. But, um, *aren't* we a bunch of rich arseholes pontificating about a better world?" Oh, Void, he was well and truly in for it now. No way out but through. "Our dragons didn't agree to bond us just so we could stand around playing soldier. The Order was supposed to be about saving Cyrna's magic, and preventing Aeris falling beneath the underclouds. So. Um. Do we ever intend to do that?"

Dorian's face burned as he felt everyone's face on him. *Yes, good, beg for action, you who lost every single sparring match.* Jameson had been a dragonaut for longer than Dorian had been alive. Dorian, meanwhile, had bonded a dragon by accident, and his abysmal performance at training stood as stark evidence that he didn't deserve to be here. But from Solaris, he felt a thrum of approval, and that kept him standing upright.

Jameson seemed to deflate. "The truth is, we don't know how the Ancient dragonauts regulated the world's magic." It seemed like it cost him something to admit.

"My father told me once that they did it by flying to the moon." Dorian knew he should probably stop talking. But he felt slightly emboldened, since Jameson hadn't yelled at him quite yet.

Graigor snorted. "Even you can't possibly believe something so childish."

Hildegard shot him a glare. "Believe it or not, Beckett, there is some solid evidence in that direction."

"'Solid' is overstating things." Jameson looked faintly constipated. "Mr. Valmont, your father had a great many delusional ideas about the nature of magic, and most of them had very little bearing on reality."

Dorian wanted to argue further, but his courage for defying the flight leader was spent. Perhaps Jameson was right. Perhaps flying to the moon was an foolish idea, and perhaps his father had suffered from delusions of grandeur. But then why did it feel so *right*?

"Things are going well, I take it." A sardonic voice cut through the chatter, one that Dorian recognized at once.

"Lady Dragonmar!" Everyone scrambled to stand at attention, even Falgar and Graigor, who still wore sour expressions.

"I can hear you arguing from my study in the highest tower," Sylvia said blandly. "I should remind you that even Illusion can't block out sound."

Jameson had the decency to look chastened. "A thousand apologies, Lady Dragonmar. We shall have more care in the future."

"See that you do. Thankfully, I couldn't overhear the specific nature of your argument. Pray tell, what has you all so heated?"

"The children chafe at order and discipline." Jameson flicked imaginary dust off his uniform jacket. "Lady Dragonmar, I begin to worry it was a mistake to add so many to our number so quickly." He then briefly, and more than a little dismissively, went over the gist of their argument.

"I see," Sylvia said. "Well, as it happens, I agree with Mr. Falgar."

"You do?" Jameson and Falgar asked at the same time.

"You will most likely work far better as a unit if you have something to work towards. And I might know just the thing."

Jameson frowned slightly, his expression as curious as it was skeptical. "Go on."

"Hildegard. Last time you were on scout patrol, you found an aether stockpile at a Kasani-controlled outpost in Thlarknia. Is that correct?"

Hildegard looked faintly surprised at being addressed. "That's right, Lady Dragonmar. At least a dozen crates, I'd say."

"Excellent." Sylvia folded her hands together. "I want you to steal it."

"You can't be serious." Jameson looked like he might faint.

"We need more aether, to maintain the Illusion over the castle as much as anything else. Taking it from a Kasani base both hurts Callahan and helps us. And if you do your jobs correctly, no one will know you were there."

The change to the energy in the room was almost palpable. After what had been a funerary mood following the training session, the new dragonauts looked at each other with hope bordering on excitement. Even Dorian couldn't help feeling cautiously optimistic. It would be good to actually *do* something again. But then he thought about his dismal performance with the sword, and prayed to all the seven gods that *he* wouldn't be the one to mess things up.

"And then, Dorian told the flight leader off! Actually told him off!"

Tai listened with half an ear as Falgar told the story with many gesticulations and hand gestures. Predictably, of course, Dorian blushed.

"Stop it," Dorian said, "I didn't tell anyone off."

"You certainly didn't hold back how you really felt," Sullivan put in. With a faint smile, he added, "Proud of you."

This just seemed to embarrass Dorian more, and he paid careful attention to his fish and mushroom pie.

Tai poked listlessly at her own supper. She wasn't sure whether the queasy feeling in her stomach was from the cream in the pie, or the fact that she felt like an outsider even among her closest friends.

She wanted to be part of their banter. Gods and Ancients, she did. And it wasn't like they were trying to exclude her. But she wasn't a dragonaut. She hadn't been there for that training session. She had nothing to contribute to the conversation.

Enough self pity, she chastised herself. She forced a cheerful expression. "Tell me more about this alleged telling off."

"Jameson said Dorian's father was delusional," Falgar complained. "He's lucky Dorian didn't punch him in the face."

"Dorian's not going to punch the flight leader in the face, Falgar," Sullivan said.

"Well maybe he should."

"Wait," Tai said. "Why did Jameson call Cyrus Valmont delusional? Last I heard, these Order types all thought pure aetherlight shone out Cyrus's backside."

Still blushing, Dorian swallowed his mouthful of pie and explained. "When I was a boy my father told me the Ancient dragonauts flew to the moon. I thought that was the Order's official line, but when I brought it up to Jameson, he practically laughed in my face."

"Jameson's a walking toadstool."

"Falgar." Sullivan sighed.

"I'm pretty sure the Ancients did fly to the moon, though." Tai frowned. "I mean, the Prophecies of Rivka Severin mention it like half a dozen times. 'And from the moon will come salvation.' 'The Savior will reclaim the light of the moon.' It's always more or less assumed that meant magic."

"Yes, but flying there directly?" Sullivan wondered.

Tai shrugged. "Why not? It's no more outlandish than any of the other Ancient legends."

"Have you seen anything about the moon in all your library research?" Dorian asked.

Tai shook her head. As interesting as that strange spell in the red ledger was, she couldn't begin to fathom what it did, much less how to cast it. In the end it was no more useful than the fish sauce or the Voidwraith on the previous pages. Except... There'd also been something about the moon, hadn't there?

A chime rang out from Cloudfire's bell tower, signaling the end of dinner.

"I've got a bottle of Sanorian brandy and a deck of cards in my quarters," Falgar said. "Anyone interested?"

"I'll go," Sullivan agreed amiably.

Dorian grimaced and shook his head. "I'd love to, but I need to do some extra training. Don't want to be upbraided about hill sprints again."

Falgar shook his head. "Look at this guy, all bloody responsible. What about you, Tai? Brandy and cards?"

"Another time," Tai said regretfully. "There's... something else I'd like to do first."

"No fun, the lot of you. Ah well, Sullivan, looks like just you and me. Perhaps we could make it a game of strip poker."

"Falgar." Sullivan chortled and followed Falgar upstairs.

Tai smirked and shook her head. A card game — fully clothed, hopefully — sounded nice, but Tai knew she wouldn't relax until she looked at that spell circle again. She might not be a dragonaut, but she would make herself useful to her friends and the Order. She *would!*

Tai's amusement left her, however, as soon as she entered the library. Toric Verity and Vale Garamond, seated at one of the aether-lit study tables, ceased their conversation to glare in Tai's direction. Tai ignored them, but her feathers stood on end under their scrutiny.

"Another one of the Dragonmar's brother's little underlings," Toric said darkly. "You know they all got dragonstones because of nepotism, right?"

"*I* didn't get a dragonstone." Tai fixed them with a flat stare before ignoring them and getting to work.

Most of the surviving rebels had scattered or gone home to Kasa-narae after the Dragon's Fangs fell. A few, like Ryslen, stayed to care for the Order's gryphons, but in day to day life she saw little of her former comrades. On days like today she wondered if she might not have been better off leaving with the rest of them.

Dorian and the others were welcome by virtue of being drago-nauts, Xander was the dragonmar's brother, and Bradford had some nebulous connection to the Order that Tai didn't fully understand. But no one seemed to know what to do with Tai. If not for the others' insistence, she doubted she'd be tolerated in Cloudfire at all. She supposed she had been naive to hope she might make at least one new friend in this forbidding place.

But while most of her time here was an exercise in frustration, she *had* found the spell circle. And although she didn't yet know why, Tai knew it was important. There was a feeling of rightness within the pages of the old red-covered tome, a feeling of coming home. Vale and Toric could sneer at her all they wanted. She'd show them.

There it was, again. Pages and pages of dry descriptions of the moon, followed by the strange and wonderful spell circle. In the center of it all sat a crescent-shaped rune, with an arrow pointing outwards.

The moon.

She ran her hand down the rest of the page. Those were lesser runes of Kassoria around the outside, she was almost certain of it. Runes governing space and time. The arrows surrounding the central glyph could mean travel or displacement, perhaps a large gap between spaces?

"Fish sauce!" Tai blurted. Realization hit her with the force of a Thlarknian mining cart.

Toric, still talking to Vale in hushed tones, turned towards Tai and gave her a dirty look. "Excuse me?"

Tai flushed. "Nothing."

Excitement coursed through her as she turned the pages back in the red-covered volume. Moon phases. Fish sauce. The tides of the undersea. Perhaps it wasn't so arbitrary after all. Perhaps this book showed things that, at one time, could only be obtained via the lost magic of Planeshifting.

She had to tell Dorian right away.

"What are you doing?" Toric stopped her halfway to the exit. "You can't take books out of the library."

"What are you talking about?" Tai clutched the red volume protectively.

"They are for Knights and Dragonauts of the Order."

"The Lady Dragonmar herself said I might train to be a knight, now if you'll excuse me." Tai moved to push past Toric but the dark-haired knight blocked her way.

"You're a novice squire. And that's all you'll ever be if you don't stop acting like you're above the rules."

Vale tossed aside his blonde ponytail and gave Tai a half-sympathetic glance. "Toric, does it really matter? It's just a book."

"Just a—" Toric looked half way to an aneurysm.

"What in the Void are you three arguing about in the middle of the night? You're giving me a Void-cursed headache." A new voice interceded, welcome in familiar.

"Captain Xander," Tai said with relief.

"Not captain of anything anymore." Xander swayed slightly and there was a strong scent of whiskey on his breath. Tai frowned. The former captain had always enjoyed his drink, but he was usually less blatant about it.

"Is everything okay, Capt... Er, Xander?"

"Everything except for these buffoons." Xander massaged his temples. "Are they giving you trouble?"

"I'd hoped to borrow this book, but they say I can't."

Xander blinked at Vale and Toric. "Last I heard that wasn't a crime."

"As if we'd trust our collection to a treasonous drunkard like you," Toric practically spat.

Vale put a comforting hand on Toric shoulder. "Let it go, Toric. He's the dragonmar's brother. We don't want any trouble."

"Dragonmar's — ugh." Toric let out an indignant huff, but departed without further argument.

"Thanks for that," Tai said.

"No problem," Xander said. "So what's in this magic book that's got your feathers all twisted?"

Tai slipped the red book into her satchel and the two of them departed the library. As they walked, Tai explained briefly about Dorian's theories regarding the moon. She didn't tell Xander what she thought the spell did yet, though. She wasn't ready to share that with anyone, not even her friends.

"Interesting," Xander said. "No wonder Hildegard was so eager to get those books out of Greystone. Wonder if she even knew what she had."

"Probably an inkling." Tai forced herself to meet Xander's blood-shot hazel-brown eyes. "But in all serious, Captain. Are you all right?"

"Again. Not a captain." He ran his hand through his shaggy brown hair. "It's a bit strange, being home, is all. Really, it was my Void-cursed mistake staying away as long as I did. Which reminds me. Have you been back to visit your family?"

Tai's wings twitched of their own accord. "Not yet," she admitted.

"They're just down the hill, aren't they? I'm not captain anymore and I can't tell you what to do, but I really think you need to go see them. Don't wait three bloody Cycles like I did."

Tai grimaced. She'd promised she wouldn't go home until she was a success. An unemployed aeronaut who'd also failed to become a dragonaut certainly didn't qualify as successful. But as they crossed into a more public section of the castle and passed some Orith pilgrims oooh-ing and ahh-ing over an old tapestry, Tai recalled her last conversation with Tanis. Their mother had gone missing, and Tai had never even known. Xander was, unfortunately, right. She really had put this off for too long.

First thing in the morning, she resolved to talk to Dorian about giving her a ride down the mountain.

Hildegard, Jameson, and Dax climbed the spiral staircase to Dragomar Sylvia's private study.

"Feels wrong," Dax observed, "Not letting the newcomers into the fold."

"We'll welcome them when we know we can trust them," Jameson said.

Hildegard snorted. She'd known Meronethian Inquisitors who

were more trusting than Jameson. "And when will that be, I wonder? Some time around their hundredth birthday? They passed the Trials, they bonded dragons. Shouldn't that be enough?"

"Our work is too important to risk on a handful of recent outsiders. Besides. They didn't *all* pass the Trials."

Hildegard rolled her eyes. "Zekador's Pants, Jame. I know you're still sore that the boy's mother liked Cyrus more than you, but it's been *twenty years.* Nursing a petty grudge against a boy half your age is *beyond* pathetic."

Jameson's expression darkened, and for a moment Hildegard worried she'd gone too far. But then he shook his head and said, "It's not like the ones who *passed* the Trials are faring much better. Falgar and Beckett Void-cursed near knocked each other out of the sky."

"I admit that the training session could have been... improved." Hildegard winced. "But let's be realistic, Jame. None of them will ever be good enough for *your* impossible standards."

Jameson sniffed. "I only wish to uphold the reputation our predecessors enjoyed."

Dax, frowning, retrieved a silver fob watch from his voluminous robe pocket. "The Dragonmar is late."

"You've somewhere else to be?" Jameson raised his eyebrows.

"I'd hoped to send a message via aether beacon," Dax said, "But it can wait."

Dragonmar Sylvia swept into the room a moment later, looking poised as ever, with a cloth-wrapped bundle under her arm. "Forgive my tardiness. I needed a word with my dear brother Xander. And to collect this, of course." She placed the bundle reverently down on the mahogany desk. Everyone, even the aloof Jameson, craned their necks to get a better look.

Sylvia unwrapped the cloth to reveal what looked like an ornate silver hand mirror. Instead of glass, however, the crescent moon at the top enclosed a flat blue circle that shimmered and cast strange patterns in the afternoon light.

"Moon glass!" The dragonmar might as well have placed a live windserpent on the table. *Trouble*. That artifact had *always* been trouble. But to the Void if she wasn't eager to get her hands on it anyway. "I thought you lost that thing years ago."

"I did," Sylvia said, "And now it's back."

Hildegard knew Sylvia well enough not to expect any further explanation. She gazed instead at the eerie swirling patterns. "We're not going to try and enter spirit realm again are we?"

Supposedly, last time Xander and Cyrus saw visions of ghosts. Hildegard had only gotten a headache.

Sylvia pursed her lips. "No," she said, "We are not going to the spirit realm. But that's hardly the only thing this device is good for."

"It's a magical amplifier," Jameson said, "Possibly the most powerful ever created."

Hildegard's mind went back to their argument during training. With a powerful enough amplifier, maybe they really *could* fly to the moon. But she wasn't about the mention that now, not when Jameson was already in such a prickly mood.

Dax, however, looked thoroughly unimpressed. "The Ancients used the moon glass to *destroy* magic. I don't see how it's supposed to help us restore it."

"It's just a tool," Hildegard replied. "For good or for ill."

"Nothing for it but to try it out, I suppose." At a nod of permission from the Dragonmar, Jameson picked up the mirror and turned it over in his hands. He'd been off with the Eastern Mountain Dragon Clan the last time they'd tried to use the moon glass, so Hildegard supposed this was all new to him. "The new moon was the day before yesterday, so there's almost no ambient magic. Therefore, if this really *is* a magical amplifier, I should be able to light that candle over there without aether."

"I wouldn't—" Hildegard began, but too late. With the moon glass in one hand and his athame in the other, Jameson had already finished drawing the rune.

The spell exploded in a violent conflagration, sending Hildegard careening backwards into a nearby bookshelf. Heat blasted against her face before Dax cut it off with an impeccably-timed barrier spell. The nascent inferno guttered and died.

"Bloody Void." Hildegard climbed unsteadily to her feet. "Is everyone all right?"

"That was... more powerful than I expected," Jameson admitted.

"You're missing an eyebrow," Dax said.

Jameson felt his own face and groaned. Sure enough, smooth pink skin shone where a bushy brown eyebrow had once rested. "Well. Eyebrows grow back. If that's all anyone's missing, I count it as a win."

"Some win," Hildegard said, but it was nice to hear Jameson being positive about something for once.

Sylvia dusted herself off, composed as ever. "I'm glad you're all no worse for wear. In the future, however, I'd kindly ask you not to burn down my study."

"Apologies, Lady Dragonmar." Jameson looked earnestly shamefaced.

Hildegard looked down at the moon glass, equal parts terrified and impressed. No doubt about it. That device was trouble. But it might, she thought, be the exact kind of trouble they needed.

CHAPTER SIX
HOMECOMING

T anis Lunstrum was mending nets when someone pounded on the door. He set aside his work with mild annoyance, but by the time he was on his feet, his father was halfway to the door.

"I can get it," Tanis said quickly. Savior's wings, but the man was *supposed* to be resting.

"No, no, best let me." Roan tromped past on his wooden leg. "There's a good chance it's that Depths-rotted Aerishman again. Why Councilor Vyr suffers him, I'll never know. Of course, my answer remains the same."

"Father." Tanis sighed and prepared himself for the old well-trodden argument. "Maybe Vyr and this Aerishman have a point. Maybe I should—"

"Don't be foolish. You're only sixteen."

"*Exactly*. I'm only sixteen. I'm young and healthy. Having a demon won't affect me the way it did Mother. If I could do magic, it would really help the town. I could contribute more, and there'd be less pressure on you." However, Tanis knew his arguments were a lost cause. Roan wouldn't listen, he never did.

"Losing my leg was unfortunate." Roan sighed. "But it could have been much, much worse. Demonic fugue could mean losing your wings. Like your mother."

This gave Tanis pause. To know the freedom of flight, only to have it brutally snatched away... that was any Orith's greatest fear. First Tai, and then Mother had left home rather than continue to live with the shame of being flightless.

But that was the point, wasn't it? They'd left Tanis and Roan to care for the village and the dying silverleaves on their own. Could anyone really blame Tanis for what dangerous choices he made in the aftermath?

Roan pushed open the front door, no doubt ready to tell the Aerishman precisely where he could take his demonic magic.

However, it wasn't the Aerishman at the door. Or rather, it *was* an Aerishman, but not the one he was expecting. It was that stocky red-haired fellow he'd accompanied up the mountain with the porter crew. And at his side was—

"Tai!" Roan practically squawked in surprise. "The little hellion returns to us at last."

Tanis schooled his face into a carefully neutral expression. Truth-fully, he'd assumed that once his sister was inside that fancy castle with those fancy Aerishmen, it would be another eight years before she deigned to think about them again.

"Come in, come in." Roan hurriedly ushered the guests inside. "You look hungry. Come have some food. Tanis even acquired some cheese recently on a salvaging expedition."

Tanis caught a flash of a grimace on Tai's face, even as she tried to hide it. *Typical Tai.* Too fancy these days for salvaged cheese. Her companion, however, perked up at this news. "I like cheese."

While Roan cheerfully set about gathering plates and cutlery, Tanis returned to the net mending. He knew he ought to be more sociable to the guests. If Mother were here, she'd give him a stern reprimand. But, well, Mother wasn't here, was she? And the tides waited for no one.

Roan needed all the nets he could get if he wanted to catch enough fish to sustain them until the next tide. While no longer as efficient a fisherman as he'd been before he lost his leg, Roan was still one of the best in the village. Tanis was proud to be Roan Lunstrum's son. He just wished he could do more in the wake of his father's injury.

Mending nets was all well and good, and Tanis brought home a meager income with his salvaging and occasional work as a porter. But none of that was full-time employment. None of that could be relied upon. If Tanis had a demon, he could do Aerish magic, and then perhaps he could make a real difference around here.

"That's impressive." Tanis looked up from his work to find his sister's Aerish companion, watching with what seemed to be genuine interest. "All that delicate knotwork."

"I can show you if you like." He demonstrated the use of the bone needle and gauge. "Want to try?"

"I'll give it a go." The Aerishman tried making a few loops with the hemp rope, and then grimaced as the knot closed far afield of where he intended. "I'm sure nobody's good at it the first time. But I suppose for now I'd best leave it to the professionals."

Tanis took the net back and preened, just a little, at being called *professional*.

"Your, um, spoken Kasani," Dorian observed, "It's, ah, improved, since we were in the forest with the porter crew. Have you been, um, studying?" He scratched his neck, as if worried he'd said something rude.

Tanis smirked. "Is useful," he said in an affected thick Toreenish accent, "When them think you no understand."

Dorian flushed, but nodded. "I... suppose that makes sense. I don't speak much Toreenish, I'm afraid. Should probably learn it, if we're going to be staying in Cloudfire. I, ah, don't think I ever properly introduced myself. I'm Dorian Valmont."

"Tanis Lunstrum." Tanis twisted a length of rope around the bone needle and pulled it taut.

"So what do you use that net for, anyway?"

Tanis cocked his head, uncertain if he was being made fun of or not. "You don't have fishing in your sky world?"

The Aerishman blushed. "We do, in lakes and things. But I always assumed people used, you know, fishing rods. Little those funny sticks with the string on the end."

Tanis snorted. "You don't know anything about fishing, do you?"

"Not even a bit," Dorian admitted.

Pleased to know something a fancy Aerish adult didn't, Tanis briefly went over the basics of how fishing nets worked, at least until Father called them over to eat.

Tanis sat across from Tai and Dorian and awkwardly dipped bread and hard cheese in his fish and mushroom stew. It was impossible not to notice the way his sister and the Aerishman seemed to almost instinctively move in concert with one another, hands brushing against each other as if drawn together by those magnets Tai used to play with when they were kids.

"So," Tanis said, "How long have you two been courting?"

Dorian flushed bright scarlet, while Tai practically choked on her cheese. "We're not..." Tai forced herself to swallow.

"Tai and I are friends," Dorian elaborated.

"Pretty good friends, I imagine." Tanis smirked. He didn't consider himself an expert on the ways of the world but he was pretty sure most *friends* didn't make such obvious doe-eyes at one another.

Mostly, it amused Tanis to see his sister so obviously flustered. Tai's absence had been a specter hanging over their household ever since Tanis was eight years old. Somehow, runaway Tai was still the responsible one, the one who had her life together. Whenever Tanis got in trouble for shirking off lessons, his parents reminded him that Tai was a model student. Whenever Tanis did a halfhearted job at his chores, his parents were quick to point out Tai's thoroughness. Tanis often wondered why, if Tai was so perfect, she'd felt the need to leave them all behind.

Maybe she was just too good for the rest of them.

"Tanis..." As if sensing his thoughts, Tai's expression fell, and she poked awkwardly at her cheese bread. "About when I left..."

Tanis squirmed uncomfortably. Just because he'd been thinking about it didn't mean he wanted to talk about it.

Thankfully, another knock at the door saved him from such an unbearable line of conversation.

"I'll get it."

Tanis shot out of his seat with utmost speed, far faster than Roan could manage on his prosthetic. He half hoped it was Councilor Vyr or his Aerish ambassador, because a drawn out-argument with his father sounded like an improvement over a serious discussion about Tai's long absence.

Instead, however, it was his best friend Lana.

"Lana," he said reluctantly. "Now isn't really a good time. My sister..."

"Never mind about that," Lana said. "I think I've found one."

Tanis's heart made a nervous flutter. "You what... really? Oh... Oh Fallen."

The meaningful glint in Lana's eyes left no doubt as to what she'd found. He glanced guiltily towards his father and their unexpected dinner guests, wondering what they would say if they knew what Tanis planned to do. He'd dreamed of this day, planned it for weeks, but now that it was actually here...

"You can't tell me you're getting droopy wings." Lana put her hand on her hip.

"No, no." Tanis waved his hands. "I'll, uh, be right there. Just give me a second."

Tanis stole back in the house and grabbed his rucksack off the hook.

"Where do you think you're going?" Roan looked taken aback.

"Lana found a skyship wreck that's nearly intact," Tanis said. "Thlarknian, by the sound of it. We have to go before any of the other salvagers get to it."

Roan looked uncertain. "But your sister…"

Tanis ignored the guilty feeling wriggling in his stomach. It wasn't like he'd wanted his thrice-cursed sister to show up at such a crucial moment. "Do you want me to find more cheese or not?"

Roan looked at hard cheese he'd laid out on top of his bread, and then at his missing leg, and Tanis knew he knew it wasn't really about cheese. "Very well," he relented. "But please do try and hurry back."

"I will, I will." And before his father could argue further, Tanis bolted out the door and took off into the warm afternoon sky.

"You're not going to be in trouble for leaving when your sister's here, are you?" Lana asked as soon as they were airborne.

Tanis grimaced. "When he finds out what we're actually doing, that will be the least of my worries."

"But it'll be worth it, right?"

Tanis wished he knew for sure. He was taking an enormous risk, he knew that. Roan certainly wouldn't be happy about it. But Roan was stuck in the past. No amount of stubborn denial could force things to go back to the way they used to be. The town of Everwood was dying, and if Tanis wanted to have a chance to save it, and his family, he needed to take drastic measures.

One day, Roan would understand. He'd have to.

Tai watched, perplexed and a little dismayed, as her brother went flying out the door. Eight years they'd been apart, and he could barely stand to be around her longer than a minute. *Suppose I deserve that.*

"Sorry about him." Roan let out a long-suffering sigh. "Sometimes I think he is a man grown. Other times I remember he is very much just a boy."

"He seems like a good kid," Dorian observed as he helped himself to another piece of cheese. "I enjoyed learning about fishing nets."

Roan shook his head. "He takes a great deal of responsibility upon himself. Too much, for a boy his age. A lot of that is my own doing. I think he feels like he has to, ever since, you know." He adjusted the wooden stump where his leg used to be.

"Can I... ask what happened?" She glanced at his missing leg and glanced away. Her mother would have been aghast to know that Tai asked before the information was freely volunteered, but Tai didn't understand how she was supposed to simply ignore it when her stepfather was missing a part of his anatomy.

"Suppose it was bound to come up eventually." Roan winced. "Fishing accident, about a year and a half ago. I was careless. Rusted hook snagged my ankle. Didn't lose the leg right then and there, but later, from the infection."

Tai pushed aside her plate, her appetite leaving her. If they'd been in Aeris, a professional Healer could have cleared up the infection before it progressed that far. But this was not Aeris.

"I'm sorry," she said, though it seemed woefully inadequate. "I should have known. I should have written more, I should have come back right away, I could have helped."

"Don't," Roan said with a sharpness that surprised her. More gently, he added, "It's not that I don't appreciate the sentiment. But it's bad enough Tanis seems to have gotten it in his head that he's the parent and I'm the child. I don't think I could take it from both of you."

Tai twitched her stunted, useless wings. "I think I might understand a bit of how you feel."

"Aye," Roan nodded at her wings sympathetically. "Suppose you might at that."

"And Mother?" Tai almost didn't want to know, but she had to ask.

Roan nodded sadly. "Yes. She lost her wings to demonic fugue."

He let out a weak chuckle. "Some few years, our family's been having."

Dorian shifted uncomfortably. "I didn't know... didn't know demons could do that. People always used to warn me how dangerous they were, but I guess I never believed it, not really." Then, perhaps worried he was being rude, he added, "I'm sorry you went through that."

"You know much about demons?" Roan asked.

"I was bonded to one for a Cycle and a half," Dorian said.

"About eleven years," Tai translated the Aerish time reckoning for her father's benefit. Most Toreenish found it strange, how the sky-dwellers measured time in groups of seven years.

Dorian nodded. "We had a careful balance, an understanding. I realize... I realize not all who wind up with demons are so lucky."

Roan steepled his fingers thoughtfully. "I'd heard demons weren't too common on Aeris."

"They're not," Dorian said. "I was always considered a bit of an oddity for keeping Hematite around. Are they... more common here in Orith?"

"In the forests and the seas, most certainly. But the border guards keep them out of the cities and towns." Roan took a rather embittered bite of cheese. "At least, they used to."

"That's what I don't understand," Tai said. She thought about all the demon-possessed she'd seen when they arrived. "Why are there so many demon-possessed in Everwood?"

Roan let out a weak, bitter laugh. "A lot has happened since you've been gone," he said. "Around three years ago, the silverleaves started to lose their glow. No one knows why. And as you know, once the glow goes, trunk rot is quick to follow. Fertilizer from glowfish helps a little, which is why I was forced to spend so much time out at sea. But unfortunately it hasn't been enough. I begun to fear our little town was doomed. But then Councilor Vyr started listening to that Void-cursed Aerish dragonaut, and that's when everything really went to the Void."

"Dragonaut?" Tai looked at Dorian, but he looked as nonplussed as she felt.

"Oh, aye." Roan poured some greenwine out of a jug and took a larger than necessary swig. "Want any?"

"No thank you," Tai said. "Tell me more about this dragonaut."

"Right, right. He's a handsome bastard and a charming enough fellow, and at first he seemed like the Savior-given miracle we needed. You see, his Aerish magic restores the trees good as new, better than the entire ocean's worth of glowfish could."

"That's good, right?" Dorian wondered.

Roan's smile was grim. "You'd think so. But the trees start to die off again after a couple of weeks. And the dragonaut can't be here all the time. He's got lofty important dragonaut business to be about."

"A temporary solution at best, then." Tai was disappointed, but not particularly surprised.

"But that handsome dragonaut, he had a wonderful idea." Roan rolled his eyes. "What if the people of Everwood could do magic ourselves?"

"It's impossible to draw magic beneath the clouds without a dragon," Tai stated the obvious.

"Not," Roan said, "If you have a demon."

Dorian dropped his cheese slice. "But... drawing magic from demons is... Void, no wonder people are going into fugues left and right."

"Desperate times and all that," Roan said. "The people are so eager to find a solution to our woes, they don't stop to think about what it's doing to us as a whole."

Tai shook her head with dismay. Which dragonaut was causing all this? Her father had described him as Aerish and male, so that ruled out Dax or Hildegard. If this had gone on for several years, that meant it had to be Jameson. But Void take her, why? She might not much care for the man, but there were leagues of difference between being a bit stuffy and hidebound, and purposefully infecting her entire town with demons. The thought that the Order might be involved in something like this made her sick to her stomach.

Except. *No.* It wasn't just the thought of demons making her queasy.

Bloody Void-cursed Aerish cheese! She knew there was a reason she didn't like it.

"I'm sorry." Tai stood up abruptly. "I have to use the outhouse."

With a glance of apology towards Dorian for leaving him to make no-doubt awkward conversation with her stepfather, Tai sprinted out the door.

The communal outhouses, shared by all their branch residents, were located in the outer branches, far from the silverwood trunk and the central hub. Tai did her business as quickly as possible, then washed her hands from the nearby spigot. Thus relieved, she could pause long enough to get a proper sense of her bearings.

It felt strange, after all these years, to be back in her hometown. She had expected to feel *more,* somehow. Like stepping back in time to her childhood. But of course it wasn't like that at all.

The town had changed, in small ways and in large. Her favorite noodle shop was boarded over. The dressmaker was now selling herbal remedies. In an illogical way, it annoyed her. How dare things not remain precisely as she left them? And yet, in other ways, she found it hard to drum up any emotion about the place. It felt like just another stop-over on another skyship voyage.

Dorian, of course, had been in awe of the shining silver trees when they arrived. As a child, Tai found the silver-white against the gray sky to be depressingly drab compared to the vibrant world above. Looking at her home through another's eyes, she supposed she could see the beauty in it. But there was decay and rot in the town, too, far more than she remembered.

Tai passed a beggar, blue-veined skin in the advanced stages of demonic possession sickness. His dirty ragged robes hung off him like they were meant for a much larger man, and from the intricate embroidery on the cuffs and collar, he must've been someone of great accomplishment once.

The beggar groaned at her, evidently in too much pain to produce words. Tai stopped long enough to press a coin in his hand, and wished fervently that she could do more. Condescending as they might have been about it, Everwood always used to take good care of their poorest and sickest residents. No one used to have to beg.

But when she looked back up from helping the begar, she noticed something else that hadn't been there before. Or rather, someone.

A majestic dragon lay sprawled on the landing scaffold, indigo scales shimmering in the silver light of the tree. It wasn't Solaris, and it wasn't Jameson's dragon Cloud, either.

"Oh, you've got to be kidding me." She knew this dragon, all right. "Meroneth's balls. Void on a stick. *Savior's depths-sodden wings.*" Tai let out a stream of curses in both Kasani and Toreenish. A Void-cursed handsome dragonaut. Of course, *of course.*

"Tai Lunstrum. Fancy seeing you here." Kadmin Crowley sauntered towards her, confident and graceful as a treecat.

Tai gritted her teeth and grasped the hilt of her athame, wondering if there was any way she could shove him off the tree and make it look like an accident. Kadmin seemed to know exactly what she was thinking, and smirked. *Curse that smirk to the depths.*

"You're not going to kill me, Tai."

"You don't know that." Tai tossed her head back defiantly, but rather than feeling tough and collected, she knew she probably sounded like a peevish teenager.

"Tanis seemed to think you'd hide with your rebel friends forever. But I know you better, don't I? I knew you'd come here eventually."

"You've been *looking* for me?"

"Don't be so self-important," Kadmin said. "I care for this town too, you know. All those years on the trade caravan. I am not the mustache-twirling villain you think I am. But since you *are* here, we might as well have a chat."

Tai didn't remove her hand from her knife hilt. "My stepfather says you've been infecting people with demons."

"That's an awfully crass way to put it," Kadmin said. "It's scarcely my fault that your trees are dying off. You'd prefer I stand by and let them? I'm simply giving your people the means for self determination."

"But at what cost?"

Kadmin ignored the question. "A little bird told me you lost at the Trials last moon."

Tai felt a chill. It was an innocent enough statement, on the surface. The Trial results were publicly posted. But how much did Kadmin *really* know? She forced her face into a neutral expression. *Don't react*, she told herself. *He'll know he's on the right track if you react.*

"It must be so frustrating to fail at your goals yet again," Kadmin continued blithely. "But I did not come to fight. I came to extend an invitation."

"You what now?"

"Those people you travel with do not appreciate you. We, however, might. Leave them behind. Join the winning side."

Tai's eyebrows climbed to her hairline.

Kadmin flashed his straight white teeth. "Think about it. You, a dragonaut, flying with the Kasani. Isn't that what you've always wanted?"

"Bond a dragon against their will? I'd rather eat rock roaches. Besides. How do you know I won't betray you?"

It hadn't been longer than a handful of moons since Tai's last clumsy attempt at espionage. Surely the man wasn't fool enough to fall for the same ploy twice, much less *suggest* it.

"I don't." Kadmin shrugged. "But those bigger and more frightening than me know how to handle traitors." He spread his arms in what was clearly supposed to be a magnanimous gesture. "Serve us loyally, and the rewards will be significant."

Tai snorted and twitched her wings. "You must think I'm stupid."

Kadmin shrugged. "Not stupid. But foolish, perhaps, to squander your talents for those that cannot see your value." He flashed that obnoxious smile again. "Just think about it, all right? I'm here for two more weeks, then I return to Kasanarae. But I'm sure you'll know where to find me either way."

And without another word he leapt onto his dragon's back and the two of them soared towards the turbulent clouds.

Tai shook her wings out and ran a frustrated hand through her hair. What in the Void had *that* been about? She sighed and walked back to the dwelling, not looking forward to telling Dorian what she'd just seen.

Unfortunately, the afternoon's surprises were far from over.

Even from outside, Tai could hear the sound of angry voices. Tai entered to find Tanis looking defiant, Lana looking sheepish, and Dorian looking outright dismayed. Roan, meanwhile, paced the length of the central living area, his wooden leg making a soft *thok, thok, thok* against the woven mat floor.

"How could this happen?" Roan kept repeating over and over. "Savior help us all, how could this happen?"

"How could *what* happen?" Tai asked. But the answer was already evident.

"You wouldn't let me work through Dragonaut Kadmin or Councilor Vyr, so I had to take matters into my own hands." Tanis met his father's gaze head on, his brown eyes blazing with defiance. But his eyes weren't the only things that were aflame.

If she softened her gaze just a bit, just on the edge of her peripheral vision, she saw Tanis cloaked in an aura of blue fire. Dorian used to have an aura like that too, back in the old days, back on the *Phoenix*. And if she relaxed her focus even further, she saw the creature itself, verdant green and lizardlike, likewise swathed in sapphire flames. Demonfire. Despite his father's protestations, Tanis had gone out and bonded a demon. A demon he intended to use as an energy source. A demon who very well might send him into fugue like their mother.

"Oh, Tanis," she whispered. "What have you done?"

CHAPTER SEVEN
MACHINATIONS OF EMPIRE

What have I done?

Tanis clung to the dull gray tree trunk, gritting his teeth against the pain. It was agony the likes of which he had never known, all his organs drenched in liquid fire.

"Okay." He panted for breath. "Let's try this again."

He lifted the tarnished and chipped silver athame with a trembling hand and attempted, once again, to draw the rune for light. The world wavered around him and the edges of his vision blackened. At some point, without being aware of it, Tanis had collapsed to his knees.

Was this what his mother had done? Was that why his father warned him so adamantly against this?

«Surely you did not think it would be easy,» the demon Malachite said with unbearable smugness.

Tanis grunted, because he couldn't trust himself to speak. He wasn't out of his depth. He *wasn't*. He just needed more practice, was all. Tanis could excel at practically anything, so long as he put in a modicum of effort. Surely this Aerish demon magic was no different. When his mother used to do magic, she did it the same way she did everything — with grim-faced stoicism. Surely, *surely*, Tanis was not so pathetic he couldn't do the same.

«We are not dragons, doe-eyed and foolhardy, to give selflessly until we are depleted,» Malachite said with a dismissive flick of his tail. «You ought to have known that when you sought me out. If you wish to take, you must also give.» His mindvoice's tone changed at once, wheedling where it once was dismissive. «I can make the pain stop. All need do is say the word.»

Tanis's hands clenched into fists. He shouldn't. He knew he shouldn't. If he kept it up, only thing at the end of this path was fugue. But sheer agony won out over good common sense.

"Fine," he breathed.

Malachite was true to his word, and the pain ceased at once. For a blissful moment, Tanis knew a feeling of euphoria as his spirit energy drained out in a stream of silver-white. Tanis felt like he was floating high above the silverwood canopy, all of his worries far, far below. But then, just as abruptly as it began, it was over, and Tanis was left feeling weakened, depleted, and so, *so* exhausted.

Malachite stuck out his forked serpentine tongue, as if actually licking his chops.

"Was it a good feast?" Tanis massaged his temples,

«It will do for now, I suppose.» Malachite made a show of examining his claws.

"*Tcch*." Tanis braced himself against the tree trunk and rose unsteadily to his feet.

Was the demon visibly larger than he had been a few minutes ago? No, surely not. Demon growth did not happen that rapidly. Not from a single feeding. But the more Tanis gave of his life essence, the more powerful Malachite would become, until at last Tanis's body could handle it no longer, and then, *fugue*. If he didn't get possession sickness first, and that would be, in many ways, worse.

Whatever the case, Tanis did not dare to try Aerish magic again tonight. He sighed and dusted himself off prepared for another evening of his father's *I told you sos*. It wasn't that he'd expected demonic possession to be all treelight and sparkles, but he'd hoped that by now he would have made *some* progress at becoming a useful mage.

"Copper for your thoughts, Tanis Lunstrum?"

Tanis jumped, so startled he almost fell off the branch. Which it was a good thing he didn't, because he didn't think he had the energy to fly back up. "Good evening, Kadmin," he said, straightening his feathers and trying not to look like a Depths-sodden fool.

"Bad day?" Kadmin wore a sympathetic expression, though it didn't quite reach his eyes. He probably thought Tanis was such a backwoods bumpkin, struggling with the magic his own people had known for centuries.

"I know I should be learning magic faster," Tanis admitted. "But it's hard, sometimes, to practice, when every time I draw energy from Malachite I feel like I'm going to die."

Fool. Kadmin surely didn't want to listen to childish whining.

Kadmin, however, nodded. "If I might make a suggestion, you could consider spending some time in Aeris."

Tanis blinked. "What, leave? Leave Everwood?"

"Only temporarily, of course. Learn the spells with the aid of aether crystal and the ambient magic. Then, when you are ready, come home, and draw from your demon with knowledge and purpose."

Part of Tanis couldn't deny he was intrigued, but he shook his head. "My mother never needed to do that when *she* learned magic."

"No, she didn't," Kadmin agreed. "However, perhaps if she had... Well. Things might've turned out differently, mightn't they?"

Tanis tamped down his upwelling of annoyance. Kadmin helped the villagers out of the goodness of his heart. The least Tanis could do was forgive him being a bit insensitive.

"Doesn't matter anyway," Tanis said dejectedly. "I can't just skip merrily off to Cloudfire. I have responsibilities here, and nowhere near the coin required."

Kadmin put his finger on his chin. "There is, perhaps, one option."

"Oh?" Almost despite himself, Tanis perked up.

"The Kasani Sky Forces are always looking for reserve soldiers."

"A soldier?" Tanis couldn't hide his skepticism. "Why in the Void would the Kasani want me to be a soldier? I've never even held a blade before."

"You'd receive training, obviously." Kadmin shrugged. "You fight for us part time, remain in your homeland the rest of the time. You'd not spend all that much more away from home than you already do with your work as a porter. And all the while, you can practice your magic without draining your spirit energy."

Part of Tanis wanted to jump at the opportunity. But doubt tugged at him like a child on his mother's apron strings. No matter what Kadmin said, fighting for the Kasani was bound to be dangerous. His father had already lost his wife and his step-daughter. It would break the man entirely if Tanis died in the distant sky for some foreign cause.

"Sorry," Tanis said, "But I don't think it's a good idea." He spread his wings to fly back to his dwelling.

"There is, of course, compensation," Kadmin said. "Three imperial gold sovereigns a week for new recruits. That's, oh, about fifteen Saviors in the Toreenish currency. You'll get more, once you prove yourself."

Tanis stopped in his tracks. "*Fifteen Saviors?*"

That was more than three times what he brought home from the trade caravans. It was even more than Roan brought home from fishing, most weeks. With that, he could get his father set up with a proper caretaker, someone expert in the care and rehab of those with missing limbs. And if he learned magic from the Aerish, and put that knowledge towards saving the silverwood trees...

"It sounds too good to be true," he found himself saying.

"I'm not asking you to sign up today," Kadmin said with a shrug. "Just think about it, all right?"

By the time Tanis landed outside his front door, he was completely worn out. He let out a silent oath as he fought to compose himself. The last thing he wanted to do was make his father worry, or worse, confirm the man's beliefs that bonding with Malachite was a bad idea. But there was no denying that the creature sapped his energy. He, who used to fly laps around the village for the fun of it, was now winded from the relatively short flight home from the central hub. Things could not continue like this. *Some soldier I would make,* he thought.

And yet, the idea wouldn't leave him alone. If he could practice magic without giving energy to Malachite, then his stamina would surely return. Wouldn't it?

Tanis pushed the door open to find his father in his customary chair, clutching his leg in his hand and wincing in obvious pain.

"Father!" Tanis rushed to his side.

"Ah, Tanis." Roan looked faintly glassy-eyed, but he shook himself off and reattached his prosthetic, standing up with a fake smile that failed to hide his grimace. "Forgive me. You... caught me at a bad moment. But I'll be all right."

"This isn't all right, Father." Tanis quickly moved to support Roan so he didn't fall over. "There has to be something we can do. Aerish healing magic, or..."

"I've tried and tried to explain to you." Roan let go of Tanis and pottered over to the sideboard to make some tea. "Not everything can be solved with magic. Those Aerish healers have some neat tricks up their sleeves, I will grant you. But even their so-called miracles cannot re-grow a missing limb." Roan handed Tanis a cup of tea, and then settled back into his chair with his own teacup. "At any rate. It's not as if we have the coin for fancy Aerish Healers. All the effort of going out fishing on a bad day, and for what? Half a crate's worth of glowfish. If I didn't know better I'd half guess they're dying out, too."

Tanis shuddered. A few blighted groves of silverwood were worrisome enough, but if the entire Depths-sodden undersea was dying... well, it didn't bear thinking about.

"I don't say this to worry you," Roan said, "But I fear we must cut down on luxuries for a time."

Tanis swallowed and nodded his understanding, suddenly feeling guilty for the expensive tea in his hand. If their financial situation was serious enough that even stubborn, prideful Roan was willing to admit it, then they were probably in far more dire straits than simply having to cut back on luxuries.

"I could... take on more porter jobs," Tanis said slowly, his mind whirring as the beginnings of a plan began to take shape. "Would you be... all right, if I were gone a bit longer this time?"

"My dear boy, we've been over this. I am far more capable than you give me credit for."

Tanis raised his left wing in a gesture of skepticism.

"Look." Roan let out a long sigh. "The fact is, you're nearly to the Third Waypost. You'll be a man grown soon. You'll always be welcome here — I'm not kicking you out, Depths curse it — but I'm certain the Path the Savior has laid out for you does not involve wasting your youth playing nursemaid."

"But—" Tanis lowered his wings, the argument dying on his lips. This was what he wanted, wasn't it? Why, then, did he feel so strangely disappointed that his father hadn't tried to talk him out of it?

His family needed the coin. That was the inevitable truth. For now, he just had to believe that his father could take care of himself.

Tanis stepped back outside in to the cool evening air. He felt a bit guilty for lying to his father. But Roan had enough to be worried about already. Far better Roan believe he was doing his customary porter work, rather than fighting in a Depths-sodden war.

Steeling his resolve and gathering his energy, Tanis leapt from the branch and took off looking for Kadmin.

So Tanis found himself, scarcely three weeks later, in an itchy, ill-fitting Kasani uniform, guarding some remote outpost in middle-of-nowhere southern Thlarknia. And that was when everything fell straight to the Depths.

"Retreat!" Jameson's voice, relayed instantaneously through his dragon, sounded loud and clear even through the near nonstop barrage of enemy arrows and fireballs.

"Zekador's pants," Falgar swore as he and his dragon Meridian narrowly dodged an enemy spell. "The briefing didn't say a Void-cursed thing about battle-magi!"

"I thought this was supposed to be a quiet outpost," Dax agreed, more than a little accusatory.

Hildegard shook her head. "I should've guessed that the Dragonmar wouldn't be the only one who's good at Illusion."

Dorian had a bad feeling about this mission from the start. He wasn't sure if it was because he still lost nine out of ten sparring matches, or the fact that nearly every training session devolved into a screaming argument. Perhaps, at his core, Dorian was simply a coward. But he did not think, even for a moment, that the dragonauts were ready for real action.

So in the end, he wasn't especially surprised when the entire mission turned out to be a Kyrizzian-begotten disaster.

What had looked like a quiet back-country outpost was nothing more than Illusion magic. Once they'd crossed the spell barrier, they'd encountered a fully fledged military base, teeming with activity. The soldiers, predictably, were less than happy to see them.

"I said, retreat!" Jameson repeated.

"What about the mission?" Graigor demanded.

From astride his white dragon, Jameson shook his head. "Lady Sylvia needs to know about this. That's our top priority."

"No offense," Graigor Beckett retorted, "But, *to the Void with that.*"

"To the— What do you — get back here!" Jameson could only sputter as Graigor and Borealis shot like arrows towards the center of the stronghold.

"Oh, for the Void's sake," Jameson said. "After them! Before they get themselves and the rest of us killed."

Dorian, who was nearest, took off in Graigor's wake. He looked on in horror as the emerald dragon Borealis rained fire down on the soldiers below. He tried to tell himself that it was self defense, that these were Janus Callahan's forces. But it was hard not to feel sick at such a wanton display of violence.

Graigor and Borealis came to a rough landing, and Graigor tumbled free from his saddle. He took a moment to right himself, then charged towards the warehouse entrance, sword at the ready. "Everyone watch out for Graigor Beckett!"

"Gods and Ancients," Dorian complained. "He's enjoying this, isn't he?"

Graigor was a better swordsman than Dorian, but Dorian was, by a slight margin, the better flyer. After a swift and graceful landing, Dorian sprung from the saddle and sprinted after Graigor. It didn't take long to catch up.

"What are you doing?" Dorian was barely short of breath, a fact which might have made him proud in any other situation. "Jameson sounded the retreat."

Graigor turned around to glare at Dorian. "Yes, and Jameson's a moon-addled idiot. The mission was to get the aether crates, and that's what I plan to do."

Dorian looked around the warehouse. There was aether, all right, so much that it made the hairs on his arms stand on end. But anyone with eyes could see there was more than just aether stored here. Massive glass cylinders towered almost to the warehouse ceiling. Inside, blue liquid glowed, along with... well, Dorian didn't know what it was. A strange concoction of ash and dust curled around itself in a spiral pattern, reminding Dorian of a sleeping gryphlet. In certain light, it looked almost alive.

"What do you suppose that is?"

"Not my problem," Graigor strode confidently ahead and pulled an ather crystal straight from the wall. "One down." The rest of the crystals pulsed ominously.

Dorian pulled Graigor behind one of the barrels just barely in time to avoid a passing guard.

"What are you doing?" Dorian repeated in a harsh whisper. "Jameson *gave us an order.*"

Graigor let out an aggravated grunt and shoved Dorian out of the way. "Much as I know Jameson *loves* playing army, guess what? We're not in one. The only thing I promised to do was not blab that Cloudfire is full of dragons. And guess what!" He gestured wildly at the chaos outside the warehouse. "That particular gryphlet is out of the bag. So. I can do what I want, actually." He stepped away from the glowing tank and marched arrogantly further into the warehouse.

"Meroneth's balls." Dorian let out an exasperated sigh and scrambled after Graigor. "Use your brain for half a Void-cursed minute. You may be decent with a sword but you can't take down a whole base by yourself."

"Not all of us are as weak and useless as you," Graigor shot back.

Annoyance and shame prickled at Dorian in equal measure. He had been told he was *useless* for his entire life. Somehow, no matter what he did, he could never seem to get away from that appellation.

"I'm trying to save your life, you insufferable—"

"Stop right there!" A burst of magical fire zinged past. A warning shot, or perhaps a near miss. Dorian supposed he should count himself lucky he and Graigor hadn't brought the entire base down on themselves with their arguing.

Dorian drew his blade and turned to face his assailant.

The attacker was a gangly teenage Orith boy, with black-feathered wings poking out of the back of an ill-fitting Kasani uniform.

"You're just a kid," Dorian blurted.

Dorian caught a flicker of blue demonfire in his peripheral vision, and sure enough, when he softened his gaze, he saw a vivid green demon about the size of a large housecat perched on the boy's shoulder. Dorian felt a chill. He'd seen this demon before. Ancients help him, he'd seen this *Orith* before.

"What are you doing here?" Dorian wondered, flabberghasted.

"Void's sake, I have to do everything." Graigor stomped forward, sword at the ready.

"Stop!" Dorian deftly stepped between Graigor and the Orith youth, just narrowly managing to block Graigor's blade with the flat of his own. "That's Tanis Lunstrum."

"I don't care if he's the Queen of Vatea," Graigor shot back, "He's an enemy combatant!"

Void take him, Dorian didn't know *why* Tanis was here in an enemy uniform, but he would *not* allow Graigor Beckett to murder his best friend's brother.

A flash of blue glinted on Tanis's wrist as he frantically tapped on his aether beacon. "Attackers in the warehouse! Help!" Only after he lowered his hand did he finally seem to recognize Dorian. "Fallen Depths," he swore in Toreenish. "It's *you*."

Graigor's green eyes flashed with fury. "Now you've done it." For a moment, Dorian feared for his life. Would Graigor go so far as to kill Dorian to get to Tanis?

"It doesn't matter." Tanis looked like he might be sick. "You're too late."

The ground shook beneath them, forcing Graigor to stumble a few paces backwards. A glass cylinder shattered and blue liquid spilled out onto the stone floor.

"What the—" Graigor brandished his sword.

"Skyquake," Dorian said. His heart thudded in his chest, and his hearing narrowed to a faint ringing in his ears. *The ruins of Icereach Citadel crumbling around him, Hematite plunging into his soul, his father... his father...*

"Not a skyquake." Tanis tugged on Dorian's sleeve. "They're going to blow up the warehouse rather than let outsiders get ahold of the experiments. We need to run. Now."

"Experiments..." Those would be the tubes, Dorian supposed.

With what felt like an unfairly momentous force of will, he forced himself back to the present moment. "Right! Running."

All previous enmity forgotten, Dorian, Graigor, and Tanis sprinted for the exit, dodging falling bricks and gushing fluid. They staggered out the door just as the building entrance collapsed behind them. They weren't out of danger yet, however. The entire base was a mess of shouting and clashing swords and falling debris.

"Solaris!" Dorian called out for his dragon.

«Just a moment!» In his mind's eye, he saw Solaris fighting off no fewer than three enemy soldiers.

"Solaris!" Dorian cried again, this time in fear and worry. But Solaris held her own, a whirling vortex of spikes and claws and golden flame.

Graigor's dragon Borealis staggered to the ground a moment later, and Graigor wasted no time climbing up onto his saddle. Dorian expected the pair of them to fly off without him, but to his surprise, Graigor held out his burly arm. "Don't stand there like a sky-puffer, get on!"

Dorian took the proffered hand and scrambled onto Borealis's back. He cast a worried glance back towards Solaris, but she sent back wordless reassurances.

"Thank you," Dorian said to Graigor. Graigor might be a stubborn blowhard, but perhaps he wasn't all bad.

"Void take it," Graigor complained. "You're one heavy bastard."

Nope, Dorian thought. *He's still an arse.*

Borealis pumped his wings, frantic to get away from the rapidly-collapsing warehouse.

"But what about Tanis?" Below them, Tanis narrowly ducked out of the way of a falling piece of mortar.

"Who cares?" Graigor retorted. "I'm not getting killed to help one of Callahan's men."

«I have him,» came Solaris's blessedly reassuring mindvoice.

The ruby dragon, having finally extricated herself from her attackers, swooped down and deftly scooped Tanis up by the shoulders. "Gah!" Tanis cried out in surprise as Solaris launched herself into the sky.

"The Void does she think she's doing?" Graigor shook his head. "On you, Valmont, if your moon-blind dragon gets us all killed."

They flew at top speed into the warm desert sky, leaving the chaos of the base behind them. Dorian craned his neck to scan for any sign of pursuit, but fortunately, the enemy seemed more interested in making sure they didn't get whatever was in that warehouse. Far below, Kasani soldiers scrambled like ants to put out their own fires. When Borealis and Solaris passed through the Illusion barrier surrounding the fortress, it looked like a quiet and sleepy outpost once again.

This time, Dorian knew better.

They landed, exhausted, on the deck of the Order's skyship *Thunderbird*. Tanis Lunstrum kicked and thrashed in Solaris's claws. Dorian felt a twinge of guilt, but surely, *surely* this was better than letting him die in that collapsing warehouse.

The rest of the crew looked worse for wear. One of Dax's wings was in a sling, and Hildegard had a bloody cut on the side of her face. Sullivan had a bandage on his arm but he looked in better shape than the rest as he hurriedly tended to their injuries. They were, at any rate, all alive, and for that, Dorian was grateful.

Jameson massaged his temples in obvious annoyance as he looked from Tanis, to Dorian, to Graigor. "I don't even know where to begin. I suppose, first things first. Were you followed?"

"Doesn't look like it." Graigor gave Jameson a crisp salute, all trim professionalism now that they were back on the ship. One might almost think he hadn't flagrantly disregarded a direct order.

"Thank Zekador for the small miracles," Jameson said. "Explain yourself. What did you hope to accomplish, charging that warehouse?"

"I'd hoped to actually complete the mission and not fly away home with my tail between my legs," Graigor said. But then he seemed to calm himself and added, "Whatever was in that warehouse, I don't think it was simply aether crystal."

Dorian nodded in agreement. "There were... tubes. Strange, glowing tubes."

Hildegard raised her eyebrows. "Tubes, you say? Most curious."

"The Kasani blew them up, rather than risk us finding out what they were," Dorian added.

«Did you recognize what was in those tubes?» he asked Solaris, not particularly optimistically. She hadn't been with them in the warehouse, but she saw everything he did through their bond.

«Those curled up ash creatures,» Solaris said. «There was something... familiar about them. And unsettling. Nocturne might have known.» A flash of shame and worry coursed through their bond. «Nocturne is probably how your Janus Callahan found out about it to begin with.»

Dorian's heart did an uncomfortable somersault. Nocturne was Callahan's own personal captive dragon, and he'd also apparently been some kind of archivist or librarian for his dragon clan. Dorian feared to even contemplate what manner arcane knowledge his stepfather had forcefully taken from the creature.

"Chances are it was something they didn't mind losing, because they have more somewhere." Hildegard tapped her fingers together. "I've suspected for years that the Kasani Empire has designs against Thlarknia. If this base is any indication, those plans are much further along than we thought."

Sullivan pursed his lips with worry. "Perhaps our unexpected guest has some insight."

At long last, they all turned to Tanis, who had given up his thrashing, and now sat sullenly in Solaris's claws. "They were willing to blow the place sky high to prevent some strangers finding out. Do you really think they'd share their secrets with a reserve grunt like me?"

"This guy's as green as they come," Graigor complained. "I want it known it was Valmont's idea to bring him along."

Jameson buried his face in his hand. "We can question the prisoner properly when we get back to Cloudfire. Meanwhile, Beckett, Valmont, escort him to the brig. We can't just let him run around free. After that I want to see everyones on deck."

"One other thing." Graigor grabbed Tanis roughly by the arm, and yanked off the bracelet containing his aether beacon. He threw it unceremoniously over the side of the skyship, and Dorian watched as it disappeared into the clouds.

"Good thinking," Dorian admitted. He might not like Graigor much, but the last thing they needed was a repeat of the Dragon's Fangs.

"Your bloody bleeding heart, Valmont," Graigor complained as he helped frog-march the angry Orith down the stairs. It was more difficult than it looked, with the boy's massive wings flaring out at every angle. "Could've just left well enough alone, but *noooo*, you had to drag home one of the enemy soldiers as a Void-cursed pet."

At least I didn't disobey orders, Dorian thought sourly.

They finally finished manhandling Tanis down into the brig, and locked him in an iron barred cage.

"Sorry about this," Dorian said with what he hoped was a sympathetic smile. Tanis only stared at him balefully.

"Why in the Void are you apologizing to *him*?" Looking utterly disgusted, Graigor spat into the cell.

Dorian flinched. "Was that *really* necessary?"

Tanis's voice cracked a little. "I really don't have any information, you know. I only joined up three weeks ago, and as a reserve at that. They don't tell me a Depths-sodden thing."

"I believe you," Dorian said, because he honestly had no reason not to. Ancients help him, he'd just been at the boy's house in Toreen watching him mend nets. What in the Void was he doing here?

"Yeah, well, Valmont's an idiot." Graigor cracked his knuckles. "Torture isn't off the table, you know."

Dorian glared at Graigor. "Torture is *very much* off the table. I just want to know… what were you doing on that base in the first place? Why aren't you in Everwood with your father?"

For a moment, the Orith youth looked terrified and guilty and vulnerable, but then he scowled and crossed his arms. "I know what you're doing. This is like that Good Guardsman Bad Guardsman thing. Your friend over there stands there all menacing and making threats while you pretend to be my best buddy. Well. I'm not going to play along!"

Dorian sighed. "We're not playing Good Guardsman Bad Guardsman." Though he was painfully aware that, from an outsider's perspective, that was probably exactly how it looked.

A shaft of sunlight cut through the trapdoor above as Hildegard poked her head inside. "You two coming? Jameson's about to have an aneurysm."

Dorian winced. "No avoiding it, I suppose." To Tanis, he said, "We'll talk later."

Tanis rolled his eyes. "I can *hardly* wait."

CHAPTER EIGHT
A NEW ASSIGNMENT

T ai ought to have known that it was a bad idea to go to the
tavern.

It had been a frustrating afternoon already, stirring in
the library, hitting dead end after dead end on her Planeshifting
research. She was close. She *knew* she was close. But she just couldn't
focus, knowing that Dorian and the others were in danger without
her. The relative safety of Cloudfire Castle felt stuffy and confining.

So when Captain Xander and Lord Bradford asked if she wanted
to grab a few drinks, she'd responded with an enthusiastic "Ancients,
yes."

That was how she found herself a few hours later, nursing her
third glass of strong Toreenish greenwine, while Xander and Bradford speculated over which Order members might be secretly
courting one another.

"Jameson and Hildegard?" Bradford suggested.

"Not a chance in the Void." Xander shook his head vehemently.
"Now, Vale and Toric, that's a possibility."

"I thought Toric was Valgrenite," Bradford said.

"Yes," Tai said, "And Vale's a man, so I don't see the problem."

Bradford leaned forward conspiratorially. "I think Vale might be a woman in disguise."

"Bradford," Xander sighed, "You can't just speculate on someone's gender. If Vale says he's a man, he's a man, and that's that."

"Sorry, sorry." Bradford seemed to cast about for a change of subject. "Say, Tai. Did, mmm, the Lady Dragonmar ever get back to you about the tree situation?"

"No." Tai sighed and ruffled her wings in consternation. She'd made her report when she came back from Everwood, but as far as she knew, it had gone into the Void where reports went to die. "Sending a dragonaut or two to help random towns once in awhile would go far towards building good will, but I doubt the dragonmar cares what someone like me thinks." She tried not to let her voice reveal too much bitterness.

"I love my sister dearly, but she's got her head so far up her own arse, she's practically a pretzel." Xander downed the last of his greenwine.

"That is *not* a mental image I needed." Bradford winced and drained his own glass. "Meroneth's balls, though. I wish she wouldn't treat me like such a child. Being in Cloudfire makes me feel about eight years old. I was the leader of the rebellion, for Zekador's sake!"

Tai nodded in sympathy. She didn't know Bradford well, but she felt a distinct kinship with him at this moment.

"My sister's not all bad," Xander said fairly. "She believes in doing the right thing — eventually. Zekador's Pants, though, if you think she's bad now, imagine growing up with her."

"I *did* grow up with her," Bradford said dryly.

Tai cocked her head sideways. "How did you meet Xander and the Dragonmar, anyway, Bradford?"

"Well," Bradford began, but before he could continue, another voice slurred voice cut into their conversation.

"I could tell you about that bitch Lady Ferran." A tawny-winged Orith man, clearly well in his cups, stumbled over to the table.

Tai froze. They clearly were referring to Sylvia, who used her grandparents' name when dealing with the townsfolk. It was one thing for Tai and her friends to complain about her, but Tai had a feeling this situation could get ugly fast. "What kind of things?" she asked carefully.

"Cloudfire used to be a prosperous town, until you barebacks showed up like you owned the place."

Tai's feathers stood on end. "Maybe we should—"

"*Used* to be prosperous?" Bradford crossed his arms. "The whole place was run by your crime cartels before *we* cleaned the place up. *You* ought to be grateful."

Tai buried her face in her hand. "*Maybe* let's not start a fight?" Tai desperately tried to think through how she might defuse the situation. To the newcomer, she said in Toreenish, "Don't worry, we're just leaving." She hastily dug out her coin purse and left a pile of coins on the table to settle the tab.

"Don't speak Rivka Sevarin's tongue to me, you Depths-sodden traitor bitch," the Orith man spat. "You're no better than one of them. No point having wings at all for the likes of you, is there?" He shoved her hard on the shoulder, grabbing a handful of feathers as he did so.

"Hey!" Xander sprung to his feet and unsheathed his belt knife. Bradford looked a bit confused, but he followed suit a moment later and settled into a well-practiced fighting stance.

"Barebacks have fangs." The drunk stranger grinned and drew his own blade as if he'd been looking forward to this all day.

Tai groaned and shook out the wing he'd grabbed. How in the Depths was she going to stop these moon-blinded fools from gutting one another?

Thankfully salvation came when the tavern door swung open, revealing Vale and Toric in their crisp blue House Ferran cloaks.

The malcontent sneered at them, but, perhaps realizing he was outnumbered, he stalked away.

"Thanks for that." Tai smiled hesitantly at Vale and Toric, but their stony expressions didn't waver in the slightest. In fact, she thought maybe they looked even more annoyed than before.

"Engaging in tavern brawls. Picking fights with the locals." Vale sniffed. "Have you given a the slightest thought to how that looks?"

"We didn't pick—" Bradford began, but at a sharp glance from Xander, he closed his mouth.

Once they returned to Cloudfire, the Order knights marched them straight to the Dragonmar's study at the end of a long spiral staircase. Toric knocked rapidly on the door. "Lady Dragonmar? A word?"

"Enter." Perhaps it was Tai's imagination but she thought Lady Sylvia sounded exhausted from the other side of the heavy wooden door.

The Dragonmar's study was best described as organized chaos. Every possible free surface was covered with books, stacks of papers, and magical gadgets whose purposes Tai couldn't even begin to name. But everything was lined up in neat little rows, and Tai had a feeling Sylvia never had trouble finding anything.

"How can I—" Sylvia cut off abruptly as she took in their bedraggled appearances and noted the strong scent of alcohol that no doubt wafted in after them. "What in Zekador's name happened to you three?"

Vale's mouth drew into a grim, frustrated line as he explained the confrontation at the tavern.

Sylvia massaged her temples. "Xander," she said, "I cannot stop you from engaging in drunken buffoonery, but in the names of all the gods, do not drag Bradford down to your level."

Bradford tugged on his collar. "Actually..." *hic...* "I, mmm, invited him, Mmmm... m'lady Dragonmar."

Tai winced. The young lordling was even drunker than she thought.

"That does not make it better." Sylvia sighed. "Vale, stand watch at the door. Toric, go fetch one of Healer Estevan's sobriety tonics.

We ought to eat least talk things through with clear heads." She glared especially at Xander.

Toric returned a few minutes later, carrying a glass flagon of a foul-smelling brownish green substance. It tasted about as good as it looked, and although Tai's buzz had already mostly worn off by that point, now it was gone entirely, leaving only a dry mouth and a bitter headache in its wake. *Party's over.*

"Now that that's taken care of," Sylvia said, "Explain yourselves."

Xander, shamefaced, ran his hand through his shaggy brown hair. "It was my fault. A lapse in judgement. I admit I've been... frustrated, stuck inside the castle."

"And I'm used to running a rebellion," Bradford put in. "Here it feels like I'm being treated like an errant child."

"So you chose to *act* like an errant child?" Sylvia massaged her temples. "I cannot prevent you going to the tavern. You are, as you say, adults. But picking fights with the townspeople? No. That I cannot allow."

"For the fifteenth time," Bradford complained. "*He started it.*"

Sylvia opened and closed her mouth several times before responding. "It sounds to me," she said, "That what you three need most is more work to do."

The three of them exchanged wary glances. That sounded like a sentence to muck the gryphon stables if ever there was one.

But what Sylvia said next took them all by surprise. "I'm sending all three of you to Kasanarae."

"*Kasanarae?*" all three repeated at once.

"Yes," Sylvia said, "Kasanarae. Bradford, you said you wanted a rebellion? Well then, you shall have one. I wish for you to travel to the Kasani capital, get in touch with the city's underground elements, and cause Emperor Callahan as many problems as you can. Our agent in the city, Faris Saunderlain, works at the docks. She'll be a good place to start looking for information."

Bradford perked up like an eager schoolboy. "Happy to, Lady Dragonmar."

"Xander," Sylvia continued, "I know it's a challenge for you, but I expect you to be the adult in the room and keep him out of too much trouble."

Xander nodded, frowning. "Will it be safe for him there? He's Janus Callahan's son."

"I know whose bloody son he is." Sylvia wore just a ghost of a smile. "Bradford, I taught you how to cast Illusion magic. I know you are competent. You might not pass yourself off as an employee in his household like I did, but I'm confident you can live in the same city unrecognized."

"Of... of course, Lady Dragonmar." Bradford looked like he couldn't believe his good luck.

Sylvia then turned to Tai, who quailed slightly under her intense blue-eyed gaze. "You, however, *are* to pass yourself off as one of the Emperor's employees."

Tai blinked. "Eh?"

Sylvia steepled her fingers together. "You mentioned some weeks ago that an enemy dragonaut was recruiting people in your hometown."

"Kadmin, yes." Tai was surprised the Dragonmar even remembered. Perhaps her report hadn't gone into the Void where reports went to die, after all.

"I want you to take him up on his offer."

"You're joking."

Sylvia shook her head. "Afraid not. We badly need more dragonstones. The enemy has at least one. I want you to steal it."

"Steal it," she repeated faintly.

"And anything else from the palace you might think is useful. Including, I think, information."

Tai was stunned. It felt like the room was spinning around her. Had the whole world lost their Void-cursed minds?

"I'm afraid, with spring Voidstorms rolling in, we don't have much time to plan," Sylvia said. "Your skyship departs the day after tomorrow."

The day after tomorrow. The dragonauts weren't due back from their mission until the end of the week at the earliest. She wouldn't have a chance to say goodbye. And yet... this was her chance, wasn't it? A way to finally prove herself, to find her place in the Order?

"Very well," she said faintly. "I'd best start packing."

The return flight to Cloudfire was as long as it was uncomfortable. Dorian wished he could fly in the Linking with the aeronauts, but the *Thunderbird* already had a full complement, which left the dragonauts with nothing to do but stew over what went wrong.

They'd failed to retrieve the aether cache, revealed to the enemy that they had a team of incompetent dragon riders, and were sent flying home with nothing to show for it but bad news.

"They know we have dragonauts, but they don't know where we came from," Hildegard kept repeating, perhaps to reassure herself as much as the rest of them. "They won't think to look in Cloudfire. Sylvia's Illusions are too good."

"Janus Callahan isn't stupid," Jameson countered. "Surely he must realize Sylvia and Xander are descended from the Ferrans. He'll put two and two together eventually."

"Will he, though?" Hildegard asked. "Void, I was in the Order longer than he was, and even I never knew about Cloudfire until two years ago."

"Yes, but Janus—" Jameson shook his head and buried his face in his bandaged hand. "Too many unknowns. What we do know, however, is that Kasanarae seems to be gearing up for a full-scale invasion, and there's Void-all we can do about it."

"What about those glass tubes Valmont and Beckett reported?" Hildegard wondered. "What are they doing that's so secret they were willing to destroy it before letting us find out?"

"Perhaps once we've regrouped, we could send a scouting mission," Sullivan suggested.

Jameson, however, shook his head. "There's too few of us and too many of them. And now we've tipped our hand, they'll be even better prepared."

«I agree,» Solaris said. «We should hold off further action until we can learn to fly together like civilized individuals.»

The others nodded in grim agreement, except for Graigor and his dragon Borealis.

«I begin to think you lack nerve, Solaris,» Borealis said. «Or has your rider's weakness rubbed off on you?»

"Don't talk to her that way," Dorian said. He was used to aspersions cast against his own strength and courage, but he would suffer none of that against Solaris.

"He's right, though," Graigor said. "When Borealis and the others accepted our Summons, they thought they'd be joining someone *competent*. If you'd just let me kill the Orith brat, he wouldn't've sounded the alarm, and we wouldn't be in this mess."

"*In this mess?*" Falgar shot back. "If you hadn't run off, there wouldn't *be* a mess in the first place!"

Graigor shook his head. "At least I *did* something. At least I wasn't a *coward*. Kyrizzian help us, how useless can the rest of you be? Especially *you*, Valmont."

Useless. The too-familiar word settled in the pit of his stomach and sprouted thorny tendrils. *Useless.* Zekador help him, he thought he'd gotten past this. He was *supposed to* have gotten past this.

It was at times like these that Dorian missed Hematite most of all. Legend had it that demons used to be humanity's guides and protectors, before icy corruption turned Lord Meroneth's heart. Dorian didn't know how much of that was true, but Hematite always used to feel like the old kind of demon — a guardian, a moral compass. He'd been bonded with the creature for so long, he wondered how much of his own sense of justice came from himself at all. Without Hematite, could he really trust his own judgement?

If he couldn't talk to Hematite, Dorian wanted to talk to Tai. She was Tanis's sister. She would know what to do. Tai *always* knew what to do.

Unfortunately, as soon as they touched down on Cloudfire's airship platform, he knew it wasn't to be.

"What do you *mean* the *Roc* has already departed?" Hildegard's face fell as soon as she heard the news.

Evidently, the Order's other skyship left for Kasanarae the previous day, carrying not just Tai, but Xander and Bradford as well.

"Hey, now, don't yell at me," said Vale, who was on dock duty. "I'm just the messenger."

As bad as Dorian felt, it was nothing to how Tanis looked. The Orith boy sunk to his knees, wide brown eyes shining with fear and misery.

"My sister isn't here?"

"I'll, uh, go get the Dragonmar." Vale cast an uncertain glance at the prisoner before departing the skyship landing.

"Not that it would have done you much good if your bitch sister were here," Graigor said pitilessly. "If it were up to me, we'd've hauled you overboard the moment Valmont's bleeding heart dragon dropped you on our skyship. In fact." He crossed his arms and sneered. "It's still not out of the question."

"You can't be serious!" Dorian stood protectively between Graigor and the Orith boy.

"Enough, both of you." Jameson sounded annoyed, almost bored. "Nobody is getting hauled overboard. The boy will have to go to the dungeons until we figure out what to do with him."

"But—" Dorian protested. He'd seen Cloudfire's dungeons. They were cold and dank and poorly maintained. Better than death, sure, but hardly a suitable place for a teenager.

"Surely you don't think we can just let him go," Jameson said.

"Well, no, but — but he's just a kid!"

"I'm sixteen," Tanis said, not helping his own case.

"Come now, is this how we treat our guests?"

Dorian felt a wash of relief as Dragonmar Sylvia joined them on the dock. Finally, here was someone with *authority*, someone who could take *charge*.

Sylvia gazed at the young Orith with raptor-like intensity. "Tell me. How did you come to be in the Thlarknian borderlands?"

Tanis swallowed. "I signed up as a reserve soldier because my family needed the money, and they said they'd teach me how to do magic. Nobody told me anything important, I don't have any secrets to share."

Sylvia nodded, her mouth a thin, thoughtful line. "I believe you," she said, "For now." To the others, she continued, "I see no need to lock him in the dungeons. But of course, sending him on his way is out of the question. Even if he can be trusted, which we have no way of knowing, they would gladly torture him for any information about the Order they think you have."

Tanis blanched. "They wouldn't do that. Would they?"

"They were perfectly happy to let you die when they destroyed the building you were in," Sullivan pointed out.

Tanis opened his mouth, perhaps to protest, then closed it again, lowering his wings and staring balefully at the ground.

Sylvia's expression was grave. "There are few limits to what Janus Callahan is capable of. For your own safety more than ours, it is best if you stay in Cloudfire."

"So, what?" Graigor asked, disgusted. "We just give him the run of the castle?"

"Not at all," Sylvia said. "One of you will have to look after him."

Jameson scoffed. "We're dragonauts, not babysitters."

"I'll do it." Dorian hadn't consciously decided to speak before the words left his mouth. "I'll be responsible for the boy."

Jameson's eyebrows shot up so high they almost disappeared in the wrinkles of his forehead. "You?"

Sylvia, however, fixed Dorian with a scrutinizing expression. "Very well. The prisoner will be your responsibility. But should he betray us or harm the Order, then you will also shoulder the blame."

Dorian swallowed and nodded. In the past two moons, he'd gotten Hematite killed, possibly ruined his friendship with Tai, and made a bungled mess of their first ever mission. He didn't think he could stand it if he failed at this, too. But taking responsibility for Tanis was the right thing to do. He knew that as surely as he knew he liked flying and pie.

"I understand," he said.

CHAPTER NINE
KASANARAE

The Azure Sky Docks greeted Xander with the air of an old friend returning home. Just being on the docks, any docks, felt like a breath of fresh air compared to being cooped up in dreary old Cloudfire Castle. Unfortunately, he wasn't about to embark on another exciting voyage; he wasn't returning to the wild freedom of the sky. None of these ships waited here for him. *No.* He and young Bradford were here on his sister's bidding. Again.

He supposed he ought not to complain. Tai Lunstrum was the one in real danger. She was bound for the Imperial Fountain Palace itself. Xander wondered with a sinking heart whether he'd ever see his former employee again.

"She's a smart girl," he told himself. "I know she'll be all right."

Xander didn't realize he'd spoken out loud, but he must have, because Bradford looked up with understanding. "My brother thinks highly of her." With a grimace, he added, "If anything, I envy her job. I know I can't do it, for the obvious reasons, but *come on.* Which would you rather do, move cargo, or lounge about the fountain palace all day?"

Xander snorted. "I doubt she'll do much lounging around. Nope, we've got the easier job, no doubt about it."

Bradford looked slightly ill.

"You'll be all right." Xander examined the boy. The minimal Illusion masking Bradford's hair and eye color might not seem like much, but unless you were a genius at it like Sylvia, less was more where Illusion was concerned. It was the clothes that truly made the disguise. Xander doubted many would look for the Emperor's wayward son in common dockhand's clothing. However, he noted with a frown, the boy's stiff, regal bearing meant no one would confuse him for a seasoned laborer, either. They'd need to work on that.

The dock master, a balding man a few years Xander's senior, looked them up and down with a bored, pursed-lipped expression. A demon sat perched on his shoulder with a hide of shimmering garnet cloaked in blue flame.

"Names?"

"Cedric Weatherbee." Xander gave the fake name they'd agreed upon before leaving. "I've over two Cycle's experience working on the docks." Not quite a lie. "This is my nephew, Brand. He's inexperienced, but makes up for it in work ethic." Almost the truth. "I'm supposed to ask for Faris Saunderlain."

"Family friend, eh?" The dock master smirked.

Yes, actually. Faris was the Order's main contact in Kasanarae. But Xander had no idea if the dock master knew that.

Bradford, for his part, gave a weak smile. "That's me. His hardworking nephew."

"Very well." The port master boredly wrote their names down in a dusty ledger. "I am Regnald Barca, but you will call me Dock Master, Boss, or Sir."

"Yes Sir," said Xander. "You work on these docks for long, Port Master?"

Regnald stared at Xander with a look of barely suppressed contempt. Finally, he said, "Cedric, you'll be with Faris's crew over there on dock thirteen. Brand, you'll be over with Stokes on dock four."

"What, we won't be together?" Bradford blurted.

Regnald gave him a flat stare. "Is that a problem?"

"N... no. No problem."

"Hmm." Regnald slammed the ledger shut. "Come back at the end of the day for your pay, and if your crew leader doesn't complain too much, there'll be more work for you tomorrow."

"Right. Okay." Bradford let out a plainly terrified breath as soon as they were dismissed. "No problem. Dock four. Right."

Xander cast the young lordling a worried glance. The boy reminded him a bit of Dorian on his first day. Utterly out of his depth. How had this green youth managed to run an entire rebellion on his own? "You'll do *fine*." He hoped to all the gods he was right.

Xander, meanwhile, had his own work to do. With all the swagger he could muster, he made his way to dock thirteen.

"Crew leader Faris?"

"Ah. You'd be Sylvia's brother, I presume?" The crew leader emerged from behind a stack of crates, and it took all of Xander's training not to let his mouth hang open. The fact that she was a woman wasn't so unusual — most dock workers were men, sure, but in a big city like Azure, female dock workers weren't entirely unheard of. But far more surprising was her tail. It was long and tufted, like a lion's, coated in fur the same color as her graying brown hair. She also had a pair of spiral ram's horns curling out from behind her pointed ears.

"Never seen an Iriya before?" Crew Leader Faris seemed to take his gawping in stride.

Xander realized he'd been unbelievably rude and fought to regain his composure. "I... haven't, actually," he admitted sheepishly, if also truthfully.

"I'm not surprised," Faris said. "Not many of us dare to leave the homeland."

"Pleasure to make your acquaintance. I'm, ah, Cedric Weatherbee. Here to—"

"To help with the crates, of course." Faris grinned, revealing pointed canines. "You can start with that stack over there, bound for the cargo hold on the *Aurora*." She handed him a wheeled push-cart, and Xander set to work.

As he moved the massive wooden crates up and down the gangplank, he did his best to listen in on the conversations around him. Faris wasn't about to talk shop about the Order here on the docks where practically anyone could overhear, and of course nobody knew him enough to confide in him. But there was a lot one could learn from some simple old-fashioned eavesdropping of his own. *Ears open, mouth closed,* as his sister always liked to say. In this way, he learned that the Thlarknians hadn't lifted their aether embargo following the sinking of the Dragon's Spire last year, and that the Emperor was just itching for an excuse to declare war. Many dock workers were worried about conscription. Lots of unrest among the common people, that was for certain. Bad news in general, but just perhaps, good news for Xander and his hopes for revolution.

"That's the *Aurora* all sorted," he reported some time later. "What's next? I don't see anything staged at dock fourteen." He gestured towards a magnificent vessel that hung suspended above the next dock over, its aether sails glimmering in the spring sunlight.

"No, there wouldn't be, that's the *Imperial Javelin*." Faris rolled her eyes. "Emperor's newest boondoggle, that. Still under construction, if you can believe it, moons behind schedule. Of course old Regnald is having fits about it. Anyway. Supposedly, she'll be the fastest ship in the seven skies, if they ever finish her. Pity they'll just use her to rain cannonballs down on the innocent Thlarknians."

"Thlarknia again." Xander frowned.

"You can work on loading the *Pride of Valgren* over there on dock fifteen." Faris pointedly moved the conversation back to work, and Xander hurried to comply.

By the time the sun sank behind the underclouds, Xander was

more tired than he'd felt in a long time. His own exhaustion was as nothing, however, compared to young Bradford's. Red-faced and drenched in sweat, the emperor's son upended his canteen all over his face.

"Do you really... do this... all day?"

Xander stifled a smirk and patted the boy on the shoulder. "Harder than it looks, isn't it?"

"No wonder my brother got in such great shape after just a year." Bradford grimaced slightly and explained, "I couldn't learn anything useful because I was too busy trying not to collapse. How about you?"

"Not sure if Faris trusts me yet. But still plenty of rumors I think we can work with," Xander said. "I suppose time will tell."

But with Sylvia working in the open, Tai behind enemy lines, and Callahan strengthening his forces, Xander couldn't help but wonder if time was in short supply.

Tai ought to have known that she would not be the only dragonaut recruit.

When she arrived at the Azure Fountain Palace, she barely had the chance to drop off her things and change her clothes before she was ushered outside onto the training grounds. Tai shaded her eyes against the afternoon sun and saw five young men and women around her own age, each dressed in the same blue-gray recruit's uniform.

"Aha," said a slender girl with the typical olive skin and gray eyes of a Kasani noble. "Fresh meat." She regarded Tai like a wolf surveying her dinner.

"Just what we need, more competition," sniffed a curly-haired boy who looked like he might have been the girl's brother.

"Come now, she doesn't look so tough," the noble girl said. She bared her teeth in what might have almost been a smile. "Enjoy it while you can, my fine feathered friend. Rarely takes long for the new ones to be sent packing."

"You're a recruit, too," said a round-faced boy who looked like he might be a year or two younger than Tai. "You're just as likely to be sent home as the rest of us."

"Hardly." The curly-haired boy sniffed. "Unlike some of us, Owain, my mother actually holds sway in the Imperial court. Of course, seems the Imperial Dragonauts will admit anyone these days, even the disgraced nephews of failed dragonauts, and worse, *foreigners.*"

His disdain, Tai saw, was not just for Tai, but for the others in the group, which included a tall girl with Sanorian features and rich brown skin a shade or two darker than Tai's, as well as a pale, slender, freckled boy who might have been Thlarknian. Other than Owain, they all stared at her with stony indifference.

"Nice to meet you all," Tai said nervously. The rest responded with baleful glares.

"Don't mind them," the round-faced boy, Owain, said. "The Taggart siblings talk a big game, but we'll see what happens once we get out on the training field. My name's Owain, by the way. Owain Barclay. I fear Denton is correct, my uncle Ambrose failed as a dragonaut, but I hope to do better, eh?"

"I'm... sorry for your loss," Tai said delicately. She'd been there when Ambrose Barclay fell to one of Hildegard's arrows.

"Eh," Owain said. "I realize it sounds callous, but between you and me, he was an arse." He winked conspiratorially. Tai forced a smile, not sure what to make of the boy. "Anyway," Owain continued, "Those two delightful people are Denton and Cressida Taggart, and over here are Judika Lewellyn and Jeziah Morne."

"I'm Tai Lunstrum," she said. Kadmin knew who she was, so there was no sense giving a fake name. Not for the first time, she wondered just what in the Void she was getting herself into. "So, you're all here to become dragonauts?"

"Obviously," Cressida scoffed.

"We're all here to *try* to become dragonauts," Denton corrected her. "Only one of us will earn a dragonstone." His casual posture, smirking while he crossed his arms, left no question who he thought deserved the honor.

All right, Tai thought. More Trials. She could handle that. Denton Taggart was just another Graigor Beckett, and this time, gods help her, she intended to defeat him. His attitude didn't bother her in the slightest. After all, she wasn't here to make friends.

"Attention!" an authoritative voice rang through the training grounds.

Tai immediately stood straight, as did the Taggart siblings and the Sanorian girl. Owain was slower to react, but noticing the others, spun into a hasty salute.

"Hmmm." A massive woman in plate-mail armor paced up and down, inspecting them as if they were gryphons for sale. "Not bad. But you'll need to do better if you wish to be dragonauts. A lot better." Her silver eyes flashed with a twisted glee that indicated she couldn't wait to put all of them through their paces.

This, Tai realized, could only be Vivienne Penregon, cousin of the Empress and leader of the enemy dragonauts.

"You are here," Vivienne said, "Because my colleague, Dragonaut Crowley, thought you showed potential. But which of you will earn this dragonstone—" she produced a plain gray pendant from her pocket and ran the chain through her gauntleted fingers — "Is up to the Emperor, and he'll only listen to me."

The Taggart siblings nodded smugly, secure in their confidence. Lewellyn and Owain stood hopeful and determined. Only the freckle-faced boy, Jeziah, looked somewhat bored, as though he didn't want to be there.

Without further preamble, Vivienne separated the dragonauts into pairs and handed them practice swords. Tai was paired with

Denton Taggart, who clearly considered himself the best. Tai looked forward to seeing how she compared.

Denton was strong, there was no denying it. Definitely stronger than Tai. But he was clearly used to overpowering his opponents without much finesse. Tai broke through his defenses almost immediately, and he looked genuinely surprised when she sidestepped his momentum and jabbed her practice sword at his chest — not too hard, she thought, but the boy still flinched as if she had actually stabbed him.

"Oh, excellent, excellent," Vivienne swept over, beaming at Tai while Taggart still irritably rubbed his midsection.

"She cheated," his sister Cressida complained. "There's no way she could have beat Denton. He and I have been training together since we were kids."

"I note you lost your bout too," Vivienne said coolly, "Which just goes to show you how much childhood games matter in the real world." She spun sharply around and gestured at Tai. "Everyone. Look at Miss Lunstrum here."

Tai awkwardly waved, uncomfortable as the center of attention.

"Miss Lunstrum is small, and a little scrawny. She has wings, which makes her a target."

Thanks, Tai thought.

"And yet," Vivienne continued, "Miss Lunstrum won her bout with very little effort. Does anyone know why that is?"

"She cheated," Cressida repeated.

"She practiced for a long time," suggested Owain.

"Taggart's gods-awful," said Jeziah.

"Taggart would not be here if he were 'gods-awful,'" Vivienne said evenly. She paced up and down the row of recruits, gazing at them each in turn. "What you need to understand about being a true warrior," she continued, "Is that battle is not a gentleman's dual or a sparring match between friends. In the heat of battle, only two things matter — your own survival, and stopping the other guy. Battle is, I fear, messy. By using Taggart's larger size against him, she pressed whatever slight advantage she could get. And so, she was victorious." Then, however, Vivienne said the worst possible thing she could say. "The rest of you should all strive to be like Miss Lunstrum. As a reward for her excellent performance, she may have liberty for the afternoon. The rest of you are to run extra laps. Come along!" she clapped her hands, and the others formed a surly line around the training grounds, glaring daggers in Tai's direction.

In singling Tai out, Vivienne had all but guaranteed that Tai would be the one the others resented. While Tai certainly did not yearn for their good opinion, she also knew she'd have a Void of a time gathering useful information if the others all excluded her. Shrewdly, she couldn't help wonder if that might have been intentional. Did the duchess suspect something?

There was one good thing, however. Being granted unexpected free time meant that she had two entirely free hours before dinner to do some quality snooping.

CHAPTER TEN
AN UNEXPECTED INHERITANCE

EIGHT YEARS AGO

Tai let out a stream of unbecoming swear words, as, soaking wet, she hauled herself onto the riverbank. *Stupid, stupid, stupid!* She pulled a bit of kelp out of her hair in disgust. She could almost hear her mother's chiding voice in the back of her mind. *It's the definition of insanity, you know, to do the same thing over and over and expect a different result. What did you think was going to happen?*

Tai shook the water out of her useless, waterlogged wings. And in her feastday best, too. Mother would never let her live it down.

Ruefully, she wondered what under the clouds had possessed her to ask Jace Farnham to dance. He could have danced with any girl he wanted, the way Lucynde and the others flocked about him with their perfect wings and perfect hair and perfect embroidered festival robes. But Tai had been caught up in the music and the lights and the general atmosphere of the Autumn Festival. And so, like an absolute Depths-sodden fool, she strode right up to him and asked him to dance with her.

Tai's face burned from the memory of it. Of Lucynde and Jessamine tittering from behind their brightly colored paper fans. Of Jace, looking surprised, and she dared hope receptive, but also perplexed.

"I'd *like* to," Jace said delicately, earning a scoff from Lucynde. "But..." He twitched his own mottled brown wing and asked, "Aren't the Autumn festival dances meant to be done *airborne?*"

In that moment all she wanted in the world was to wipe the smug looks off of Lucynde and Jessamine's faces. She thought maybe she could fly just from pure spite alone, like some kind of heroine in a fantasy tale. So, like a cursed, Depths-sodden fool, she leapt from the branch, straight down towards the Everwood River. And now, here she was, soaking wet and utterly humiliated.

Tai had no desire to climb back up the ladders and face her family or her peers. Thankfully, this being the Autumntide Festival, there was still plenty to do on the ground level.

Tai made her way over to the market stalls, where Aerish merchants traveled all the way from the distant world above to pedal their wares. The trade caravans came through a few times a year, often coinciding with the seasonal festivals. But everyone knew they saved their best for Autumntide.

Tai didn't have much spending money, but just looking around was enough for an evening's entertainment. She wandered between the stalls, admiring brightly colored bolts of silk and confections of spun sugar. But most captivating of all were the clockwork pieces, gears and cogs and bolts forged with greater precision than most Orith smiths could dream of. While none of the products were magical in nature — even aether crystals would cease to glow beneath the clouds — many of them had obviously used magic in their manufacture. Tai picked up a silver pocketwatch and admired how the casing seemed to shine different colors in the light of the silverleaves. It must have been smithed with techniques long lost to the Orith people.

"Anything catch your eye?" The teenage merchant spoke

Toreenish with the lilting, almost musical accent that was common among the Aerish traders.

Tai set the watch down, embarrassed. It probably cost more than her parents gave her for pocket money in a year. "N...no," she said quickly. "Just looking."

"You've got good taste." The trader was young, probably not more than a year or two older than Tai. But he was already extremely good looking, lean and athletic, with smooth olive-tan skin and sleek black hair tied back in a ponytail at the nape of his neck.

"Beautiful." Tai was not entirely referring to the watch.

"They say in the Ancient times, they forged this metal using dragon fire. Of course, these days we just use aether forges." He flashed a charming smile. *Clouds above,* he was attractive.

"What, dragon fire, really?" *Majestic creatures of the sky, who flew alongside Orith and Aerish alike...* Tai looked at the fob watch again in fascination, then shook her head. She really needed to stop wasting the handsome trader boy's time. "Sorry, but I really can't. I should... go."

She once again became aware of the fact that she was soaking wet and probably still had riverweed in her hair.

The trader boy wrinkled his nose, seeming to guess her line of thinking. "Why *are* you all wet, anyway?"

"I... fell in the river."

"You must be pretty clumsy." He smirked. Savior help her, even his smirk was charming. "I thought all you Orith were supposed to be good at falling."

"We are," Tai said, slightly defensive, "But water is still wet."

"You couldn't fly away from the water?"

Tai wished the ground would open up and swallow her into the Depths. "I... can't fly at all."

"Oh, well, that's understandable then."

"I— what?" Tai was taken aback. When people learned of her condition, they usually reacted with some combination of pity and scorn. She supposed this boy's nonchalance ought to bother her, but if anything, she found it refreshing.

"Well," he said, "I can't fly, either." He moved his shoulders up and down to demonstrate that he had no wings whatsoever.

"That's... true." Tai felt her mouth twitch into an involuntary smile.

"I'm Kadmin, by the way." He extended his hand in what she recognized as an Aerish gesture of greeting. "Kadmin Crowley."

"Tai Lunstrum." She took his hand.

He let go of the handshake and stepped back in surprise. "You're the one the captain was looking for."

A moment later, she heard the unmistakable sound of wingbeats as Tanis came fluttering to a perfect landing beside her. *Show off.*

"There you are," Tanis said. "Mother's just about having a fit. And why are you all wet?"

Tai scowled. "I wasn't gone *that* long."

"Some Aerish woman's looking for you," Tanis said. "I don't know why, but it sounded important."

"That would be Captain Brielle. I think I'd, uh, better come with you. To smooth things over. Ay, Falgar!"

Another Aerish teenager, lanky and sandy-haired, looked up from where he was lounging against a stack of crates. "Mmm?"

"Man the till until I get back, yeah?"

Falgar gazed languidly between Tai and Kadmin and gave a knowing smirk. "All right. But you owe me next time I want to skive off to go flirting."

Tanis snorted, and Tai felt her cheeks burning. Kadmin wasn't flirting with her, surely not. He was just... helpful. That was all.

"I'll see you up top." Tanis took flight once more. *Show off, show off.*

"This is a lot of ladders," Kadmin commented somewhat breathlessly as they made their tedious way back up towards her family.

"Yeah, sorry about that." Tai twitched her wings. "They're for small children and the elderly. Everyone else is supposed to fly."

"They make *old people* climb these things?" Kadmin's tone conveyed disbelief. "Meroneth's balls, but you all must be strong."

Tai wasn't certain she'd ever blushed as much as she did this evening. *Strong!* The handsome Aerish boy said she was *strong!* Granted, he also extended that compliment to Orith retirees, but she'd take it! "Oh, you know, it's not so hard."

"That sort of thing would be useful for climbing skyship riggings," Kadmin commented.

"Skyship?"

"Yeah, you know. Big flying boats in Aeris?"

"I know what a skyship is." Tai allowed herself a self-indulgent moment to relish in the possibility of flying in one. In Aeris, it wouldn't matter if she couldn't fly. In Aeris, everyone could fly, because they had something better than wings. They had magic.

"You ought to apply for an apprenticeship in Cloudfire," Kadmin said.

Tai lowered her wings, crashing back into reality as surely as she'd crashed into the river. "I'd be laughed off the docks if I tried to get a job on an Aerish merchant vessel."

"Aw, now, don't say that," Kadmin said.

Tai shook her head. "I know how these things go. You have to study with the Merchant's Guild in Silverlake for *years* before the Aerish will even look at you. But I can't join the Merchant's Guild. I can't join any guild. I can't even get an apprenticeship, because that's part of the Path, and I can't Fly the Path if I can't even Fly."

"That's stupid," Kadmin said bluntly.

Tai let out a weak laugh. Calling the Path stupid simply *was not done*. But Kadmin was a foreigner, ignorant of their ways. There were plenty who would have been outraged and offended at Kadmin's words.

Tai looked nervously around, and, hardly daring to believe her own audacity, whispered, "It *is* a bit stupid."

"Sounds like you're making excuses," Kadmin continued. "You

know what my Mistress always told me. Where there's a will, there's a way."

Tai opened her mouth to argue, then snapped it shut again. Depths swallow her, what was she doing, complaining about every little woe to this handsome Aerish merchant? He must find her unbearably dull and whiny.

At long last, they reached the highest branches. It didn't take long to find her mother, standing across from a tall Aerish woman in a tricorn hat, both of them in a towering temper.

"She's just a little girl!" Reora cried.

"She's a girl who has the right to know where she came from," the woman, presumably Brielle, snapped back.

"Um, hello." Tai cleared her throat.

Both women glared at her. But Trader Brielle's expression softened, and she said, "Tai. Why don't you sit down?" She gestured at one of the lantern-lit tables laid out for the festival goers to relax and enjoy themselves.

"All... all right," Tai said. She looked around nervously, wondering what she could possibly be in trouble for this time.

"There's no easy way to say this, so I'd best get right to the point," Brielle said. "Tai, your father is dead."

Tai blanched. "Roan? He can't be." She looked around frantically and finally saw him laughing at the gaming table with the rest of the village fishermen. She glared at the Aerish trader woman. "He's right over there, don't joke about things like that."

"Not Roan," Reora said, looking like she'd rather be anywhere else on Cyrna. "Your birth father. Meron Altmore."

Tai blinked. Whatever she'd expected, it hadn't been that. "...Oh."

Tai hadn't seen hair nor feather of Meron since he and Reora split up ten years ago. She didn't even know if he was alive. Well, she knew now, evidently. Far from giving her any sense of closure, Tai felt hollow.

"Your father left you something," Brielle said. "A rather *large* something, in fact."

Tai blinked in befuddlement. "Why would he do that?" But curiosity won out, and she followed up with a more plaintive, "What is it?"

"A skyship," Brielle said. "More specifically, *my* skyship, that is, the skyship of which I am captain. The *Winds of Fortune.*"

"A skyship?" Glorious images danced through her mind, of flying freely through the Linking, under her own power...

Reora, however, shook her head. "Just what, pray tell, is a thirteen-year-old girl going to do with a skyship?"

"To be honest," Brielle said, "I am not really certain what Meron's logic was in... that is, I rather thought that I, as captain and de facto co-owner..." she shook her head. "It doesn't matter. Meron left the ship to you, and it's up to you to decide what to do with it."

Tai blinked several times. "Well, I'd fly it, obviously."

Brielle's smile was strained. "Flying a skyship is a trifle more complicated than saying you want to do it. The simplest thing for you to do, I think, is to sign the rights over to me. I will pay you fifty golden Saviors for the vessel. Barring that, however, you can do whatever you like. Sell it yourself, repurpose it into one of these quaint little tree houses, crash it into the Void-cursed ground. It will no longer be my concern." Her jaw visibly twitched at this last bit.

"We would be happy to accept your generous offer of fifty gold," Reora said quickly. "Let's get this done quickly so you can be gone from here and back on your ship where you belong." The look Reora shot the other woman was pure venom. Tai was slightly taken aback; she knew her mother had a tendency to be prickly but this was beyond the pale.

"Now wait just a second." Tai ruffled her wings. She was the one who'd inherited a ship, so why was it up to Reora what she ought to do with it?

"Dear, you are only thirteen. You don't know what you want."

"I, more than anyone, want to agree with you, Madam Reora," Brielle said, her tone one of extreme caution. "But the terms of Meron's will were precise. It has to be Tai's decision."

"*Fifty golden Saviors,* Tai." Reora drummed her fingers against the table.

Tai stared at the merchant. That was more money than she'd ever seen in her life. Even *one* golden Savior was a lot of money. She could buy a *lot* of magnets with fifty. And yet, she couldn't help but thinking that it was an insulting amount to offer for a skyship. An *entire skyship.*

"I guess what I want to know is, if he apparently thought so much of me to leave me a ship, then why did he never come see me? Why didn't he even so much as write me a letter?"

"Meron was a complicated man," Brielle said with a sigh. "He cared about you deeply. He kept a sketch of your likeness on his nightstand in our stateroom. I suppose... I suppose, deep down, he was ashamed of what happened, of how things ended with your mother."

Reora glared daggers at Brielle, and Tai felt a sudden dawning comprehension. She'd said *our* stateroom, not *his* stateroom. "You're my stepmother."

This time Brielle's smile turned ironic and, she thought perhaps, a little bitter. "In a manner of speaking. Meron, as you likely know, was not the marrying sort."

"If you ask me," Reora said through gritted teeth, "You should take this woman's offer of fifty gold so that we might wash our hands of her."

"There's something else," Brielle added with an air of great reluctance. "It was... always your father's intention that, when you were old enough, he would make you his apprentice."

"Tai can't be an apprentice," Reora said sharply. "She's Flightless."

"With all due respect, Reora," Brielle said, "That is under Toreenish law, not Kasani. And the *Winds of Fortune* is a Kasani ship." She cleared her throat. "As I said. Meron wanted to make you his apprentice. In honor of his memory, I would... extend you the same invitation."

Brielle looked like she'd just swallowed one of the sour citrons the Kasani traders sometimes brought. Tai inferred that she couldn't expect much of a welcome if she took the trader up on it. But *all the same...*

"Absolutely not," Reora said. "I forbid it."

Tai felt like she'd fallen in the river all over again. "It's my ship," she said, "And therefore my choice."

"You're thirteen years old and my daughter." Reora impatiently brushed her aside. "Therefore the choice is mine."

"Though it pains me to admit it, your daughter is right," Brielle said. "Meron's will was very clear. I doubt you'd wish to contend with the Kasani inheritance lawyers."

Tai's mother looked like she might actually start spouting wraithsmoke. But ultimately, she lowered her wings in surrender. "Tai, I cannot stop you from doing this. But as your mother, I can highly, highly discourage it."

"I... probably shouldn't," Tai admitted. But *oh*, by the Fallen, she wanted to.

"We can do the paperwork of signing over the *Winds of Fortune* now." Perhaps too eagerly, Brielle fished through her handsome leather satchel and handed Tai an official-looking piece of parchment, along with an Aerish-style quill pen and ink pot. *A feather,* Tai thought distastefully. Might as well make a pen out of a finger.

Tai picked up the document and skimmed it. She knew some written Kasani, mostly so she could read books she found at the market, but this contract was rife with words she didn't understand, such as "heretofore" and "beneficiary." One sentence, however, stood out more than the others.

"I have to decide tonight?"

"Of course," the Aerish tradeswoman said primly. "We are merchants, we must keep traveling. Even Meron would not expect us to hang around all moon."

Tai bit her lip in consternation. She picked up the pen, and tapped it a few times on the table. Signing over the ship was the right thing to do. She knew it was. Fifty gold was a hefty sum. She could likely make more on the open market, but she was a thirteen year old flightless Orith, what in the Depths did she know about commerce? The offer of an apprenticeship sounded far more alluring, but it also meant leaving home for moons at a time. Surely she couldn't do that, could she?

She hovered with her pen over the page, ready to sign away her rights to the ship, and her last memories of her father.

"If I may," the handsome apprentice, Kadmin, interjected. "She has until the end of the evening. There's no need to make her sign right now."

Brielle's nostrils flared, and Tai thought that if she'd had wings, she surely would have flared them too. But then she relaxed her posture and said, "Very well. Since Falgar was evidently left in charge, I'd best go back and make sure the entire stall hasn't burned down in my absence. But if you don't find me by the time the market closes at eleven bells, you should know that the ship defaults into my name and you also forfeit the fifty gold. So don't tarry with your decision."

Tai wasn't sure that was true, but she didn't know nearly enough Kasani to parse the legalese, so she had no choice but to take Brielle at her word.

Brielle rolled up the contract and tucked it inside a wooden tube, then began the long descent back to the market level. For the first time, Tai felt rather sorry for the Aerish. Being flightless was one thing. But these fragile wingless folk couldn't even jump to the ground level without grievous injury or death.

Tai turned her attention to her mother, who was still seated at the festival table, face buried in her hands. To her alarm, she realized her mother was crying.

"Mother? Are... are you all right?"

Reora was always so calm and composed. Tai didn't think she'd seen her mother cry even once.

"Meron, you bastard," Reora sniffed. "How can you keep tormenting me, even from beyond the grave?"

"I—" Tai began, but she realized she had no idea what to say.

"I apologize." Reora gathered herself, and straightened her feathers. "I shouldn't speak ill of the dead."

"Do you... want to talk about him?"

Tai had very few memories of her father. When she tried very hard, she could vaguely recall a wiry man with bronze skin and black wings that tickled when they wrapped around her. But that was a long time ago, buried in the far recesses of her memory.

Reora sighed, clearly also lost in memories. At length, she said, "He was an independent spirit, hated to be tied down. It was... foolish of me, I think, to assume I could keep him for myself. He was brilliant. Adventurous. Could make anyone laugh even when they were about to cry." She smiled and shook her head, wiping away an errant tear. "But... he had itchy wings, as the old saying goes. He tried, gods know he did. And I tried... maybe I tried too hard. Maybe if I'd been less clingy, less stifling..."

Tai shook her head vehemently. "Don't say that. Father made his choices."

At that moment, Tai very nearly made up her mind. If she left to go on this apprenticeship, she'd be no better than her no-good father. Roan was the only father she'd ever known, the only father she needed. And Tai was needed here. Surely, she was. Who would peel the tubers in her absence? Not Perfect Tanis, that was for certain.

So why, then, did the thought of doing the right thing make her feel like she'd swallowed a basket of poisoned mushrooms?

Tai spent the rest of the evening listlessly wandering the upper levels of the village, admiring the colorful lanterns, watching the aerial dancers become progressively clumsier as the greenwine continued flowing. But her mind was wholly occupied with dreams of the sky, of magic and skyships and a world where it didn't matter if she was flightless.

If she left to become an apprentice, this might be her last Autumntide here in Everwood. Who knew where her travels would take her? Signing away the ship was the right thing to do. The *responsible* thing. She had to keep reminding herself of that, over and over, even as her heart called out for glorious adventure beyond the clouds.

Soon enough, she found herself back at her family's wattle and daub dwelling. Perhaps tinkering with her dragon would help clear her head. Of course, if she was *truly* responsible, she'd get a head start on tomorrow's chores, maybe even earn some rare praise from her mother.

Golden lantern light flickered in the windows, which immediately struck Tai as odd. Tai had been sure the lights were all turned off when they left several hours prior. She pushed open the door to find Tanis, Reora, and Roan all huddled over the kitchen table, examining a pile of cogs and bolts that looked suspiciously like her incomplete dragon, as well as the remains of Mr. Squeakers and a few of her other failed experiments.

"The lodestone ought to be helpful with navigation." Reora held up Tai's expensive magnets.

"Re," Roan said gently, "These are Tai's. I'm not sure we—"

"Oh, nonsense." Reora waved him off. "We want to give our boy the best possible start, don't we?"

"What are you doing?" Tai demanded.

The three of them jumped as if struck by an Aerish aetherbolt.

"You're back." Reora made a show of straightening her feathers. "Have you signed the paperwork?"

"Not yet." Tai frowned. "Why's my clockwork dragon in pieces all over the table?"

"We've just received the most wonderful news." Reora blatantly sidestepped the question. "Tanis has been granted an apprenticeship in the Navigators Guild."

"Con...congratulations." Tai could manage her jealousy later. Right now, she wanted to get her feet back under her. "But... my stuff..."

"Mother thought this might be useful for my apprenticeship." To Tanis's credit, he had the decency to look sheepish. "Since I'll be so much younger than the others, if I could make, say, a compass, that could give me an advantage. At least. I hope." He stared at a discarded magnet in consternation, and Tai could tell her eight year old brother didn't know the first thing about constructing a compass.

"Those are *mine*." Her voice, embarrassingly, cracked.

Reora's nostrils flared. "Oh, use your brain, Tai. What were you realistically going to do with these gadgets? You and your brother are both far too old for silly toys. Tanis is beginning his apprenticeship. He *needs* them."

The fact that Tai herself would never be able to have an apprenticeship hung in the air with the weight of a physical object.

"I can't wait to show Lana and the others." Tanis bobbed up and down with excitement.

Tai had to exercise great restraint not to smack him across the face. *He's only eight*, she reminded herself. *I will not cry, I will not cry…*

"Whatever is the matter with you, Tai?" Reora at long last seemed out of patience. "It is only a possession. I didn't raise you to be so materialistic. Tanis is your brother."

"I don't — I mean — I know he is, I just—" Tai spread her arms and her wings in desperation, unable to form words. Unable to say how *frustrating* it was to have nothing that was truly *hers*.

"Of course," Reora added with a tone of obviously forced calm, "If you were to sign over the rights to that ship of Meron's, and bring fifty more gold into the family coffers, we might be able to purchase new supplies for Tanis's apprenticeship, and then you could keep at least some of these trinkets." She shook her hand dismissively at the pile on the table.

"So you would take my gold, as well?"

"Don't be ridiculous! It's the family's gold. You're a child whose not even had her first flight. Fallen take it, Tai, since when did you become so selfish?"

Tai ruffled her wings, sending several black feathers loose. Tears pricked at the corners of her eyes. "Don't you get it? It's not about the gold or the gadgets or any of that. It's about being my own person! Just because I can't fly doesn't mean I don't have a *brain*!"

"If you don't wish to be treated like a child, then you shouldn't act like one."

Tai wiped away her tears with the drab, unadorned sleeve of her robe. She had *one* thing that was wholly her own. She had a ship.

"Mother," she said, "I'm sorry I'm flightless and I'm sorry my father left and I'm sorry I keep reminding you that you don't have a perfect family."

"Tai, for the Savior's sake…"

"Tanis? You can keep the gadgets. Best of luck with your apprenticeship."

"See, now," Reora said, "That wasn't so—"

"Roan," Tai cut her mother off. "Take good care of Mother and Tanis for me, yeah? You're a decent sort. Mother was lucky she met you."

"Tai, what are you—"

"I won't be the family burden anymore," Tai said. "I'll be back when I've made a name for myself."

Tai strode out into the cool night air, past the ladders and the scaffolds and the platforms, past places where she'd tried and failed to fly so many times. She didn't bother to flap her wings this time. She didn't need to. She'd be airborne soon enough. Tai jumped, and she felt the wind rush through her hair and through her feathers, until she came to a graceless landing in the damp undergrowth.

"There you are." Brielle was wiping down the market stall counter with a damp cloth, clearly about to close up for the night. "I was beginning to think you wouldn't come."

"I knew you would." Kadmin gave a cocky smile. She was becoming increasingly fond of his smile.

"I've decided." Tai placed her palm down on the counter. "I want to be your apprentice."

CHAPTER ELEVEN
BABYSITTING

PRESENT DAY

"Here we are." Dorian swallowed nervously as he showed Tanis around his living quarters. "I've set up a kind of sleeping area for you over there. I'm working on getting a larger apartment so you can have your own room, but for now those curtains should give you some privacy."

Tanis looked at the brocade bedcurtains surrounding the makeshift sleeping alcove and then at Dorian, expression unreadable. It was a little unnerving how quiet the young Orith was, but Dorian couldn't blame him. Dorian hadn't been a chatterbox, either, when he'd moved into a new place full of strange new people. *Gods*, he wished Tai were here.

"It's getting late, but if I can get you anything..." he trailed off, trying to think what things he would have liked when he was sixteen, which wasn't *so* terribly long ago. "A book to read, perhaps, or a snack?"

"A silver platter full of dainty little pastries."

Well. *That* was certainly something Dorian would have enjoyed at sixteen, though finding such a thing was another matter. "I'll see what I can do." Dorian made a quick mental inventory of what might be in the castle's well-stocked kitchens.

Tanis sighed. "I was being sarcastic."

Dorian flushed. "Right. Of course you were."

"It doesn't matter." Tanis shook his head. "I don't think prison is supposed to be comfortable."

"You're not in prison."

"Oh, so I can leave, then?"

"Ah. Well. No."

Tanis flopped down on his makeshift sleeping pallet, wings spread wide, hands behind his head. "Right then. Prison."

Dorian let out a long sigh. He didn't know what else to say to the boy; everything felt like empty platitudes. He'd do everything he could to make Tanis's stay comfortable, but at the end of the day, the boy was right. He was a prisoner.

«You know, Solaris,» he said as he drew the curtains shut on his four poster, «Even when you found me in those Ancient ruins, I don't think I felt as out of my depth as I do right now.»

Solaris sent back a burst of amusement. «You simply misremember.»

The best anyone could say about the next few days was that Tanis didn't cause any trouble. He followed every rule to the letter, and while he might glower, he never complained. However, he never said much else, either. Mostly, Tanis spent his time staring ahead, his face a mask of quiet insolence. The other dragonauts started referring to him as Dorian's shadow. If Tanis disliked this monicker, he gave no indication.

"Your Order is sure wealthy," Tanis commented one afternoon after training, as they traversed hallways lined with rich tapestries and marble statuary.

Dorian jumped, half surprised to hear the boy's voice for once.

"It's impressive, isn't it? I imagine some of this has been here since the Ancient times."

Tanis, however, wrinkled his nose. "Oh, it's impressive all right. Impressive how your Lady Dragonmar lets the Orith people suffer, knowing full well that she could do something about it."

Dorian frowned and recalled his brief visit to Everwood. The dying silverleaves and the desperate people. The demons. "I'm sure it's more complicated than that," he began, but he was painfully aware how hollow it sounded. As useful as telling Tanis he wasn't a prisoner. So Dorian took the coward's way out and said, "I imagine you're hungry. Let's go to the kitchens."

Tanis ruffled his wings, but offered no further comment.

"Why, hello!" Dax Vesper sidled in across from them at the dining hall table, grinning and carrying a tray full of hand pies.

Tanis shot the Orith dragonaut a baleful glance. "Just because we're both Orith doesn't mean we're friends."

"Of course, of course. I know that. But I *also* know what it's like to be one of only a few Orith in the castle. So I'm around if you ever want to chat."

Tanis looked thoroughly unimpressed. "There'd be more Orith in the castle if your Order weren't so obviously prejudiced against us. Besides. You left our people by choice. I was hauled here in a drag-on's thrice-cursed talons. Our situations are not the same."

Something like grief briefly flashed across Dax's face. "Do not assume you know my situation. Did you not also leave your people behind in fighting for the Kasani?" But he perked up at once, and said. "But enough about me. What about you, Dorian? How are you?"

Dorian blinked. It was a simple enough question, but he found himself caught off guard all the same. "Fine, I suppose."

"Young people can be difficult." Dax leaned back on the bench and steepled his fingers. "The key is don't even try to make them think you're cool. It's a losing prospect."

Dorian swallowed a bite of meat pie. "I just wish Tai were here."

Dax nodded sagely. "Yes, I imagine you must miss her terribly. You're in love with her, are you not?"

Dorian felt warmth rush to his face. "What? No, no. We're... we're friends, that's all."

"Uh huh." Dax's voice radiated skepticism. "That look of panic on your face when her ornithopter malfunctioned at the Trials. That's a look you reserve for your friends, is it?"

Dorian crossed his arms. "I care about my friends."

"And you're so keen to protect her wayward little brother, because that's what friends do."

"I'd help Tanis even if he wasn't Tai's brother," Dorian said, though even as he said it, he wondered if it was true. He *hoped* it was true. Sighing, he added, "I just wish I could talk to her."

Tanis sulkily prodded at his pie. "Yeah, well. I can't talk to *any* of my family, least of all my turncoat sister. I haven't seen my mother in almost a year, and now I can't even visit my father. He's missing a leg, you know? I gave up my apprenticeship to care for him, and now he's got no one."

Dorian looked alarmed. "You gave up an apprenticeship?"

Tanis shifted in evident discomfort. "Truth be told I kind of *hated* underseas navigation. But *still*."

Dax lowered his wings. "I understand more than you realize."

Tanis fixed him with a flat stare. "Do you, now."

Dax seemed to take a moment to consider. "Your surname is Lunstrum, is it?"

"That's right."

"You're not Reora Lunstrum's boy, by any chance?"

Tanis abruptly flared his wings, hitting Dorian in the side and nearly knocking him off the bench. "Sorry," Tanis said quickly, while Dorian righted himself. "But Reora... she's my mother, yes. Do you know her? Is she all right? Where did she go?"

Dax drummed his fingers on the table. "I'll explain all I can. But I'm afraid it requires bending the rules just a little." He shot Dorian a questioning glance.

Dorian nervously massaged the back of his neck. Tanis was *his* responsibility. But Dax was a dragonaut, higher ranking than Dorian, and had always been friendly to him. And ultimately, Dorian wanted what was best for Tanis, rules be cursed to the Void.

"I'm going to go clear the trays," Dorian declared. "I'll pretend not to hear whatever you two discuss while I'm gone."

Tanis's mouth gave a twitch that might have almost, *almost* been a smile.

Later that night, Tanis stole quietly out of the quarters he shared with Dorian. His feathers ruffled uncomfortably against the poorly fitting wing-holes in his borrowed Aerish tunic. He missed his comfortable silk robes, with embroidery on the cuffs and collar. He'd even settle for the scratchy wool uniform the Kasani army provided. In this pathetic old thing, he might as well be naked.

"Are you sure this is all right?" He met Dax Vesper near the staircase. Dax, Tanis noted, looked resplendent in embroidered silk robes of aquamarine. No tatty old tunics when you were a dragonaut, apparently.

"Mind you," Dax said, "Don't go telling the Dragonmar. But you're with me, so you should be all right."

Tanis had to admit that there was a certain thrill in breaking the rules. He didn't trust Dax Vesper, not exactly. Not yet. But he was also well aware he wasn't exactly spoiled for choice where allies were concerned.

Tanis looked around, wide-eyed, as Dax showed him the beacon tower. Aether crystals, near as many as the Kasani kept in their Thlarknian laboratory, lined the walls in a spiral pattern. In the center of the room, an engraved slab of wood sat on a stone plinth. Dax inserted a small crystal into a depression in the middle, and the spell circle sprung to life, a complicated array of Aerish runes hovering above the dais in glowing electric blue.

Tanis didn't think it would ever cease to amaze him how quickly and readily magic worked here above the clouds. No need to draw from Malachite up here. He felt the demon stir sullenly within him. He didn't speak directly, but Tanis understood his meaning. *Do not forget my presence. Do not forget you let me in your soul.* Tanis let the creature have a bit of his spirit energy. Just a trickle. To calm his nerves, he told himself.

"It's easiest just to send encoded messages," Dax said, "But with a circle as advanced as this one we can do voice communication. We just have to do this, this, and this." He ran his hand over the floating runes, rearranging them too quickly for Tanis to follow. There was a crackle of magical energy, and the crystals on the wall blinked in what appeared to be some kind of pattern, bathing the room in flickering blue light.

Tanis thought he'd done rather well, going from no magic at all to flinging fireballs in a matter of weeks. But the deft way Dax manipulated the flowing Aerish sigils made it starkly clear how far he had yet to go.

"This is Winter Winds, calling Shining Path, address code Frost Wing Fallen Position Three," Dax said.

"This is Shining Path, Addressing Stone Cloud Connection Six," came a rough, masculine voice from the other end. "State your business."

"Good morning, Gideon," Dax said with just a hint of irony. "I need to speak to the mayor on a matter of some import."

There was a pause on the other end, a magical thrumming buzz. "The mayor is a busy woman."

"Indeed, so," Dax said cordially. "But the dove has come to roost."

The crackling buzz lasted longer this time. Finally, the other voice came back. "Very well. Stand by."

There was a longer pause this time, so long that Tanis wondered if perhaps they'd lost the connection. Then a voice, magically distorted yet so achingly familiar, piped up from the other end.

"Tanis?"

"Mother," Tanis choked out in return.

They exchanged approximately a minute of pleasant greetings before Tanis spilled out his every insecurity, every worry that gnawed on him for the past several years. He tried to stop himself, but the words kept coming, like poison he had to vomit up if he had any hope of recovery. He talked about his failure in the Navigator's Guild, his worries about his father, his fool decision to join the Kasani army. His subsequent failure at Thlarknia and subsequent kidnapping. He told her of Dorian, who claimed to be Tai's friend, and he complained about the fact that Tai wasn't even here. And through it all, though he tried to hide it, there was just the slightest hint of accusation. *Where are you? Why did you leave?*

Reora, however, didn't sound impatient with his blubbering. "Well." Reora's voice caught, though whether it was from emotion or a crackle in the magical connection, Tanis couldn't say. "Of course you know I'd rather you *hadn't* left your apprenticeship."

Tanis was glad she couldn't see him wince. So typical of his mother, to focus on that.

But then Reora continued, "But I suppose I've been a poor role model, these last few years. I wouldn't have left if I had a choice. I need you to know that. Every day I wish I could have brought you here, but... well, I fear that's impossible."

Conflicted emotions made a toxic cocktail in the pit of Tanis's stomach. *Wouldn't have left if she had a choice, wanted to bring him along...* a likely story. It was like when Tai left all over again, only a thousand times worse. *Oh, sorry, it was against my will, I'd've stayed if I could,* meanwhile she was off living her best life while Tanis was left cleaning up the mess. "Can you at least tell me where you are?"

She had to be in Aeris somewhere, or perhaps even here in Cloudfire, if she had access to the aether network. Maybe he could join her. Maybe he could even help her, with whatever it was she was doing. If she got him out of here, he might even consider forgiving her.

"I'm doing important work, and one day, I'll be able to tell you about it," Reora said. "But that day has not yet come."

"Of course it hasn't." Tanis supposed he'd been a fool to think any differently. Yet there was a traitorous part of him that refused to give up hope. *One day.* She'd tell him one day. Savior only knew when that day would come.

"It's for your own protection." Dax stepped in and put a comforting hand on Tanis's shoulder.

Tanis shuffled his wings in annoyance and brushed the older Orith aside. Adults were always claiming to do things for Tanis's protection, but most of the time, it was to save their own sorry hides.

To Reora's credit, however, she sounded genuinely regretful from the other side of the connection. "I'm afraid he's right. But... if possible, I'd like to talk to you again."

He should tell her no. She'd abandoned him. He should tell her to go straight to the depths. But his traitor heart won out yet again, and he said, voice plaintive, "I want to talk again, too."

Tanis returned to his quarters some time later to find a frantic Dorian overturning pillows and pacing about in consternation.

"Tanis, thank all the gods," he breathed. "I've been worried sick."

"You won't find me under a pillow."

Dorian tugged on the ends of his long copper hair. "Meroneth's balls, boy, you're my responsibility. You can't just wander off like that."

"He was all right." Dax came to his defense. "He was with me."

"I know, I know. Just... maybe *tell* me next time. I was worried you'd gotten hurt, or..."

"Or that I went to the beacon tower and ratted you all out to Janus Callahan," Tanis said flatly. He was tired of people pretending they were controlling him for his own good. He wished they would be honest.

Dorian looked crestfallen. "Yes, or that."

"Rest assured, he has not been in communion with any Kasani forces," Dax said smoothly. "And I remind you that you *did* say you'd allow me to help the boy." He let out a long breath. "Still, I apologize if I stepped out of line. In the future, I shall not abscond with your charge without permission."

Dorian scratched his neck. "You're right. I did say that. And I'm sure you did what you thought was best."

Dax made his farewells and departed, leaving Dorian and Tanis alone in an awkward silence.

"I... know this is hard for you," Dorian began.

"Spare me," Tanis said, before flopping down on his sleeping pallet and staring at the high vaulted ceiling. He sighed. "I'm sorry for being rude. But you'll forgive me if my worries about my family outweigh any desire to spare your feelings."

Dorian's expression seemed genuinely distraught, and Tanis *almost* felt guilty. Dorian had seemed nice, that time, when he'd visited their home in Everwood. He'd been so interested in fishing nets. Tanis didn't *want* to bear the man any ill will. But Dorian was still Tanis's jailer. They could never be friends.

Dorian continued scratching his neck, something Tanis noticed he did a lot when he was thinking. "If you wanted, we could go back down to the village. Pay your father a visit."

Tanis opened his mouth to let out another snarky one-liner, but then he paused. "Is that... is that allowed?"

"As long as I'm with you, I don't see why not."

Tanis twitched his wings. In truth, he didn't understand these Order people at all. He'd been nothing but rude to them, yet they kept bending over backwards to accommodate him. But they also kept him prisoner. It didn't make sense. However, none of that changed the fact that if he had an opportunity to go home, he was going to take it. Maybe, just maybe, he'd even find an opportunity to escape for good.

"I'd like that," he said.

CHAPTER TWELVE
IMPOSTERS

When Bradford unloaded the last crate from the dolly, he could finally pause to catch his breath.

Meroneth's Balls. He downed the remaining contents of his water canteen, and inwardly groaned as he tried to coax out the last drops. He looked longingly at the water barrel, several docks away, and wondered if he could get there and back before the dock master —

"No time for lollygagging." *Nope.* There was Regnald now, with his demon Garnet perched on his shoulder. "You wanna lounge around all day sipping tea, take your chances with the fancy folks in the upper city. Down here, you're expected to work."

Bradford winced and slung his canteen strap back over his shoulder. *Fancy folks in the upper city.* Was it just a figure of speech, or did Regnald suspect something? Bradford checked to make sure his Illusion was still intact, then swiftly rolled the dolly back to the staging area before the dock master could find something else to complain about.

Bradford's biggest fear was that everyone would soon find out he wasn't just a clueless newcomer, but a nobleman, and not just a nobleman, but the son of the thrice-cursed emperor. He was supposed to lead a rebellion, which he couldn't very well do with his head on an executioner's block.

Some rebel leader he was, though. Lately he seemed incapable of doing anything except hauling crates around, and even that, he did poorly.

"There're laborers lined up around the city walls hoping to get your job," Regnald said. "So don't think I'd even blink before replacing you with someone faster."

Bradford swallowed, nodded, and hurried to move the cart along as fast as his exhausted legs would take him. "Is it true?" he asked one of the other laborers, as they began unloading their carts. "Is it really so hard to find work on the docks right now?"

"Eh," said his teammate, a gangly fellow with a scar on his face. Bradford struggled to recall his name. Stokes or Spokes or something like that. "Seems like fewer ships coming in than there used to be. Maybe that's why."

"Why are there fewer ships?"

"No idea," Stokes-or-Spokes said. "Taxes, probably. Folks are always complaining about taxes. But there's no point tying yourself in knots over it. Regnald might be a crotchety old pain in the arse, but do a decent day's work and he'll see you're taken care of. Just, you know, don't slack off, complain, or talk too much."

The dock worker raised his eyebrows at this last bit and point-edly went back to unloading his cart. *Point taken.* Bradford did not know how he was supposed to glean useful information from these workers if he didn't talk to them, but as his governess Tahlia always used to say, *Keep your ears open and your mouth closed.*

From elsewhere in the docks a bell sounded, jangling and metallic and shrill. Bradford was in the middle of wheeling the cart back to the loading dock, but Stokes-or-Spokes raised his hand in warning. The other workers stopped what they were doing, and gestured at the sky with worried expressions.

"What's going on?" Bradford expected to see a warehouse on fire, or Voidstorm clouds, or worse.

Stokes-or-Spokes shook his head. "Inspection," he said, and from the grave look on his scarred face, Bradford thought perhaps a Voidstorm might be preferable. Ancients help him, even Regnald looked concerned.

Bradford looked up where the others were pointing, and saw a burnished golden shape appear, followed by the now-familiar sound of a dragon's wingbeats. But Bradford knew this was not Solaris come to pay a cordial visit.

Conflicted emotions, gnawing dread merged with foolish hope, warred in the pit of his stomach. Not just any dragon. *Thunder*. And that meant, on her back, her rider...

Bradford watched, transfixed, as Thunder landed and a stocky giantess of a woman dismounted. He couldn't look away, even as his heart tried to break free from his chest.

Even the surliest dock workers stood straighter in the imposing dragonaut's presence. She carried herself with perfect poise and effortless strength. No doubt Vivienne could go toe to toe with the most hardened dockside toughs. Moving boxes all day wouldn't leave *her* an exhausted and disheveled mess.

Bradford felt especially disheveled now compared to Vivienne with her polished steel armor and sleek braided hair. He recalled a golden summer afternoon almost two years ago now, near the stables at Callahan Manor. They'd been practicing the sword, as they often did in those days, and Vivienne beat him every time.

"Perhaps you're just not as strong as you think you are," she'd said, storm-gray eyes alight with the challenge.

You were right, Vivienne, the present-day Bradford thought ruefully. *I was nowhere near as strong as I thought I was.*

Back then, all Bradford wanted in the world was to be stronger, to be *better*, to *impress her*.

He sincerely doubted she'd find him impressive now.

Vivienne was no longer the playful and charismatic bodyguard who'd accompanied her cousin Saedra to backwater Frostvale. Now she was an Imperial Dragonaut, and she worked for Bradford's father. She'd *enslaved a dragon,* for the Ancients' sakes. Whatever they'd once been, he didn't see a way for them to be anything but enemies now.

Bradford pulled his woolen worker's cap down as far as it would go to shield his face. He was under Illusion, sure, but he'd mostly only changed his hair and eye colors. Would it be enough? A traitorous part of him even hoped she *would* recognize him, though he knew full well how disastrous that would be.

Vivienne inspected the next skyship over, close enough that he could see her every movement, close enough that he almost fancied he could smell her, an enticing combination of linseed oil and orange blossom.

"What've we got here?" she asked the worker in charge of loading the other ship. Although as well-muscled as any dock worker, the man seemed almost scrawny compared to Vivienne. Bradford struggled to remember his name. Bartel or Martel perhaps?

The apple at Bartel-or-Martel's throat bobbed as he read out the ship's manifest. Kasani oranges, wheat germ, bolts of linen fabric. Standard cargo for a typical ship, really. Bradford himself had paid little attention to what was *in* the crates. He only cared about the fact that they were *heavy.*

Vivienne tapped on the side of a wooden crate, her face drawing into a frown. "Something's off here. Let's open this one, shall we?"

Bartel-or-Martel nodded obediently and pried the crate open with a metal crowbar. Bradford couldn't see the contents from where he stood, but from the sharp intake of breath from both the dock worker and Vivienne, he knew it probably wasn't oranges or bolts of cloth.

"Aether crystal," she said, "Is not on the manifest."

Bartel-or-Martel looked like he might throw up. "I didn't know, My Lady Dragonaut, Ma'am. You've got to believe me."

Vivienne pursed her lips. "That remains to be seen. Jenkins! Take this man in for questioning. Perhaps he's honest, but if it turns out he's lying and I let him go, then that's going to be a lot of tedious paperwork on my end. Darius, I'll need you to track down the captain of this ship, the—" she examined the name written on the hull — "*For Skying Out Loud?*" She shook her head and rolled her eyes. "These ship names keep getting more and more ridiculous."

Two men in garrison guard uniforms, presumably Jenkins and Darius, marched into action, with a complaining Bartel-or-Martel in tow.

"They're not *really* going to arrest him, are they?"

It wasn't like Bartel-or-Martel was in charge of the crate's contents. None of them were. Vivienne, *his* Vivienne, wouldn't do such a thing. *Would she?*

Stokes-or-Spokes shrugged. "If they can't get anything out of him, they'll probably let him go. Though they might rough him up a bit. Those garrison guards can get pretty nasty." He said all this in a deadpan monotone, as if discussing the weather.

"But he's not a troublemaker. He didn't do anything."

"For all we know, he really *is* a smuggler," Stokes-or-Spokes said. "Anyway, just be glad it was Vivienne and not the other one, Kadmin. Vivienne's at least fair. If it were Kadmin, he'd rot in the dungeons for a year and be thankful for it, to the Void with any innocence or guilt."

Unbelievable. Bradford fumed, but there was little he could do for Bartel-or-Martel from where he was, and he had problems of his own to contend with.

Vivienne strode up to inspect their ship next. Bradford stood against the crate and tried to make himself look small and uninteresting.

"*Fair Elena*, out of Archibald's Landing," Vivienne read off of the clipboard she carried. "What are you loading today?"

"'Cording to the manifest, we've got rolled oats, Vatean silk, and sixteen counts of raw aether ore," Stokes-or-Spokes answered.

"Someone actually willing to pay the tariffs," Vivienne said. "I'm impressed. Let's make sure everything's above board, shall we?"

She tapped against several of the crates, but didn't ask them to open any. The dragon, Thunder, sniffed at a few boxes as though she could discern the contents.

Like her rider, Thunder was intimidatingly large, and Bradford felt dwarfed in her shadow. He thought he'd gotten used to dragons during his time in Cloudfire, but even Solaris and Northstar, the largest dragons, seemed almost puny compared to this majestic golden-bronze beast.

Thunder sniffed Bradford, too, and he could feel the heat of her dragon breath like an aether-powered hair dryer.

"Everything looks to be in order," Vivienne said. "We'll need Captain Abergavenny's approval before signing off, though, so if you could just... if you could just..." she trailed off, and, to Bradford's horror, looked right at him.

"Lady Dragonaut," interjected one of her garrison guard goons, Darien or Darius, or whatever his name was. "I hate to interrupt, but if we could cut this short, I've received word that Kadmin wishes to see you at once."

"What in the Void does that idiot want?" Vivienne sighed, massaging her temples. To Stokes-or-Spokes, she said, "Make sure your captain signs the manifest. Gotta keep the thrice-cursed paperwork in order." Then, without another word, she climbed on Thunder's back and took off into the bright spring sky.

"Everyone reattach your jaws to your skulls and get back to work," barked Regnald. "I'm not paying you to stand around gawping."

Bradford's heart thudded in his chest as he watched Vivienne depart. She'd recognized him. He was almost sure of it. Would she tell his father? *Don't panic,* he tried to reassure himself. *You don't know she knew it was you.* But he had a sinking feeling all the same.

"*Back to work,*" Regnald reiterated. "Don't make me tell you again."

"Right sir. Of course sir."

Bradford half expected heavily armored palace guards to come descending down upon him at any moment. But for the time being, he still had a job to do. As he wiped the sweat from his brow and scrambled to get more Void-cursed crates onto the Void-cursed dollies, he solemnly swore never to look down on common workers again.

Tai closed the desk drawer and exited the empty office with as much nonchalance as she dared. There'd been nothing of interest in there, at least not worth reporting back to Sylvia. Still, the Azure Fountain Palace was large, with plenty of snooping left to do.

She felt a pulse of magic coming from a door at the end of the hallway. Curious, she knocked, and when no one responded, she tentatively tried the doorknob. The door opened, bathing the hallway in blue aetherlight.

«Ah. One of the candidates.» The mindvoice did not seem particularly surprised at her presence.

"What the..."

Celestian, Kadmin's dragon, lay sprawled luxuriously on a finely-woven rug, turning the pages of a massive leather-bound book.

"Are you *reading?*" Tai blurted.

«Is that so surprising?» Celestian asked. «My bond with Kadmin enables me to read your human script.»

The script was Kasani, specifically, and not universal to all humans, but Tai felt no need to correct him. Curiosity getting the better of her, she knelt on the floor next to the dragon and inspected the volume. What sort of books must be interesting to someone like Celestian?

"The *Voyages of Tanazar Felanthryn*. Huh."

Celestian's silver eyes shone with amusement. «You thought I'd be reading some dusty old spellbook?»

"Well, yes, actually," Tai admitted. To her embarrassment, she'd never really given much thought to how dragons kept themselves entertained when they weren't flying about. It had never occurred to her that one might *read adventure novels*.

«There is much wisdom to be gained from fiction,» Celestian said. «For instance, this chapter I am reading now is about when the human Tanazar Felanthryn infiltrated the court of the Thlarknian high king. Even our enemies, it seems, have things they can teach us.»

"Of course. Well. Um. Its, uh, nice to meet you." Tai felt distinctly wrong-footed, and, strangely, like she wanted to pick up and read the *Voyages of Tanazar Felanthryn* herself. "I'm sorry I interrupted your reading."

«No matter,» Celestian said, slightly bored. «Most of the candidates come looking for me eventually. I figured it was only a matter of time before you came along.»

Tai made her awkward farewells and retreated back out into the hallway to discover it was no longer empty.

"There you are."

Tai started, flaring her wings and scattering a handful of loose feathers.

"My, my, you are a jumpy one."

Tai relaxed, just a fraction. It was one of the other candidates. Lewellyn, Tai thought her name was, the tall Sanorian with the intricately braided hair. If another candidate was here, chances were she hadn't strayed too far out of bounds. But she still felt like a child caught riffling through her parents' possessions.

"I ..." Tai's throat was dry. Void take her. *Why* had she ever thought she could be a spy?

"Hey, hey, calm down." Lewellyn smiled. "Pretty much everyone sneaks off to see the dragons the first chance they get."

Tai felt some of the tension leave her winged shoulders.

"Celestian said the same," Tai admitted with a sheepish smile. "I do love dragons," she added, for good measure.

Lewellyn nodded enthusiastically. "Yes, me too. Ever since I was a child. I was ever so excited when Kadmin recruited me. Pity that it's all a farce."

Tai's wings twitched, but with a force of effort, she stilled them. *Pity it's all a farce.* Lewellyn couldn't possibly suspect her already, could she? "What do you mean?"

Lewellyn rolled her eyes. "The Taggart siblings. They're not even that good, but their mother is someone important, Countess of something or other, and one of the Empress's chief advisors. So everyone knows the dragonstone's probably going to go to one of those two. Personally, I just hope it's Cressida. She may be stuck up, but at least she's not a thrice cursed idiot like her brother."

Tai bit her lip, not sure whether to laugh. "Is Duchess Vivienne the type to play favorites based on rank?"

"Surprisingly, no," Lewellyn allowed. "She's fairer than many. But even though she's in charge of our training, it's the Emperor who decides in the end. And gods only know how his mind works."

"Still, seems to me like the rest of us have a chance," Tai said. "I fought Denton Taggart, and I didn't find him especially impressive. I figure the rest of us just have to make sure we're too good to be ignored."

Lewellyn barked a good-natured laugh. "I like you, new girl. We should team up."

Tai responded with a thin-lipped smile. She wasn't here to make friends, but the pragmatic part of her knew she needed allies if she wanted to survive more than a week in this place. "We're still competing for the same dragonstone," she reminded the other candidate.

"No reason we can't work together until then," Lewellyn said. "So what do you say? Friends, until we inevitably have to betray each other?"

Nothing worth doing is easy.

"Friends," Tai agreed. "Until we inevitably have to betray each other."

CHAPTER THIRTEEN
MAKING INROADS

Dorian was so distracted after yet another disastrous training session that he utterly failed to watch where he was going.

"Gah!" came a startled feminine voice.

"Oh, sweet Ancients, I'm sorry." To his absolute horror, he realized he had barreled headlong into none other than Dragonmar Sylvia herself.

Tanis stepped to the side, looking like he was trying hard not to laugh. Dorian, meanwhile, could only fight to contain his mortification as he helped the fallen dragonmar to her feet. "Meroneth's balls. I didn't hurt you, did I?"

"Language," the dragonmar said vaguely. "But worry not. Nothing's hurt but my pride." She dusted herself off and smiled wanly. "I'm afraid I was the one who didn't watch where she was going. You have my apologies."

"Erm," Dorian replied eloquently.

"I know that look." Sylvia put her finger on her chin in a way that was again so familiar, and yet Dorian still could not place it. "Something's bothering you."

Dorian flushed and scratched the back of his neck. "Ah, nothing severe. Another day, another lecture from Jameson about my woeful inadequacy."

Dorian reached behind his back, stretching his tired muscles. He felt like he spent every spare moment in training, but he still couldn't seem to impress the exacting flight leader. He supposed he ought to be used to it, growing up with Janus Callahan, but he'd been foolish enough to hope that life among dragonauts might be different.

Sylvia's expression softened somewhat. "Jameson is... difficult to please. Not impossible, I don't think. He's not like Janus Callahan." Dorian's eyes widened. How did she know he'd just been thinking about his stepfather? "But if it means anything," the Dragonmar concluded, "I am nothing short of *in awe* of how far you've come."

Gods help him, she actually sounded like she meant it.

"Oh." Dorian felt his flush deepen. "Erm. Thank you, Lady Dragonmar."

Dorian examined the dragonmar, once again trying and failing to puzzle out where they'd met before. She looked exhausted, he realized, with dark circles under her eyes, her wavy brown hair sticking out at odd angles.

"Are... are you all right, Lady Dragonmar? I mean, is there... I mean, is there, ah, any way I can help?" He scratched his neck again, realizing he probably had very little to offer.

Sylvia smiled sadly. "I appreciate it more than you know, but I fear there's little you can do, unless you know how to cool the Toreenish ambassador's finicky temper, and quell the unrest in the town while you're at it."

Tanis shifted his wings in derision. Dorian glanced uncertainly between his ward and the Dragonmar. Perhaps he *did* know how to cool tempers in the city, after all.

Clearing his throat and steeling what courage he could gather, he said, "All due respect, Lady Dragonmar, but, ah, *why* can't we help the Orith?"

Sylvia raised her eyebrows. "What do you propose?"

"Well." He swallowed and scratched his neck some more. "We could, ah, feed magic to the silverleaves."

"If only it were that simple," Sylvia sighed. "Anything we did would be like throwing water droplets on a wildfire."

Dorian shook his head. "That may be so, Lady Dragonmar. But if Callahan's dragonauts are already doing it, how must it look if we don't?"

"As far as any of my spies can gather, Kadmin was acting independently, and only in the town of Everwood. Still..." Sylvia placed a thoughtful finger on her chin. "Perhaps you have a point. It *would* build a great deal of good will with the locals if we at least *tried*."

Dorian nodded eagerly. "Yes! Yes, we should do that."

"I will... have to give it some thought." She gave him that look he found so hauntingly familiar, simultaneously happy and sad.

Well. That wasn't a yes, but it wasn't a no, either. And more importantly, the Dragonmar hadn't told him off simply for asking.

"You're headed for Everwood tomorrow, correct?" Sylvia asked.

"Yes, Lady Dragonmar," Dorian confirmed. "At least this way Roan will know his son is safe."

Sylvia closed her eyes. "No parent should be left wondering what became of their child. Still, I trust you to monitor their conversation, and make sure he doesn't give away any of our secrets."

"Of course," Dorian said. "And thank you."

Sylvia turned on her heel and departed, seemingly in a hurry.

"Well." Dorian let out a long sigh. "I suppose that could have gone worse."

"She's not going to let you go feed the silverleaves," Tanis predicted. "Trust me. 'I'll think about it' almost always means no."

"You're probably right," Dorian agreed. "But it was wroth a try."

"She seems to like you, at any rate," Tanis mused. Then, wrinkling his nose, he added, "Can't imagine why."

Dorian snorted. "She's like that with everyone."

Tanis stared at Dorian, face screwed up into a puzzled expression.

"You all right?"

Tanis opened his mouth and closed it several times before finally answering. "It's nothing," he said. "Never mind."

And yet, even though it might be his imagination, Dorian thought he saw approval in the adolescent Orith's eyes.

The next day, Tanis sat uncomfortably in his childhood home, squirming under his friend Lana's disapproving gaze. Moons had passed since he'd seen her last, and this was the way she looked at him, with a mixture of pity and disgust.

"That's... the same demon we found that day?" Her eyes kept straying towards Malachite and then darting away, as if that were less rude than staring openly.

"No," Tanis said sardonically. "I've got a whole pile of demons on rotation. Five or six by now."

In the past, his best friend would have laughed at his sarcastic joke. No longer. She blinked and looked away as if he'd said something dirty and offensive.

"It's just... he's gotten rather powerful, hasn't he?" Lana fiddled with her collar, which was embroidered with an intricate floral pattern. That was new; she must have reached a new Waypost on the Path in his absence. He'd missed so much during his imprisonment. No wonder it felt like there was a gulf as wide as the undersea between them. "I thought the whole purpose of going to Aeris was so you didn't have to draw energy from him."

"And I haven't been." Tanis crossed his arms, defensive.

"You've certainly been feeding him, though," Lana accused.

Tanis was, in fact, feeding Malachite a trickle of silver-white spirit energy right at that very moment. He cut it off, embarrassed, and the euphoric feeling vanished abruptly. Malachite gave a huff of annoyance, and Tanis massaged his aching head. *You and me both.* He glanced at Malachite, who was now the size of the living room table. The demon hadn't grown *that* much in Tanis's absence, had he? Depths take him. Perhaps he had.

"Ah, leave him be." Roan unexpectedly came to Tanis's defense. "The boy's well aware how dangerous demons can be, he doesn't need us to remind him." But Tanis's father had that look on his face, the one that seared into his soul as surely as the harshest criticism. The dreaded, all-encompassing *concern*. "I just want to make sure you're all right."

"I'm fine, Dad. I'm much more concerned about *you*."

That was why he'd been so desperate to come back, after all. Roan, however, seemed to be getting along just fine without Tanis. He said he missed Tanis, and he was probably telling the truth. But he was not, thank the Savior, destitute. Tanis supposed it evened out, in the end, two fewer hands to help out, but one less mouth to feed. Tanis's stomach turned over at the thought that he might have ever been a burden.

"My dear boy," Roan said. "If I've told you once, I've told you a hundred times. It's my job to look after you, not the other way around. So tell me, boyo. These Aerish, how are they to work with?"

Finally, a question about something other than Malachite. "Yeah, you know, decent enough." He undid his ponytail and tied it back up in a messy top knot, just to do something with his hands. "Mostly just chores and stuff. They don't trust me enough to tell me anything really important."

This was the truth, mostly. He couldn't hide everything from his father, of course. It was now patently obvious that he was not simply working as a porter. But he'd left the details intentionally vague. He saw no need to make his father worry more than necessary.

"I note you're speaking Kasani, though," Lana said. Lana spoke the Aerish trade tongue too, but made it no secret that she resented having to learn it. "You decided to become one of them now, like your sister?"

Tanis ruffled his wings in annoyance. "I'm not one of them, and neither is Tai. It's just... rude, to leave Dorian out of the conversation."

Dorian waved awkwardly from where he sat, absently fiddling with a spare length of fishing rope.

"If he were truly your friend, he'd learn our language," Lana said in Toreenish.

"We're not friends," Tanis replied, also in Toreenish. They *weren't*, so why did he feel so guilty for saying so? "We're just... colleagues."

Surreptitiously, Tanis sent more spirit energy to Malachite, and felt instantly better. He hoped his father and Lana wouldn't notice. Dorian *did* seem to notice, and frowned. He did not, however, pass judgement, for which Tanis was grateful.

It was with conflicted feelings that he eventually said his farewells and climbed back up onto Solaris's saddle.

"Hold on tight, it's a bumpy ride near the cloud layer," Dorian warned.

Tanis adjusted his harness, but he didn't mind the turbulence, not really. It came nowhere close to the turbulence of his thoughts.

His mind kept replaying his conversations with Lana and his father over and over. "We're just concerned about you." "Demons are dangerous." Did they think he didn't know that? Did they assume him wholly ignorant of what Malachite was doing to him? He'd bonded the demon in the first place to *help them*. *Fallen*, Lana had even *encouraged* it. How dare they cast judgment now, when sometimes it seemed like letting Malachite feed on him was the only thing that made life bearable?

He'd managed to restrain himself during the visit, only allowing Malachite a tiny drab of spirit energy at a time. Now that they were airborne, however, he opened the floodgates, letting his life force flow freely into the demon. His worries and frustrations drained away in the wake of the demon-induced euphoria, and he was far, far too tired to care about the consequences.

Soon, blissfully, consciousness left him.

Startled market-goers scrambled out of the way as Dorian and Solaris came to a haphazard landing in Cloudfire's town square.

"Come on, come on, don't you dare die on me." Dorian prayed to all seven gods as he lifted the unconscious Tanis from Solaris's back and set him down gently on an unused stone bench. Silver-white spirit energy streamed out of Tanis while the demon, Malachite, gorged himself unrestrained.

Heart pounding, Dorian unsheathed his athame and traced a series of sigils into the air. Protection, connection, banishment, and stasis. He drew out his own life essence and wove it together in a web with Tanis's, creating a makeshift barrier. "Nahiira help me, let this work."

Dorian was no Healer, but he knew a thing or two about demons.

To his relief, the gushing torrent of spirit energy slowed to a trickle. Malachite, deprived of his feast, stared at Dorian balefully. *You have won the battle, but not the war,* his expression seemed to say.

Tanis blinked awake, gasping for breath. "What — where am I?"

"Thank the Ancients." Dorian realized he'd all but forgotten to breathe. "Are you all right?"

"I think so." Tanis tugged at his hair, which had come out of its topknot. "What happened? Weren't we flying through the cloud layer?"

"We were," Dorian said. "But you lost consciousness. This was the safest place I could think to land."

"Lost consciousness..." Tanis's eyes widened. "Malachite! Oh, Fallen, I went into fugue, didn't I."

"Not quite, thank Nahiira." If it had been a real fugue, there would have been little Dorian could have done. "I combined your spirit energy with mine to create a barrier. It won't hold forever, of course, but it kept Malachite's attack from progressing too far."

"Fallen." Tanis buried his face in his hands. "Thought that was only supposed to happen with big high level demons, ones that had been around for years."

Malachite was large and powerful for a demon who only possessed his host a few short moons ago, but Dorian saw no benefit in pointing that out. The boy was clearly terrified. The last thing he needed was a lecture. "Would you like some tea?" he asked instead.

Tanis twitched his wing as if startled by the question. But then he shrugged and said, "Yeah, okay."

The bell by the door chimed as Dorian and Tanis stepped inside the tea shop. Powerful aromas greeted them; jasmine flower and cinnamon and other spices Dorian couldn't name. Everyone else in the shop was Orith, feathered wings of black and white and gold gathered on rich scarlet poufs around low wooden tables.

"I shouldn't have let Malachite take so much of my energy," Tanis said despondently as he sat down. "I just... after my Father, and Lana..."

"It can be rough, returning home," Dorian said delicately. He hadn't actually been back to Frostvale since he left over a year ago, but he imagined returning would be an uncomfortable experience.

"My parents did their best," Tanis said with a sigh, "But it was always Tai this, Tai that. She wasn't even there, and she still managed to get more attention than me." He smiled ruefully. "I always thought if I proved myself useful, if I held things together, then maybe... maybe I'd be worthy of all that attention too."

Dorian's heart ached at this, because he thought he knew a bit of how Tanis felt. For the first few years after he'd been taken to live in Callahan Manor, he'd been so, so desperate to win his new guardian's approval. But no matter what he did, he always fell short. It wasn't until much later that he learned that Janus had always been determined to hate him, and that it hadn't been Dorian's fault at all.

But thankfully that wasn't the case with Tanis's father. He'd met the man twice now, and he could see that clear as day. "Your father loves you," Dorian said. "Honestly, I think he just wants you to have the chance at a normal life."

"Whatever my life is," Tanis said with a sigh, "I fear it's far from normal."

A gray-winged woman with tiny embroidered stars and moons on her sleeves arrived at their table a moment later and took their orders in Toreenish. Dorian, whose Toreenish was atrocious, attempted to order a passionfruit tea. He must have said something else, though, because the server flushed scarlet and raised her hand to her mouth, half stifling a laugh. Tanis stepped in and corrected him, and the server nodded and winked before sweeping off to get their tea ready.

Tanis chortled. "You really *can't* speak Toreenish, can you?"

"Sweet Meroneth," Dorian groaned in Kasani. "What did I say?"

"The grammar was all over the place, so not a lot that made sense." Tanis made what appeared to be a valiant attempt at keeping a straight face, but eventually surrendered into fits of laughter.

Tanis's resemblance to his sister was more pronounced when he laughed. The same dimples, the same pointed chin.

"It's not your fault, I suppose," Tanis said. "It's just you said *asa*, meaning sister, when I think you meant *asha*, meaning tea, and then when you said you *wanted* it you said *kahari*, which means to desire, but more, um, sexually. And of course, *kierath*, meaning *passionfruit*, is a rather loaded term in both of our languages, so when you tried to say you wanted some passionfruit tea, you instead said you wished to make passionate love to that lady's sister."

Dorian could feel his face burning. "Oh," he said. "Oh, no."

"Hey, hey, don't worry about it." Tanis awkwardly patted Dorian on the arm. "It's nice that you tried. I mean, most Aerishfolk wouldn't even bother. Plus." His brown eyes sparkled with barely suppressed mirth. "I know you *actually* want to make passionate love to *my* sister, so that makes it doubly funny."

Dorian let out a high pitched choking noise. He was saved having to respond, however, when the server returned, carting two steaming pots of tea.

She also handed them each a small saucer containing what appeared to be a sugary, gelatinous cube. Not wanting to make a complete fool of himself, he waited for Tanis to eat first before taking a bite. It was good, he thought, sweet yet also salty, with a hint of candied ginger.

Now that they had their tea, Tanis sat up straight and ruffled his wings, clear signs of one steeling himself for a tough conversation. "I... know I shouldn't give Malachite so much of my energy. I try to stop, but... he's just always there, poking and prodding at my thoughts." He scratched his head as if he could feel the demon's physical presence there. "And when I finally do let go, let him feed, it feels so—"

"It feels great," Dorian finished for him. "I know. Believe me, I know."

"Until it doesn't anymore," Tanis sighed.

"Until it doesn't anymore," Dorian agreed.

Dorian had been, in many ways, lucky to have Hematite as a demon. Hematite had no desire to send Dorian into a fugue, no desire to take more energy that was sustainable. So they'd reached a balance. But it had taken a great deal of trial and error to get that far.

"You... did something, back on that park bench," Tanis continued. "Somehow, I don't... feel him as strongly. I mean. He's still there, but I can resist him. Fallen Depths, I can at least *think*."

In Dorian's peripheral vision, he could see the ghostly form of the demon now, blue flames flickering in sulky indignation. "I strengthened your spirit aura by combining it with my own," Dorian said. "It formed a sort of shield to temporarily weaken Malachite's influence."

Tanis's face fell. "Temporarily?"

"I'm afraid so. But you should be able to create the shield yourself, with meditation and practice."

"I forgot you had a demon too," Tanis said thoughtfully.

"I did," Dorian said, heart aching as he prodded at the empty place in his soul where Hematite once resided. "But Hematite wasn't like other demons. He was... a friend."

"Were you *kahari kierath*?" Tanis waggled his eyebrows.

Dorian's face turned scarlet. "What? No. Of course not, why would you even—"

Tanis chortled. "Relax, relax, I'm just messing with you. So you and your demon were friends. You should be grateful. Most of us are not so lucky." His expression became grave once more, and he held his teacup close to himself like a child's toy. "It's funny. I thought for sure I'd be able to handle possession. But look at me now. Only a few moons, and he's already driven me nearly to a fugue. Pathetic, right?"

"No!" Dorian waved his hands. "It's... these things take practice. You're far from the first person to ever let a demon get out of control."

"Funny," Tanis said. "I used to think I might like to be an aeronaut. You know, like my sister." He absently traced a spiral pattern on the glossy table. "But nobody'll take me the way I am now."

"You can be possessed and still be an aeronaut."

"You can be possessed and be an aeronaut, or you can be Orith and be an aeronaut, but no self-respecting skyship captain would take on someone who is both."

Xander would, Dorian thought, but he supposed it didn't matter. Xander didn't have a ship anymore. If it hadn't been for Hematite, however, they'd've lost far more than just the ship. "Having a demon on board can be thrice cursed useful, actually."

"Maybe." Tanis seemed unconvinced. "But, um, back to that meditation thing you mentioned."

"Yeah?" Dorian asked.

"Can you teach me?" Tanis placed his palms on the table.

The youth's expression was so hopeful, so imploring, that Dorian knew he couldn't answer any other way. "Of course."

Two weeks later, however, Dorian began to fear that helping Tanis was a lost cause.

"I can't do it," Tanis complained, for what must have been the hundredth time that afternoon. "I don't care what you say, it's just not possible!"

Dorian screwed his eyes shut and prayed to all seven gods for patience.

"You've only been at it for two weeks. Of course you're not going to be perfect. But Ancients help me, you have to actually *try*."

For a few glorious moments, Dorian almost thought he might actually reach the boy. He'd thought Tanis wanted to learn. So far, though, all Tanis seemed to want to do was complain. A guilty part of Dorian almost preferred when Tanis was sullen and monosyllabic.

It was a pleasant day in early summer, the skies above Cloudfire a flawless blue. Falgar and Sullivan had gone flying, and Dorian wished fervently that he could be up there with them, but a promise was a promise.

"I'll never be able to resist Malachite's influence," Tanis moaned. "I'm doing everything you say, but it just... doesn't... work." The Orith youth screwed up his face in concentration.

Through Dorian's peripheral vision, he saw Tanis's swirling blue-white spirit aura congeal and solidify into a crystal barrier. It was impressively solid, Dorian admitted, but unfortunately it was brittle as well. Too brittle. At the first test of pressure from Malachite's verdant claws, the shield dissolved in a puff of energy, which Malachite lapped up like a hungry cat.

"You see," Tanis said, and now he looked genuinely dispirited rather than simply petulant, "It's impossible. Maybe some people just aren't meant to resist demons."

And just like that, Dorian's annoyance drained away. He remembered an afternoon not unlike this one, on the deck of the *Phoenix*, holding a trembling sword in his unsteady hand. *My body just wasn't meant to do this,* he had said. *That remains to be seen,* Xander had replied.

"Hey. These things take time."

He put a reassuring hand on the boy's shoulder, but Tanis irritably shrugged away. "Easy for you to say. I bet you never had to struggle with anything."

"Ha!" Dorian's laugh came out like a squawk.

"What? It's true. I've heard all about the so-called dragonauts." He rolled his eyes. "My sister was bloody obsessed when we were kids. I got to hear *all about* how you all are the best of the best, the 'finest humanity has to offer.'" He gestured with his hands. "Sorry, I wasn't born excellent like the rest of you."

Dorian wasn't sure whether to laugh or cry. Even steeped in cynicism, this was the closest Tanis had ever come to a genuine compliment — and it was utterly unfounded. "I," he said with a sigh, "Am *far* from the best humanity has to offer." He decided now would be a good time to change the subject. "Your technique is getting better, but the spirit barrier is too fragile. It doesn't need to be solid, it just needs to be consistent. It's like—" he waved his hand vaguely, scrambling for words to describe what he meant. "Back in your house in Everwood. Remember that fishing net you showed me?"

"Yes." Tanis frowned, clearly nonplussed.

"Well, it's sort of like that. You weave the spirit energy together so that it can flex and bend without breaking, but it's still a consistent enough web that Malachite can't get through."

"You want me to turn my spirit energy into a fishing net?" Tanis's tone was skeptical, but Dorian could tell from the glint in his eyes that he liked the idea.

Tanis closed his eyes and breathed in and out, moving thin silver-white tendrils of energy. Several times, he let out a frustrated swear as the energy snapped and dissolved into nothingness, but each time, he got farther than the time before.

As he worked, Tanis asked casually, "So if you're 'far from the best humanity has to offer,' how'd you end up with a dragon bond?"

Dorian winced. "Kinda hoped you'd ignore that comment. It's a, um, long story."

"We've got nothing better to do." Tanis, seeming to sense Dorian's discomfort, grinned.

Dorian could find no way to get out of it, so he told Tanis everything. About his time on the *Phoenix,* about how he could barely hold a sword properly, about his disastrous first flight. He talked about Sullivan's broken arm, and the collapse in Greystone Citadel, and Solaris, weak and injured and desperate for help he was too inept to give. He told Tanis about Tai's outburst in the galley and how he, an hour later, hesitantly asked for help to get stronger.

Eventually, he realized he'd been droning on for an embarrassingly long time. *Stop making everything about yourself,* said the imaginary voice that sounded like Janus Callahan. Although, Tanis *did* ask. "I guess what I'm trying to say is, I know what it's like not to be good at something right away."

Waving aside his incomplete spirit web and starting over, Tanis nodded thoughtfully. "I... had no idea."

"There's no reason you'd be expected to," Dorian said. Though it was a strange feeling to be around someone who *overestimated* him for once.

"So you think there's still hope for me, then?" Tanis wondered.

"Of course. Tell you what." Dorian dusted his hands. "Let's take a break and do something other than meditation."

"All right," Tanis said, frowning. "What did you have in mind?"

He grinned and gestured towards the barn-shaped hangar below, where the Order stored their ornithopters. *"Go flying."*

CHAPTER FOURTEEN
FLYING LESSONS

Tanis was skeptical at first as he approached the array of flying machines lined up in the cavernous stone hangar bay. What could this Aerish contraption offer, really, that was better than the perfectly good wings on his back? But Dorian looked so eager and excited that Tanis felt obligated to humor the man. *Like a scampering gryphlet cub,* he thought.

"You'll want these." Dorian handed him a pair of googles.

"Why?" Tanis wondered.

"Just trust me."

Tanis shrugged and put them on.

Dorian climbed onto his dragon Solaris, leaving Tanis to choose an ornithopter and adjust the safety harness. "I don't exactly know what I'm doing," he admitted.

"You'll be all right. Just kick off with your legs, and the aether engine will handle the rest. But if you need help, you can talk to me through the aether beacon."

"Aether beacon." He prodded the blue crystal mounted near the front of the vehicle's wooden shaft. Not so different from the one he'd worn during his short-lived stint as a Kasani soldier. "Got it."

Dorian and Solaris launched themselves out of the hangar's cave-like opening and into the summer sky. With nothing to lose, Tanis shrugged and followed suit.

And in that instant, everything changed.

"Zekador's poorly fitting pants!" Tanis didn't actually know much about the Aerish god Zekador or why his pants were the wrong size, but he figured if he was going to fly like an Aerishman, he might as well swear like one. And this moment warranted a good swearing.

Wind blasted in Tanis's face, drawing back the skin around his mouth. Thank the Savior for the goggles, or he wouldn't have been able to see the crest of Cloudfire Mountain receding below until the shimmering alabaster castle looked like a child's toy.

This was nothing like flying with his own wings. Even the fastest wingracer in Toreen couldn't match this speed. It wasn't even like flying on Solaris, though he suppose the time she'd carried him in her claws came close. This was wild and unrestrained freedom. It was terrifying. It was *incredible*.

Tanis briefly entertained the idea of running away, trying to shake his captor and make a bid for freedom. Ultimately, however, he decided it was a lost cause. Fast as this ornithopter was, Solaris was faster. And traitorously, at the moment, Tanis found he didn't particularly *want* to leave.

Tanis wasn't sure how long he flew in circles above Cloudfire. Half a bell, maybe a bell. Eventually, though, the vehicle slowed, the wind in his hair lessened, and the vehicle gave the slightest lurch.

"It's not malfunctioning, is it?" Tanis poked at the main crystal, concerned. He'd simply unclip the harness and fly to safety if it failed, but wrecking one of the Order's expensive ornithopters would most likely get him in a lot of trouble.

Dorian wheeled around on his scarlet dragon and flew in close formation to inspect the aether crystal. "Nearly to shatter point," he said with a sigh. "We'd best head back."

Tanis did his best to hide his disappointment as he followed the dragon and rider back to Cloudfire Castle.

"That was excellent," Dorian said as soon as Tanis unclipped his harness and removed his flight goggles. "You're a real natural at this."

Tanis smirked and twitched his raven-black wings. "Born to fly," he said. "Just wish I could have done it for longer."

"Yes." Dorian's mouth drew into a concerned line as he removed the engine's crystal and examined it. "Seems the charges run out faster and faster these days. This is the sort of thing the Order is supposed to be trying to prevent."

Tanis took the crystal and turned it over in his hands, but he simply didn't know enough to say if there was anything wrong with it. It was blue and pointed, and warm to the touch, shining with a faint inner light. Was it true what the Order believed? Was Aerish magic really dying? And if so, did it have anything to do with the silverleaf blight back home?

Tanis thought of the experiments he'd been set to guard at the Kasani base. Those had something to do with manipulating ambient magic. Fallen, but he wished he knew more about it. He was beginning to realize there was a lot he didn't know.

"Kadmin mentioned some kind of artifact once," Tanis said casually, testing the waters. "Some kind of mirror thing that was supposed to amplify ambient magic."

"The moon glass," Dorian said at once, as if this were common knowledge. "Yes, it exists, but it's dangerous. Flight Leader Jameson tried to use it for a simple flame spell, and it literally blew up in his face. He lost an eyebrow."

"He *what*?"

"He's lucky it was *just* an eyebrow."

"So there's a moon glass here, in the castle, right now?"

"Yes," Dorian said, "But don't get any ideas. It's well guarded, and it'll be more than just my job on the line if we take it out to go joy riding on an ornithopter."

"Fair, fair." Tanis set the failing aether crystal down.

As soon as he did so, an uncomfortable presence reasserted itself inside him. Malachite, not just requesting spirit energy, but outright *demanding it*. Tanis made a startling realization that he'd barely sensed the demon's presence the entire time he'd been airborne. Malachite seemed determined to make up for it now, though.

Not now. Tanis groaned inwardly. Compared to the thrill of flying, the euphoria of spirit drain felt like a pale imitation. An *inconvenience*. Irritated, without really thinking about it, he wove his spirit energy into a fishing net, just like he'd practiced. To his surprise, it held. Malachite bounced against the barrier like a moth against a paper windowscreen. He could still sense the demon's presence, but no longer was it so immediate, so insistent.

"Would you look at that." Tanis laughed. "I did it."

"Hey now!" Dorian's face broke into a grin. "I knew you could—"

«Oh, come now.» Malachite sounded well and truly annoyed. «This is not what we agreed to.»

"Malachite..." Tanis began, dismayed.

Malachite prodded the barrier, gently at first, but then with increasing aggression until he finally took a swipe that knocked Tanis backwards.

"Stop it!"

Tanis drew his belt knife and stumbled towards the creature, slashing out wildly in self defense. Silver-white spirit energy sprayed out of the demon like a punctured cask of sparkling greenwine. Malachite staggered away, but so did Tanis. He toppled precariously, out of the ornithopter hangar and into the empty sky below.

"Whoa there!" Dorian caught his wrist just before he plummeted, and pulled him gently back into the cavernous hangar.

"Thanks." Tanis dusted himself off. His spirit barrier, for the moment, remained in place, and Malachite twitched his tail, sullen but unwilling to strike again.

"Sorry I had to do that," Tanis said to Malachite as he resheathed his knife. "But Depths take it, no means no."

«No matter,» Malachite said sulkily. «You will give me your spirit energy eventually. Humans always do.»

"You should be careful." Dorian's face was ashen-white. "You nearly fell halfway down the mountainside."

"Oh, that." Tanis shook out his feathers. "I'd've just flown back here."

"Ah, right." Dorian looked slightly mollified. "Wings. I keep forgetting. Still, you ought to be careful." Scratching his neck, he asked delicately, "Ah, how much combat training did the Kasani give you, exactly?"

Tanis wrinkled his nose. "Not much," he admitted. Crestfallen, he added, "That bad, huh?"

"No, no!" Dorian waved his hands. "I mean. You hit the mark. Which was, ah, far more than I managed when I was new to the sword."

"Well, that's something."

Dorian shook his head and massaged the back of his neck. "What I'm saying is... You've got good natural coordination, but your footwork... well... since you're learning so quickly anyway... maybe it's time we started practicing your sword skills."

Malachite reacted with dismay, which at the moment seemed like evidence enough that it was a good idea. "Sure, why not? Let's do it." But as he stood up, he wavered, and nearly fell out the hangar a second time. He moved sheepishly back towards the wall. "Though maybe... maybe some rest, first."

"Ah, yes, I should've warned you." Dorian flushed and scratched his neck. "You... probably don't want to keep that spirit barrier up all the time. It takes a lot out of you, as do ornithopters for that matter. It'll keep Malachite from draining your spirit energy in the short term, but if you burn yourself out, you'll just be all the more vulnerable. But don't worry. I've just the thing. Let's go to the kitchens."

Tai was surprised to learn it would be the better part of a year before the Imperial Dragonauts selected their newest dragonaut.

She supposed that made sense, because they needed to determine not only who was the most skilled, but who would fit best with the team. Tai thought ruefully of the Order's single day of Trials and the dragonauts who could scarcely tolerate one another, and thought perhaps this was one area where the Kasani dragonauts got it right. If Tai did her job, though, she planned to be be long gone with the dragonstone before that year was up. If only she could figure out where they kept the Void-cursed thing.

Days fell into a comfortable rhythm as Tai threw herself wholeheartedly into her training. Her tentative alliance with Lewellyn paid off. Soon, the young nobleman Owain joined them as well, and together, they rose to the top of the class.

As long as she didn't think about it too hard, she could almost say she enjoyed her time in Kasanarae. But the reality of her mission was never far from the forefront of her mind. These people wanted to enslave dragons. Lewellyn and Owain were her allies, but never her friends. She couldn't let herself forget that.

"We've got special guests with us today, so look sharp!"

The candidates straightened at the sound of Duchess Vivienne's voice during training one bright summer afternoon.

Special guests, indeed. Behind Vivienne, no less than three dragons circled and came to a landing. First, Vivienne's gold-bronze dragon Thunder landed at her side, followed quickly by Kadmin riding Celestian. Tai once again admired how Celestian's purple-blue scales glittered in the sun, but she quickly looked away, lest Kadmin think she was admiring *him*.

Last, but not least, a black and silver dragon made his delicate landing in the training field. This one was smaller than the others, almost sickly in appearance. Tai's breath caught in her throat when she realized this must be Nocturne, Chronicler of his clan, and the unwilling bond to the Emperor himself. All these weeks here, and she'd not seen the Emperor even once. Tai craned her neck to get a better look at the man, but it wasn't Janus Callahan seated on Nocturne's back.

The whispers cut off as each candidate fell to their knees. A fraction of a second too late, Tai followed suit. Saedra Alansae Adrienne Rachelle Penregon Kasani climbed down from the saddle, looking poised as ever in an elegant midnight blue riding habit with a sapphire circlet on her brow. Tai's heart beat a frantic rhythm. She was less than a gryphon's length away from Dorian's former lover. Callahan's wife. The bloody thrice-cursed *Empress*.

"You may rise, for you are all the future hope of the Empire," Saedra said.

Although curvier than Tai — most people were, she thought ruefully — Saedra was more slender than her cousin Vivienne, and softer, somehow, both in manner and appearance. But the two of them were obviously related. Saedra and Vivienne shared the same silky dark hair, the same intelligent silver eyes, and the same natural charisma that flowed from their very being. Tai felt small and inadequate next to the Empress's regal bearing.

Saedra gave them each a perfunctory greeting. When she reached Tai, however, she paused, meeting Tai's brown eyes with her gray ones.

"I know you," the Empress said.

Oh Void, oh Void. "Your... your Imperial Highness."

"You were at Goose Head."

Saedra remembered. Of course she bloody Void-cursed remembered. But perhaps the Empress just had uncommonly good facial recognition. Tai could have been any random soldier. Saedra didn't necessarily *know* that Tai was a spy. Tai's ears rang with the sound of her own pounding heart. "Your Imperial Highness," she said again.

"It's funny," Saedra said, too quietly for anyone else to hear. Almost too quietly for Tai to hear. "I spent a year hoping to see him again. And when finally I did, he had eyes only for you."

Nope. Saedra knew, all right. *Void, Void, Void.*

Rather than calling for the guards, however, Saedra abruptly turned and addressed the next candidate. Tai was left with her feathers sticking straight out, trying to quell her panic. And, shameful though it was to admit, there was a tiny, ridiculous, illogical part of her that thought, *Dorian had eyes only for me?*

"If chosen to bear a dragonstone," Saedra addressed the group, "You will be part of the most elite force in the Kasani Empire. Just by being here, it means you are among the best. You should be proud." She stepped aside, ceding the floor to Flight Leader Vivienne.

"As part of your training," Vivienne said, "It is important that we see how you get around controlling the dragons themselves. These three dragons here are bonded to myself, Lord Kadmin, and, of course, Emperor Callahan, who could not be here today because of the rigors of running the empire, so her Imperial Highness is here in his stead."

Tai glanced at the Empress, and then at Callahan's dragon Nocturne, and suppressed a frown. It was Saedra's empire too, wasn't it? Why was she out here training recruits while Janus handled the affairs of the state?

Dragons reflected their riders. This much, Tai knew. Thunder was large and powerful, like Vivienne. Celestian was sleek and athletic, like Kadmin. But Nocturne, lying listlessly on the ground with his head in his obsidian claws, looked more than just frail. He looked ill.

Tai's mind raced at the implications. Could the Emperor be unwell?

"As you may have guessed," Vivienne said, "The bonds with these dragons differ slightly than the dragonaut bonds of old." *Understatement of the Cycle.* "You will no doubt become just as close to your bond as the Ancients were with theirs." *Doubtful.* "The means of control, however, comes not just from the bond itself, but also from the dragonstone."

Tai raised her eyebrows. This was information the Order did not have.

"There is much about these wondrous artifacts we don't know."

Dragonaut Kadmin twisted the silver chain around his finger. "But we know enough to exploit them. So today, each of you will borrow one of our dragonstones, and attempt to control our dragons."

Excitement slowly overtook the fear in Tai's heart. Could it really be that easy? Were they just going to hand her a dragonstone and send her on her way?

"We will, of course, be accompanying you, so that we might take over in the event things go wrong," Vivienne said. *Well, so much for that.* "As there are only three dragons, the three top performers in training so far shall have the first three flights. Candidate Lunstrum, Candidate Lewellyn, and Candidate Barclay, come forward."

Tai, Lewellyn, and Owain shared triumphant glances before approaching the magnificent dragons. Denton Taggart wore a face like a thunderstorm, eyes brimming with resentment.

"You'll be with me, naturally." Kadmin waved her over with that cocky little smirk of his.

Ugh, how did I ever think he was attractive? She wanted to punch that stupid smirk off his face. Instead, she gritted her teeth and forced a smile.

Regardless, Celestian was, in her opinion, by far the most impressive of the captive dragons, and she felt honored to fly with him. But what of Celestian's own feelings? He claimed to have come to an understanding with Kadmin, but surely it must chafe to have his dragonstone handed off to a novice.

"Is this... all right?" she asked the dragon.

"Of course it is," Kadmin answered in Celestian's stead. "It's what we're here for."

She fought to hide her annoyance. Kadmin used to always answer for *her* when they were courting, too. Reluctantly, Tai slung the silver chain around her neck.

"Oh!"

A flood of sensation — Celestian's senses, no doubt — washed over her, so sudden and powerful that she nearly staggered backwards.

"Sorry!" Tai smiled faintly. "Was not expecting that."

«You are afraid,» Celestian observed. «Afraid... and guilty?»

Tai's heart lurched. "Can he read my thoughts?" If so, then she might as well have just signed her own death warrant.

Kadmin only laughed and shook his head. "Only the ones you choose to project. And your loudest emotions." He cocked a single eyebrow. "Really, Tai? Afraid?"

Tai glowered at Kadmin. "Celestian must be mistaken. I'm not scared." That was, of course, a bald-faced lie, and she was certain Kadmin knew that. But better Kadmin to think she had embarrassing cold feet about riding a dragon, than for him to guess her true feelings.

«Does it bother you, that I have this?» Tai thumbed the borrowed dragonstone and addressed Celestian directly.

Celestian cocked his serpentine head, his draconic face bearing a curious expression. «I believe you are the first human to ever ask me that,» he said. «But to answer your question, no, I do not mind. It is a matter of practicality, is it not? You must learn to fly.»

Tai twitched her inadequate wings and thought longingly of her years working on skyships. *Must learn how to fly*, indeed.

"The Coercion spell is easy, but it takes concentration," Kadmin explained. "Hold the dragonstone tight and then focus on moving Celestian's left foot."

Tai did so. Sure enough, Celestian tapped his left front foot three times just as she commanded. Fascinated, and a little horrified, she tried the same with the right foot. Celestian complied at once.

«Sorry about that,» she said to the dragon.

«There is really no need to apologize,» Celestian said. But luckily, she thought he found her attitude puzzling rather than annoying, or worse, suspicious.

Nevertheless, Tai dropped the pendant and let it hang limply from its chain. It was unnatural to have so much power over another creature.

"In the sky, instinct always trumps careful forethought,"

Kadmin continued in his insufferably smug instructor-voice. "Coercion should always be a last result, not a first one. Let's try it, shall we?"

Tai nodded climbed up onto the dragon's back. Celestian's saddle was made from stiff black leather, and felt nowhere near as comfortable as the well-worn dragon saddles the Order favored. Of course, Dorian had always just flown bare-back on Solaris before they came to Cloudfire, so she supposed she ought to be grateful there was any saddle at all. Kadmin seated himself behind her and put his arms possessively around her waist, crushing some of her feathers. Tai wrestled her wings free of his inconsiderate grasp.

Oh, I remember this. She used to *hate* it when Kadmin pulled on her feathers. Back in the old days, she hadn't dared complain. She had been a foolish girl, still thrilling in her first romance and believing it was true love. Now, she couldn't complain either, but for wholly different reasons. Dorian, Tai noted, had never been anything but painstakingly gentle with her when they flew together on Solaris.

Then Celestian launched into the sky, and all thoughts of Kadmin were driven from her mind.

The dragonstone made all the difference. Riding on Solaris, while pleasant, did not greatly differ from riding a gryphon or an ornithopter. But *this*. This was flying in its purest form, what the Linking only sought to imitate. This was pure unity of thought and purpose, wholeness. Her wings were Celestian's wings and Celestian's wings were her wings, beating their defiance against the humid Kasani sky.

"Lunstrum," came Kadmin's slightly muffled voice, "What — are — you doing?"

Tai flushed. Apparently, in her excitement, she'd flapped her own wings, repeatedly hitting Kadmin in the face and giving him a mouthful of feathers. *Amusing*, but not terribly safe. With an effort of will, she stilled herself.

«You fly amazingly well,» Celestian said. «Not at all like the ninnies Kadmin typically brings here. You have flown before, I take it?»

«About a Cycle as an aeronaut,» Tai answered. She had to carefully avoid spreading her wings and hitting Kadmin in the face yet again. Praise from Celestian felt more valuable, somehow, than if it had come from the Queen of Toreen herself.

«It shows.» Celestian spoke in a way that made Tai feel warm all over. His mindvoice took on a playful tone as he added, «Shall we do some showing off?»

Tai grinned. «Oh, indeed.»

Tai didn't care about holding back, didn't care what the other candidates thought. This was just her, and Celestian, and the sky. The pair of them took off with an exhilarating corkscrew turn. Kadmin clung to her back, taking hold of of feathers for purchase. This time, she didn't mind as much.

«This is more fun than I have had in moons,» Celestian said with a telepathic chuckle. «But I fear if we keep this up much longer we will make my rider ill.»

Good, Tai thought, but thankfully stopped herself before projecting that thought too loudly.

"That was... excellently done," agreed the slightly queasy-sounding Kadmin. "However, I think we should land now. The other candidates will want their turn."

Tai sighed as reality settled back in. Yes, that was right. She was a spy in enemy territory, and Celestian was not her bonded partner, but a slave under Kadmin's thrall. For a few glorious moments, she'd been able to forget all that. But Celestian himself would never have the privilege of forgetting.

«You really need not feel sorry for me,» Celestian reassured her. Tai winced, realizing she must have been thinking more loudly than she intended.

With no small sense of melancholy, she brought Celestian down to a graceful landing. Before surrendering the dragonstone back into

Kadmin's custody, she scratched Celestian affectionately behind his horns, in the spot where Dorian's Solaris always seemed to like it.

«I enjoyed flying with you,» she said.

«And I you,» Celestian said. «I am not permitted to pick favorites, but if you were chosen to receive the dragonstone, it would not be such a bad thing.» An odd emotion crossed through their connection. *Uncertainty? Regret?* But it was gone before she could grasp it.

After Lewellyn and Owain landed with their respective borrowed dragons, Cressida Taggart joined the Empress on Nocturne, and the quiet Jeziah rode Thunder, leaving Denton Taggart to take his turn with Celestian.

Despite Nocturne's obvious weakness, Cressida was competent and flew with no-nonsense efficiency. Jeziah, to Tai's slight surprise, flew excellently. The Thlarknian youth was a bit gawky on the ground, but in the sky he moved with natural grace.

Denton Taggart, however, was terrible. He seemed less interested in flying, and more interested in imposing his will. He refused to let up control even for a moment, micromanaging Celestian's every wingbeat. Tai flinched, not wanting to watch, but unable to look away. Even without the connection they'd briefly shared, Tai could tell the dragon was in pain. They didn't make it far before Kadmin seized control and brought them to a safe landing. For once, Tai was glad Kadmin *could* take over.

"This is, I suppose, a teachable moment," Kadmin said. "Can anyone tell me what Mr. Taggart did wrong?"

Tai's wings gave an agitated twitch. *Teachable moment, my arse.* Couldn't Kadmin tell that Denton was hurting the dragon?

Lewellyn tentatively raised her hand.

"Miss Lewellyn," Kadmin prompted her.

"Right, Sir. Mr. Taggart tried too hard to maintain control of the dragon and didn't let him use his natural instincts. Sir."

"Quite right," Kadmin said. "Your control was, I must say,

commendable. But that doesn't matter if you do not let the dragon be a dragon. I venture to guess Celestian knows more about how to fly than you do."

Tai relaxed slightly, and almost cracked a smile. Denton, predictably, bristled.

Kadmin, however, seemed to take pity on the boy, because his expression softened, and he said, "I will reiterate that your control was impressive. Why don't you show the others your competence by having Celestian pace across the length of the training grounds?"

Tai bit back an angry protest. Surely Kadmin wasn't going to encourage this sort of heinous behavior.

Apparently, he was.

Denton's expression turned self-satisfied, and he did precisely as Kadmin instructed. Under Denton's thrall, Celestian pranced across the training grounds in an exaggerated, undignified gait.

Some of the other candidates laughed at the flourishes and poses. To Tai's disappointment, her almost-friend Owain was among them. Tai, meanwhile, had her hands balled so tightly into fists that her fingernails threatened to break skin. Bad enough that Denton was controlling the dragon. Did he have to humiliate him, too? Couldn't the others see how twisted and wrong this was?

Celestian finally returned to Kadmin, inclining his head towards his rider in a way that conveyed perfect stoicism. But Tai wondered how the dragon truly felt.

Denton held the dragonstone in the air like he'd just won a trophy. "There, now, you see, stupid dragon? I'm the one who's in control." He slapped Celestian carelessly across his indigo muzzle. A few stray sparks escaped the dragon's snout, but if Celestian wanted to react more than that, the Coercion prevented it. "You can't do anything to stop me. I can do anything I want to you."

Denton swung the dragonstone amulet, and as he did so, Celestian's left foreleg jerked backwards at an unnatural angle, causing the dragon to collapse to the ground. Not even Coercion could prevent the dragon from letting out a telepathic cry of shock and pain.

"Hey now, that's not—" Kadmin began, but Tai didn't hear the rest of what he said over the outraged ringing in her ears.

She didn't recall deciding to act. Next thing she knew, she'd closed the distance between them. A moment later, they were both on the ground, a tangled mess of limbs and feathers, as each punched and kicked and clawed at the other like a pair of feral gryphlets.

"Get off me, get off me!" Denton Taggart at last extricated himself, shoving Tai violently aside. "What in the Void was that for?"

"This is sick!" Tai rose to her feet and rubbed her arm where Denton struck it. "Can't you all see how sick this is? Celestian's not an ornithopter, not an object to be used and abused. He's a living creature!"

"Technically they're made of pure magical energy," Denton began.

Tai was perfectly ready to attack him again, and he must have realized it, because he backed off at once. "Okay, okay, I'll stop, I'll stop! Just stop trying to murder me, Void Eternal."

"It isn't right," Tai said, deflated. "It just isn't right."

Tai's heart pounded as she stalked back to rejoin the others. The rest of the candidates wore expressions somewhere between shocked and terrified. Owain, perhaps, looked a bit impressed, while Lewellyn only looked dismayed. *You've gone and done it now,* her almost-friend's expression seemed to say.

And now that the moment was over, she realized that yes; she *had* done it now. Might as well announce her true allegiance from the highest parapet. Empress Saedra in particular glared down at her with sharp-eyed intensity.

"My goodness," the empress said. "Brawling during a training session. Is this really the front we wish to put before the outside world?"

Vivienne's expression was grave. She turned towards Cressida and said, "Miss Taggart, if you please escort your brother to the infirmary. Miss Lunstrum," the stocky dragonaut let out a long sigh, "I think it's clear to everyone here that you struck the first blow. I appreciate your sentiment, truly I do. But Her Imperial Majesty is correct. I can't simply allow the candidates to attack one another. I'm afraid I have no choice but to dismiss—"

Tai's heart sank to her boots. She was going to be expelled from the fountain palace, and forced to return to Cloudfire empty handed, and all of this would have been for nothing. Failure, again. *Void curse it!*

"If I may, Flight Leader." Kadmin stepped forward.

Tai's wings twitched, uncertain. She didn't want to owe Kadmin anything, but at the moment, she'd take whatever reprieve she could get.

"Go on." Vivienne's eyes narrowed.

"There is no need to dismiss a promising candidate on her first offense." The ghost of a smile, one she'd once thought so charming, played at his lips. "She did, after all, break the rules standing up for *my* dragon."

At this, Denton Taggart had the decency to look abashed, though his sister Cressida glared daggers in Tai's direction.

"For once, I agree with you," Vivienne said. "But I can't simply let this slide. What do you propose?"

"Let her stay on as a candidate," Kadmin said smoothly. "But in recompense, I would have her act as my *personal* squire. That way, I can make sure she stays out of further trouble."

Was that a malicious glint in his dark green eyes? Or was it just Tai's imagination?

Almost against her will, Tai glanced over at the Empress. Surely this was the part where Saedra announced that Tai had been a spy in Goose Head, and she was a spy here. But while she continued to look at Tai with a shrewd expression, Saedra said nothing.

Tai swallowed. "That is... more than generous, my lord dragonaut."

Tai's relief, however, was short-lived. She was saved from expulsion this once. But *Void Eternal!* Kadmin Crowley's bloody *squire.* The thrice-cursed man wasn't likely to let her out of his sight. She'd get no skulduggery done under his careful scrutiny.

I am in serious trouble.

CHAPTER FIFTEEN
THE WINDS OF FORTUNE

FIVE YEARS AGO

"All hands on deck!" Captain Brielle's voice rang across the *Winds of Fortune.*

"Not now," Tai groaned. After almost three years on the skyship, she dreaded hearing the captain's voice.

Tai gritted her teeth and hooked her left toe around a bit of rigging as she reached desperately for the tangled line. "Almost got it!"

She leaned out to her full height, which, regrettably, wasn't much, and grasped her hand outward — and missed.

"No!"

She knew a moment of unnatural stillness as her foot fell free of the rigging, leaving her suspended in thin air. Her stomach plummeted, followed quickly by the rest of her, and she hit the deck with an awkward thud.

"Ow." She stood upright and rubbed a sore spot on her bottom.

To her enormous bad luck, she'd landed right at the captain's feet, and straightened herself just in time to make eye contact with Brielle Tagenal's flinty gaze.

"Did you untangle the line?" Brielle glanced up at the still clearly tangled line and back down at Tai, mouth twitching in disapproval.

"I... almost had it."

"Useless ground-dweller," the captain muttered under her breath, just loud enough so that Tai could hear. More loudly, she said, "Falgar, get that line untangled now, before we fall out of the sky!"

"Yes Captain." The more experienced deckhand scrambled to work.

Tai, meanwhile, remained frozen under Brielle's paralyzing stare. She supposed she ought to be used to the captain's disapproval by now. Even after nearly three years, she couldn't seem to do anything right on this Depths-sodden ship.

It wasn't like she didn't try. Savior help her, she couldn't remember the last time she wasn't giving it her all. Every day she worked herself to the point of exhaustion, untangling lines and swabbing decks and cleaning the aether engine and changing out crystals. But it wasn't enough.

She still was not permitted to fly in the Linking. She wasn't "ready." The captain was never especially forthcoming about what being "ready" meant. Tai suspected it was just Brielle's way of saying "never."

The problem was, Tai really *had* started leagues behind everyone else. It wasn't *just* that she knew nothing about sky sailing. She didn't know about life in the sky *at all*. She'd never used magic before, much less enchanted an aether engine. She could barely even speak the same language as everyone else. Tai used to pride herself on knowing how to read the Kasani trade tongue, but it turned out there was a wide gulf between reading a language and parsing orders shouted out at a rapid clip.

Fortunately, she found she enjoyed learning Aerish magic, so she at least picked that up at a reasonable rate. The precise ways the runes and sigils and energy flows fit together reminded Tai of the clockwork gadgets she used to tinker with back home in Toreen. She was confident she'd catch up with the others eventually, she just feared it wouldn't be fast enough.

"Almost three years you've been on my ship," Captain Brielle said brusquely —*My ship*, Tai was not fool enough to correct her— "And yet you still can't do the simplest of tasks."

The captain then launched into a long-winded rant about maintaining proper standards. Tai was getting better at understanding her rapid-fire Kasani, but she still ended up missing every fourth word or so.

"I will try harder," Tai promised. But she didn't know how she could try any harder than she already was.

"Swab the deck." Brielle brusquely handed Tai a mop and a bucket. "It's all you're good for."

"That was utterly unfair of the captain," said Falgar, once he'd returned from untangling the rigging. Other than Kadmin, Falgar was the only person on this ship who acted like she was a sentient being capable of speech.

"Thanks," Tai said, "But I'm used to it by now."

"I've seen how hard you work." Falgar crossed his wiry arms. "It's a heap of gryphon dung that she hasn't let you in the Linking yet."

"It's not so much different from being at home." Tai gave a sad smile and lifted her mop. "Everyone can fly but me."

"Ah," said Kadmin, joining them, "But this is the sky! Anyone can learn to fly. You just have to work hard if you want the recognition you deserve."

"Right, because the rest of this time has been a relaxing vacation." She ruffled her wings in agitation. She knew she was being whiny, and she hated that about herself. Kadmin was only trying to make her feel better.

Kadmin had been an enormous source of help and support over the past three years, teaching her magic, drilling her in the Kasani trade tongue, and generally showing her the ins and outs of life on a skyship. She'd've given up long ago if not for his unwavering faith in her. But *all the same.* "I'm starting to think no amount of effort is going to make Brielle let an Orith in the linking."

"The old captain was Orith," Falgar pointed out unhelpfully. "Your dad, wasn't he?"

Tai ran her hand through her hair. "For all the good that's done me."

"See, this is your problem," Kadmin said. "You need to stop using your wings as an excuse. From where I'm standing, you have a lot more body parts than just your wings. Most of them are quite fetching. You claim Brielle won't let you in the linking. But who said anything about *let*?"

Tai gaped at him. Part of her was thrilled he'd called her *fetching,* but that didn't make what he said any less outlandish. "But... but She's the captain."

"It's your ship," Kadmin said. "Doesn't that, technically, make you the boss?"

Tai bit her lip. Kadmin was right, technically, but...

"Sometimes," Falgar put in, "It's a lot easier to obtain forgiveness than permission."

Tai's opportunity to ask forgiveness rather than permission came sooner than she expected, on an overcast afternoon some three weeks later. Captain Brielle was sick with the fireflu, or so she claimed.

"Fireflu my arse," Falgar said knowingly. "I know a hangover when I see one."

Either way, the shipboard Healer warned that the captain might become immune to Healing magic if she relied on it too heavily, so Brielle announced that she would retire to her cabin to try and sleep off whatever was wrong with her head.

"Now's your chance." Kadmin elbowed her meaningfully in the side.

"Eh?"

He gestured towards the central Linking circle, where the rest of the ship's aeronauts disappeared back into the Linking under the not-so-watchful eye of Brennan, the first mate. From his bloodshot eyes and hangdog expression, Tai guessed that Brennan had also been at the Narean whiskey last night. But unlike the captain, he didn't have the luxury of taking a day off.

"He'll still turn me away," Tai predicted.

"Only if you look like you're breaking the rules," Falgar said. "Just walk in like you own the place. Which, technically, I suppose you do."

"All right." She frowned and put on her most confident face as she followed the rest of the line of aeronauts entering the Linking.

"You're not on the roster," Brennan noted at once.

Tai might have quailed right there, but she couldn't bear the thought of backing down in front of Kadmin and Falgar. So she said, "Last minute change of plans. Captain said I'm to enter the Linking today. Unless you want to wake her up and ask her?"

"Fine, whatever." Brennan waved her on.

Tai couldn't believe her own daring. Void, she couldn't believe it had been so easy. Before she could talk herself out of it, she stepped into the circle and crossed into the ship's pocket dimension.

Tai laughed with delight as she floated suspended midair. In a way, it felt like coming home. Not in the way Everwood was technically home, but *truly* home, the place where she always should have been. She marveled at the dancing motes of magical light, and the smooth efficient way her fellow aeronauts swam through the sky. They towed the ship along much far greater swiftness and efficiency than sails and rudders could manage. Falgar and Kadmin took up empty positions near the rear of the formation, and Tai, not sure what else to do, followed suit.

And so, just like that, after years of waiting and failure and frustration, Tai Lunstrum performed her first flight.

They flew over towns and cities and jagged mountain peaks. Before long, they left the floating islands behind and sailed over empty sky, with nothing but the roiling underclouds below. Somewhere underneath those clouds was her homeland. She thought of Mother and Roan and Tanis, and wondered what they would think if they could see her now.

Over time, her arms and wings grew tired, but she found she didn't care. She'd fly until she collapsed from exhaustion, if this was what it took. She never wanted to relinquish this sensation, not ever.

"What do you think?" Kadmin asked. "Do you like it?"

She faced her friend, grinning and breathless. "I love it."

And then, without warning, before either of them could change their minds, Kadmin kissed her, and she kissed him back, clinging to each other with desperate want and need, drunk on the Linking and high on glory. Tai swore the motes of magic danced around them in celebration of their fledgling romance.

"Get a room, you two," Falgar said.

Embarrassed, they disentangled themselves. Fortunately, the other aeronauts in the linking were so busy with their work they didn't appear to notice Tai's and Kadmin's blatant show of fraternization.

Tai expected to be reprimanded for entering the Linking without permission. But Kadmin and Falgar were more than willing to vouch for her, and even the rest of the crew could find no fault with her flying skills. So Captain Brielle, in the end, ran out of excuses to keep her from the regular flight rotation.

The moons that followed were some of the happiest in Tai's life. Between her blossoming romance with Kadmin and her ever-increasing skills as an aeronaut, things finally seemed to be going right for once.

Until one fateful afternoon in the height of summer, when Tai gazed out at the pink-tinged evening clouds, and noted something on the horizon that didn't belong.

"Um, guys?" she asked Falgar and Kadmin. "What's that?"

The white and pink clouds below gave way to ominous black

clouds on the horizon. And those dark clouds came closer and closer like an inky undersea tidal wave.

"Meroneth's cold and shriveled balls!" Falgar swore. "That's a Voidstorm!"

Tai felt her blood freeze and her bowels liquify. They'd skirted the edges of Voidstorms occasionally, and the violent turbulence always meant a lot of tedious cleanup afterwards. But unless they sharply changed course, they were looking at facing this one head on. At this point, the more experienced aeronauts at the front of the formation finally noticed. Tai witnessed a great deal of pointing and shouts of alarm.

"We should have never gotten this close. Who the Void is on watch right now?" Kadmin's silver-gray eyes flashed dangerously. "Brennan, of course, the useless sod. Probably fell asleep. Tai, go get the captain."

Tai blanched. "Wait, what?" Brielle might not be hungover today, but she was still off duty. Interrupting the captain on her rest rotation seemed only marginally less intimidating than the storm.

"Do it!" Kadmin's face was a rictus mask of fury, and Tai hurriedly scrambled out of the Linking, not needing to be told again.

Savior help her, but this furious, decisive Kadmin was a completely different person from the one she'd stolen kisses with these past few moons. But she supposed she couldn't expect delicate niceties, not when the situation was life and death.

"Captain!" she pounded hard on Brielle's stateroom door. Already, the ship was rocking so badly she had to brace against the wall for purchase. She could barely hear over the sound of the aether sails flapping violently in the wind. But she had to try anyway. "Captain, there's a Voidstorm!"

Tai was at the point of trying to break down the wooden door before it thankfully slid open, revealing a disheveled and bleary-eyed Captain Brielle.

"Lunstrum, what the—"

"Voidstorm," Tai repeated, not wasting time. "We're about to fly right into it!"

"Meroneth's balls." Brielle bit out a curse and scrambled hastily to the crow's nest to get a better look. "All hands in the Linking, all hands in the Linking at once! Pull hard to port if you don't want to get blown to pieces!"

Tai didn't waste time or ask for clarification before plunging back into the Linking. She flared her wings against the gale-force winds, fighting with all the strength to steer the ship back on course.

The wind caught her, and she tumbled backwards, end over end, lost and disoriented in a haze of black clouds.

"Void Void Fallen Depths *Void*!" she let out a litany of curses in both Kasani and Toreenish.

«Well, now.» a thrumming voice resounded in her head, not unlike the wild demons who sometimes dogged Everwood's town border. «What have we here?»

Tai fought to right herself, sure she must be hallucinating in all the chaos. "What the—"

Dark clouds and mists swirled around her like smoke, causing her hair and feathers to stand on end. And then, to her astonishment, the black fog came together to form a creature, long and serpentine, who stared at her through menacing amber eyes.

"Voidwraith," Tai managed to choke out, her voice dry.

No doubt about it. This *definitely* had to be a hallucination. The Ancients had summoned Voidwraiths to commit their terrible atrocities, but *wild* Voidwraiths? Living in the underclouds and inside Void storms? Those were surely just tales to scare naive young sailors. Weren't they?

«She who walks between worlds,» the smoke creature said, with just the barest hint of wry amusement. «An outcast below, and an outcast above. You will never fit in with these Aerish, you know, no matter how hard you try. But nor can you return home. Such a pity.»

"I—" Tai had no idea what to say. *Stupid hallucination. You don't know me.*

«You could find home here, though,» the creature said. «You could be one with the storm.»

"Yeah." Tai managed to swallow. "Don't think so."

It was the most difficult thing Tai had ever done, but she tore her gaze away from the monstrous creature and flew away from the black smoke with all the strength she had.

In the end, miraculously, the *Winds of Fortune* avoided the brunt of the storm. They were well off course now, almost certainly not going to make their deliveries on time, and the aether engine and secondary sails took severe damage from the wind and turbulence. But they were alive. They'd be able to limp back into the nearest port for repairs; everything else could be sorted after.

Once they were certain the worst of the danger had passed, Kadmin, Falgar, and some of the other more experienced aeronauts left the Linking to assess the damage, while Tai and the others remained to make sure the ship was safely spell-anchored and out of the storm's path until they could plot a new course.

"Thought we'd lost you back there," said Arnault, a burly aeronaut who'd barely said more than two words to her before now.

"Wasn't feeling too confident about it myself," Tai admitted, shaking out her feathers.

"Guess the winds saw some reason to spit you back out." Arnault sounded dubious as to what reasons those might be.

"You... make it sound like the winds were intelligent," Tai carefully hedged. She wanted to tell someone about the wraith, but she was fairly certain Arnault would think she was out of her mind. She wasn't even sure she wanted to tell Kadmin.

"Likely just sailor's fancies," Arnault confirmed. "But some hear strange voices when the wind takes them. Voices that prey on their hopes and fears. Voices that will say whatever they need to in order to get you to stray from your course. But, ha, we aeronauts do tend to jump at shadows after a long voyage. It's probably nothing."

"Yeah," Tai laughed weakly. "Probably nothing."

Despite everything, she felt a surge of triumph when she finally exited the Linking. Savior help her, they'd *done* it. They were *alive*. She found Kadmin, fully intending to plant a celebratory kiss on his mouth, to the Void with whoever was watching. But one look at Kadmin's ashen face told her that romance was the farthest thing from his mind.

"What happened?"

"Brennan is missing," Kadmin said. "We think he fell overboard."

Tai's stomach did an uncomfortable flip flop. "Oh," she said. Right now she was too stunned to feel much emotion, but she knew it would come. Fallen Depths, it would come. "Did... did anyone else..." she couldn't seem to bring herself to use the word *die*.

Kadmin's head gave a spasmodic little jerk to the side. She couldn't tell if that meant yes or no. But Falgar joined them a moment later, looking graver and more serious than she'd ever seen him before. "It's the Captain," he said. "She fell from the crow's nest."

She felt a brief moment of relief. "Oh, well, that's not so bad." Tai herself had fallen from the crow's nest just that morning when trying to untangle another line. But Falgar's horrified expression told her that it was, in fact, *so bad*.

"Tai." His voice came out like a croak. "We're not Orith. We can't fall from things the way you can."

Tai and her friends pushed through a crowd of worried aeronauts gathered around the crow's nest. And there, splayed out on the deck at an unnatural angle, lay Captain Brielle Tagenal, her neck clearly broken, her eyes gazing lifelessly up at the evening sky.

CHAPTER SIXTEEN
RESPONSIBILITY

PRESENT DAY

Xander was nursing his second mug of ale when Faris came stumbling into the tavern.

"Whiskey," she said to the barkeep, "Neat."

"Yes, ma'am." The barkeep handed her a plain glass tumbler of amber liquid, which she drained in one.

"Another," she said, without so much as flinching. This one, however, she only sipped from before joining Xander at the rough wooden bar table.

"Long day?" Xander asked, deadpan.

"Like you wouldn't believe." She took another sip of whiskey and then straightened herself like she was preparing for battle. Most of the patrons of the Twisted Gryphon were friendly to the rebellion's cause, but she leaned forward and spoke quietly, to prevent their words finding unwelcome ears. "It's done, at any rate. Donovan's team will attack the central aether cache on Kassoriasday."

"So. That's it, then. It's really happening." Xander drummed his fingers on the table. He supposed he should be glad that, after weeks of planning, it was finally time to start *doing*. But this meant the mission was in Donovan's hands now, and the lack of control left Xander feeling itchy. Donovan was a hard worker and a genial fellow, but was he ready to take a risk of this magnitude? Was Xander ready to let him?

Faris seemed to understand his line of thinking. "Donovan knows what he signed up for. He'll do a great job." He wasn't sure whether she was trying to convince him, or herself.

"Can't help thinking I should be there with him." Xander sighed and drained his mug, signaling the innkeeper for another. "Not shouting orders from the sidelines."

Faris snorted. "And supposing you get yourself arrested, who'd lead our merry little band?"

"Well, you could." Xander thought that much was obvious. Faris knew practically everything that went on in the city of Azure. She was still pretty tight-lipped about how she got involved with the Order in the first place, but if there was ever a shoe-in candidate to lead the underground, it had to be the iron-haired Iriya woman.

Faris, however, shook her head. "Nuh uh. No way." She swirled her glass around. "Call me a coward if you wish, but my responsibility is always to my family first, and the Order second."

Xander took a swig of his drink. "I'd never call you a coward for that." For much of Xander's life, family and the Order were one and the same. It was oddly refreshing to think that for some people, that didn't have to be the case.

But he also understood Faris's reticence to get her family further involved. Her husband, Teonard, had been arrested the previous moon for protesting the war in Thlarknia. With two children to look after on her own, Faris still had plenty to lose.

"If I had a lick of sense I'd take Tair and Luka and fly somewhere far from here," Faris said. "But I can't abandon Teo, not when there's still a chance I can save him. Besides." Her hand shook slightly as she took a drink of whiskey. "We've already fled one nation in defiance of their corrupt government. I won't do that again."

Xander nodded. Despite her tail and horns, it was easy to forget, sometimes, that she came from the mysterious empire beneath the clouds. Here in the city, Faris, Xander, Tai, and even Bradford all wore the same mantle of *foreigner*. But unlike their Orith neighbors, the sunken content of Iriya had almost no contact with the world above. Xander couldn't even begin to imagine what she must have gone through to get here. The only thing he knew was that his sister, somehow, had helped. He wondered if he'd ever get the full story from either of them. Gods knew a straight answer from Sylvia was rarer than a purple-haired dryad.

"You're one of the bravest people I've ever met," Xander reassured his friend.

"You're kind to say so," Faris said with a sigh. "I can strategize, but it's... easier, I think, when I have some distance. I can't stop thinking, today's the day we send Donovan into danger. But tomorrow it might be Tair, or Luka. I just don't think I can make that kind of decision."

Xander let out a long sigh. Her meaning was clear. She was good at organization and strategy, but making the tough choices was *his* job.

"The reason we're doing this," Xander said at length, "Is so that one day Tair and Luka won't have to."

Xander didn't have children of his own, of course, but he had people he cared about just as much. He thought of Tai, in the heart of enemy territory, and Dorian, off doing gods-knew-what for the Order's ends. And Bradford, here with the rebels.

As if summoned by his thoughts, the tavern door swung open and Bradford stalked in, looking exhausted and more than a little disheartened.

"Whiskey," he told the barkeep, "Neat."

"That's the same thing I ordered," Faris commented.

The barkeep gave Bradford his drink. Bradford took it with a rudimentary thanks and joined Xander and Faris at the table, burying his face in his hands.

"Long day, I take it," Faris said drily.

"Oh, you know," the Lordling replied. "Regnald didn't fire me, so I suppose that's a start."

"That *is* a start." Faris patted him on the shoulder. "Keep that up, and you may even get on his good side one day."

"A feat worthy of the Imperial Medal of Valor." Bradford's glum face gave way to a wistful smirk. Everyone knew it was impossible to get on the grumpy dock master's good side.

Faris finished her drink and dusted her hands. "Sorry to be rude, Brand, but I'm afraid this is my cue to leave. Donovan's watching Tair and Luka, but I can't expect him to babysit all night. Not when he's got a heist to plan."

They said their farewells and Bradford watched her depart with a worried frown. "Heist, eh? So it's finally happening?"

"Evidently." Xander could not dismiss his misgivings.

"And nobody thought to invite me." Bradford examined his drink with an air of despondence bordering on petulance.

"Thought you had more sense than to throw your life away bloodying the emperor's nose," Xander replied blandly.

"I'd be satisfied with giving him a hangnail at this point," Bradford sighed. "Not one new recruit since Donovan joined. Not one! It's just... I don't understand why it was so much easier before. Back in the Dragon's Fangs, people respected me. They listened to what I had to say. But I begin to think it was only because they already knew me as Viscount of Frostvale. Now I'm just some nobody dock worker." He shook his head. "How do you do it, Uncle? How did you manage to earn their respect?"

Xander was briefly taken aback. "I... listen to what they have to say, I suppose," he answered honestly. "If you want to be a leader, the people have to think you *want* them to succeed."

Like he wanted Bradford to succeed. Like he ought to want Donovan to succeed. *Oh, Void.* Perhaps he'd been looking at all of this the entirely wrong way. They weren't just sending the man into danger. They were also giving him an opportunity.

Bradford sighed and slumped his shoulders. "I just... maybe I'm not cut out for this leadership stuff."

Xander couldn't help but smile. "That," he said, "Remains to be seen."

The magic flowed out of Solaris and through Dorian, bathing the dais in multihued pastel light. The shimmering trees took in that power, and it seemed they stood taller, the leaves glowing brighter. Dorian stood taller, too.

"May your light shine bright and may you never go hungry," said Falgar, quoting what was evidently an old Toreenish proverb. "We of House Ferran care only for the health and prosperity of all peoples, above and below the clouds."

Dorian couldn't help but be impressed. His friend tried to turn everything into a joke, but when he needed to take things seriously, he delivered.

Most of the audience burst into thunderous applause, though predictably, there were some jeers from the crowd as well. Cries of "Dirty foreigner" and "Go back to the sky" could be heard even amidst the cheering.

"No sense holding out for universal approval," Dorian sighed. He thought this was a pretty good turn-out, all things considered. "At least the High Councilor of Silverlake didn't turn us away outright."

"That old man in Westhaven was bang out of line," Falgar complained.

"He had his reasons." Even now, awash in the sparkling lights of Toreen's largest and most opulent city, Dorian wondered if they were doing the right thing.

Feeding magic to the trees came from a place of altruism, but it was a temporary solution, and dangerous, too. Sooner or later someone was bound to figure out it wasn't "demons" fueling their spells. And then it would be only a matter of time before word of dragons in Cloudfire made it back to Emperor Callahan in Kasanarae.

"I suppose I should be thankful the Dragonmar let us help the Orith at all," Dorian said with a sigh. "After that disaster in Thlarknia I thought she would keep us locked away forever."

"I told you, mate," Falgar said. "The dragonmar likes you for some reason."

Dorian wrinkled his nose. "Can't for the life of me fathom why." Jameson certainly didn't share Lady Sylvia's opinion, and neither did most of the Order knights. One of the best things about these missions, he thought, was that he could avoid Cloudfire Castle as much as possible.

It wasn't that the last few moons had been so terrible, not really. In the weeks immediately following the disastrous attack on the aether cache, everyone had been on high alert, worried Callahan would swoop in and attack from out of nowhere. But after several moons of relative quiet, they allowed themselves to relax. Perhaps the enemy really didn't know where they kept themselves hidden. Life fell into a comfortable rhythm, and Dorian did his best to keep himself so busy he didn't have much time to feel worried or despondent.

He held his own against the other dragonauts now, and won as many sparring matches as he lost. He even could keep up with the others on those Void-cursed hill sprints.

Nevertheless, Dorian couldn't help feeling like they were all killing time waiting for something to happen. These missions of good will were the only times Dorian got to feel like he was actually taking direct action *towards* something.

Today, Dorian felt especially fortunate to be in Silverlake, the Toreenish capital.

The trees stood so tall they nearly reached the cloud layer. Nestled among the branches was a dizzying array of catwalks and bridges and balconies, all connecting buildings that were themselves works of art. Onion-shaped structures made of opulent crystalline glass hung among the trees like Mystictide decorations, all seeming, like the trees themselves, to glow with their own inner light. And to think the Orith managed all this without magic.

The dais was nestled high in the branches, so high that Dorian refused to look over the edge.

"You're a dragonaut, and you lived on a skyship for the better part of a year," Tanis pointed out when he noticed Dorian's discomfort. "You can't tell me you're afraid of heights."

Dorian shook his head, moving closer to the reassuringly solid tree trunk. "I like heights just fine, but I'm not an Orith. If I fall from this platform, *splat*." He palmed his fist in demonstration.

«I would catch you before you went *splat*,» Solaris reassured him. «Although, I may not be able to pass myself off as a demon in that case. And the lie about Illusion will only take you so far.»

Dorian had expected Solaris to be annoyed about having to pretend to be a demon, but the dragon mostly took it in stride. He sure wished they didn't have to do it, though. All this lying and deception made him itchy.

"Tarheyvak vienav," came the disdainful voice of a local youth flying past. *Stupid Foreigner.*

Falgar wrinkled his nose and stuck his tongue out at the retreating Orith.

"Falgar," Dorian chided him, since Sullivan wasn't around.

"I know, I know, representatives of Cloudfire, veneer of professionalism, blah blah." Falgar stretched his arms behind his head. "Still, you'd think they'd be a bit more grateful, since we came all this way to save their magic trees and all."

"They're not magic, they're bioluminescent," Tanis said. "Anyway, I think most people *are* grateful. But you all said it yourself. This whole thing is to make you Aerishmen look good, not selflessly trying to help people."

Dorian winced. "*I* want to help people."

Tanis's expression softened just slightly. "I know you do. But surely you understand not everyone's going to see it that way."

"Well!" Falgar dusted his hands. "The High Councilor has invited us to a feast, so we've got that going for us."

Dorian forced a smile. Toreenish cooking was delicious, but Dorian had never been fond of being the center of attention, especially as an obvious foreigner unfamiliar with the local customs. Too many bad memories of his first Mystictide Festival in Frostvale when he was ten years old, and tried to eat the decorative centerpiece.

Dorian and Falgar were given pride of place in the council hall, where they sat on colorful silk cushions around a low-slung table. Well-dressed servants flitted about handing out local delicacies on ornate silver trays. Once Dorian got past his utter terror of using the wrong utensil, he had to admit the food was very good. Each bite came with a burst of delightful and unfamiliar flavor, a miniature culinary adventure.

"I could get used to this." Falgar fluffed a pillow and leaned back against it luxuriously. "Sure you won't have some of the greenwine?" He waved his copper goblet. Like many things in Orith, the green liquid glowed faintly.

"Ah, no," said Dorian. He took a sip from his own goblet, which contained plain water. "I feel it's best to keep a clear head for this sort of thing. Still a long flight back to the castle ahead of us." He liked ale and cider well enough, but the strong Toreenish alcohol invariably gave him a sour stomach. Fortunately, his hosts didn't seem to mind.

"Ah, well." Falgar clinked his wine goblet against Dorian's water one. "Suppose one of us has to be responsible. Pity Sullivan's not here. Can't imagine he's having too much fun, holding down the fort with only Graigor and Jameson for company."

Dorian nodded ruefully. While Dorian and Falgar fed magic to the trees of Silverlake, Hildegard and Dax were off on a scouting mission. Sullivan, however, had drawn the worst lot, stuck guarding Cloudfire Castle with Graigor and Jameson.

Dorian didn't *like* to think ill of his colleagues, but Jameson and Graigor weren't who *he'd* choose to spend the evening with, either. In fact, being away from Graigor's constant taunts and Jameson's unending scrutiny felt like a miniature holiday.

"Ah, excuse me," said an unfamiliar voice in heavily accented Kasani. "You are the dragonaut Dorian Valmont?"

Dorian sat up, surprised to be addressed directly. "I'm him," he said, "I mean, that's me."

He found himself addressed by an Orith youth, perhaps a year or two younger than Tanis. He had all the gawky, gangly long limbs of adolescence, and his voice cracked when he spoke.

"Only..." the boy swallowed. "Is it true you flew a dying ship through the underclouds?"

Dorian nodded. "Erm, yes, I suppose I did."

The Orith boy's eyes were wide. "So amazing! I want to be just like you when I grow up. I've been accepted into the merchant's guild, and I know they'll let me get on a merchant's ship, I just know it! I've even got a demon just like yours, see?"

Dorian's "demon" was an Illusion that Dragonmar Sylvia had conjured up before they departed, to explain away the fact that he could do magic beneath the underclouds. But of course, the Orith boy didn't know that.

Dorian softened his gaze, and sure enough, he saw the creature in his peripheral vision. A large creature, too, near the size of the low-slung table, with scales of sapphire to match his cloak of blue fire. "I, ah, that's—" He took a hasty sip of water, simultaneously glad that it wasn't greenwine and partially wishing that it were.

The look Falgar gave him was both pitying and amused. "What my friend *means* to say," Falgar said, "Is that we are glad to be of service."

The Orith boy nodded and then hurriedly scampered away.

"See now?" Dorian lightly elbowed Tanis. "Orith with demons *can* be aeronauts."

Tanis shook his head, mouth pursed into a thin line. "That kid was way too young to have a demon."

"He's not that much younger than you, pipsqueak," Falgar chided, noting the obvious demonfire in Tanis's aura.

"I'm sixteen. That's practically an adult," Tanis shot back. "How old are you, exactly? Eighteen?"

"Twenty-four." Falgar smugly took another sip of greenwine. "You have a point, though. That's a pretty big demon for a young fellow."

Dorian squirmed guiltily. "He didn't *look* like he was in any danger from it," he said. But he still didn't like the idea of someone taking on a powerful demon on *his* account. Especially after he'd seen what Malachite did to Tanis.

"What about you?" Falgar asked Tanis. "You going to try and banish Malachite, when all this is over?"

Tanis twitched his wings, looking surprised by the question. When Tanis had collapsed on Solaris's back, Malachite had been quite a bit larger than just the table. Now, the demon was about the size of a hunting cat, able to curl up in Tanis's lap — not that he was inclined to. "I honestly hadn't thought that far ahead. I'll need him to be able to cast magic, if... if I ever return back home."

The question hung in the air, unasked and unanswered, yet still tangibly palpable. Would Tanis be allowed to return to Everwood eventually? The Order couldn't intend to keep him prisoner forever, could they?

Falgar frowned and cleared his throat. "Does it... hurt the demon, to reduce his power like that?" He waved his hands. "I mean, I know he probably deserves it, but still. Seems a bit cruel."

«It does not hurt,» Malachite allowed. «It is, however, *irritating*.» His blue demonfire flickered.

Dorian frowned. "If your arrangement with Tanis isn't working for you, couldn't you just leave? Find another host who's more biddable?"

«You will not reduce my energy any faster with all these irritating questions,» Malachite griped. «But no, I cannot simply find another host. I am bound to my host as long as he lives. Even if Tanis Lunstrum did banish me outright — and most hosts get bored of the attempt long before that happens — then I shall simply be forced to return. It is the tragic lot of our kind. It is not all bad, however,» Malachite conceded. «We demons get delicious spirit energy, and the hosts experience euphoria in return. Young Tanis and I had a good arrangement, before *you* came along.»

"A good arrangement?" Falgar interrupted. "From what I understand, you nearly sent him into a fugue."

Malachite cast Falgar a baleful stare, but offered nothing else in response.

"Wait," Dorian said, frowning. "Even after you're banished, you come back? To the same host?"

Dorian thought of Hematite, who was supposed to have been seeking out Dorian's father on the day they met in the ruins of Icereach Citadel. His demon had broken the rules by saving Dorian's life instead of Cyrus's.

"I'm surprised you don't know all this already," Tanis said. "You banished a demon yourself, didn't you?"

Dorian shook his head and examined his water cup, really wishing it were greenwine now. "Not intentionally."

"What happened?" Tanis sounded genuinely curious.

"He... gave his life for me. For all of us." Briefly, he told Tanis the circumstances of the *Phoenix's* final, tumultuous flight.

"So that's how you wound up in the woods that day," Tanis said. "I always wondered. None of the other ships we scavenged were in such good condition. And *never* with any survivors."

Dorian nodded and swallowed a mouthful of water. Perhaps he *should* ask for greenwine.

"Fish roll?" one of the Toreenish servers asked, presenting him with a tray of small silver fishes wrapped in grape leaves.

"No thank you," Falgar said.

"Yes please." Dorian took a bite, the complex flavor temporarily distracting him from thoughts of Hematite's sacrifice. "Delicious!"

"If you say so," Falgar said dubiously. He took another swig of greenwine.

Fish rolls, unfortunately, were only a momentary diversion. Dorian leaned back against the silk cushion and observed the rounded ceiling, painted with silver serpents and winged deer and other creatures Dorian had never heard of. Hematite would have loved all this. The food, and the ambiance, even the silk pillows. Now, more than ever, he wished his demon were still around to enjoy it.

«Solaris.» He reached out to his dragon, frowning.

«What is it?» Solaris and Meridian were nestled high in the trees, out of sight of the party-goers.

«What Malachite said just now … about demons coming back?»

«What about them?»

«Hematite,» Dorian elaborated. «He could come back too, right? He's not necessarily... gone forever?»

«Ah.» A heavy sadness reverberated through their connection. «As to that.»

Dorian's heart sank. That was a *no* if he'd ever heard one.

«It is *not* a no,» Solaris said. «Rather... I do not know.» She shook her serpentine head. «Ordinarily, Meroneth would have called Hematite back to himself before things got so far. But in the under-clouds, all bets are off. We are, I fear, in uncharted territory. There may, I fear, be little left of our old friend. But if there is... well... Meroneth has never been kind to those of his servants who defy him.»

Dorian's heart sank. That made twice that Hematite had defied what demons were supposed to do. And both times, in doing so, he'd saved Dorian's life. He deserved better than complete nonexistence or some kind of cosmic punishment as a result.

"You all right, mate?" Falgar asked, sensing his distress.

"It's nothing," Dorian sighed. "Thinking I should've had some greenwine after all."

"Well, it's not too late," Falgar said. "You can—"

«Look out!» Solaris's mindvoice cut through the conversation, clear and urgent, all traces of melancholy replaced with white-hot terror.

Dorian sprang to his feet and drew his sword. And not a moment too soon, because an arrow struck the wall directly behind the space Dorian just vacated.

Cries of terror displaced sounds of merriment as the feast goers scrambled to get to safety. A black-clad man in a billowing cape strode into the hall, crossbow at the ready. Dorian couldn't make out his face. The attacker wore a pointed bird-like mask, not unlike illustrations he'd seen of old plague doctors.

"Death to the interlopers," the masked attacker said in flawless Kasani, "The Fallen Realm for the Orith!"

Dorian sprang to his feet and drew his sword, but before he'd stepped more than a pace towards the attacker, he froze. *Ashe Valerian's head separating from her body, her blood drawing a neat arc across the afternoon sky...* It felt like a grave sin, somehow, to kill this man without even seeing his face. To kill him in an Orith Council Hall, a religious building, no less. Dorian's stomach churned, and he suddenly regretted having so many fish rolls.

"Fallen Realm to the Orith," Dorian said. "What does that mean?"

The attacker didn't answer, but only drew back his crossbow string to loose another arrow. Not a moment too soon, Solaris and Meridian burst into the feast hall. Startled, the attacker let go of the bowstring. The shot went wide and hit a wall-mounted lantern, which fell to the floor and shattered.

Shouts of alarm rose up in the feast hall as one of the silk pillows caught fire.

«We must go.» Solaris head butted him from behind, practically forcing him to fall backwards onto her saddle.

"What— But the fire—" Dorian scrambled for purchase and hastily grabbed Tanis's hand to pull him onto the saddle behind him. Solaris sprinted through the wide Council Hall door and took off into the cool evening air. Falgar and Meridian followed shortly after.

"We can't just leave," Dorian stammered, still too shocked to fully understand what was going on. "What about the other feast goers?"

«They will be fine,» Solaris said. «The Toreenish authorities have the situation well in hand.»

"You heard what that guy said," Falgar added. "Fallen Realm for the Orith or whatever. It was us he was after."

"Yes, but all the same—" He craned his neck back towards the Council Hall, scanning for signs of smoke or flame. Had the Orith put out the fire in time?

He tried to turn Solaris back around, to better inspect the damage, to confirm that there were no casualties. But Solaris was adamant. «We must go back to Cloudfire and report to the dragonmar.»

Dorian deflated, the fight draining out of him. Void curse him, why had he hesitated? If that beautiful Council Hall burned to the ground, it would be Dorian's fault, because he hadn't stopped the attacker in time.

"Were we followed?" he asked with a resigned sigh, once they were clear of the city.

"Doesn't look like it," Falgar said. "But that whole feast hall saw our dragons. And they know we're from Cloudfire. Even Mistress of Illusion Sylvia is going to have a Void-cursed time covering this one up."

Dorian's heart pounded in his chest. *Why hadn't he acted?*

Nobody would call their return flight anything other than despondent.

"We did the right thing, getting out," Falgar said. "It wasn't cowardly. It was just good common sense." He sounded like he was trying to convince himself as much as Dorian.

At long last, they landed on the castle ramparts, as exhausted as if they'd run there instead of flying. It felt like centuries ago, not mere hours, that he'd been enjoying fish rolls with the people of Silverlake.

"We need to report to the dragonmar," Falgar said.

Dorian nodded, but before following his friend, he turned towards Solaris, who was obviously distraught.

«I am sorry,» Solaris said at last. They were the first words she'd spoken since they left Silverlake.

"You did what you thought was right," Dorian said. "No one can blame you for that."

«I am a coward.» Solaris's mindvoice was so raw, so emotional, that it took Dorian aback.

"I... what? No, of course you're not."

She shook her serpentine head, practically radiating guilt.

"Solaris..."

«I blamed myself, you know, when Nocturne was taken.» Solaris said it casually, but he could sense it deep down in her, a hurt that she kept carefully buried these past two years. «He always tried to teach me about the history of dragonkind, and I always wanted to be off flying and proving myself in the moon dance. And then, all of a sudden, one day, he was not there anymore. I thought perhaps, if I had been a better student, perhaps I could have prevented...» she shook her serpentine head. «And then I found you, and you displayed courage and determination beyond what I had any right to ask for. And yet... after Hematite died...»

Dorian's heart caught in his throat. "You're worried I'll get *you* killed, too."

«No!» Her mindvoice was so forceful that a few stray sparks escaped her nostrils. More calmly, she reiterated, «No.»

"Then what..."

«Do you not see? It is *your* death that I fear. You humans, you do not know how fragile you are. My species is long-lived. Even with your extended lifespan, I know we must say our farewells one day.

But to see it happen before its time... That is not something I can bear.»

«Oh.» Dorian's heart did an uncomfortable little flip-flop. *Oh.*

"Are you coming?" Falgar looked at the two of them with slightly impatient puzzlement. "The dragonmar's going to want to hear the report from both of us."

"Right." Dorian swallowed. "I'll be right there."

He rubbed Solaris's neck just behind her horns where she liked it, trying to convey all his reassurances. *I don't intend to die any time soon.* Yet he also knew his intentions mattered little, in the grand scheme of things.

It was with a heavy heart that he followed Falgar back into the main castle and up the spiral staircase that led to the dragonmar's study. It wasn't even in particular that he feared for his life, though he did, of course, worry about disappointing Solaris.

But no, the leaden feeling in his stomach came from the fact that this almost certainly meant the end to their missions of goodwill.

Dorian would once again be useless.

CHAPTER SEVENTEEN
FORBIDDEN CONVERSATIONS

"You need to start giving thought to plotting your escape." Reora's voice was warped and distorted across the aether beacon connection, but Tanis would recognize that tone anywhere. It was the voice she used when she fully expected to be obeyed.

Tanis wavered uncomfortably, holding onto the aether beacon plinth for purchase while he fought to keep his woven spirit barrier in place. He knew he ought to relax the barrier, but the last thing he wanted was to deal with Malachite on top of everything else for this conversation. Besides. With all the sword training he'd been doing, he could maintain the shield all day with sheer physical force alone. Maybe. Most of the time.

"It's not that simple, Mother." He tried to keep his tone even but he was painfully aware how childish he sounded.

Escape from Cloudfire Castle was a daunting prospect at the best of times. But when he was honest with himself, a part of him didn't want to leave just yet. He was learning so much here, not just how to protect his spirit energy from Malachite, but how to fly an ornithopter and fight with a sword and even advanced Aerish spellwork. Prison warden or not, it twisted him up inside to think of betraying Dorian, who he'd started to regard as a friend.

"What about you, anyway?" Tanis asked. "Have you been to visit Father yet? At least tell him you're alive?"

"I want to," Reora said, and her voice sounded genuine enough that he almost believed her. "There are just... things I must do here, first."

Things she must do here first. But she'd never tell him what those *things* were, or where *here* was, or how long it might take to do them. And meanwhile his father was all alone. Perhaps Tanis really *ought* to think about escaping. Did he really want his parents back together, or was he just trying to assuage his guilt over his own absence?

No, he decided. He wanted all his family together. Well, save perhaps Tai. She was welcome to it, of course, but he'd long ago given up any optimism for that happening. But the rest of them, himself and Roan and Reora, they were a team. And Tanis would do almost anything to fix what had been broken.

"It's not safe for you there." Reora, as ever, would not be dissuaded from her course. "Just last week there was an attack against Aerish meddlers in Silverlake. For you to continue associating with the likes of them will lead to nothing but trouble."

"I heard about that," Tanis hedged. One thing he did *not* want to do was tell his mother that he'd been present for that attack. It might be one way to lure his mother away from whatever she was so wrapped up in, but if Reora decided to single-handedly storm Cloud-fire Castle, Tanis didn't see it going well for anyone.

Tanis shook out his black feathers and sighed. It seemed like his whole life was secrets upon secrets upon secrets. Not that his mother, he thought ruefully, had any branch to rest on in that regard.

"They're really not so bad, these Aerish, you know. That whole thing in Silverlake... they were only trying to help."

"We do not need help from arrogant foreign interlopers."

Tanis couldn't see her from across the aether connection, but he could easily visualize the familiar way Reora always pursed her lips when she talked like this.

"They can do all sorts of things with magic," Tanis insisted. He wasn't sure why it was so important to change his mother's bad opinion about the Aerish, but all of a sudden it seemed *incredibly* important. "With that moon glass of theirs, we might even be able to—"

A sharp crackle of magical energy on the other end. "A *moon glass?*"

"Yeah, I mean, they keep it locked up most of the time. I'm just saying if they *did* use it, I think these Aerishmen could do a lot of good."

"I... I see." Reora's voice was contemplative, and more than a little disturbed.

He was about say his farewells when another voice interrupted the communication. "Tanis Lunstrum." It was the male voice he vaguely recognized as the mysterious Gideon, who ran the signal beacon on Reora's side. From the way his mother talked about him, Tanis guessed Gideon was someone important. Too important to trust Tanis with any of the details of what he and his mother were doing, he thought bitterly.

"Ah, hello there," Tanis said awkwardly.

"This moon glass," Gideon said without preamble. "I wish to know more about it."

Tanis blinked several times. Had Gideon been listening in on their entire conversation? "What do you want to know?"

"Where do they keep it stored?"

Tanis's feathers stood on end. "Fallen if I know."

"I would be very interested in finding out." Gideon, like Reora, was clearly someone used to obedience.

"Yeah well." Tanis put on his best teenage demons-may-care voice. "Don't tell me much around here, do they?"

"Your mother tells me you are a resourceful boy," Gideon said. "I feel I should remind you it is by my grace that she may use our signal beacon at all. If you wish to keep up these conversations, I'd suggest finding all you can about the moon glass."

The spell circle abruptly cut out, bathing the room in darkness. Tanis staggered backwards from the sudden cease in energy flow.

"Are you all right?" Dax scrambled into the room, catching Tanis before he could fall backwards onto the rear wall panel.

Tanis clutched the side of his head, while Malachite used the distraction to shove past Tanis's barriers. The demon lapped up Tanis's spirit energy, and in his distracted state, Tanis let him. Might as well at least get some calming euphoria out of all this. He hadn't expected the severing to be so... jarring.

"How much of that did you hear?" Tanis asked.

"None, I was watching the door." Dax's face fell. "Should I be concerned?"

"Only... how much do you know about this Gideon guy?"

Dax's frown deepened. "He's a great man. But life has made it... necessary for him to be harsh at times."

Tanis regarded the Orith dragonaut. How much could Tanis trust him? How much could he trust any of them? He didn't like how Gideon held further communications with Reora over his head. But he could hardly justify siding with his prison wardens, either. In moments like this he felt like Malachite was the only one who understood him. He'd regret giving the demon so much energy in an hour or two when the euphoria wore off, but right now he didn't care. Right now we only regretted holding back.

With great effort, he finally reconstructed his spirit barrier. He'd do no one any good if he collapsed from fugue right here and now.

All in all, Tanis was sick to the Depths of being yanked around from one person to the next, always in service of someone else's agenda. He was beyond done with them all. He just wanted, if possible, to see his family together again.

One day, he vowed to himself. *One day I'll be strong enough on my own.* And then he'd make everything right without Gideon *or* the Order's help.

If there was anything more humiliating than being Kadmin Crowley's squire, Tai didn't even *want* to know what it was.

It wasn't even that the individual duties were all that bad. Mostly, it was just boring day-to-day chores, such as keeping his chambers tidy and making sure he had the correct uniform.

But the chores themselves paled compared to Kadmin's Void-cursed *smugness* about the whole thing. Tai dreaded hearing her own name, always with the same singsong inflection, drawing the single syllable into two.

"*Taiii*, my tea is cold. Warm it up for me."

"*Taiii*, the epaulets on my uniform are tangled, straighten them out."

"*Taiii*, it's been such a long day, I require a foot massage."

At this last, Tai flat out refused. "I will *not* give you a foot massage."

"You will if you wish to continue being a dragonaut candidate." He pulled off his boot and waggled his vile sweaty toes in her direction. Good gods, she wished she could punch that smug look off his face.

"Complain to Flight Leader Vivienne for all I care," Tai said coolly as she drew him a bath instead. "I won't massage your feet." Consequences could go to the Void, she still had *some* pride.

"You're no fun." Kadmin sulkily slunk off to the bath, but to her great relief, he did not press the issue further.

One tiny silver lining was that if Empress Saedra recognized her as a traitor, she didn't act on it. Tai spent the first week after the ill-fated flying lesson with one head over her shoulder, certain she was about to be surrounded by palace guards. But as more time passed and that didn't happen, she allowed herself to relax, just a little.

"*Taiii*, please arrange my stockings by color and length."

Tai suppressed a groan. Sometimes she thought a traitor's death might be preferable to this nonsense.

Grumbling a few choice Toreenish phrases under her breath, Tai set to work. If she hoped to win and steal a dragonstone, her only option was to play along.

Unfortunately, winning and stealing a dragonstone felt less and less likely with each passing day. Kadmin scarcely let Tai out of his sight. Not only was snooping out of the question, but Tai also had to forego all her extra training sessions. She could tell Lewellyn and Owain were surpassing her in the rankings, and she had almost no recourse. She had, after all, earned this punishment.

"I know I deserve it, but the man is bloody insufferable," Tai complained to her almost-friends one evening over dinner.

"Don't know what you're complaining about." Lewellyn tugged at the end of one of her braids. "It would be *wonderful* to spend all day with Kadmin Crowley."

There was something decidedly moon-eyed about her expression, and Tai lost her appetite for the lake trout she was eating. "Ugh. Don't tell me you fancy him."

"You mean you don't?" Lewellyn asked. "I thought everyone fancied Kadmin."

"It's true," Owain put in. "The man's dreamy."

"Not you, too!"

Of course, there'd been a time when Tai wasn't immune to his charm. Owain and Lewellyn just didn't know Kadmin like she did. Tai opened her mouth to respond when Commander Vivienne strode into the dining hall, dressed in full battle armor. Conversations hushed at once.

"I have received word," Vivienne said, "That terrorist elements in the lower city have attacked the royal aether stores."

The dining hall erupted into nervous whispers. An attack on an aether warehouse could take out more than a city block if things got out of hand. But Tai had even more reason to be afraid. *Terrorists. The underground.* Were Xander and Bradford involved?

"His Imperial Majesty has ordered Kadmin and I to get a handle on the situation," Vivienne continued. "Gryphon-mounted units will be called in as needed. Soldiers, you already have your orders. As for the candidates," and now she turned to Tai and the others, "It is imperative that you stay in the palace until we return. Any attempts to leave will cause your immediate removal from consideration. Is that understood?"

"Void take me," Lewellyn whispered, "An entire aether cache. Aren't those usually well-guarded?"

"Supposed to be," Owain said. "But if Vivienne and Kadmin can't handle it, then I say, there's not a lot the rest of us can do."

Lewellyn's frown deepened. "Well, I can't just sit here worrying about it. Shall we go to the training grounds?"

"Your mind is always on work," Owain said. "I have a bottle of twelve year Narean single malt, and I can't think of a better time to share it."

Lewellyn looked dubious, but then shrugged. "Might as well. Tai, you coming?"

"Maybe." Tai's mind was on anything but whiskey. With Kadmin busy, this would be the first time in weeks she was out from under his thumb. If there was any time to find the dragonstone and abscond with it, it was now. "I'll, um, join you in the barracks later. I, ah, have to use the privy."

Tai hurried out of the dining hall, but not before she heard Lewellyn ask worriedly, "Do you think she's okay?"

Tai could feel her almost-friends' eyes on her all the way down the hallway until she rounded the corner.

Doing her best to look like she knew what she was doing, Tai strode past the library, past the training grounds and the candidate's barracks, and up the sapphire-carpeted staircase to the chapel where the highest-ranking priests and magi conducted their business.

With forced confidence, she strode up to the Imperial Archmage's office door and knocked.

"Yes, yes, what is it?" came a churlish voice.

Tai swallowed. She'd never met Archmage Rigellan, but she'd heard he could be grumpy. Well, she didn't need to impress the man, just keep him talking long enough to get a good look around. Taking a breath and praying for courage, she pushed open the doorway — and bit back a startled cry. The man seated at the polished mahogany study table, poring over pages of complicated rune work, was most certainly *not* Archmage Rigellan.

"Yes?" Emperor Janus Callahan's jaw twitched. "What do you need? As you can see, I'm rather busy."

"I'm sorry." Tai's voice came out like a squawk. "Erm, didn't mean to bother you, ah, Your Imperial Majesty. I'll just... I'll just go."

Tai backed away, but the Emperor raised a hand to forestall her. "Wait."

Janus Callahan stared at Tai for a long moment, his mouth drawn into a tight, thin line. His pale blue eyes seemed to pierce her soul. Quailing under his penetrating gaze, she turned her attention to the pile of diagrams on the table. He'd sketched out some strange looking cylinders, labeled with... "Liquid aether?" she read out loud. Then, horrified, she added, "Sorry. Didn't mean to look."

The Emperor's mouth twitched in what might have been the barest hint of a smile. "I'd hoped to use it to create moon glass. Rigellan swears he is close to that lost technique, but he's sworn he's close for nearly a Cycle now. One begins to lose faith. Still, liquid aether has... other uses. But forgive an old man's ramblings. You're Tai Lunstrum, aren't you? The recruit Lady Vivienne was so excited about."

Tai blinked. "Vivienne was excited about me?"

"Oh yes," the Emperor said. "Intelligent and skilled in battle, as was proper for the dragonauts of old. Of course," he added in a voice of perfect nonchalance, "It might be more because of the incompetence of the others than any exceptional talent on your part."

For all her purported intelligence, Tai did not know how to respond to that.

"No need to be so nervous, girl." Callahan waved at her as if she were an irritating insect. "Should you win the dragonstone, we'll be colleagues of a sort."

"I... suppose that's true, Your Imperial Majesty." Her eyes strayed to his obsidian stone pendant on its heavy silver chain. It was easy to forget, sometimes, that the Emperor was also a dragonaut. He never came to their training sessions, never flew with the others. The few times they practiced with Nocturne, Empress Saedra always came in his stead.

Closer up, she saw the dragonstone wasn't solid colored like the others she'd seen — it was less black and more of a mottled charcoal gray, interlaced with almost imperceptibly small veins of bluish white. It took her a moment to recall what it reminded her of — the beggar back in Everwood, languishing from possession sickness. Tai realized she was staring, and forced her eyes away from the dragonstone, turning her attention instead to the Emperor himself.

She half expected *him* to bear the blue veins of possession sickness, but he looked healthy enough. In fact, it struck Tai how *normal* the emperor looked. An unassuming man in his middle years, he a wore plain but well-cut blue woolen doublet, and kept his graying mousy hair tied back in a tight ponytail. He wore no crown; if not for the wood-cut prints in the broadsheets, she might not have recognized him at all.

"Right." Tai swallowed. "Well, again, sorry to have bothered you. If that's all, I'll just...."

Emperor Callahan shook his head in irritation. "Sit down." He waved irritably at a chair near the window. Unassuming in appearance or not, this man was still the Emperor. This was not a request.

Tai sat.

Callahan, however, did not sit. He gazed contemplatively out the leaded-glass study window. A thin crescent moon hung in the sky above the city of Azure. In the distance, Tai caught a flash of light that could have only been dragon fire. She thought of Xander and Bradford and the attack on the aether cache, and her worry increased.

"All this senseless violence over aether." Callahan spoke so quietly, Tai wasn't sure if she was supposed to hear.

"Your Imperial Majesty?" Tai asked. She shifted uncomfortably in her chair and wondered if it was possible to ask to be dismissed without provoking the emperor's ire.

Callahan shook his head. "Nothing, nothing. Just... all this squabbling over what's down there, when what really matters is what's up there."

Tai looked at where Callahan gestured. The tiny sliver of a waxing crescent hung in the sky, just a few days removed from the new moon. "The moon, Your Imperial Majesty?"

"If only she would reveal her secrets," the emperor said wistfully. "Then, perhaps, we could undo the mistakes of our forebears. Then, perhaps, I would not have to go through with this thrice-cursed fool's errand." He clutched his damaged dragonstone, and his face contorted with pain.

"Your Imperial Majesty!" Tai scrambled to her feet. She had no reason to like the man, but she imagined it meant nothing good if he keeled over right in front of her.

"It's nothing." He waved her aside, regaining his composure. "In the end, of course, it is not my life that is in danger. The sacrifices one must make for the greater good... pray you never have to make such choices, Candidate Lunstrum."

"Your Imperial Majesty." Apparently, repeating the man's title over and over was the only sentence she could form. So much for being intelligent and skilled in battle.

"Lady Vivienne tells me you're good with magic." Callahan was once again the picture of cold indifference. "Tell me your thoughts on this spell circle here."

He fetched a scrap of yellowed parchment off the Archmage's desk and proffered it for Tai's examination.

"That's—" Tai cut off, breath caught in her throat. She recognized Dorian's cramped, efficient script, annotating the runes and the spell circles. This must be one of the pages Dorian transcribed with

Empress Saedra all those moons ago. But next to Dorian's transcriptions were a list of numbers, as well as runes in what she assumed must be Callahan's own hand, or perhaps Archmage Rigellan's. Runes she'd seen only one other place before — in the old Planeshifting spell.

"Those are the runes the Ancients used." She tried and failed to keep her expression impassive.

"Very good," Callahan said. "Few people recognize them as such. Thankfully, my dragon Nocturne has a near perfect memory. This one represents the moon, and this one, the source of all magic, the seven gods combined. Of course, even Nocturne does not know everything about how to work the spell."

Burying her emotions as deeply as she could, Tai turned her attention to the spell. "It appears to distribute ambient magic. I'd have to do some calculations." The Emperor did not protest as she fished her notebook out of her satchel, so as surreptitiously as she could, she wrote down the numbers in the margins and the strange Ancient runes. "Connected in this way..." Her eyes widened. "My gods, the power needed for such a thing must be enormous."

"I see you have a clever eye," Emperor Callahan said. "You are correct. In Ancient times, the moon powered the spell."

"Isn't all magic powered by the moon?"

"Forgive me, I misspoke," Callahan said. "I mean, the Ancients cast this spell *from the source*."

"You mean they were—" Tai cut off abruptly. Dorian had mentioned something similar, but Callahan was not to know that. "You're suggesting the Ancient dragonauts were *on the moon* when they cast the spell?"

"Indeed," Callahan said.

Tai felt a chill and hoped the Emperor didn't notice her feathers standing on end. Dorian had told her to look out for something like this, hadn't he?

"Archmage Rigellan thinks I'm mad," Callahan continued, "But Nocturne and I know pieces of Ancient lore that even he has barely fathomed." Callahan took a seat at last, leaning back slightly and steepling his fingers. "Tell me, Candidate Lunstrum. Do you know why the world's magic is in such a sorry state?"

"Because the Ancient Dragonauts betrayed their bonds in some kind of ritualistic sacrifice, releasing Voidwraiths and sinking the continents of Orith and Iriya," Tai answered immediately by rote. But even as she said it, she wondered if that was the entire story. The Great Betrayal had been a heinous crime, but why had it affected Cyrna's magic so profoundly?

Callahan noted her expression and nodded. "I see you are catching on."

Tai didn't feel like she was catching on at all, but she was nothing if not curious, so she nodded for the emperor to continue.

"When the Ancients sunk Orith and Iriya, they cut off the flow of magic between the moon and the floating lands, thereby damaging the ambient magic, perhaps irreparably. One day, soon if the calculations are correct, Aeris *will* fall beneath the underclouds to join the rest of the Fallen Realm." His hands clenched into fists and he looked pained. "No one wishes more than I that it were not so. But to finish what the Ancients started, to sink Aeris on *our* terms, is the only way to prevent catastrophe."

"But it would be the end of magic," Tai said, even though, of course, she knew that already.

"Not everywhere," Janus said. "Some small amount of magic will remain above the clouds, not enough to keep the continents afloat, but enough to get by on. Cloudfire, as you surely know, will remain above the clouds. As will one or two cities in the highest peaks of Narea and northern Thlarknia. But you are correct, I fear. For the vast majority of people, magic will be gone."

It surprised Tai to discover that his regret was probably sincere. She had thought the emperor wished to end Cyrna's magic out of some megalomaniac thirst for power, evil for evil's sake. But of course, that was not the case.

"You truly believe there is no other way?" Tai let the words escape without thinking.

Callahan's pale blue eyes flashed in annoyance, and Tai was sure she'd stuffed her mouth full of feathers this time. But he shook his head in resignation and continued staring out the window. Tai almost thought that his ire was not for her at all, but for that sliver of crescent moon.

"They say that the moon is the source of all magic. They say that the dragonauts of old flew to the moon once a Cycle to maintain some kind of giant spell circle there. They *say* that if dragonauts could fly there now, that we could effectively reset the entire thing, undo this entire debacle, restore the magic to what it used to be. But unfortunately, practical reality cannot be based on the nebulous, '*they say.*'"

Tai swallowed. "All due respect, Your Imperial Majesty. But... why not?"

Callahan wore a resigned, almost pitying expression. "We've learned much since the Ancient days. But flying to the moon? That, I fear, remains lost to the sands of time. Gods only know how the Ancients managed it. I... tried to do it, early on, you know. With Nocturne. The air got thinner the higher we flew. Soon, I couldn't breathe. Soon, there wasn't even enough air for Nocturne's wings to flap against. We didn't get anywhere *near* the moon. Saedra was furious, naturally. She only married me for politics, but I think she cares in her own way. 'You are Emperor now, you cannot throw your life away on such frivolities.'" Callahan sighed and ran a hand almost lovingly down the edge of the parchment sheet.

"You can't just fly there." The realization dawned on Tai, making her feathers stand on end. Of course. It all seemed so obvious. "You have to... you have to planeshift."

Callahan barked out a laugh. It sounded a bit unnatural coming from the emperor, who struck her as the serious sort. "If you've rediscovered the lost art of Planeshifting, Miss Lunstrum, then by all means, I would love to hear it."

Tai thought she might, in fact, have rediscovered the lost art of Planeshifting. But she certainly was not about to tell Callahan that.

"There is... something else." Callahan drummed his bony fingers against the desk, as if considering how much he should tell her. Tai had the impression that it had been far too long since he could discuss his theories with anyone. "Something I've discovered in my studies, something not even my former colleagues know about."

"I'd be... very interested to hear what that is." Tai tried her best to project an air of polite neutrality while inside her heart raced with excitement and fear.

"Using the moon circle to reset the flow of magic... well. It truly *would* reset it. I'm afraid it would not bring those poor betrayed dragons back to life. But everything else the Ancients did that day would become undone."

Tai wrinkled her nose. "I'm afraid I don't understand what you mean. Unless..." her eyes widened. *Oh.* He couldn't mean *that.* He just couldn't!

Callahan nodded. "The flow of magical energy would be powerful enough to take Orith and Iriya and drag them right back up into the sky."

Tai realized her mouth was hanging open. She closed it, but her mind still reeled at the implications. For many in her home country, the sudden restoration of Orith would be cause for celebration. It was what the Prophecy of the Savior was supposed to portend. But it would also be chaos. Utter, complete chaos. Tai thought of her stepfather, and the rest of the undersea fishermen. Entire livelihoods, rendered obsolete in an instant.

And what about the Iriya, living in their secretive enclaves on the other side of the undersea, who shunned all outsiders and attacked all ships that came near? Who in the Void even knew how *they* would react.

"Void Eternal," she swore.

"Yes," Callahan said sadly. "I fear eternal Void is the only—" he was cut off by an abrupt knock at the door. "Enter," he said with an exhausted sigh and a knowing glance at Tai that seemed to say, *An Evil Emperor's work is never done.*

The door swung open, and time seemed to grind to a halt. Tai stared at the newcomer, and the newcomer stared back. *Oh, Void. Oh, Void, Oh, Void, Oh, Void.* She might've narrowly scraped by without Saedra or Kadmin figuring out her true allegiance, but there was no way she would get so lucky three times.

"Ah, Corynne, you are back from the lower city sooner than expected," Callahan said. "With good news, I hope?" There was a slight tone of accusation in his voice, as if to say it had *better* be good news.

Corynne Beckett pried her eyes away from Tai and stood at stoic parade rest before the Emperor. Void, but Tai had been seven kinds of fool to have assumed that Corynne would have just gone back to a quiet life in Adenthul after escaping from the Dragon's Fangs. Of course she was still in the Kasani military. Of *course* she was.

"The aether cache has been secured, Your Imperial Highness." Her jaw was set in a line of barely-suppressed fury.

"Yet you do not seem happy about it," Callahan observed.

"Your Imperial Highness. Sir. Dragonaut Crowley and Celestian found it necessary to set half the block on fire weeding the rebel elements out. There have been at least half a dozen civilian deaths that I know about. Sir." Tai thought she could hear the woman's teeth grinding.

She thought the rapid pounding in her chest must be audible, too. *Void, Void, Void.* Kadmin had set a city block on fire? With Celestian? Gods, but she hoped Celestian hadn't been in on the plan. Though if he'd been Coerced, that was, in many ways, worse.

Meanwhile, Tai had her own rather pressing and immediate set of problems.

Callahan drummed his fingers on the desk. "Thank you for bringing this to my attention. Guardswoman Beckett, I don't believe you've met Candidate Lunstrum. She is one of our most promising dragonaut candidates."

The left side of Corynne's jaw twitched seemingly of its own accord. She'd met Tai before, all right. *Void on a stick!*

This was surely it, Tai thought. Corynne was about to tell Callahan all about how they'd met already, that Tai had been the one who captured her when she lost her bond with Borealis, that Tai was, in fact, affiliated with Bradford's rebellion. Any moment a squadron of burly guards would burst in here to drag Tai off to the dungeons and that would be that.

Callahan smirked as if enjoying himself. "Oh, don't mind Corynne, Miss Lunstrum," he said. "She's just upset that you're gunning for *her* old job. I'm not completely unfair, of course. When Archmage Rigellan solves the trick of recreating dragonstones, Guardswoman Beckett here is more than welcome to try for one. But she lost the first one we gave her, and the one we have remaining should go to someone else. Fair is fair."

"Fair's fair," Corynne agreed. Her cold green eyes did not leave Tai for even an instant.

"Anyway, Corynne and I have delicate matters we must discuss, so I'm afraid you are dismissed." Callahan made a shooing motion as if Tai were an errant gryphlet. Then, perhaps realizing he was being rude, he added, "For what it's worth, I enjoyed our discussions on magical theory. I can make no promises, but I shall take it into account when it comes time to decide who gets the dragonstone."

Tai was too stunned to be either offended at Callahan's dismissal or pleased at his praise. All she could do was nod silently and get out of the office as quickly as possible.

There were now three people in the fountain palace who recognized her — Kadmin, Saedra, and Corynne. It strained all bounds of plausibility that they would *all* be ignorant of her true intentions. And if Kadmin was willing to set whole city blocks on fire to get rid of the rebels, then the gods only knew what he'd do if he thought Tai might have information on their whereabouts.

The only thing Tai knew for sure was that she and her friends were all in serious danger.

CHAPTER EIGHTEEN
AERONAUTS ADRIFT

FOUR YEARS AGO

Tai, Falgar, and Kadmin stood on the empty deck of the *Winds of Fortune*, gazing over the railing at the floating island of Kasanarae approaching in the distance. *Void-cursed finally.* As owner of the ship, Tai was acting captain, at least for the time being. *Some captain I am.* Limping into port with a damaged ship and a disgruntled crew was hardly how she'd envisioned her first official landfall.

"Arnault resigned this morning." Kadmin, who was acting as first mate, joined her at the railing. Tai knew him well enough by now to guess that more bad news was to follow. Though after seeing Captain Brielle's lifeless broken body splayed out on the ship's deck, she supposed any news seemed manageable by comparison.

Tai sighed and lowered her wings. "And I suppose you'll be next."

Kadmin didn't answer right away, and Tai felt like her heart was being squeezed in a gryphon's claw.

"We said we'd stick with you 'til the end, and we intend to do that," interjected Falgar, who was nearby folding aether sails. "Won't we, Kadmin?" he shot his friend an extremely pointed glare.

"Yes, yes, of course we will," Kadmin snapped. He relaxed slightly and shook his head. "I apologize. You know I don't intend to go anywhere. I just wish... wish we all had more experience being charge, is all."

"You and me both." Tai ruffled her feathers in consternation. "We're as green as glowyrms in springtime. I get it, I get it."

The best that could be said for the weeks following that ill-fated Voidstorm was at least no one else had died. But it seemed like their crew was plagued with every other kind of minor disaster. Contracts fell through, deliveries ran late, and now, with Arnault's pending departure, she'd lost nearly every crew member except for Kadmin and Falgar. And it was only a matter of time until they left, too. *Gods*, she didn't want to lose them. Especially not Kadmin.

Though he still wore a face like a thundercloud, Kadmin took her hand in his and squeezed it. It was a small gesture, but she appreciated it all the same. It meant his anger wasn't directed at her specifically.

Despite everything else going wrong, Tai's relationship with Kadmin felt so *right*. Tai had never been in love before. It was a heady, exhilarating feeling, almost as good as flying in the Linking. But Tai's greatest fear was that he, too, would eventually grow tired of her and leave.

Tai had never felt more out of her depth in her entire life. Ancients help her, she was barely ready to be a full aeronaut, much less a captain. But with Brielle and Brennan both gone, and the rest of the crew resigned in disgust, she saw no way to finish her apprenticeship. "It would be so easy," she said with a weak little laugh, "If I had then faintest clue what I was doing."

"Isn't that always the way of it." Falgar chortled.

Kadmin let go of Tai's hand and gazed out at the island in the distance. "There may... be a way for us to continue our education."

"Do elaborate," Tai said hopefully.

Kadmin nodded. "Here in Kasanarae there's an academy for aeronauts. It's supposed to be the best in all of Aeris. We'd learn everything we need to know about flying, plus how to manage the business if we decide to go that route."

"What do you mean 'if' we decide to go that route?" Tai asked. "What else are we going to do with a big old cargo ship?"

"There are other things we could learn to do as well." Kadmin counted off his fingers. "We could crew a warship, do our service for the Kasani military. If we're very lucky, we could crew luxurious pleasure vessels. Bump elbows with the most powerful folks on Aeris."

"I like that idea of a pleasure vessel way more than fighting in some war," Falgar put in.

"Fine," Tai pointed out, "But you keep forgetting. The *Winds of Fortune* is a cargo ship. Not a warship, and certainly not a pleasure vessel."

Kadmin feigned great interest in a spare bit of rope he found on the deck. "As to that."

"Void Eternal, spit it out, man." Falgar rolled his eyes.

Kadmin sighed and slumped his shoulders. "The school is expensive. More than we can afford, even with the pay-off from that last contract."

Falgar rolled his eyes. "Why suggest it if it's not a viable option? Way to get our hopes up."

"We're not completely without assets." Kadmin drew in a deep breath and let it out. "We could sell the ship."

Tai froze. "Sell... sell the ship?"

How could Tai even *consider* selling her last inheritance from her father?

"I hate to say it, but Kadmin might have a point," Falgar put in. "The last two captains bloody Void-cursed *died*. Three if you count Brennan. *Maybe* the ship is cursed and we're better off without it?"

Kadmin shot him a flat stare. "The *Winds of Fortune* is not cursed, Falgar. But selling the ship still makes good logical sense."

Tai's wings twitched. She didn't think the ship was cursed, but she also realistically knew that there wasn't much that she, a largely untrained teenage apprentice, could do with an entire skyship and almost no crew. This academy of Kadmin's was a tempting prospect. Perhaps, if she did well, worked her way up through the ranks, she might even afford to buy the *Winds of Fortune* back one day.

Right. Keep telling yourself that.

"I'm not sure..."

"Otherwise," Kadmin said with an air of resignation, "We're going to have to look for other work, and I find it doubtful that we'd all wind up on the same crew."

Tai's heart clenched. She didn't want to lose the ship, but she wanted to lose Kadmin even less. Their young romance had been the only bright spot in several miserable weeks. If Kadmin left, then she would well and truly be alone, and what good would a ship do her then?

"I'll have to think about it," she said.

But deep down, she already knew what her answer would be.

CHAPTER NINETEEN
TROUBLE BREWING

PRESENT DAY

Vivienne Arasine Penregon Kasani, Duchess of Pennytree, Flight Leader of the Imperial Dragonauts, and Captain of the Empress's personal guard, knew that the newcomer was trouble from the moment she arrived.

She never quite understood why Kadmin spent so much time in that Toreenish backwater recruiting struggling Orith. It all seemed wonderfully altruistic on the surface, but Kadmin never really struck Vivienne as the altruistic sort. Indeed, after his behavior at the aether cache, she began to doubt he had even the slightest amount of human empathy. When he showed up with that Orith girl and situated her among the dragonaut candidates, it didn't take the Imperial Archmage to sniff out an ulterior motive.

«We would know all about ulterior motives,» said Thunder, her dragon.

«Oh, you know that's not the same,» Vivienne chided.

Nobody else knew that, unlike the other dragons, Thunder had entered her bond willingly. It was strictly forbidden among drag-onkind before the rogue dragon Solaris's bold act of defiance, so Thunder had to pretend to have been captured. But Thunder and Vivienne both knew the truth.

Of all the Imperial Dragonauts, Vivienne had always been an oddity. She didn't care about vengeance, or personal glory, or even reviving the might of the Ancient empire. Vivienne wanted the same thing she'd always wanted — to protect her queen, and to defend her nation. Even if it was from themselves.

Vivienne stood back, frowning, as she watched the new recruits at their sparring practice.

The girl was worried about something. They all were, since the aether cache. But this girl more than most. Vivienne could tell by the rigidity of her movements, the absence of her usual fluid grace. The difference was subtle, but it was Vivienne's job to read people's body language. No doubt about it, something was bothering the girl. And Vivienne, never one to leave a mystery alone, would be cursed to the Void if she didn't find out what it was.

"Rynne." She beckoned Corynne Beckett over from the training area. "Can I have a word?"

"Of course, Commander." The guardswoman kept her head down, but Vivienne could sense her bitterness seething just below the surface. A pity, really. It couldn't have been easy for Corynne to first lose her dragon bond, then watch raw recruits vie to replace her. But Emperor Callahan was not one to forgive mistakes.

"Tell me what you know about recruit Lunstrum."

Corynne froze, another subtle cue that Vivienne might have missed were she not so experienced at reading people. "Why do you think I know anything about any of the recruits?" Corynne's tone held an air of practiced nonchalance. "I only got back two nights ago."

"And you've been watching that girl like a gryphon on the prowl ever since," Vivienne said. "Come now, Rynne. You know me too well to think you can fool me."

Corynne's green eyes darted back and forth like a frightened rabbit. Finally, she sighed and spread her hands in surrender. "She worked for the Lord Bradford's failed rebellion in the Dragon's Fangs. She's the one who caught me when Borealis—" her voice caught. "When I fell."

Corynne's eyes met Vivienne's, and Vivienne nodded in understanding. *Bradford.* Their shared secret, their shared treason.

"Have you told anyone of this?"

"I saw no need," Corynne said. "Kadmin's a rat bastard, but he's no fool. He brought her for a reason." With a bitter smirk she added, "Besides. It's above my pay grade to interfere in *dragonaut* business."

"Hmph." Vivienne shook her head. "Well, keep it quiet, for now. I'll handle this."

Bradford. Handsome, charming, often *insufferable* Bradford. She remembered him as an arrogant fop, but he'd been an arrogant fop with potential. However, that was before. Before his father married Saedra, before the Empire and the Rebellion. Who Bradford was now, she couldn't even begin to guess.

Bradford.

Moons ago, there had been a moment, just a moment, where she thought she saw her old friend among the dock workers. She'd convinced herself she was just seeing things. But she hadn't been, had she?

It *couldn't* be a coincidence. That new girl showed up, and not a week later, she saw someone who looked like Bradford on the docks? And now, it turned out the two of them were colleagues? No. Definitely not a coincidence. Bradford's rebellion was in the city, probably even behind the attack on the aether cache. There was nothing else for it. She was going to have to talk to Kadmin.

Vivienne found Kadmin in the lounge, drinking from a brandy snifter and chatting amiably with one of the serving girls. Her hands curled into fists. So bloody typical. The man on probation after what happened at the aether cache, and here he was, acting like he was on some kind of frivolous holiday.

"Where's Tai Lunstrum?" Vivienne demanded.

"I gave her the afternoon off to spar with those friends of hers." He spread his arms gregariously as if to say, *see what a benevolent master I am?*

Vivienne glared daggers in his direction.

Kadmin gave the serving girl a long suffering expression. "Sorry, Angelyne, but I have to take this. It's the boss."

"Of course, My Lord," the servant, Angelyne, curtseyed and left.

"If this is about the uprising," Kadmin said, a trifle petulantly, "I don't see that you have any reason to complain. I seem to recall that I did all the work."

Vivienne ground her teeth. He did all the work, all right, commanding his dragon to burn down the entire street corner, civilians and all. Vivienne hadn't slept in days as she tried to clean up the mess and offer compensation to the families of the people who died, as if *compensation* could ever come close to making up for such a heinous crime. And here was bloody Void-Cursed Kadmin, drinking with the Void-cursed serving girls.

Vivienne was going to have to handle this carefully. She didn't know why the girl Tai Lunstrum was here, but right now, she didn't think anyone deserved what Kadmin would do to them if he decided they were a spy or a traitor.

"I am curious about your candidate selection process," she said in a careful, clipped tone.

"Ah." Kadmin steepled his fingers. "So you've figured it out about Lunstrum, have you?"

Vivienne blinked. This wasn't the answer she'd expected.

"Do use your brain, Flight Leader." Kadmin turned his brandy snifter in his hand. "You know who that girl is, right?"

"Enlighten me."

"She," Kadmin said, "Is Dorian Valmont's little bitch. The pain-in-the-arse Valmont boy is too well protected to abduct him outright without causing a fuss. But once he finds out we have his little girlfriend in custody, he won't leave a stone on Cyrna unturned until he gets her back. Which will deliver him, and by extension his dragon, right — to — us." He drummed his fingers against the side of his glass.

"Why do you care about the dragon?" Vivienne demanded. "There's a whole world of wild dragons for you to capture." She spat out that last bit with no small amount of bitterness.

Kadmin hesitated for the barest fraction of a second, but he waved it off. "His Imperial Highness wants that dragon specifically for some reason. Something about her being Nocturne's heir apparent. Honestly, not my business to ask why. It's more important that the Emperor gets what he wants."

"You don't plan to recruit the Lunstrum girl at all. You plan to use her as a hostage."

"That's right," Kadmin said in a singsong voice. "And much as I enjoy playing with my toys, I fear it had best be soon. You and Beckett and the Empress keep asking too many inconvenient questions. Still, when I deliver Solaris and the Valmont brat to the Emperor, he will reward me handsomely indeed. I suspect soon there will be a new Flight Leader. And I intend for it to be me."

"Tai!"

Tai paused swinging her sword at the practice dummy to find Lewellyn striding across the training grounds, with her hands behind her back and a worried expression on her face.

"Lewellyn, hello. Care to join me for some sparring?"

Tai should be using her rare afternoon off to look for the dragonstone. But right now she felt an almost compulsive need to hold a practice blade in her hand.

If she trained hard enough, then maybe, *maybe* she could postpone thinking about the fact that Kadmin Bloody Crowley burned *an entire city block to the ground.* If she pushed herself to exhaustion, she wouldn't have to think about Celestian, who she flew with, who she even liked, ending a dozen lives in an instant with his dragon fire. Maybe, if she swung her sword hard enough, she wouldn't have time to stew over her fear that Xander and Bradford might be among those charred and blackened corpses.

They can't be dead. If Xander and Bradford had died, Kadmin wouldn't shut up about it. But that was, of course, assuming their bodies were even recognizable.

She swung her sword in worried frustration, sending the practice dummy spinning.

"Good strike," Lewellyn said flatly. Lewellyn, however, wasn't dressed for sparring. She wore a plain gray apron dress over an undyed linen chemise, and she looked like her mind was on anything except training. "Can we talk? Somewhere in private?"

"Of course." Tai re-racked the practice sword and followed her almost-friend out of the training grounds, apprehension mounting.

Lewellyn led Tai into an empty courtyard, where one of the palace's namesake burbling stone fountains muffled their conversation from prying ears. "Do you think it's... right, what we're doing?"

Tai's feathers stood on end. "What do you mean?" Of course, Tai knew what Lewellyn meant. She'd have to be a Void-cursed fool not to.

Lewellyn's gaze narrowed slightly, in an expression that clearly said, *don't patronize me.* But her expression fell once more into a worried frown as she said, "That attack on the aether cache. Kadmin just *set all those people on fire.* I mean. Are we going to be asked to do that kind of thing?"

Tai's breath caught in her throat. *Xander. Bradford. Don't think about it.* "I... hope not," she answered, mouth dry. "I mean. You saw how furious Vivienne was. I... don't think Kadmin was supposed to do that." But it was a weak reassurance and she knew it. Being a dragonaut meant occasionally having to make hard choices. That was true for the Order as well as the Empire.

"Maybe." Lewellyn bit her lip. "But what about forcing these dragons to bond against their will. It's not right, is it?"

Tai lowered her wings. She considered lying, making up some gryphon-dung platitude to maintain her cover, but she knew she couldn't do that.

"No." Tai sighed. "It's not right."

"But *you're* still here," Lewellyn idly ran her hands under the fish-shaped fountain spout. "You still keep training for a dragonstone, even though you know it's wrong."

Guilt and deception atop guilt and deception. Void, but Tai hated this sometimes. "I... have my reasons." She wished she could think of something more inspiring to say.

Lewellyn shook her head, tears pooling in the corners of her dark eyes. "I just... I came here because I wanted to be like the Ancients, you know? Foolish of me, perhaps. But when I heard the Kasani had dragonauts, I just..." she shrugged helplessly.

"I understand," Tai said. And she did, more than Lewellyn realized.

"I've been training with Nocturne during flight practice," Lewellyn said. "I know you mostly ride with Celestian and he seems to like Kadmin for some reason. But Nocturne... gods, look at him, he looks like he's dying. It's obvious he didn't ask for any of this. And am I going to have to do that to some other dragon? I just... don't know if I can do it."

"Then don't." Tai let the words out before she'd given them due consideration. "All this, the Empire, enslaving a dragon... it isn't worth your soul."

Lewellyn's eyes searched Tai's, looking half way between hopeful and desperately sad. "Are *you* going to leave?"

Tai's heart sank. "I... I don't know," was the only honest answer she could give.

Lewellyn's face fell, and it was like twisting a knife in Tai's gut. Lewellyn's expression vacillated between disappointed and hopeful and resigned before landing on annoyed. "I knew it."

"Lewellyn..."

"I thought you, out of all the candidates, might understand. But you're a coward, just like the others, aren't you?" Lewellyn tossed back her braided hair. "You probably just want me to drop out so you have less competition."

"That's not—" but before Tai could even think of something to defend herself, Lewellyn stalked away.

"*Gah.*" Tai ran her hands through her hair in frustration. What in the gods' names had *that* been about?

Did Lewellyn see Tai as a fellow champion of dragon's rights? Could she be an ally in truth? Or had Lewellyn been trying to do precisely what she accused Tai of doing — encouraging Tai to resign so that she herself had a better chance?

Tai let out a long sigh. She *liked* Lewellyn, Void curse it. She wanted to believe the best of the other girl even if they were ostensibly on opposite sides. And while she'd known from the beginning that this day would come when their almost-friendship blew apart, that didn't make it hurt any less when it did.

Lewellyn, Corynne, Saedra, Kadmin. This just felt like the latest in a series of small dangers, small endings. Though she couldn't tangibly say why, she felt an unshakable certainty that her time in the Kasani Fountain Palace was drawing to a close.

Which meant she'd better steal that Void-cursed dragonstone, and soon.

No more messing around, Tai thought. It was time to get to work.

"All right, my friends." Bradford grinned that disarming little grin he used to save for the pretty girls back home in Frostvale. "I know we all want to go home to our dinners, so let's do this efficiently. Stokes, you take those heavy crates from the *Point of Opinion*. Martel, they need help over there on the *Stubborn Aria*. I suspect there'll be a bonus if you show up where you're needed. Don—" he cut off abruptly, feeling the grin fall off his face. He'd been about to call for Donovan, but of course, Donovan wasn't here. Donovan hadn't been here for quite some time.

Life had returned to something of a steady rhythm in the aftermath of the attack on the aether cache. The garrison did more inspections than before, and the Emperor still hadn't lifted the curfew, which meant drinking sessions at the Twisted Gryphon were almost always cut short. But life, as always, moved on, at least for Bradford. Unfortunately, moving on wouldn't be so easy for Donovan, who was still in jail, or Jorgen, who'd taken a guardsman's arrow, or any of the myriad strangers who died in the fire, whose names Bradford hadn't even known.

Bradford's insides squirmed with guilt at that thought. He ought to know their names. They deserved to have their names remembered. Donovan had been lucky to *only* get arrested. When that dragonaut Kadmin Crowley had arrived, he'd set the whole city block on fire trying to get to the rebels. Dozens had died, many of them ordinary folks who'd never even heard of the rebellion. And gods help him, Bradford didn't even know their names.

"Rona." Bradford plastered his smile back on and gestured at one of the rare few female dock workers. "You're with me."

Bradford tried to keep his hopes up. The tighter the empire's grip, the easier it was to break. If anything, his father's heightened security only added fuel to the anti-Imperial sentiment in the city. Only question was, what did they do with it?

Rona glanced at Bradford, her expression as flinty as her storm-gray hair. "And what exactly will we be doing?"

"Loading these crates onto the *Sky's the Limit,* naturally. Unless you've any better ideas." He winked and flashed his most flirtatious smile, but he wasn't much feeling up to charm for charm's sake, and Rona could obviously tell.

"Nice try," she said, "But I'm old enough to be your mother."

In her late fifties, Rona was quite a bit older than Bradford's mother, but that was neither here nor there. He tried another tack. "Whoever loads crates fastest gets a free round at the Gryphon tonight before curfew."

Rona rolled her eyes, but he could swear she almost, almost smiled. "And compete with a young strapping lad like you? Hardly a fair contest."

Bradford snorted. "You never know."

After several moons working on the docks, he could now move the crates back and forth with swiftness and efficiency. He no longer had to pause to catch his breath, and the painful blisters on his hands had long since hardened into calluses. But he had a feeling he was a long way from entirely keeping up with people like Rona, who'd been on the docks their whole lives.

"You've a son around my age," Bradford said to Rona, hoping he remembered correctly. Over the past few weeks, he'd followed Xander's advice and put extra care into listening to the dock workers and showing that he cared. So far, it seemed to work, too. The difference in their attitudes was remarkable.

"Oh indeed, which is why I can tell when you're up to no good," Rona said, but this time, her smile came readily. "You remind me of him sometimes."

"He must be quite handsome and charming." Bradford winked to let Rona know he was only joking. Though if the boy *was* handsome and charming, all the better. "What was his name again?"

"Rybalt," Rona said.

"Rybalt," Bradford repeated. He had always struggled remembering people's names. No matter how hard he tried, names and faces always seemed to bounce around in his mind like ice in a cocktail shaker. Because of it, he'd despaired of ever being more than a mediocre viscount. What kind of leader didn't remember his subjects' *names*? But people's *stories* were different altogether. Those, he remembered vividly.

Those civilians who died at the aether cache all had stories too, he thought. Ones they'd never get a chance to share.

Bradford pushed aside his lingering feelings of guilt and focused instead on Rona. "Rybalt used to work on the docks too, didn't he?"

Bradford hoisted a heavy grain sack over his shoulder and plopped it down on the pushcart.

"He did." Rona's voice cracked. "He's in the army now, though, fighting in Thlarknia."

"Ah." Bradford knew this was a delicate subject. "You must be very proud."

"Proud, yes, but also worried sick." Rona heaved the cart towards the waiting skyship. "Don't know what the Empress was thinking, supporting her husband in this boondoggle of a war."

"The Emperor is bang out of line," Bradford agreed.

"Well now, don't say that too loudly. Gods know who might be listening." Rona looked nervous, but he dared hope, also intrigued. Rona wasn't part of the underground yet, but Bradford was always on the lookout for new allies.

"Oy, Brand, a word," the thunderous voice of Regnald boomed across the docks. Bradford winced.

"Go ahead," Rona said. "I can handle this cartload myself."

"If you're sure." With an apologetic nod to Rona, he steeled himself for whatever Regnald had to say.

"You've been working on the docks for a few moons now," Regnald said. Garnet, his blood red demon, perched on the dockmaster's shoulders and shot Bradford an accusatory glare.

"That's right," Bradford confirmed. "Surely you have no complaints about my work?"

"You and that uncle of yours seem to have made a lot of friends in your time here." The boss leered at Martel, who gave Bradford a friendly wave as he walked past.

"If we're going to work together, I see no reason we shouldn't get along." Bradford wondered what Regnald's angle was. The boss remained a tough nut to crack.

"See now, here's the thing about dock trash like yourself," Regnald said. "You blow in with the wind, and the wind will blow you out. Nobody sticks around long enough to *make friends*. I don't need you riling the rest of the workers up into some kind of fraternal brotherhood. You're trouble, Brand Weatherbee. And I don't like trouble." Garnet the demon swished her crimson tail back and forth in time with Regnald's words.

You do not know how much trouble, Bradford thought, followed by, with dawning realization, *He thinks I'm gunning for his job.* Well. That was a cursed sight better than Regnald suspecting him of treason. Bradford could work with this.

Everyone has something they want, Xander liked to say. If Bradford wanted Regnald for an ally, it was simply a matter of finding out what that was, and seeing that he got it.

"You're not blowing through here in the wind, though, surely." Bradford tested the waters. "You're practically a permanent fixture in this place."

Regnald puffed his chest out. "Three Cycles this Stone Moon."

"Twenty-one years is a long time indeed. I imagine it must be rough, seeing people come and go. Makes sense that you don't want to get too close."

Regnald's eyes narrowed. "Indeed."

"Me, though, it's as you say." Bradford shrugged. "I'm just dock trash, blowing through with the wind." He flashed his most charming grin. "So I figure, might as well enjoy myself while I'm here."

"Hmph," said Regnald, but Bradford thought the man's posture relaxed slightly. Bradford was just about to try his luck with some friendly questions when the shrill metallic sound of alarm bells rang throughout the skyport.

"Another inspection?" Bradford blanched. "So soon?"

"After what happened at the aether cache? We're lucky the drag-onauts and the garrison don't hang around micromanaging our every move." But Regnald's face was ashen. "But that ain't the inspection bell. Voidstorm's coming."

Voidstorm. A frisson of nervous energy traveled down his spine.

Bradford knew, academically, that Voidstorms had increased the past few Cycles. But the surrounding mountains kept Frostvale well protected, and the volatile storms in his homeland were comparatively rare. Maybe once, twice a year at most.

Bradford recalled hiding in the root cellar while preternatural winds made their assault on the world outside. His mother, and later Stewardess Tahlia, used to keep the children preoccupied by making Illusions dance across the earthen cellar floor. When Bradford reached his teen years, there'd been stashed brandy bottles and card games with Graigor and Corynne. Sometimes Dorian, too, if Tahlia was in one of her moods to try and make them play nice together.

Bradford gazed out over the edgecliffs. There it was. Billowing black clouds approached from the distance, like a bottle of ink spilled across the bright afternoon. "*Voidstorm.*"

"Don't just stand there gawping," Regnald barked. "Get to the shelter!"

"Right!" Bradford scrambled to follow his boss into one of the nearby warehouses.

They took shelter behind a stack of crates alongside several other workers, including Rona, Martel, Stokes, and a new recruit Bradford had never met before. The new guy, in particular, looked like he might throw up. "These storms keep getting worse and worse. We're going to die, aren't we?"

"Of course not," Martel said, with what seemed like an undeserved amount of confidence. "The boss is going to protect us."

"Regnald?" Even Bradford couldn't hide his skepticism.

"Not him directly. *Him.*" Martel nodded towards Garnet, whose blue flames flickered in the dimly lit warehouse. "Demons protect people from Voidstorms. Everyone knows that."

"Didn't take you for a priest of Meroneth, Martel," Stokes said, but he looked at Regnald and the demon, Garnet, with increased interest.

Despite growing up around Dorian's Hematite, Bradford didn't know much about demons. *Protection from Voidstorms.* Was it possible? Allegedly, Hematite had helped Dorian and the others pass through the underclouds, but Bradford always assumed that was unusual demon behavior. He gave Regnald's demon another curious glance. There was something oddly beautiful about the creature, sapphire demonfire shining against crimson hide.

The storm roared overhead, and sure enough, Garnet hopped nervously about the warehouse, darting between rafters, silver eyes glowing and sapphire flame flaring high. Was he actually doing something, protecting them from the storm? Whether Garnet's doing or not, the warehouse didn't collapse on top of them. That, Bradford supposed, was a start. Eventually, the sound of roaring wind died down, and soon the bells rang, signaling it was safe to go back outside.

"Back to work," Regnald grunted without preamble, as if nothing at all unusual had happened.

All around them, other dock workers milled about, patching sails and sweeping up shattered cargo crates and otherwise trying to create order out of the chaos. Bradford remembered this from growing up in Frostvale, as well. Bradford had never been required to participate, but he used to watch in fascination as the farm hands used rudimentary Healing magic to repair broken branches in the orchards. Today, however, Bradford assumed he was required to aid in the clean up, so he hurriedly cast about for a way to make himself useful.

All in all, however, the docks had fared a lot better than his family's orchards after a typical Voidstorm. In the area immediately surrounding the warehouse, there was hardly any damage at all. He glanced over at Garnet, who'd returned to his customary spot on the dock master's shoulder. The demon looked exhausted, but also somewhat pleased with herself. Thinking back, his family's manor house itself never used to take much damage either, at least not compared to the orchards. Had that been Hematite's doing?

"Void," Regnald swore and spat off to the side, bringing Bradford harshly back to the present. "I can't believe it, now of all times? The Void-cursed dragonaut bitch is back."

Bradford's heart caught in his throat. *Vivienne? Here? Now?* Inspections had increased since the failed uprising, but this was the second in as many days. "We just had a Voidstorm."

"Probably wants to ensure we handled it correctly." Stokes rolled his eyes.

The sun had barely just peeked back out from the clouds when Thunder's massive bronze-gold wings blocked it again as the dragon circled for a landing. Bradford hung back, resorting to his usual strategy of making himself look uninteresting. For whatever reason, unfortunately, it didn't work this time.

Vivienne looked Bradford in the eye and made a beeline right towards him. She was a wild gryphon, and he was her prey. Even as his heart thudded with terror, Bradford couldn't help admiring the beauty of her hawklike gaze. He found himself desperately hoping that *she* hadn't torched any civilians at the aether cache attack. *Not Vivienne.*

"I wish to speak to this dock worker alone," Vivienne said.

Regnald and the others wasted no time getting back to their duties. Anything to avoid speaking to the dragonaut. Bradford could only nod mutely as Vivienne ushered him straight back into the warehouse they'd just vacated. She gave her athame an irritable flick, and Bradford's paltry Illusion dissipated.

"You," she hissed.

"Me." Bradford wished he could supply something more intelligent.

"Listen. I don't know what you're doing here, and frankly, I don't care. But that girl. Tai Lunstrum. She's with you, isn't she?"

"Ah—"

Vivienne shook her head. "I suppose it doesn't matter. I'm here to warn you. Kadmin's been onto her the whole time. He plans to use her as a hostage against your brother. Anyway. Thought you should know."

"I— what?"

But Vivienne had already turned around and strode out of the warehouse. In her clear, commanding voice, she shouted, "All right, people, let's see what damage the Voidstorm brought about this time."

Tanis paled when he heard the request over the aether transmitter.

"I... that's impossible. I can't do that, High Councilor."

"Then I suppose," High Councilor Gideon said, "That you don't care what happens to your dear Mother, or if you are ever allowed to speak to her again."

Tanis tugged nervously at the ends of his silky black ponytail. "What... what exactly do you plan to do with that information?'

"I don't see how that's any of your business," Gideon said. "Just know that I can do far worse than preventing your Mummy Dearest from using the aether beacon."

"Do as he says, Tanis." Reora's voice crackled in the background, causing a chill to run down Tanis's spine. He'd never heard his mother sound so frightened before. "If you do, we can find a way to get you out of there."

"I..." Tanis had no idea what to do or say. He owed the Order no loyalty, he knew that. But the thought of providing such sensitive information made his stomach churn.

"You've become attached to your kidnappers." Gideon's voice took on a falsely paternal, saccharine quality. "It's normal to feel that way. It's your mind's defense mechanism, the way you subconsciously protect yourself from the horrors happening around you.

But I must remind you, these are not your friends, they are not your people. We are."

Tanis swallowed. "Of course, High Councilor. You're right, High Councilor." Tanis wanted to throw up. But seeing no choice, he quickly apprised the High Councilor of everything he knew about Cloudfire's security, and the comings and goings of the dragonauts.

"Good," Gideon said. "You see? That wasn't so hard."

The connection abruptly blinked out without so much as a *Thank you.*

"You're welcome," Tanis grumbled under his breath at the unlit beacon.

Tanis leaned against the wall and took several deep breaths. He felt wretched, and not just because of what he'd just done.

"Are you all right?" asked Dax, who waited outside the chamber to make sure no one walked in on them.

Tanis swallowed and nodded. He wondered how much he dared tell the Orith dragonaut. How much did Dax already know about Gideon? He surely wasn't too far embroiled in Gideon's schemes, or else *he* would have simply provided all those intimate details. But Dax was a dragonaut first and foremost. Tanis couldn't rely on him not to make things worse.

"You look ill," Dax said. "You should go to the infirmary."

Tanis shook his head. "I'll be fine."

Using the meditative techniques Dorian had taught him, he strengthened his mental barriers to keep Malachite at bay. At the moment, he wanted nothing more than to drop the barrier and let the demon eat his fill. But if Tanis did that, he might not be able to stop Malachite from draining him until he collapsed. He was so much better, these days, at blocking the demon. But when he let up his barriers even a little, it was harder and harder not to let the demon drain his spirit energy entirely. He knew he wasn't supposed to keep his barriers up all the time, but it was much easier to do that than to try and force his demon to use restraint.

One day, Malachite would be banished in truth, and even now,

Tanis wasn't sure how to feel about that. Certainly, it wasn't like he *enjoyed* being bonded to the creature. But it felt like giving up, in a way.

The Order wasn't about to let Tanis go any time soon, so it wasn't like he could continue with his original plans. Dragonmar Sylvia even said that once they got their security figured out — something that, Tanis realized guiltily, he was actively undermining — they could go back to sending the dragonauts to help the trees. So it wasn't like Tanis *needed* to cast magic beneath the clouds. But maybe that was the problem. Tanis's father was doing fine without him. The town was doing fine without him. He should be happy about that, but instead he just felt hollow. He'd never in his life felt *needed,* only like extra baggage dragged from one place to the next. Guiltily, he wondered if that was why he ultimately caved and gave Gideon the information he wanted. At least he had *something* that was useful to *someone.*

Savior help him, but Tanis felt like he'd been dragged out of the depths. Malachite pawed at the barrier, so he tightened the woven energy all the further. Conflicted feelings aside, this one thing, at least, was something he could control. Something he *had* to control.

The room spun around him, and he clung to the wall for purchase. That wasn't supposed to happen, was it? Tanis took several deep breaths and shook out his feathers. *Water.* He just needed some water, then he'd be just fine. He was late for sword practice with Dorian, anyway, and his prison warden might get suspicious if he tarried much longer. *Just push through the discomfort. You'll be fine. Fine, fine, fine.*

He didn't notice, in his exhaustion, that he'd left a wide gap in his woven spirit armor. Malachite noticed, however, and flicked his forked tongue in anticipation.

CHAPTER TWENTY
NO TURNING BACK

Dorian couldn't shake a sense of melancholy as he headed down the hallway towards the training grounds. He'd hoped they might resume their missions of goodwill soon, but his most recent meeting with Jameson put an end to that.

The Orith fire fighters had prevented any permanent damage to the Council Hall, thank all the gods and Ancients. But the Toreenish government made it clear they wanted no more "help" until the reasons behind the attack were sorted out. Dorian understood the logic and the need for safety, but Void curse it, all this waiting made him itchy. He didn't look forward to sharing the bad news with Tanis, either.

Hardly for the first time in her interminable moons-long absence, he wished Tai were here. She would know what to do, she might even know what to say to the Toreenish High Council to get them to change their minds. He missed her dry sense of humor and her intellectual curiosity. He even missed how she used to yell at him sometimes. Everything in Cloudfire felt so dull and lifeless without his best friend by his side.

"Dorian, hey, Dorian!"

Dorian paused at the sound of jogging footsteps straining to catch up with him.

"Falgar?"

Dorian was surprised to see his friend still in the castle. Falgar and Sullivan had Nahiirasday afternoons off, and the two of them almost always spent it flying or strolling the town together, at least when they were not locked up together in their shared quarters.

"Sullivan and I are going to the Thirsty Cloud," Falgar declared. "We were hoping you might come with us. You know. Have a drink together. Like the old days."

Like the old days. Like back on the *Phoenix.* Dorian thought longingly back to those golden evenings around the rough, round wooden galley table, drinking cheap ale out of wooden mugs and laughing at their own antics. But of course, it could never be like the old days. He liked Falgar and Sullivan very much, of course, but as long as Tai wasn't there, it would never, ever be like the old days.

"I wish I could," Dorian said, "But I'm due to meet Tanis in the training grounds."

Part of Dorian hoped Falgar would argue further. Part of him hoped he could miraculously spend an afternoon free of responsibility. But Falgar just sighed and said, "Yeah, all right. Maybe next time."

"Yeah." Dorian felt like the world's biggest arse. "Maybe."

If turning his friends down made him feel wretched, it was nothing to how he felt when he finally arrived at the training grounds.

Tanis swung his sword against a practice dummy, his narrow boyish face screwed up with determination. But there was a stiffness to his movements, a feverish sweat on his brow, and a glassy sheen in his bloodshot eyes. Small things on their own, but together they painted a worrisome picture. Malachite perched on the practice dummy, tail swishing back and forth, sticking his tongue out in anticipation of a feast. Tanis whaled on the practice dummy like he was repelling invaders.

"Hey, hey, slow down," Dorian said. "Are you all right?"

A flash of irritation crossed Tanis's face, but disappeared just as quickly. He took a swig of water from his canteen and winced. Tanis had a slightly lighter complexion than his sister Tai, but right now he looked nearly as pale as Dorian, almost corpse-like. And that sweat. That wasn't ordinary sweat from exertion. Dorian hesitantly put his hand on the boy's clammy forehead, anticipating a fever, but his skin was cold, unnaturally so.

"Maybe we should take the day off," Dorian suggested gently. "You look like you could use some rest."

Tanis, however, shook his head. "No," he said. "I have to train today. I'm so close, I can almost — I'm so close." Again, his eyes took on a glassy expression.

"I don't think it's a good idea. If you push it too far, the flow of energy could backfire, and you—"

Tanis scowled. "You're not my father, and you're not my older brother, either, even though I know how much you want to wed my sister."

Dorian raised his eyebrows. "That's not—"

"I'm training," Tanis said. "You can help me or not, but unless you plan to drag me back to your apartment and lock the door, you can't stop me. Which I suppose would be your right, *prison warden*."

Dorian sighed and massaged the back of his neck. "All right," he said, against his better judgement. "We'll do the training session. But I want you to go straight back to your room and get some rest after this."

"Fine, fine." Tanis twitched his wooden practice blade in agitation.

Side by side, Dorian and Tanis began their warmup exercises. By now, Tanis could usually move through the forms with fluid grace, but today, his movements were jerky and stilted, and he kept wincing in pain. In his mind's eye, Dorian examined Tanis's meditative barrier. The shining blue aura flickered, brittle, as if the slightest provocation might shatter it.

Dorian's worries mounted. Tanis ought not keep the barrier up at all during training, and the fact that he found it necessary was cause for concern. The frail, flickering energy reminded Dorian of Tanis's very earliest attempts. It surely wouldn't hold long enough to finish the session, and if Malachite broke through with Tanis already in such a state... "I think we should take a break."

"No," Tanis insisted. "I can do this." He took a long, rattling breath. "I *have* to do this."

Dorian saw what Malachite intended a fraction of a second too late.

"No!" Dorian lunged forward, but he was too slow.

Tanis's fragile barrier burst into a million crystal shards. Seizing the opening, Malachite charged and knocked Tanis to the ground. The demon's blue-flame aura shone blinding bright as the demon gorged himself on a feast of Tanis's energy. Tanis's face briefly bore a glassy expression of agony and ecstasy combined, before it faded into utter blankness.

"No, no, no!" Dorian tried desperately to create a barrier of his own, the way he had that day Tanis collapsed in town, but it did no good. His outsider's magic was as nothing compared to Tanis's gushing torrent. The Orith boy lay on the training room floor, twitching, flecks of spittle forming at the corners of his mouth. Tanis's glassy eyes stared blankly at some unseen point in the distance.

Fugue. Oh, gods, that was a fugue. A real one, this time. But how could that be? Tanis had been doing so well resisting the demon. Dorian's mind reeled as he tried to puzzle out what could have caused this. The boy must've kept his barrier up all the time, not giving it a rest like Dorian had told him. And if, in the rare times he did let go, the demon fed unrestrained like this... Well. Dorian supposed he could see how this would happen. Strained to the breaking point, Tanis's aura was left utterly powerless against the demon's onslaught. *Void take him,* Dorian should have paid better attention. He should have done a better job explaining the consequences. He should have called the boy's bluff and *locked him in his bloody room*. But he hadn't, and now, despite all their best preventative measures, Tanis was in a demonic fugue.

"Like the *Void!*"

Not knowing what else to do, Dorian heaved the boy over his shoulder. *So light.* If they got out of this alive, he really needed to make sure the boy ate more. But at least this way, he made for an easy burden as Dorian ran full tilt towards the infirmary, trailing Tanis's silver-white spirit energy in their wake.

"Estevan!" Dorian burst into the infirmary, heaving for breath. "Healer Estevan, it's Tanis, he—"

Dorian cut off at the horrific tableau before him.

Jakob Sullivan stood over an already-occupied infirmary bed, head bowed in prayer, his hands balled into fists to keep them from shaking. On the other side, Healer Estevan muttered nervously as he traced complicated Healing runes into the air. Crimson blood spattered his white Healer's robes.

"Dorian." Sullivan looked up, his face drawn, eyes red with tears. "Thank the gods you're here. We'd just made it into town when a man in a bird mask showed up out of nowhere, and he — he — Falgar's been stabbed!"

Tai ground her teeth as she folded the last of Kadmin's fine silk shirts. Savior help her, but she needed to find the dragonstone and get out of here soon. Not just because she was certain her disguise would fall apart at any moment, but also, just to be free of that *insufferable bastard*.

"Will that be all, *Your Lordship?*" Tai almost, *almost* hid her sarcasm. It was late in the evening, around the time she usually went to bed. Not that she was much looking forward to going to the barracks tonight. She hadn't spoken to Lewellyn since their disagreement in the courtyard earlier that day, and couldn't say she relished returning to their shared quarters.

"Come over here." Kadmin waggled his finger like she was a puppy. "Come, have a drink with me. Let's chat. We never get to do that anymore."

For all the shirts Kadmin owned, he hadn't even bothered to put one on. He lay sprawled on the divan, wearing his uniform jacket open and revealing his leanly-muscled chest. She'd found his chest attractive, once. Now she just found it nauseating. How dare he sit there, all demons-may-care, after he and Celestian murdered all those innocent people?

Kadmin's dragonstone, which represented his connection to Celestian, lay carelessly slung over the armrest. Tai suppressed the urge to roll her eyes. "I'll pass, thanks."

"Aw, don't be like that. Come, have some wine."

Tai opened her mouth to tell him where he could shove that wine, but she stopped short as the outline of an idea began to form. By the looks of him, Kadmin was already well into his cups.

"Better than going back to the candidate barracks, I suppose."

Kadmin smirked. "That's the spirit. As they say, rank has its privileges."

Forcing a smile, Tai sat as far away from Kadmin as the divan would allow.

Kadmin yawned and raised his arms in an unconvincing stretching motion so that he could then put his arm around Tai's shoulder. It took everything in Tai's power not to flinch.

"It feels like we never get to talk anymore," Kadmin drawled.

"Yeah, well, busy with training," Tai said. "And I mean, I'm sure it would be inappropriate, you know, for you to be seen... fraternizing."

"Ah." Kadmin pulled Tai closer. "But I *love* to fraternize."

For a terrible moment she wondered what Dorian would think if he found her here, with her former lover's arm around her winged shoulders. She, of course, owed Dorian nothing; she and Dorian were not together. For all she knew, he fell in love with someone else in her moons-long absence. That thought did not make her feel better.

"Wine?" Kadmin brandished the emerald bottle.

Gods, yes. Tai wanted to upend the entire thing directly down her throat. But right now, it was crucial that she keep a clear head. So although she had no intention of drinking it, Tai poured herself a goblet, and then topped up Kadmin's.

For a time, they spoke casually, mainly about trivialities. Kadmin, in his typical fashion, did most of the talking, but tonight Tai was more than happy to shut up and listen.

"Of course, Lady Vivienne disapproves of my actions at the aether cache, she disapproves of everything." Complaining about Lady Vivienne seemed to be Kadmin's favorite topic. "All I'm saying is, if those rebels didn't want to be burned alive, they shouldn't have attacked an Imperial aether cache. I mean, that's a pretty basic thing to not do, isn't it?" He chuckled at his own joke. Tai did her best not to be sick.

Kadmin sloshed around his near-empty wineglass and Tai schooled her face into careful neutrality as she moved to refill it. Unfortunately, the bottle was empty.

"Ah, oh dear, I'll open another, why don't I." She sprang to her feet and made her way over to the wine rack, swearing under her breath as she wrangled with the temperamental corkscrew. Void, but she always hated these things. Why couldn't the Kasani just keep alcohol in wooden kegs or clay jars like normal people?

She finally popped the cork loose and scrambled back over to the divan, pouring a fresh measure into Kadmin's goblet. Tai's, of course, remained full and untouched. Fortunately, Kadmin didn't seem to notice or care. He simply accepted the goblet and took a grateful sip.

"Anyway, it's all about striking a balance with the lesser unbonded," Kadmin said.

Tai fought to keep the disgust from her expression. "Lesser unbonded?"

"Yes, well, you'll understand if you bond a dragon one day." He waved his hand condescendingly. "Sometimes you've got to give people the carrot, other times the stick. Those people in your hometown, I gave them the carrot. See how beneficent I can be. But those rebels at the aether cache... well. I fear they needed the stick." His gray Kasani eyes swam with some unreadable emotion. Self-righteousness, perhaps, violently shoving away the faint vestiges of guilt. Tai guessed Kadmin probably wanted her to tell him he'd done the right thing in killing all those people. Of course, she was not going to do that.

"Carrots and sticks," she said blandly as she refilled his goblet. *Here is one delicious fermented grape-flavored liquid carrot for you. You can take the stick and shove it up your... calm down, Tai.*

Kadmin droned on for the next half-bell or so, pausing only for Tai to give the occasional nod or "Mmm hmm" or "I see." He complained about Lady Vivienne, cast aspersions on the other candidates, and boasted loudly about how he and Celestian cast the fireball that sent the *Phoenix* crashing down beneath the underclouds. Tai flinched at this last one, but covered it quickly by refilling his goblet yet once more. He most likely had no idea that she had been on that ship when it crashed.

"And yet the rogue dragonaut survived." Kadmin shook his head in disgust. "I don't understand it, Tai. I really, really don't. But, well, you know the man, perhaps you could tell me." Tai froze, but Kadmin barreled on. "How could such a bumbling incompetent keep eluding our grasp? How is it he stripped us of half of our dragonauts? How..." his voice caught in a hiccup that was almost a sob. Void, but he really was drunk. "...How did he kill Ashe?"

Ashe. The auburn-haired dragonaut Dorian had beheaded back in Goose Head. Nobody around here seemed to talk about her much. "Did you... did you care about her, then? Ashe?"

"I loved her, Tai," Kadmin said. Tears pooled in his red-rimmed eyes. "I'm not sure you could ever understand love like that."

Tai wisely chose not to say anything.

Kadmin seemed to finally, *finally* remember who he was talking to, and hastened to add, "It was different with me and you. We were kids back then. I thought it was love with you. I really, really did. But I was just a kid. I never meant to hurt you. Just a kid, just a kid. Ashe, though, *Ashe*."

Kadmin drained the rest of his goblet and buried his head in his hands, weeping openly. Not knowing what else to do, Tai awkwardly patted him on the shoulder. *The man I love killed the woman he loved.* She despised Kadmin, but no one could deny it was a cruel twist of irony.

"There there. It'll be okay. You should get some rest."

With some regret, some trepidation, she hoisted the intoxicated dragonaut up and guided him gently towards the adjacent bedchamber.

"Taking me to bed, just like the old days," he slurred.

Tai did not dignify that with a response.

For such a skinny bastard, he sure was heavy. All the intoxicated flopping around didn't help. But in a few hours, he was going to wake up hungover and furious. The least she could do was make sure he was comfortable. As gently as she could, Tai deposited Kadmin on the soft feather mattress. Sure enough, it was less than a minute before he started snoring loudly.

"Right. Okay."

Her heart thudded in her chest as she stepped out of the bedchamber and back into the sitting room. Kadmin's dragonstone remained where he'd left it, flung casually over the side of the settee.

Moving quickly before her courage could fail, Tai took the dragonstone, shoved it unceremoniously down the front of her tunic, and strode casually out into the hallway. Tai half expected alarm bells to blare, or for Kadmin to wake up fully sober and shout for the guards. But so far, it was just an ordinary evening in the Kasani fountain palace. Tai felt the dragonstone against her chest, warm and thrumming in time with Tai's heartbeats.

She'd reached the main entrance hall and almost dared to hope she could make a clean getaway when she heard the unmistakable sound of footsteps. Tai froze in her tracks.

"Candidate Lunstrum." Lady Vivienne looked graver than Tai had ever seen her. "Thank the Ancients I found you. I've been looking everywhere."

"For me?" Tai tried to keep her expression politely puzzled. Although it gave off no visible light, Tai was certain the dragonstone between her breasts must glow like a Void-cursed beacon.

"At eleven bells, Thunder will take over guard duty from Nocturne. I can buy you as much as ten minutes."

"Ten... ten minutes?" Tai didn't need to fake her confusion now.

"To run," Vivienne elaborated. "You must be gone from this place at once. Go back to your contacts in the city. Or back to wherever your rogue dragonauts are hiding. Or anywhere you like. Just don't stay here."

Tai's heart felt like a snare drum. *She knows. Oh, gods, she knows.*

"I don't understand," she lied. Despite abstaining from the wine, her mouth felt as dry as a hangover.

"I think you do," Lady Vivienne said evenly, and oh, by all the gods and Ancients, Tai wanted to quail under the intensity of that gaze. Her stolen dragonstone throbbed against her heart. How had Vivienne known she planned to flee? Moreover, why was Vivienne allowing it?

There was no time to puzzle it out. Tai licked her lips, trying to coax some moisture into her mouth. "All right then. I'll go."

After all, Tai had what she came for.

CHAPTER TWENTY-ONE
BROKEN HEARTS AND BROKEN DREAMS

THREE YEARS AGO

Tai forced open the shutters, letting in the fresh city air. If fresh one could call it; the humid Kasani breeze brought in a whole plethora of aromas, savory and unsavory alike. Shaking her head, she set the pie on the windowsill, and then set about cleaning up.

It didn't take much effort. She had few possessions, and hardly any space in the tiny apartment to store them besides. With the chipped walls and creaking floorboards, even her best attempts at cleaning felt like polishing dung.

Well, polished dung was better than unpolished dung, and Tai intended to see her own reflection in the shining shite. Kadmin was visiting tonight, and he couldn't *stand* a messy apartment. "No girl of mine should live in squalor," he would say. Yet his tone always somehow conveyed that she was the perpetrator rather than the victim, and he certainly never offered to help.

Life in the Kasani capitol was filled with disappointment after disappointment. The first came when she was told, in no uncertain

terms, that the Kasanarae Academy of Flight was for Kasani pupils
only. The fact that they were happy to accept Falgar, who was
Vatean, however, led Tai to believe that they really meant *Aerish*
pupils only.

Tai was outraged at this injustice, but there was little to be done
about it. As Kadmin quite rightly pointed out, making a fuss would
only compromise Falgar's education, and cement Tai's reputation as
a troublemaker. So, after selling her ship in hopes of an elite aeronaut's education, Tai was unceremoniously tossed out and forced to
make a living in an unfamiliar city.

If there was any silver lining to be had, it was that she at least got
a fair price for the ship. Nearly three times what Captain Brielle had
offered all those years ago. Even after funding Kadmin and Falgar's
tuition, she had a tidy sum left over. Enough to live off of, for now.

But Tai knew her savings wouldn't last forever, and local skyship
crews were far from enthusiastic about hiring an unproven Orith girl
with an incomplete apprenticeship. Her best hope was that when
Kadmin graduated and got admitted to a crew, he'd use his Acad-
emy-trained influence to get her an apprenticeship on the same
vessel. It pained her to think how far behind the others that would
leave her, but it was surely better than nothing. For now she just had
to be frugal, and take on odd jobs doing mending and laundry to
ensure her savings lasted until Kadmin finished school. Flying freely
in the Linking now felt like a distant memory.

At least she had Kadmin. That was what she kept telling herself,
over and over, as she slipped ruther and further into the dull gray
humdrum of day to day life. At least she had Kadmin. But even he
seemed to be slowly slipping away from her, and the prospect terrified her. He was the only bright spot in an otherwise dreary land-
scape. If he grew bored with her, she truly would be left with
nothing.

For the first moon or two after he started at the Academy, he
visited her apartment every day. They would share their meals
together, talking and laughing and making love late into the night.

Bedding Kadmin made Tai feel simultaneously grown up and rather rebellious. *What were her mother say?* But Tai was eighteen now, no longer the naïve little girl she had been when she left Toreen.

Unfortunately, as Kadmin became busier and more engrossed with his school work, his visits dropped in frequency, from every day, to a few times a week, to thrice a moon if she was lucky.

Tai understood this, expected it, even. The Academy's curriculum was rigorous, of course it would take a lot of his time. But lately, even when she saw him, he seemed distant, even irritable. Criticism slowly overtook affection in their interactions, just a little at first, but then more and more. A snide comment here, a churlish remark there, until it seemed like he was annoyed at her more often than not.

"Are you really going to wear that?" "I'd be on latrine duty for a moon if the sergeant found my quarters in such a condition." "Surely you have nothing to complain about. It's not like you have any real responsibilities."

This last had the effect of stabbing her in the chest and twisting the knife. Did Kadmin think she *enjoyed* being locked up in this dismal apartment doing tedious odd jobs for a pittance? Of *course* she wanted to be at the Academy with him and Falgar, or better yet, on a ship somewhere flying in the Linking.

She told herself things would be better after Kadmin graduated. Then she'd prove her worth, to Kadmin and to everyone else. But as time passed, it became more and more difficult to believe. Could Kadmin really get her an apprenticeship? Would he even want to? It made her feel wretched and disloyal to question his intentions, but when he spent so much of their precious rare time together offering nothing but disparagement, she really began to wonder.

Sometimes, being Kadmin's lover felt just the same as being Brielle's apprentice, or Reora's daughter. Perhaps Tai was doomed to always fall short of people's expectations.

Tonight, however, would be different. Tai was sure of it. Tai was *determined* to make it so. She'd lit scented candles, donned her best Aerish gown (modified in the back to fit her wings), and even baked a pie. Her mother always used to tell her that a way to a man's heart was through his stomach. If Tai made everything perfect tonight, then perhaps, *just perhaps*, Kadmin would remember why he'd fallen for her, and they could go back to the way they were in the beginning.

There was a knock at the door, and Tai nearly jumped out of her skin. He was here early! She straightened her feathers and ran a nervous hand through her hair before opening the door, only to find that it was not Kadmin on the other side.

A freckle-faced boy in the blue-gray uniform of the Academy stood politely outside with a sealed envelope.

"Are you Tai Lunstrum, miss?"

"Yes, that's me. Can I... help you?" Tai's heart sank. She thought she knew what was in that envelope.

"I've a message from the Kasani Academy of Aeronautics, miss Lunstrum." The youth handed over the envelope and then departed with a bow, clearly not wanting or expecting a response.

Tai let out a long sigh as she unsealed the envelope. Somehow, she doubted the administrators had seen the error of their ways and were begging her to come study. Sure enough, it was Kadmin's handwriting that greeted her. His penmanship had improved significantly since coming to the Academy, but there was no mistaking his cramped, slanted style.

Tai, the letter read,

A thousand apologies, but something came up and I cannot make our appointment. I know you will understand.

All the best,

Kadmin.

Tai felt her hand curl into a fist around the crisp Academy-issue paper, ice settling in the pit of her stomach. She ought to have expected this. His exams were coming up. He was busy. But *Void Eternal.* They hadn't seen each other in almost two weeks! She had really thought, just this one evening, he *might* make time for her.

She scanned the letter again, looking for any signs of regret, any evidence that he actually cared. No, *Dear Tai* or *My Dearest, Tai,* just a simple, curt greeting of *Tai*. And then at the end, *All the best.* Not *sincerely* or *yours truly* or, she'd been foolish enough to hope, *love*. The message was as cold and impersonal as a tax bill.

Exams are coming up. Remember, exams are coming up. How would she feel, if he failed his exams and got expelled and it was all her fault? No. If she wished to win and keep Kadmin's heart, she knew the most important thing was to be supportive. And that meant he'd have his pie, Void curse it, even if he didn't have time to share it.

Tai covered the still-cooling pie with a cloth napkin and loaded it into a wicker basket. Then she extinguished the candles, locked her apartment (not that she had anything valuable to steal), and strode confidently towards the Academy campus.

People stared openly as she passed, but Tai was used to it by now. Even among Azure's immigrant population, winged Orith were rare. Her appearance marked her as an outsider. Back home, she'd been stared at for having small, stunted wings. Here in Kasanarae, she was stared at for having wings at all. Being gaped at was just part of life's irritating background noise.

Once she reached the Academy campus, she didn't have to look long to find Kadmin. He sat on the edge of a fountain, laughing and joking with several other Academy students, including a stunningly pretty Kasani woman with long silky hair and, as the saying went, curves in all the right places. Tai was suddenly conscious of her own short-cropped hair and flat, skinny figure. The group of students passed a wineskin around, each taking a hearty swig. Whatever they were doing, it didn't look like studying.

Feeling equal parts hurt and outraged, Tai stormed forward, ready to tell Kadmin precisely what she thought about his "study session."

Before she'd moved more than a few paces, however, the beautiful Kasani woman said something Tai couldn't hear, and Kadmin burst out laughing, his eyes sparkling with mirth and affection. Tai didn't think he'd ever laughed like that to anything Tai said. Then, without warning, Kadmin kissed the woman on the mouth. He'd never kissed Tai like that, either, not even that first time in the Linking.

Many thoughts flickered through her mind at that moment. But the thought at the forefront was not, *How could you,* nor was it, *Wasn't I good enough?*

No.

It was, *I sold my ship for you, you bastard.*

Suddenly, abruptly, Tai wanted nothing to do with any of it anymore. She dropped the basket on the ground, and only vaguely noticed as the pie fell out of it and spilled cooked cherries and apples onto the sidewalk. *Impolite to litter,* her mother's imaginary voice intoned, but Tai couldn't make herself care. She ran back to her shabby apartment as fast as her feet would carry her. Tai refused, absolutely *refused*, to let Kadmin see her cry.

Tai never found out if Kadmin knew she'd seen him that day. She had no idea what he thought when she abruptly disappeared from his life, if he even cared, if he even bloody *noticed*. All she knew was that she never wanted to see him again.

CHAPTER TWENTY-TWO
STRESS BAKING

PRESENT DAY

Dorian stared in horror between Sullivan and Tanis, unsure what he could do, how he could help. He was no good with Healing — Stewardess Tahlia, who taught him magic, always warned that a miscast rune could do more harm than good.

But with Tanis shuddering in his arms, and Sullivan and Estevan desperately trying to staunch Falgar's bleeding, Dorian knew he was on his own.

"Okay." He let out a deep breath. "Okay. I can do this."

Forcing his hand steady, Dorian grasped frantically for what little knowledge he remembered. *Connection, at a thirty-degree angle from Restoration... How much was thirty degrees again? Oh,* curse his lack of training. It wasn't like he had a bloody *protractor.* No other spells required this level of precision.

"Just need to staunch the flow of spirit energy... there!" he released the spell, and to his great relief, the great gushing torrent slowed.

Slowed, but did not cease.

"Not enough power," he complained. He drew from Solaris, but didn't want to draw too much. If he hurt his dragon on top of everything else, he didn't think he could bear it.

«You will not hurt me, but I would warn you if you did,» Solaris reassured him.

That was something, Dorian supposed.

His frantic and inexpert efforts were cut off, however, when Hildegard burst into the room, dressed in civilian clothes, her ponytail askew. She must have come as soon as she heard about Falgar, and looked just as alarmed to find the Orith youth twitching on the brink of death. "What in the Void happened here?"

"Tanis," Dorian gasped out. "Fugue."

"Meroneth's balls." Hildegard tossed a few more runes into the air, more sophisticated than Dorian's, and joined the flow of her power with his. And yet even that was not enough to stop Malachite's feasting.

"I have an idea," Hildegard said. "But it's risky."

One risky idea was better than the zero ideas Dorian had, so he nodded and said, "Do it."

"Try to keep him stable. I have to go get something."

Dorian nodded and kept working. He felt sweat beading at his temple. Keeping him stable was easier said than done.

Thankfully, Hildegard returned a moment later, carrying a cloth bundle under her arm. She unwrapped it to reveal what appeared to be a crescent-moon hand mirror, but with strange, swirling blue aether in the place of glass.

"The moon glass," he said. "But what—"

"It's dangerous," Hildegard said, "But it might be the only way."

Hildegard took Dorian's hand in his, and together, they funneled power through the strange object into the healing circle. The ornate silver handle vibrated in Dorian's hand, becoming steadily hotter until, unable to bear the pain, he dropped it.

"Oh, no!" Dorian gasped, certain that he'd both destroyed an irreplaceable magic artifact and killed his best friend's brother.

But the moon glass appeared intact, and Tanis, though unconscious, was at the very least breathing. The uncontrollable flow spirit energy sputtered and ceased.

"Did that... work?" Dorian didn't dare hope.

Tanis blinked awake, looking confused. "What—" and then, abruptly, he collapsed again.

"Tanis!"

"He's alive," Hildegard confirmed, "But he's in a bad way."

Healer Estevan, his white robes still splattered with blood, knelt down beside them. "Your friend Falgar is still asleep, but he should be all right. As for this one... well, thanks to you, he may yet pull through. But we're not out of the woods yet."

Muttering something about getting too old for this, Estevan tried to lift Tanis's unconscious form.

"I'll help." Dorian quickly scrambled over.

Together, Dorian and Estevan lowered Tanis onto an unoccupied hospital bed. Even with his massive wings, Tanis seemed so light, so fragile.

"I'll need to perform an exorcism," Estevan said, all business despite his exhausted demeanor. "You've done well so far, but that is a spell that requires utmost concentration."

Dorian nodded. Healing magic was tricky enough, but exorcism was one of the most difficult and dangerous spells around. Dorian knew he'd only get in the way if he tried to help.

"Will he be all right?" Dorian's voice was small.

Estevan's face was drawn. "If exorcism were easy, almost no one would carry a demon. But if he survives the night, he'll just as likely survive the next ten Cycles."

Dorian swallowed and nodded. Knowing it was crucial to give the Healer privacy, he left the infirmary. By all the gods, he felt wretched.

"You probably saved his life, you know," Hildegard said.

"Can't help but thinking it's my fault he was in danger to begin with. If I'd paid better attention…"

"Tcch." Hildegard waved a dismissive hand. "Strange though… that moon glass. Have you used it before?"

Dorian shook his head. "Seen it, but never used it." He inspected his palm, which was pink where it came in contact with the handle. "I can see why one would want to use it sparingly."

Hildegard nodded. "Funny thing. When I tried to use it a few moons ago, it was… worse. A lot worse."

"Burned off Jameson's eyebrow if I recall correctly."

"I think with us both drawing from it together, it worked more… predictably. Not less powerfully, but like we could share the energetic load." She ran her hand through her auburn ponytail. "I need to go to the library and make some notes. It's definitely given me a lot to think about."

A lot to think about indeed. Worries over Falgar, Tanis, and the mysterious moon glass swam together in his mind. He missed Tai, he missed Hematite, he missed Captain Xander, he even missed Bradford. Right now, he thought he could do with a lot *less* to think about.

For the moment, however, he headed for the kitchen. There was nothing he could do to help his friends directly, but when they woke up, they were likely to be hungry, and it had been far, far too long since Dorian baked his signature ginger plum pie.

Dorian had forgotten how reassuring it could be to lose himself in the rhythm of kneading dough. As his hands moved through the gooey flour, he found he didn't think so much about his fears or worries.

Cloudfire's kitchens were remarkably well-equipped, even better than the manor house in Frostvale. He had everything he could ask for, from big sacks of flour to great wheels of cheese to stasis-preserved fruits and vegetables from all across Cyrna. There were even fresh brown eggs all times of year from the castle chickens, including Henrietta and Mrs. Pennyfeather, who once lived on the *Phoenix*. Dorian wondered if it was one of their eggs he cracked into the ceramic mixing bowl. He'd been fond of the shipboard chickens, and felt oddly guilty for not visiting them enough since they'd come to Cloudfire.

«I am surprised you are not down here in the kitchens more often,» Solaris observed. «You were always off in the galley back on the *Phoenix*.»

Dorian smiled ruefully. In truth, baking was something he and Hematite used to enjoy together. For a time it had seemed too painful. These days, he went flying or to the training grounds if he wanted to let out some stress.

«More practical, that way,» he told Solaris wistfully. «If I'm stronger, I'm better equipped to rescue your kinfolk.»

Solaris responded with a flash of guilt. «I never meant—»

«We've been over this,» Dorian replied, gently but firmly. «I love training and flying. And gods know I love my life here more than my old life in Frostvale. But I enjoy this, too. With everything that's been going on, it's easy to forget that, sometimes.»

«If nothing else,» the dragon said coyly, «I imagine your fancy new muscles make kneading the dough a lot easier.»

«You're lucky you're not here corporeally, or I'd fling an egg at you.»

«Such wastefulness! And anyway, our training together has made me quite nimble. Difficult to say if you would miss or not.»

Dorian stuck out his tongue and got back to work. He was so deep in concentration that he didn't initially notice someone else entering the kitchens.

"Gah!" Dorian staggered backwards, dropping the mixing bowl and splattering batter across the stone countertop. "L... Lady Dragonmar. Forgive me. You, um, startled me."

"Oh dear," Dragonmar Sylvia said. "That was not my intention. Here, let me help you clean that up."

Sylvia set about with the efficiency of someone well used to spending a lot of time in the kitchens. Dorian raised his eyebrows in mild surprise. Everyone in the Order took part in chore rotations, but he'd always imagined the Dragonmar more at home in some lofty tower, not scrubbing cook pots. Tonight, however, she'd foregone her usual sky blue silks in favor of a practical woolen tunic, with her wavy hair tied back in a matching kerchief. Again, it struck him how familiar she was, and again, he couldn't remember why.

"I'm, um, sorry to be down here so late," he said. "I, um, was just worried about Falgar and Tanis, and I thought baking a pie, it might... I might..."

Sylvia seemed perfectly unperturbed to find one of her drago-nauts in the kitchen in the middle of the night. "I am not Janus Calla-han," she said. "I do not give a spark in the Void who uses my kitchens, so long as you clean up after yourself. And that's never been a particular problem with you. Honestly, I'm surprised not to find you down here more often."

"Solaris said the same thing." Dorian frowned. The Dragonmar had always been cordial to him, but today, she spoke like an old family member. *Who are you, really? Why do I know you?*

"I am sorry I messed up the crust you were making," Sylvia said. "Can I help you with a new one?"

"It's fine, I've still got enough dough left over," he assured her. "But um. If you want to grate the ginger. The root, that is. Not me." He ran an awkward hand through his dark red hair.

"Of course." Sylvia smiled wryly and got to work.

Dorian thought wistfully back to another night baking another pie in the *Phoenix's* cramped but cozy galley. He wondered what Tai was doing right now, if she found what she was looking for in far-off Kasanarae.

"So, um, what are *you* doing in the kitchens in the middle of the night?" Dorian wondered.

"As it happens," Sylvia said, "I, too, enjoy a bit of stress baking." She finished grating the ginger and started removing pits from the plums.

"Gotta be pretty stressful, being the dragonmar," Dorian said.

Sylvia's returning smile was rueful. "You have no idea."

"Just being in charge of Tanis is a lot of work, I can't imagine being responsible for the whole castle." Dorian scratched his neck with his free hand. He hoped he wasn't overstepping.

Sylvia laughed, but not in an unkind way. "Just wait until you have children of your own."

Dorian felt his face burn bright red. "That... that would be quite some time from now." Unbidden, he imagined Tai at his side, teaching a gaggle of red-haired, raven-winged youths how to fly an ornithopter and bake pies like this one. But he pushed the daydream aside. He didn't even know if Tai wanted children one day, much less with *him*.

"Do you have children, Lady Dragonmar?" Dorian realized that, despite living in the castle with her for the better part of a year, he actually knew very little about Dragonmar Sylvia as a person.

Sylvia looked surprised by the question, then thoughtful. "Yes," she said, "But they're quite grown up now."

"Do you talk to them much?" Dorian wondered.

"Now and then." Sylvia gazed wistfully out the leaded glass window. "The thing about parenthood is, you never really stop worrying that you're failing them, even when they're very clearly doing just fine for themselves."

Dorian chuckled and molded the crust dough into the pie pan. "I pretty much feel like I'm failing people all the time, so one more thing to worry about probably wouldn't change much."

Sylvia snorted. "You'd think that, wouldn't you?" She paused a moment before continuing, "Tell me, Dorian. Are you happy here in Cloudfire?"

Dorian stopped short. Was he? It wasn't a question he'd ever considered. "I... um," was the most eloquent thing he could come up with. "I miss the *Phoenix,*" he finally admitted. "I miss Captain Xander and I miss Tai and I miss Hematite."

"The demon?"

"Yes. The demon." He sighed and poured the plum and sugar mix into the pie pan. "He was always kind to me. Not like Tanis's Malachite at all. And Tanis... gods, even after everything, he still went fugue, and I can't help thinking it's all my fault. And Falgar got attacked, and if I had been there, maybe I could have... maybe..." he shook his head. He was certain he sounded pathetic, and surely the Dragonmar didn't want to listen to all this moaning. But once he got going, he found it hard to stop. "It's just a lot, all on top of the constant looming fear that I'll never be good enough, because I never passed the Trials, because..."

"Enough of that, now." Sylvia's voice was firm. "If Jameson is still making you feel that way, he and I have words."

Dorian waved his flour-covered hands to forestall her. "That's... that's not necessary. I mean, it would probably be even worse, if I needed the Dragonmar to come in and fight my battles for me."

"Ah, my dear boy," Sylvia said, and her expression was understanding, maybe even a bit respectful. "Dorian... there is something you should know..."

But before Sylvia could continue, the gold dragon Meridian's mindvoice reverberated across the kitchens.

«Please, you must come to the infirmary at once. Dragonaut Falgar is awake!»

"This," Falgar declared, "Is delicious pie."

"I mean, it's all right," Graigor grumbled. He glared at Dorian as he helped himself to a third slice.

It was about an hour later, and Dorian, Sylvia, and the other dragonauts were all gathered in the infirmary. Ser Vale had brought the completed pie up from the kitchens, and though Dorian didn't consider it his best work, he was glad to have it, if only for something to do with his hands.

Falgar had come through the Healing all right — of course he had. Estevan was an expert at his craft. But Dorian couldn't get over how pale his friend looked. He couldn't stop thinking about how close Falgar had come to dying. And Dorian hadn't been there.

"I... I'm sorry." He couldn't stop repeating it, but nor could he think of anything better to say.

"Enough, enough. Stop apologizing." Falgar shook his head. "I love you, mate. You're one of my best friends, but you need to stop blaming yourself for everything."

"Besides," Sullivan said, "Think of what might have happened to Tanis if he'd gone fugue when you weren't there."

Dorian swallowed. He blamed himself for what happened to Tanis too. But his friends might have a point.

"And how... how is Tanis?" he scraped up the courage to ask. Gods help him, he almost didn't want to know.

Estevan's face was grave. "He will live. However..." the elderly Healer drew in a sharp breath as if preparing for battle.

"What is it?"

Estevan sighed and shook his head. "The Exorcism was unsuccessful, I'm afraid. Their spirit energy was simply too entangled for me to extract the creature without killing the boy, or worse."

Dorian wasn't sure what *or worse* meant, but he also knew now was not the time to ask. "But... but you said he'll live?"

Estevan nodded. "He has a long road of recovery ahead of him, and a long journey towards banishing that demon if he doesn't want this to happen again. But yes. He will live."

Dorian let out a long sigh of relief. "Good... that's good." It would have been better, of course, if Estevan had been able to sever the bond with Malachite, but Dorian would take what he could get. "And... Falgar?" He glanced nervously at his friend.

"I guess Sullivan can no longer claim to be so holier than thou," Graigor said.

"Oh, good one, because I got stabbed full of holes." Falgar pointed both index fingers in Graigor's direction. He turned slightly towards Dorian and Sullivan and made an exaggerated eye roll.

Jameson sniffed. "This is not the time for jokes."

"It's always the time for jokes," Falgar said. "Anyway, I'm *fine*. Between Sullivan and Stevvy here, I've had more Healing magic than I'll ever know what to do with. Void, though, it'd be nice to go on a single date with my boyfriend without being attacked. 'Least it wasn't the bloody city watch this time."

"Meroneth's balls, Fal, that man *stabbed* you," Sullivan said. "I wasn't sure I'd be able to help in time. If I'd finished my Healer's training I might have..."

Falgar sat further upright and patted Sullivan on the arm. "Now you sound like *him*." He winked at Dorian.

Healer Estevan sniffed. "You dragonauts are far too cavalier with your lives. Just because you're more durable than the rest of us doesn't make you invulnerable."

Falgar crossed his arms, then grimaced. "It was that hooded bloke who brought swords into this, not me."

"Hooded bloke?" Dorian's heart sank.

Falgar nodded. "He was dressed just like that arse who attacked us in Silverlake. Might've been the same guy, who knows?"

Dorian's heart sank further. So it really was Dorian's fault, then. If only he'd stopped the attacker the first time!

"How sure are you?" Jameson asked. "If someone's attacking our own, it's crucial we get to the bottom of it."

Falgar shook his head. "Might have been the same guy, and might not have been. I couldn't see his face. He had the whole assassin get-up going on. Black cloak, plus a black mask over his nose and mouth, one of those bird beak get-ups like he was afraid of catching the plague."

If Dorian was chagrined, it was nothing to how Dax looked.

"Those cloaks and masks," Dax said, "Are the uniforms of the Toreenish border guards."

"Bloody town watch," Falgar said. "I bloody knew it."

Dorian frowned. "Aren't they the guys who are supposed to keep demons away from towns? Why would they want to attack dragonauts?"

"They believed you were there with demons, remember," Dax pointed out. "Still, this is not normal behavior for the border guards. I wonder... They obscure their faces to protect themselves from demonic possession. The demons need eye contact to establish a bond, you see. But that also means that nearly anyone could impersonate a border guard, if they wished."

Hildegard nodded gravely. "Do you suppose they work for Emperor Callahan?"

"Could be," Falgar shrugged. "With my charming personality, it's not like I have a whole lot of other enemies."

"There are plenty in town who want to see the Order gone,"

Dax nodded and folded his hands together, expression pensive. "Tell me, Falgar, did your assailant have wings?"

Falgar grimaced. "Couldn't tell under the cloak."

Hildegard, thankfully, was as ever the voice of reason. "Orith or Aerish, it doesn't matter. The important thing is, how do we prevent it happening again?"

Dragonmar Sylvia cleared her throat, her expression uncommonly grave. "This lends evidence to something I've suspected for a long time. Someone on the other side has been far too aware of our movements. I fear there is a traitor among us."

CHAPTER TWENTY-THREE
ONWARD

The knock at the door sent Xander's heart plummeting. Nobody visited the lower city apartment he shared with Bradford, especially not this time of night. If someone was here now, it either meant the city guard had caught onto them at last, or something even worse was afoot.

Xander set down his charcoal, abandoning the sketch he'd been working on, and moved to answer the door.

"Faris." Relief that she was not from the city watch warred with the knowledge that she wouldn't come here unless it was a genuine emergency. "Bad news?"

"I'm afraid so." Faris swept in and sat down without waiting for an invitation. "Rona Hargreaves from the docks has been arrested."

Xander's stomach fell to the floor. "Rona... no, I just spoke to her. She was at the tavern last night." His hand curled into a fist. "Void Eternal. She wasn't even part of the underground yet. What in the Void could she possibly have done to offend the garrison?"

"Evidently messing with the war recruiters," Faris said with a sigh. "She was trying to agitate people out of signing up to be cannon fodder, so of course, they dragged her off to the palace dungeons for 'disturbing the peace.'"

"Void." Xander massaged the back of his neck. "What are they going to do to her? Do we know?"

"That remains to be seen, but it would surprise me if they didn't ship her off to Thlarknia." Faris grimaced. "Reunited with her son in the cruelest way possible. Janus always did like ironic punishment."

Xander shook his head and covered his face in his hand. "Rona's too old to go to the front lines. Void, it's my fault," he said. "First Donovan and that whole catastrophe, and now... If I hadn't been stirring up so much agitation — if I'd warned the fool woman to be more careful—"

"Don't you go blaming yourself," Faris chided him. "Rona's an adult. She knew what she was about."

Xander snorted. "Rona is a dock worker who just wants to make ends meet. Can't say we did her any favors, getting involved in her life."

Faris helped herself to some of Xander's wine, then paused when she saw the sketch on the table. "Is that me?"

Face reddening, Xander yanked the piece of parchment away. "Just a doodle. Helps me think."

"I'm flattered," Faris said. "But Xander, you know I'm a married woman."

Xander massaged his temples. "It's nothing like that." Xander didn't think of Faris that way. In fact, he'd never thought of anyone that way in his life, much to his parents' chagrin. "I just... like to draw people."

"You've got quite the skill," Faris said. "But I hope you don't make it a habit of drawing underground members. If the city garrison finds this, it'll lead them right to us."

"I burn the sketches when I'm done." Feeling defensive, he tossed the unfinished sketch into the hearth. Only a few embers remained of that morning's cookfire, but the paper still blackened around the edges.

Faris snorted. "Something of a pity, I suppose. I love the way you've drawn my hair."

The door swung open again, and Bradford tumbled inside. "Tai's in danger," he announced at once.

"What?" Xander's stomach filled with ice. He had to have heard wrong. *Not Tai.* Briefly, frantically, Bradford relayed what the enemy dragonaut Vivienne had told him. "Void take it. I Never should have let her go on that thrice-cursed fool's errand."

"Vivienne Penregon told you this?" Faris raised her eyebrows.

Bradford had the decency to look abashed. "She recognized me, even through my Illusion. We... knew each other, back in Adenthul."

Faris let out a string of Iriya that, from her tone, Xander guessed was impolite indeed. "She could be on her way with your father's troops at this very moment."

"Vivienne wouldn't do that."

"You're sure about that, are you?" Faris's tone radiated skepticism.

"I... don't know." It sounded like it pained Bradford to admit it. "But Void take it. Why would she lie about something like that?"

Xander stood abruptly. "Enough yammering. I'm going after her."

"Like the Void, you are." Faris put a warning hand on Xander's arm. He angrily snatched it away.

"If you think I'm going to just let Tai rot in the palace dungeons, then think again. She's—" She was what, exactly? His former employee? That felt ludicrously weak. "She's like a daughter to me."

"Let's just use our brains for half a second." Faris dusted her hands on her apron. "Has it occurred to you that one of Callahan's highest ranking officers planting the idea in your head to storm the castle dungeons just *might* be a trap?"

"If she wanted to arrest me, she could have done it then and there." Bradford rumpled his curly brown hair in agitation. "Anyway, she didn't say Tai'd been arrested. She just said we should watch out for her."

"Then, at the very least, we should go look for her," Xander said.

Xander downed the rest of his drink and strode outside into the night. Faris, grumbling, and Bradford, ashen-faced, hurried after him.

It was late enough at night that even in a busy city like Azure, most of the streets were dead and empty. A full moon hung in the summer sky, bathing the city in an eerie silver cast. Despite the warm weather, Xander felt a chill, and wished he'd thought to grab his coat.

They'd just made it to the upper city gates when the sound of wingbeats and a flash of blue aetherlight caused them to stagger to a halt. A dragon shot up into the sky, letting out a panicked cry that pierced the summer night. A few moments later, a formation of gryphon knights took off in the dragon's wake.

Xander's heart sank. the gryphon knights seemed to have come from the upper city, but the dragon...

"Did that dragon take off from *your neighborhood?*" Faris asked, ashen-faced.

"I believe so, yes," Bradford replied gravely.

They sprinted back the direction they came, to find his apartment and the entire city block overflowing like an anthill full of city guards.

"I guess," Bradford said faintly, "It's lucky we weren't there when they arrived."

"Let's go." Faris put a warning hand on his forearm. "You two can stay at my place for now. Whatever happens, you don't want to be found here."

Xander nodded, selfishly mourning the loss of his art supplies and his expensive Narean whiskey. What had a dragon been doing in the lower city to begin with? Was it looking for them? And if so, how in the *Void* were they not in chains already?

Somewhere in the distance, alarm bells clanged out an angry retort. Xander had a sinking feeling that the garrison's activity in the coming weeks would make the aftermath of the aether cache attack seem like a calm day on the crystal fjords of Narea.

After everyone dispersed to give Falgar and Sullivan some privacy, Dorian found Jameson standing in the hallway. He gazed out an arrow-slit window, wearing a pensive expression.

"Are you all right, Flight Leader?" Dorian asked.

Jameson jumped as if aether-stung. He looked for a moment like he wanted to give Dorian one of his signature tellings off, but then he slumped his shoulders and shook his head. "Forgive me, Dragonaut Valmont," he said. "It is nothing."

Dorian frowned. It certainly didn't look like *nothing*, but he knew better than to pry. "Well," he said uncertainly, "If you ever want to talk about it..."

Jameson almost, *almost* smiled. "Have you ever been in charge of anyone, Mr. Valmont?"

"No," Dorian said. And then, kicking himself, he amended, "Yes." Of course he had. "Tanis." *And look how well that turned out.*

"Of course." Jameson shook his head sadly. "Then I suppose you understand better than many, what it is to have someone under your charge endangered on your watch."

Dorian felt like he'd been gut-punched. "Yes."

"I can't help feeling like it's my fault, somehow." Jameson's pale hands curled into fists. "Falgar is one of my men. I should have protected him."

Dorian barked out an ironic little laugh, which he regretted at once. "Sorry," he said. "I didn't mean to... that was insensitive." He let out a long breath. "Just, well, I know a thing or two about blaming myself, too."

Jameson *did* smile this time, and shook his head. "You're really nothing like your father, you know that?"

Dorian's smile turned rueful. "I've been told."

"You fly excellently. I suppose I don't say that enough. I reckon Xander was right, that first night you arrived. You *will* be better than Cyrus one day. If you're not already."

"*Oh.* I, um..." Dorian's flush deepened. Praise from Jameson was so rare, he did not know how to accept it when it came. "You... you knew my father when he was young, didn't you?"

"Yes." Jameson's tone was guarded.

"What... what was he like?"

"He was an arrogant, self-important piece of gryphon dung," Jameson said. "As I said. You are nothing like him."

And just like that, the Flight Leader turned on his heel and departed down the spiral staircase.

The streets of Azure were eerily quiet after curfew. It made Tai's feathers stand on end, thinking that every dark corner hid soldiers and palace guards and a sobered up, angry Kadmin.

The tension followed her until she arrived at the apartment where, last she heard, Bradford and Xander were staying. The building looked intact, not a burnt out husk following the aether cache attack, at least. *Thank Zekador for the small miracles.* But assuming Xander and Bradford were alive and not in prison, how would they react when she showed up in the middle of the night, bringing trouble on her heels?

She pounded on the door. No answer. This late at night, they were probably asleep, if they were here at all. Feeling guilty, she tried again, louder. "Xander? Bradford? It's me."

Nothing.

Hesitantly, she tried the door handle, and was surprised when it swung open without protest.

"Captain Xander? Lord Bradford?"

As far as she could tell, she had no audience but the spiders in the wall cracks. Two beds sat in the corner, neatly made up and unoccupied. A half-finished wine bottle, still open, sat abandoned on the rough wooden table alongside two glasses, one with wine still in it. The hearth still shone with a few dull embers, as well as a partially burnt sketch in what was unmistakably Captain Xander's drawing style, depicting a spiral-horned Iriya woman Tai didn't recognize. All of this bore signs of recent use. But wherever Xander and Braford were, it wasn't here.

Where had they gone off to in the middle of the night?

Tai stepped back into the cool night air, mind racing, trying to figure out what to do.

The sound of wingbeats cut off her thoughts. She spun around, heart racing, searching for the source of the noise.

«Thank Zekador I found you. I am not too late.» Celestian's indigo scales glittered in the lamplight, his silvery eyes shining with fear.

"Celestian!" her voice came out as a terrified squawk. She'd gotten Kadmin good and drunk, but like a Void-cursed fool she'd forgotten all about the dragon. "Don't you feel what your bond feels? Shouldn't you be raucously drunk right now?"

«I feel what the person holding my dragonstone feels,» Celestian corrected her. «At the moment, the human Kadmin Crowley is passed out drunk, but what *I* feel is like I just fled through the streets of Azure in a frantic hurry. So I shall only ask you this once. What do you think you are doing?»

Tai lowered her wings. If Celestian wanted to take the dragonstone by force, she realized there was little she could do to stop him. "Look. I know you think Kadmin's working for the greater good or whatever, but you can't seriously want to remain bonded to him. After... after the aether cache..."

Celestian pawed the ground uncertainly. But then he straightened his serpentine neck, his draconic expression resolved. «I am sorry, but I must have the dragonstone back. If I stray too far from it, there is a strong possibility that I might Unravel.»

"Unravel?"

«Die,» Celestian elaborated. «Permanently.»

"Oh." Tai swallowed. Whatever else may have happened, she didn't want the dragon to *die*.

Celestian breathed out an agitated puff of sparks. «The palace guards will be here any moment. If you give the dragonstone to me, I can buy you some time to run. But if they catch you, there will be little I can do.»

Tai swallowed. Void take it, she was so close! It itched like the spot between her wings she could never quite reach, to have the dragonstone in her hand but be forced to return to Cloudfire empty handed.

"Is there any way I can free you?" she asked.

«You would have to destroy my physical form,» Celestian replied. «However, my Compulsion to defend myself would outweigh anything you might do even with the dragonstone.»

Tai glanced from Celestian's wicked-sharp teeth to his wicked-sharp claws to the wicked-sharp crescent blades on his tail. *Not* a fight she could win with a rusty old athame. *Couldn't have stolen a sword while you were at it, could you?*

Celestian twitched his bladed tail in agitation. «I know you do not approve of Kadmin or the Imperial dragonauts — I do not always either, given what he made me do to that city block — but sometimes we must do things we find distasteful, for the greater good.»

"Burning an entire city block is more than just distasteful," Tai shot back.

To Celestian's credit, he was genuinely distraught, she could feel the emotion emanating off of him in waves. «Yes, I... am aware of that.» He craned his long indigo neck behind him, as if searching for interlopers. Tai was painfully aware of the guards that were likely on their way. If she didn't get out of here soon, it would be too late. «You labor under the assumption that I wanted or asked for any of this. All I am trying to do is to prevent disaster. If you know of any way to fly to the moon and restore the lost magic without all this horrible nonsense, I would love to hear it.»

Tai's heart thudded in her chest, in time with the thrumming of the dragonstone hidden down her tunic. Her mind went back to the Planeshifting spell she'd worked so diligently on back in Cloudfire, and how *close* she'd been to figuring it out.

Celestian's silver draconic eyes lit up. «You *do* know something.»

Tai felt a moment of panic. *He can sense your strongest emotions, fool!* She licked her lips and swallowed. "I... might."

More wingbeats heralded the approach of gryphon-mounted guards. *Void Void Void...* No more time to stand around deliberating.

"Do you trust me?" she asked Celestian.

«As much as I trust any human.» Which was no answer at all.

"Come with me. Then we can find out together whether or not the Order knows a better way."

Celestian turned his long purple-blue neck towards the approaching guards, knowing they were out of time. Finally, after a heartbeat that seemed to last forever, he nodded. «Very well.»

Tai wasted no time. She vaulted onto Celestian's back, and the two of them took off into the summer night. Despite everything, it felt good to be airborne again. But she had little time to enjoy it, because the gryphons were hot on their heels.

Tai took a deep breath and tried to find her center. This would work. This *had* to work. "I'm going to borrow some of your magical energy. Is that okay?"

After a barest moment's hesitation, Celestian nodded. «Do it.»

Tai closed her eyes tight and searched for calm. She would have loved another moon or two to study and perfect the spell, but she didn't have it. She probably didn't even have a minute.

Tai traced sigils into the air, clearly and confidently. Magic, Tai had learned during her long years in the sky, was not just about sigils and symbols. Those were useful tools. But what really mattered with magic was understanding the energy and the way it flowed. She could, after years of working with skyships and Linkings, see the way the power moved through the circle.

The magic flowed beyond the circle, beyond Tai's direct control, taking on a life of its own. The power streamed through her, from the natural environment, from the aether stone on her athame, and from Celestian. Even Tai's own life energy flowed outward into the swirling vortex of energy. Tai let it. This was her Void-cursed fool plan, let her be the one to deal with the consequences She desperately clung to Celestian's neck ridges as her life force drained away, like she'd seen the demon Malachite do to Tanis back in Everwood all those moons ago.

Tanis... Mother and Roan... Home. For a wild moment, she wished she'd had a chance to see her family one more time before taking off on this wild misadventure. Then, the world seemed to fold in upon itself. Tai was up-side-down and in-side-out, her senses blasting a bizarre array of sound and color that her brain couldn't even begin to process.

The last thing she remembered before blacking out was Celestian, frantic and terrified, crying «What have you done?» before the world dissolved into nothingness.

CHAPTER TWENTY-FOUR
NEW BEGINNINGS

THREE YEARS AGO

Tai clutched her rucksack close to her chest. It contained her few possessions, the last remnants of the pointless misadventure that was the past five years of her life.

Should've just taken Brielle's Void-cursed pay-out when I was thirteen, she thought ruefully. Then at least she'd have gold. Now she was stuck, destitute and heartbroken, in a foreign country with no ship, no job, no boyfriend, and nothing to show for all the blood and sweat and tears of the past five years.

Gods above. Her brother Tanis would be so smug when she showed up on their doorstep. He'd be, what, thirteen now? Almost fourteen? Older than Tai had been when she left. *Sweet Ancients.*

Despite everything, she missed her family. Tai knew it was probably for the best, going home. But no matter how she turned it over in her head, she felt like a failure. She'd promised she wouldn't come home until she was successful, and she was far from that. But what choice did she have?

"Tai? Tai Lunstrum?"

Tai froze in surprise at the sound of her name. For a wild moment, she thought perhaps it was Kadmin. But no, of course it wouldn't be. She hadn't heard a word from Kadmin since that day in the fountain square, not that she cared. The sooner she could forget that Kadmin ever existed, the happier she'd be.

But to her embarrassment, she finally remembered that Kadmin was not her only acquaintance in Kasanarae. Zachary Falgar shouted and waved, elbowing through the crowd to reach her.

"Falgar!" She embraced her old friend, feeling an odd combination of happiness and regret. She'd been so wrapped up in self-pity and desperation to make Kadmin love her that she'd hardly spoken to Falgar at all since he started at the Academy. Some friend she was. "I... should have come by to visit," she said, slightly awkwardly.

"Never mind about that." Falgar waved her off. "What brings you to the docks?"

Tai sighed and lowered her wings. "I'm going home. To Toreen."

"What, like for a visit?"

"Forever."

Falgar wrinkled his nose. "Why in the Void would you go and do something like that?"

Tai let out a weak chuckle. "Believe it or not, Fal, some people *want* to live near where they grew up."

"Yeah," Falgar retorted, "But I never got the impression *you* did."

Falgar was right, of course. The thought of returning home with nothing to show for it made a leaden lump in her stomach. But there was no sense staying here, either. "I don't know if you heard, but Kadmin and I, erm, ended things." She felt another wriggling guilty sensation as she remembered that she'd never *actually* broken up with him. But after nearly a moon without either one of them making contact, she thought it was safe to say that the relationship was over.

Falgar's expression darkened at the sound of Kadmin's name. "I hadn't heard that," he said, "But it doesn't surprise me. Have you booked a berth already?"

"Not yet," Tai admitted with a grimace. In truth she didn't expect there to be many ships bound for Cloudfire that would grant her passage for the paltry amount of coin she had left. Perhaps someone would let her swab decks or do other chores in order to make up the difference. They may not want her as a proper aeronaut, but surely nobody would complain about cheap labor. "But enough about me," she deflected, laughing weakly. "What about you? How's the Academy?"

Falgar shifted in obvious discomfort. For the first time, she noticed he was wearing brown trousers and a plain linen shirt, not the blue-gray Academy uniform Kadmin always wore. "Yeah. About that..."

"Don't tell me you're giving up, too?"

Falgar grimaced. "Didn't have much of a choice in the matter, if we're honest. Thing is, the commandant at the Academy never liked me. There was this whole misunderstanding about his daughter..."

"*Misunderstanding*, eh?"

"It wasn't my fault!" Falgar waved his hands. "She seduced me! Granted, she didn't have to try very hard... but, ah, the point is, the Commandant was already *primed to dislike me,* as it were. So when exams came around and Kadmin Crowley and I ended up getting identical answers in rune theory, who in the Void do you think the Commandant was going to believe?"

Tai raised her eyebrows. "I'm guessing you *didn't* cheat off of Kadmin's exam?"

"Of course I didn't! I may be foolish, but not that Void-cursed foolish."

"I knew it." Tai couldn't keep the venom out of her voice. "He probably copied off of you because he was out drinking with that Kasani girl instead of studying." She ruffled her feathers. "Which, by the way, you could have told me about her, instead of letting me fawn after Kadmin like some kind of moon-blind idiot." She sighed and shook her head. Falgar was not the object of her ire. "Sorry, sorry. That was uncalled for."

Falgar ran his hand through his sandy curls. "Nah, I probably should've thought to reach out. I'm, er, sorry to be the one to tell you this, but that man *always* had some new Kasani girl or another on his arm."

"Of *course* he did."

Falgar raised his hands helplessly. "I thought you two were broken up already! Kadmin didn't want a fart in the underclouds to do with me once he got his cooler, richer friends. I'd assumed it was the same with you. I... should have checked in with you. And for that, I'm sorry."

Tai shook her head. She hadn't been a spectacular friend this past year, either. "So you got expelled for cheating even though Kadmin was the one who cheated off of you."

"Got it in one," Falgar said.

"What a rat bastard."

"On that we can agree." Falgar chortled. "Anyway, it ain't all bad. Got a cushy job on a small cargo ship that used to be some rich lady's pleasure cruiser, if you can believe it. And the captain's a right fair gentleman, not grasping for position all the time like Brielle. There's only one other crew member besides the captain and me, which means there's always a ton of work to do, but my crew mate's got a really nice arse, which might make me forget all about the commandant's daughter."

"Falgar!" Tai smiled and shook her head. "Well, I'm glad you found something, at least." *At least one of us did.*

Now it was Falgar's turn to shake his head. "I just don't like the idea of you slinking off home with your tail between your legs."

"I'm Orith, not Iriya. We're the ones with wings, they're the ones with tails."

"It's just an expression. But hey, why not come work with us? Ol' Tight Pants may be nice to look at, but he's kind of an uptight prig, so gods know I could use more than just him for company. And I know the Capain's still hiring."

Tai blinked. "Your captain would hire an Orith?"

"I mean, he's not exactly picky. He hired me." Falgar winked.

"Not exactly reassuring," Tai said, but she still agreed to meet Captain Xander of the *Phoenix*.

Xander was, understandably, skeptical at first, but once she showed her knowledge of aether engines and skyship maintenance, he was eager to have her on board.

And so Tai became as an aeronaut once again.

This time she promised not to make the same mistakes as she had on the *Winds of Fortune*.

First, she was going to dedicate herself wholeheartedly to her work, not just in skyship maintenance and flying in the Linking, but learning the ins and outs of running a trade business as well. If she ever again found herself in charge of her own ship, she wanted to be prepared.

Second, she vowed that she would never, ever again develop personal feelings for a crew member. That way led to nothing but pain.

She almost kept her promise to herself. For two long years, she kept it. She kept everyone at arm's length, even Falgar. And while they might not be a happy crew, they were a functional one. Until one bright day just at the end of winter, when a bumbling, awkward, copper-haired young Aerishman stumbled on board and changed their lives forever.

CHAPTER TWENTY-FIVE
AWAKENING

PRESENT DAY

The first thing that Tai thought when she woke was that she, not Kadmin, had too much to drink. *Void Eternal.* This was the mother of all hangovers.

Her second addled thought was that this was not the candidate's barracks in the Fountain Palace, nor was it her chambers in Cloudfire castle, nor her old cabin on the skyship *Phoenix*. For a wild, bizarre moment she thought she was back home in Everwood, but no, that wasn't right either. She was in an unfamiliar bed, gazing up at an unfamiliar ceiling.

Her head felt run through with a pickaxe, but through her muddled thoughts she surmised she must be in Toreen. This unfamiliar chamber had the same rounded wattle and daub walls as her childhood home, and she thought she smelled fish and mushroom soup. There was nothing as quintessentially Toreenish as fish and mushroom soup.

So, she was in some strange house in Toreen. How did she get there? Like grasping at ephemeral sparks, her memories returned in

fits and starts. Kadmin, the dragonstone, Planeshifting, Celestian...
Oh, sweet Savior's wings! Celestian!

Frantically, Tai reached for the dragonstone. It was gone. At some point, someone evidently changed her out of her clothes and into a simple linen nightgown. But *where was the dragonstone*? She scrambled off the mattress to look for it, but the room spun nauseatingly, and she had to cling to the nightstand for purchase.

"Oh, good, you're awake!" A masculine voice, familiar though she couldn't quite place it, preceded a broad-shouldered young Orith man entering through the beaded curtain. He carried a fragrant bowl of soup, which he set gently down on the end table.

For a wild moment, she almost thought it was Dorian, but no, that wasn't right. This stranger looked nothing like her friend. He was Orith, for one, with wings of black and brown. Well. One wing. Brown striped feathers covered half his back, while the other side held only a severed stump.

Tai felt a surge of pity for the stranger. She knew more than most what it was like to be an Orith who couldn't fly. The one-winged man had a broad, open face and a friendly smile, though his hazel-brown eyes shone with concern. "You shouldn't be walking around just yet. You went through quite an ordeal. You'll need time to recover."

"My—" Tai began. She grasped at her chest where the dragonstone had once rested.

"Ah, right, the necklace," the stranger said. "It's right over here, with the rest of your clothes."

"You took my clothes?" Tai couldn't quite hide the accusatory tone. She didn't even know this person.

The stranger at least had the decency to look abashed. "I didn't, no, of course not. It was the Lady Mayor who did that. Ah, Fallen, I've got to report to the Council." He winced apologetically. "The mayor will want to know right away that you're awake."

"I know you," Tai said. She wished her head wasn't so Void-cursed fuzzy.

The one-winged man smiled. "We grew up in Everwood together."

"Jace!" she blurted, remembering at last. Jace, from her hometown, for whom she'd once nursed a secret crush. She felt her face redden as she remembered foolishly asking him to dance at the Autumn festival when she was thirteen. Ancients, but she hoped he didn't remember that. "You're Jace Farnham. But what—"

She cut off abruptly, looking anywhere but at the stump where his wing used to be. It would be rude to pry, and for once, she avoided blurting the first thing that came to mind. *For once.*

Jace, however, seemed to know full well what she'd been about to say. "The wing?" He shook his head sadly. "Possession sickness, I'm afraid. A lot of us in Everwood got it after we started taking on demons. My wing started rotting, and they had to remove it before the rot spread to the rest of me. Then I had to get rid of the demon before the rot started up again somewhere else."

"Depths," Tai said, "I'm so sorry."

"All's well that ends well, I suppose," he said, and she couldn't quite decide if his smile looked forced or not. "Here in Lost Hollow, I fit right in."

"Fit right in?" Having grown up as a flightless Orith, she found that hard to believe.

"I must go fetch the mayor. You should eat your soup before it gets cold. You need to get your strength back."

"All right," she said, frowning. "I guess... I'm still not sure what happened to me."

"I found you when I was out on patrol. I'm a border guard here in the town, you see," Jace explained. Tai wondered how it was that someone with one wing was allowed to be a border guard, but she decided it was best to keep her mouth shut for now. "You were just laying there outside the town walls, unconscious, curled around a dragon, of all things. Of course I had to go straight to the High Councilor for help. He wanted to take you in himself, but, well, the mayor insisted I bring you here instead."

"The mayor and the High Councilor..." what did such important people want with her? Then again she supposed it wasn't every day a dragon came crashing into town.

"Celestian..." she forced the name out through the icepick sensation in her head.

"The dragon's all right, as far as we can tell," Jace picked up the dragonstone and handed it to her. "You and the dragon can catch up while I go fetch the mayor."

"Oh... okay." Tai had about a thousand more questions, but before she could formulate a full sentence, Jace was gone.

Tai let out a long sigh and draped the dragonstone around her neck. She was sure Celestian would be furious with her.

«Celestian?» She quested out nervously.

«Good, you are awake. For a time I feared you would get yourself killed with that fool stunt.»

Tai winced. «I'm sorry I got you involved in this.»

Celestian's prickliness subsided. «I know.» Tai could see in her mind's eye the way he moved his whipcord tail back and forth. «How much do you remember?»

She rummaged through the fragments of that hectic night. «I cast the Planeshifting spell. Or, at least I tried to. I wanted... wanted to prove we could Planeshift to the moon.» She let out a bitter laugh. «You can see how well that worked. I was aiming for Cloudfire. I don't know where I am, but this isn't Cloudfire.»

«You were asleep for the better part of a week.» Celestian's mindvoice radiated genuine concern.

"A *week*." Tai felt cold. "I... Didn't realize the spell was going to do that. And it didn't even work."

«You drained your own spirit energy to spare me draining mine,» Celestian said, with what might have been the vaguest hint of gratitude. «The result, I think, was not unlike a demonic fugue. You will feel fatigued for a time, and will need to work to regain your strength.»

Tai once again sat upright, and once collapsed back down, head pounding.

"A hangover with no booze, and a fugue with no demon," she grumbled. "Isn't that just the way of it?"

«There is some silver lining,» Celestian said. «Since you do not have a demon draining off of you, your spirit energy will recover all the more quickly.»

"Thank Zekador for the small miracles." She ate another spoonful of soup. "So, if I was unconscious, why are you still here? Why didn't you take the dragonstone and go back to Kadmin?"

The burst of emotion she felt from Celestian made it clear he was affronted. «I did not intend to simply abandon you to die.»

Tai felt unexpectedly warm. "Oh. Well... thank you."

«However, once you are recovered, I suppose it is... best that I return to Kasanarae. Planeshifting is... clearly not the solution either of us had hoped for. It is best we... return to the original plan.» In her mind's eye she saw him twitch his tail back and forth, and she could tell even he wasn't sure what he really wanted.

Tai slumped back against the headboard. "We could always try again," she said weakly, but she and Celestian both knew she'd do no such thing in her current state. *Void take it.* She was going to have to make it a priority to figure out how to free Celestian, or else she really would have to send him, and the dragonstone, back to the enemy. She was no better than Kadmin if she kept him here against his will.

«There is no need to make any major decisions until you have recovered,» Celestian reassured her.

"I guess I understand why I passed out." Tai massaged her temples. "But why here? Why didn't we end up in Cloudfire like we were supposed to?"

«I am no expert,» Celestian said, «But I believe it has something to do with what you were thinking about at the moment you made the transition."

"I was thinking about Cloudfire," Tai said. "The spell said to visualize the destination."

«Perhaps,» Celestian said, «But were you thinking about it hard enough?.»

Tai's wings twitched as she fought the urge to be defensive. "I was distracted trying to get away from those guards." She thought back, trying to remember. "I was thinking... I was thinking..."

The bead curtains rustled, signaling Jace's return. And this time, he was not alone.

"Tai," breathed his companion.

The implications of everything that had happened hit her like the winds of a Voidstorm.

"Mother." Ancients help her, she'd been thinking about her mother. And now her mother was here.

In some ways, Reora Lunstrum had changed little since Tai had last seen her more than a Cycle ago. Still that thin, severe face, the sharp brown eyes, the graying black hair tied up in a rigid bun. But the lavishly embroidered robes of the Mayoral Office were new, as, unfortunately, were the emaciated stumps where her wings used to be. *Both* of her wings. Had she suffered from possession sickness too, like Jace? Or was this an artifact of the fugue that had nearly claimed her life?

"Thank the Savior you're awake," Reora said. "I feared you were dead."

There were many things Tai could have said upon seeing her mother for the first time in eight years. Profound things, emotional things, intelligent things. But what came out of her mouth was, "What are you doing here?" Followed, rather plaintively, by, "And where exactly is *here*?"

Reora, thankfully, seemed to take Tai's confusion in stride. "This is Lost Hollow," she said. "A haven for flightless Orith. Welcome home."

CHAPTER TWENTY-SIX
CRIME AND PUNISHMENT

«You are certainly in a mood today,» the dragon Meridian commented as Falgar angrily dismounted and tore off his flight goggles.

"Thrice cursed right I am," Falgar spat. Then, feeling guilty, he ran a placating hand down her golden-scaled neck. "None of it is your fault, though, and I shouldn't take it out on you."

«Flight Leader Jameson means well,» Meridian provided, but Falgar just shook his head.

"It's not bloody Jameson I'm upset with," Falgar said. Then, with the slightest hint of a smirk, he added, "Though the man is an uptight prick, I won't deny it."

Jameson wasn't so bad once you got to know him. He loved his bureaucracy and his rules, but he truly believed in the Order and what they stood for, and wanted to see Cyrna's magic restored. That he thought the only way to accomplish that was to have no fun ever again — well, they could work on that.

No. The problem was Graigor Bloody Beckett, and if things kept continuing the way they were, Falgar feared there'd be another stabbing on their hands and he, Falgar, would be the perpetrator.

Falgar didn't know what the man's bloody *problem* was. Falgar had tried reaching out to him, tried going to the tavern with him, tried extra training sessions with him, tried discussing dragons, which was the only thing they really had in common. He'd been so certain that if he and Graigor could find *some* commonality, then the rest of the team would follow. But the stubborn arse of a man rebuffed him at every turn. It was like he *wanted* to keep the dragonauts in discord.

Every time Falgar dared hope he and the rest of the dragonauts would come together as a team, Graigor Beckett would charge in like a dragon-riding wrecking ball and within minutes they'd all be back to bickering. It was as if the Flight had a wound, and Graigor's sole purpose was to pick at it.

Therefore, it was with great disappointment that he arrived at the communal baths and found them already occupied by the person he least wanted to see. He'd all but given up on friendship; now seeing him always meant trouble.

"Graigor." Falgar wondered if he should just go use the bath in his private quarters, even though it was all the way upstairs.

"Don't worry, I was just leaving." Graigor wrapped a towel around his stocky midsection. They'd just gotten out of training, so he couldn't have been in there more than a few minutes. "Don't need a thrice-cursed Valgrenite ogling me, thanks."

Falgar thought he might actually see his own brain from rolling his eyes too hard. "Believe me, if you and I were the last two people on Cyrna, I still would not ogle you."

"Hmph," Graigor replied eloquently as he set about putting his trousers back on.

And yet, Falgar thought uncomfortably, *There but by the grace of Sullivan's friendship go I*. Falgar sank luxuriously into the steamy aether-heated bath and recalled a fateful afternoon in arse-nowhere Thlarknia. Sullivan had accused Falgar of being a bully, and gods help him, he had been right. But Falgar had come around eventually, hadn't he? Why, oh why, did Graigor refuse to do the same?

«Perhaps,» Meridian interjected, «Because no one has treated him to the brutal honesty that you were afforded.»

Falgar grimaced. «Oh, yeah. Go around insulting my peers when we're supposed to be learning to get along. I'm sure that'll go well.»

"Been doing some thinking," Graigor said conversationally as he pulled his too-tight tunic over his head. Graigor seemed to think that wearing tight clothes showed off his muscular physique when, in reality, it made him look like an overstuffed sausage. But Falgar would not tell him that because he, unlike Graigor, was capable of tact. Most of the time. *See? Personal growth.*

"Thinking? That's new."

Oops. Maybe not that *much tact.*

"That guy who attacked you seemed to know a lot about your movements, where you were trying to go."

"Going to a tavern on the weekend!" Falgar covered his mouth in horror. "What a weird, unpredictable move! Never know what I'll do next."

Graigor rolled his eyes. "I reckon the traitor probably tipped them off. If, of course, the attacker wasn't the traitor himself."

Falgar sank deeper into the sudsy water. If only he were a fish, then he wouldn't have to listen to Graigor's prattle. Graigor had been on about the alleged traitor ever since Falgar got out of the infirmary, but so far, nobody had come up with the faintest shred of evidence. "You know, Graigor, the way you keep obsessing over this thrice cursed traitor makes me think maybe you protest too much."

Falgar didn't actually think Graigor was the traitor. An arse, yes. But a traitor? Well, frankly, Falgar doubted he had the brains to pull it off.

"I notice Valmont skulking about a lot," Graigor said. "I think he might report to Callahan."

Falgar fixed Graigor with a flat stare. "Valmont. Reporting to Callahan. Come on now."

"Well, why not? Callahan raised him, didn't he? I know Lady

Sylvia likes to fawn over the useless bastard, but that's just the perfect cover, isn't it?"

"Use your brain for half a second. You've known Dorian longer than I have. Do you really think he's capable of that kind of deception?"

Graigor chortled. "Probably not. He hasn't got a duplicitous bone in his soft body. But I think you've got a blind spot where your little boyfriends are concerned. Let's not pretend for a second that you and that boy toy of yours would have won the Trials if you didn't work for the Dragonmar's brother. The Dragonmar rigged the whole thing from the start."

"Oh, shove off," Falgar said. *Oops. That* wasn't tactful. But really. *Boy toy? Really?* "You passed the Trials too in case you forgot. Does that mean Lady Sylvia rigged it in your favor, too?"

"Nah, I got in on sheer talent."

Falgar sank further into the bathwater, running the soap through his sandy curls. "Of *course* you did."

Graigor smirked. "Sylvia rigged the trials in favor of Xander's merry band of little bitches. Your bird-brained Orith friend would've gotten a dragonstone too, except, ah, *someone* sabotaged her ornithopter right at the last minute."

Falgar's eyes narrowed. "Zekador's poorly fitting pants. You sabotaged Tai's ornithopter. You cheated to beat her in the Trials!"

Graigor snorted. "If I had, I wouldn't bloody well admit it, would I? Anyway, I didn't cheat. I just got lucky that *someone* prevented your chicken bitch little *friend* from cheating." He folded his muscular arms, his face radiating smugness.

"Ugh, that is *it.*" *Tact* could go straight to the *Void.*

He climbed out of the bathtub, not caring that he was naked and dripping wet and covered in soap, and he punched Graigor hard in the face. Graigor's nose made a satisfying crunch.

"Aaaagh, what in the Void, man?" Graigor held his hand up to his bleeding nose.

"I'd go see Healer Estevan if I were you."

"You assaulted me! You thrice cursed stupid Valgrenite, you assaulted me, naked, in the baths! You're going to pay for this!" Graigor stormed out, still clutching his nose.

Falgar took a deep breath and let it out, unfolding the fresh tunic he'd set aside. He would, no doubt, indeed pay for this. Graigor was going to raise the unholy Void, and Falgar would face consequences. But at the moment, he couldn't prevent a wicked grin from sliding across his face.

Meroneth's balls, but he'd enjoyed that.

Despite everything, things seemed to go well for the Kasani underground in the weeks following Tai and Celestian's disappearance. Janus Callahan tried to keep the incident hushed up, of course, but but no one could stop the rumor mill. Day to day, Xander's mood varied wildly from proud of his former employee to terrified for her safety.

Xander had been afraid that the incident would only tighten the viselike grip the garrison had on the city, but to his great relief, it seemed to have the opposite effect. With only one dragonaut left, Callahan's forces were simply spread too thin to fully enforce his reign of terror.

Not that the underground had done much to take advantage of it, at least not yet. Grand sweeping gestures like blowing up the aether cache had already proven to do more harm than good. But that didn't mean Xander and his friends were twiddling their proverbial thumbs. They just became more *strategic* in choosing their targets.

The underground's current focus was the *Imperial Javelin,* a massive warship still under construction at Azure's main sky docks. This was the ship that was supposed to bring Callahan ultimate victory in Thlarknia, and probably conquer Pazarae and Narea while he was at it.

With construction nearly completed, Callahan announced a grand dedication ceremony with music and fireworks and free-flowing wine. Xander almost had to hand it to his former friend. Everyone loved a party. But Xander had no intention of enjoying the festivities.

After the attack on the aether cache and the disappearance of one of his dragons, Callahan desperately needed a show of strength, and the *Imperial Javelin* was it. So, of course, it became the underground's responsibility to make sure the dedication was a complete fiasco.

It was just little things, at first. Things Callahan's men would chalk up to incompetence rather than malice. A broken plank here, a missing crate there. Poor Dockmaster Regnald was tearing out his remaining hair over it, but if he suspected Xander or his allies, he kept it to himself.

Bradford, meanwhile, put his charm and charisma to excellent use. Before long, the city's anti-Callahan sentiment reached fever pitch. All it took was one jovial comment that the *Imperial Javelin* referred to parts of Callahan's anatomy he found lacking, and soon the dock workers would speak of little else. Xander didn't particularly want to think about Callahan's anatomy, but even he found it slightly amusing.

Tonight, though, they were done with petty pranks. Tonight, he would finally get to take real action.

"You don't have to go, you know," Faris told him as they scrubbed skypuffer droppings off the landing docks. "Let the team handle it. They're more than capable enough."

Xander grunted and shoved his mop into the bucket of sudsy water with perhaps more force than was necessary. "I'm going, and that's that. I stayed behind when Donovan attacked the aether cache, and look how that turned out."

"You remained free to fight another day."

Xander shook his head. "If I'd been there, I might have turned the tide. Aldric is loyal, but he's reckless, and Martel and Stokes are too green to know their arses from their elbows. I don't want it on my conscience if they get arrested."

"Then send someone else you trust," Faris said. "Me, for instance."

"And let you get arrested like Rona and Donovan? No, thank you. I have few enough friends left in this Void-forsaken city. Besides, you've your kids to think of."

"Just because I reproduced doesn't mean I need to be placed in a glass jar." But Faris's shoulders slumped, and he knew he had won. "Just answer me this, Xander. When was the last time you had a day off?"

Xander grunted noncommittally.

"It's unhealthy to never relax, you know."

Perhaps that was true for most people, but it had never felt that way to Xander. Relaxing meant helplessness, it meant being bereft of anything but his fears and his anxieties and his whiskey bottle. Xander didn't want to bloody relax. Not while Rona and Donovan still rotted in prison. Not when Sylvia and Dorian and Tai were gods-knew-where, doing gods-knew-what. Not when there was so much work to be done.

"I can relax when I'm dead," Xander said, and he hoped he wasn't unconsciously summoning that day to come sooner.

And so, despite Faris's protests, Xander found himself several hours later outside Lady Philhelmina Taggart's townhouse, his hooded woolen frock coat the only armor against the evening chill.

Aldric was already waiting outside, towering over the two recruits he'd brought along like a lord holding court. "The thing we're looking for is brass and spherical, about the size of a grapefruit."

"Do we have any idea what it does?" asked Stokes, who Xander had the impression was well-meaning but not too bright.

"Not a fart in the underclouds," Aldric said. "But Lady Taggart's as puffed up as a parade gryphon ready to show this thing off at the ceremony, so when it goes missing, she looks a fool in front of the Emperor, and the Emperor looks a fool in front of the city. A win for us."

"And who knows," Xander put in, stepping out of the shadows. "Perhaps the artifact may be of some use to the underground as well."

Aldric fixed Xander with a withering stare. The pinch-faced young rebel had never quite warmed up to Xander the way the others had, and Xander didn't have to be a Kassorian telepath to guess what he was thinking. This was not the Order, and unless they could be turned against the Emperor, the Kasani underground had little use for Ancient artifacts.

"Good of you to join us," Aldric said with barely concealed sarcasm. "Though the three of us could have handled this ourselves."

Stokes and the other recruit, Martel, shuffled uncomfortably. Clearly, they didn't share Alrdric's confidence.

"I've already had the lecture from Faris," Xander said. "Are we going to do this or not?"

"Yes, it would be a pity to miss out on the fun," said a too-familiar voice.

Xander's heart sank to his boots. "Brand," he said, remembering just in time to use the lad's fake name. "What in the Void are you doing here?"

"Don't be a hypocrite, Uncle," Bradford said. "If you insist on participating, then you can hardly stop me from doing the same."

Xander could think of no reasonable response to this, so he settled for a disgruntled "Hmph."

"Let's just get this over with before Lord and Lady Taggart return from the theater," Aldric said.

The townhouse was almost trivial to break into. Stokes might not have the common sense the gods gave a skypuffer, but his lock picking skills were unparalleled.

"Impressive," Xander said, and he swore the lad's ears turned pink from the unexpected praise. Xander thought of Dorian, who'd joined his crew unskilled but diligent, and he resolved to be more patient with Stokes from now on.

They crept up the manor house staircase, keenly aware of every creaking floorboard. Perhaps Faris was right, he thought, too late. Perhaps this mission would have been a lot easier with fewer of them there.

Still, they were here, so they made their way into Lady Taggart's study, summoning an aetherlight to illuminate the fine wood paneling in eerie blue.

"She wouldn't just leave it lying around," Bradford mused. "It's going to have to be — ah!" He turned excitedly towards a fancy-looking lockbox bedecked with Azure Lake mother-of-pearl filigree.

"You sure that's not just where she keeps her extra coin?" Aldric looked at it dubiously.

"It's worth checking out. Stokes, can you work your magic?"

"Not magic, Mr. Weatherbee, just nimble hands." He waggled his fingers.

Stokes fiddled with the chest lock for quite awhile longer than he had with the outside door. An encouraging sign, Xander thought. If the lockbox was that much more secure than the townhouse itself, then what was inside must be valuable indeed. But the longer Stokes worked, the more worried Xander became. Any moment, one of the servants might awaken, or worse, the Taggarts might return from the theater, and then the game would well and truly be up.

"A ha!" Xander flinched at Stokes's too-loud expression of triumph.

A moment later, he opened the chest, revealing the object inside.

"Well I'll be a wingless gryphon," Xander said. "Brand, turns out you were right after all."

Xander reached into the box and retrieved the artifact. It reminded Xander of the cloaking device Hildegard once made for the *Phoenix*. It was spherical and brass, with several rune-engraved rings surrounding it. But these runes were nothing like the ones on the cloaking sphere, and most likely served a vastly different purpose.

Idly, Xander turned one of the bands in a random direction. Nothing happened, of course, but if he just clicked it *there, there, and...*

"What the—"

He staggered backwards in surprise as the entire room lit up with light and color.

"Oh, good, because that's subtle," Aldric complained.

"It's beautiful." Martel sounded awed.

And it was. Motes of light danced around them, pearlescent ribbons of color sparkling in the otherwise dark room. Floating land-masses hovered amidst the whorls and eddies of light, easily recognizable as smaller versions of Kasanarae, the Westlands, and the Northern Reaches.

"It's an Illusion," Bradford said, awed. "I've never seen one that sophisticated, not even the Dragonmar's."

"It's not just an Illusion," Xander said. "It's a map. Look." Far away in the projection, the whorls of magic coalesced and formed the Voidstorm that was predicted to ravage the Sanorian coast at this very moment. The strands of magic represented actual magical currents in the sky. "By the gods, any skyship captain who owned this would be a rich man. Surely Taggart doesn't know what he has, or she'd be using it already."

"We've got to bring it back to the Order," Bradford said eagerly.

"Now wait just a second," Aldric cut in. "You can't just unilaterally decide what to do with it."

"Thought you didn't care about artifacts." Xander tried and failed to hide his smugness.

"At least turn it off." Martel looked frantic. "If a servant stops by and sees the bloody light show..."

"I wouldn't worry about that." Xander froze. He knew that voice, and it was decidedly *not* one he wanted to hear right now. "They already know you're here."

With a feeling like ice settling in his stomach, Xander turned off the device. He blinked several times as his eyes adjusted to the comparative darkness. It was easy enough to make out the figure in the doorway, however.

"Faris." Xander sighed. "What are you doing?"

"I told you to stay home. I warned you not to come here tonight." Faris wore a pained expression. She looked like she'd rather be anywhere else on Cyrna. "I'm sorry, Xander. That rat bastard Kadmin Crowley took my children. I have to do what he says or else..." Her voice caught, leaving the rest of the grisly sentence to Xander's imagination.

"But how did they even find you?" They'd been so careful, Faris most of all. Xander's brain simply refused to accept what he was seeing.

"I didn't want it to have to come to this, Alexander Kane." Another feminine voice, this one unfamiliar, though Bradford tensed up at once in recognition. "But you really need to have more care with what you leave lying around."

A moment later, the sound of armored footsteps greeted them. Fully a dozen armed and armored garrison guards strode in, led by none other than the dragonaut Vivienne Penregon herself. And in Vivienne's hands, she held a dreadfully familiar bit of partially-burnt yellowed paper, depicting a sketch of Faris Saunderlain, who bore an expression far more serene than the pained and conflicted one worn by the real Faris who stood before them.

"Well," Xander said. "Void on a stick."

Heart sinking, Xander slowly set down the map device, and raised his hands in the air. There was no fighting off this many soldiers.

Bradford gazed at Vivienne, hopefully, desperately. "Viv—"

"That's Duchess Penregon to you, Bradford." Vivienne's voice was hard as iron, and Bradford's face fell.

"Bradford?" Stokes's eyes were wide. "I thought his name was Brand."

Aldric's mouth narrowed into a shrewd expression. "Wasn't the Emperor's estranged son named something like that? Never noticed it before, but our boy Brand sure looks like that fellow from the wanted posters."

Martel looked both scared and impressed. "Brand was the traitor prince?" He turned to Lady Vivienne, puffing out his chest slightly, as if this new piece of information might somehow grant him clemency. "You've caught the traitor prince."

Vivienne let out a long sigh. "We have, indeed, caught the traitor prince." To Bradford, she said, "What in the Void are you doing here, Bradford? You should've left town when you had the chance. I can't just let this one go. Breaking into a noblewoman's house? Causing a disturbance in the company of known members of the underground? No. I'm sorry, Brad. All of you. It seems I have no choice but to arrest you."

The dragonauts of Cloudfire stood at attention at the crack of dawn as the Dragonmar paced back and forth inspecting them like prize gryphons. From the look in her sharp blue eyes, Dorian could tell that she didn't like what she saw.

"You have been working together for more than half a year now. During that time, I had hoped that you *might* come together as a team."

Dorian swallowed. It wasn't as if they'd made *zero* improvements these past moons. Surely they deserved some credit. Training sessions almost never devolved into shouting matches anymore. That had to count for something, right?

"Fighting," Sylvia said. "In the washroom."

Dorian looked warily at the others. Most wore expressions of puzzlement, except for Falgar, who looked abashed, and Graigor, who looked defiant. *Well, Void.*

Sylvia continued. "All these moons later, and you still bicker like children. There is no time for that, not when we have greater concerns."

Falgar let out a derisive snort. Dorian winced, certain his friend was destined for even more telling off. But Sylvia fixed him with a level gaze and said, "Something to share, Mr. Falgar?"

"Forgive me, Lady Dragonmar," Falgar said. "But what greater concerns? Ever since the attack in Silverlake, we've just been sitting around here twiddling our thumbs. And in case you didn't notice, it hasn't kept any of us safe." He absently thumbed the part of his shirt that Dorian knew hid the pale-white scar left after Estevan's Healing. "I'd say I'm sorry for striking Dragonaut Beckett, but truth be told, I think it was inevitable after being cooped up in here for so long."

Sylvia closed her eyes and took in a deep breath, as if praying for patience. "I recall you argued something similar, before I sent you to Thlarknia. Do you have any reason to believe another mission will go any better?"

The dragonauts exchanged worried glances. They didn't have any reason to believe that, and Sylvia probably knew it.

"Nevertheless," Sylvia said, "It is clear that being cooped up is bad for morale. My scouts have detected a strange magical energy in the forest. Magic that should not be there. Magic that could only come from a bonded dragon. Possibly even more than one."

The others erupted into nervous whispers. "Callahan's forces, do you think?" Sullivan wondered.

"Maybe another rogue dragonaut like Valmont," Falgar said hopefully.

Sylvia let the whispers die down before continuing. "The energy comes from a nearby Orith village the locals refer to as Lost Hollow."

Dorian felt a light brush of feathers against his arm. He turned to the side, expecting to see Tanis, but the Orith youth stood on the periphery of the group, still looking sickly but otherwise in good spirits. The feathers came from Dax Vesper, who flared his wings out and looked like he'd been punched. "Lost Hollow... oh. Oh no."

"The people of Lost Hollow are reclusive and hostile to outsiders, so my scout could not get near," Sylvia said. "However, I do not think they will turn away our dragonauts if we send them."

"I can go, milady," Jameson volunteered at once.

"If anyone, it should be me," Dax hastily put in. "As an Orith I can... perhaps help smooth things over." He shifted his weight uncomfortably, and Dorian had the distinct impression Dax knew something he wasn't letting on.

Sylvia shook her head. "I admire your initiative and have no doubt that you both would do a commendable job. But since Dragonaut Falgar seems to have become restless cooped up inside the castle, he is the one who should go. Sullivan, since I trust you to be level-headed and not cause a diplomatic incident, I want you to go with him."

Graigor Beckett's hands curled into fists. "You can't be serious. He *assaults* me, and you're *rewarding* him?"

"Going on the mission is not a reward, and staying here is not a punishment."

"He gets to go on a camping trip with his Void-cursed boyfriend, meanwhile I'm stuck here with these—" His pale eyes flashed dangerously, but he seemed unable to come up with suitable insults for the rest of them.

"Surely, your quarrel is with Dragonaut Falgar. With him removed from the situation, I see no reason you can't get along with the others. I expect the rest of you to be flying with *perfect teamwork* by the time Falgar and Sullivan return. After that, we can solve any lingering issues between Mr. Falgar and Mr. Beckett. Do I make myself clear?"

"Yes, Dragonmar," Graigor said through gritted teeth. But the pulsing vein in his forehead suggested to Dorian that this was far from over.

"Falgar, Sullivan, prepare for the journey. The rest of you, get into five-point formation. And remember. *Perfect teamwork.*"

Once airborne, Dorian searched for the euphoria that usually came with flying, but for once, it proved hard to reach.

Somehow, never once in his time as a dragonaut had it occurred to him that Falgar and Sullivan would go on a mission *without* him. He already hadn't seen Tai or Xander or Bradford in moons, and now, his two remaining friends were *also* about to leave.

"Copper for your thoughts, Valmont?" Hildegard flew up next to Dorian. Starfire's amber scales glinted in the early Autumn sunlight.

Dorian flinched, embarrassed to have made his brooding so obvious. But at least there was one friendly face here in Cloudfire. "Oh, sorry Hildegard. You... probably don't want to know."

"As flight-second, it's my duty to tell when something is bothering one of my dragonauts, and you, Valmont, are clearly bothered."

Hildegard sat in her flight saddle with a stiff upright posture, which Dorian recognized as her not-to-be-rebuffed pose. At times, Hildegard reminded him of Tai with her stubbornness.

Dorian wasn't sure how much he dared be vulnerable. Anything he said to Hildegard could go back to Jameson — or to the Dragonmar. But he might as well talk to her, if he was going to talk to anyone.

"It's silly," he said, "And I don't want to seem ungrateful, because Cloudfire is a beautiful place, and I've learned so much from you and Jameson and Dax. I never imagined I'd get to meet other dragonauts who aren't trying to kill me."

"I swear Jameson is trying to kill us all sometimes," Hildegard said, "But I get your point. You think you should be happy here, but you're not."

"It's ridiculous, but most of the time I just miss the *Phoenix*," he admitted. "I mean, I shouldn't feel nostalgic for the tiny cramped little galley, or that rock-hard bunk I had to sleep on, or the washroom I could barely fit inside with its finicky little shower, but... the crew. They were like family. I never had a proper family before."

Hildegard frowned. "That's not—"

Dorian kicked himself inwardly. "You and the rest are great! It's just—"

"We're not as close yet." Hildegard nodded in understanding. "I get it."

"I suppose," Dorian said, "I technically did have family even before the *Phoenix*, but I didn't know Bradford was my brother until like a year ago, so... ah, I'm rambling, aren't I. What about you, Hildegard? Do you have family?"

Hildegard looked relieved at the change in topic. "My mother died when I was young, and my father was a bit of an arse. He died a few years back. Good riddance, I say."

"I'm sorry," Dorian said. He realized he'd probably asked an incredibly personal question.

"Eh, don't be. Ever since I was a teenager, the Order's been the closest I've had to an actual family. Not so different from your crew, I guess."

"So... so then you understand," Dorian said, brightening slightly. "What if you had to go — go somewhere else? And some of the Order people came with you. But then they got sent away, and it was just you." Holding onto Solaris's harness with one hand, he awkwardly smoothed his hair with the other. "I suppose I must not be making much sense."

"No," Hildegard sighed, "You make perfect sense. I... know it will take time, and Jameson can be a bastard. No denying it. But maybe... maybe one day the rest of us could be part of your family too, yeah?"

Dorian gave a smile that was almost genuine. "Yeah, maybe. One day."

Unfortunately, Graigor was flying close by at that moment, close enough to hear. "A family? What a bunch of saccharine tripe. Your own family didn't even want you, Valmont, which was why you got dropped on Janus Callahan's doorstep. What makes you think someone like the Order would?"

Dorian knew Graigor well enough by now to take his insults in stride, especially because this one wasn't even particularly true. He grew up in Callahan Manor because his parents were *dead*, not because they rejected him. But Hildegard was clearly taken aback, and opened her mouth to say something. To Dorian's surprise, however, it was Dax who broke the formation to fly forward and confront Graigor. "Just because Healer Estevan fixed your nose doesn't mean it can't be broken again." The white-winged Orith's pale face was a mask of fury. Dorian didn't think he'd ever seen Dax so upset before.

"Whoa, whoa," Dorian waved his arms placatingly. "We're supposed to be getting along. Let's not have another fight on *my* account."

Graigor spat contemptuously, a wad of spittle floating down to join the underclouds. "Pathetic," he said, before wheeling Borealis around and flying back to the landing rampart.

"What was that about?" Dorian stared at Hildegard and Dax in shock.

"Graigor shouldn't have said those things." Dax shook out his massive snowy wings, mouth pinched with anger. "Completely out of line."

The training session thus ended, and everyone headed to the dining hall to get breakfast. Dorian was hungry too — these training sessions always started far too early. But he found he didn't want to stop flying just yet. "You all go ahead," he said. "I want to practice maneuvers a bit more."

"Never thought I'd see you hesitating to get food, Valmont," Graigor said.

Dorian rolled his eyes. There wasn't any real venom in Graigor's words. It was all by rote, at this point. "I'm in no danger of starving," he replied, also by rote.

"I mean it." Dax cracked his knuckles. "I can re-break his nose."

"Thanks for standing up for me," Dorian said. Perhaps he wasn't completely friendless in the castle after all. "But I don't want *you* getting in trouble."

"Perhaps you're right," Dax said with a wistful sigh. "She won't send me to Lost Hollow even if it makes the most sense that I go, so Savior knows what punishment she'd concoct instead. Anyway, are you sure you won't come to breakfast?"

Dorian's traitor stomach gave a grumble. "I probably should, but I want to fly just a bit more." He circled towards the landing parapet, intending to ask Tanis for his thoughts. He froze, realizing his young ward wasn't there. "Where's Tanis?"

"Probably had to use the privy," Dax said. "I can go find him, if you want. Finish your flight and I'll meet you in the dining hall?"

"Thank you," Dorian said. He smiled at the Orith dragonaut, allowing himself to hope he'd made a friend. But he couldn't let go of his feelings of unease as he wheeled Solaris up higher into the morning sky.

CHAPTER TWENTY-SEVEN
LOST HOLLOW

Tai's recovery from her failed Planeshifting seemed to drag on for Cycles. At first, she was so weak she could barely walk the perimeter of her mother's dwelling. Eventually, she could make it as far as the town square. After three weeks, she could cross the entire small village and, if she chose, ride the clever pulley lift to the Council Hall. But it would still be moons before she was back to her old self.

Tai wanted to return to Cloudfire as soon as she could walk again. She was happy to see Jace, and thrilled to know her mother was safe, but the sooner she delivered the dragonstone and set Celestian free, the better.

Unfortunately, Jace, Reora, and, to her surprise, Celestian, presented a united front. She absolutely must *not* leave the village until she was fully recovered. And so she spent the next several weeks slowly rebuilding her stamina and doing odd jobs around the village to prevent herself from going stir crazy.

At first, the townsfolk only trusted Tai with the simplest of tasks. Washing vegetables, peeling potatoes, scrubbing pots. On a good day, she was allowed to feed the gryphons, but never to ride on them. Tai dreaded hearing the term "fragile constitution." But thanks to her connection to Celestian, the townsfolk eventually began making magical requests as well. Tai soon spent her days scrying for wild mushrooms, levitating water out of the well, and performing minor Healing spells on all the townsfolk's bumps and bruises.

Unlike in Everwood, where demon possession was practically an epidemic, Tai hadn't seen a single demon within Lost Hollow's sturdy wooden walls. People spoke reverently of the town's High Councilor, who supposedly performed miracles, but for most of the average townsfolk, magic was strange and mysterious.

It thrilled Tai to be useful, but something didn't sit right, like a feather sticking out in the wrong direction. Every day she spent here might be the day Kadmin arrived with an army in tow. Every day she cast spells for the villagers was a day she failed to set Celestian free.

"Can you sense Kadmin?" she asked Celestian one day as she peeled carrots.

«Vaguely,» Celestian said. «He does not hold the dragonstone, so he does not have any real control over me. But fragments of our connection remain. I can tell he is alive, but not where he is. I believe it is the same for him.» He left the unspoken hanging in the air. *At least, I hope it is.*

Tai stared over the balcony at the shining grove of silverleaf. The peaceful villagers were busy at their work, and guilt churned in her stomach. "Do you intend to return to Kadmin when all this is over?"

«I am not sure,» Celestian admitted. «To be free, really free... is not something I allowed myself to consider. Yet I wonder, too, if it is not my duty to return.»

Tai frowned. "I understand not wanting to stay here with me, and I know you think Callahan's plan to end magic is a necessary evil, but why Kadmin specifically?"

Celestian replied with a burst of mirth. «You, too, were once taken in by Kadmin's charm.»

"Yes, and I learned my lesson." She stuck her tongue out.

"Puberty, egads, it messes with your head. But I never got the impression dragons much cared if humans are handsome. He enslaved you, and you still gave him a dragonaut sword. Why do that?"

Celestian shook his head. «He was decent to me. Never outright abusive.»

Tai set the fully peeled carrot into the bowl and grabbed another one. "You can't just summon someone a dragonaut sword because they *weren't outright abusive.*"

«Since when are you the ultimate judge of who gets a sword?»

Tai sighed and lowered her wings, removing the carrot skin in one smooth spiral. "I suppose I'm not."

Idly, she wondered if Falgar and Sullivan had earned their dragonaut swords yet. There were so many things she'd missed out on back in Cloudfire.

Tai felt a hollow ache in the pit of her stomach when she realized it had been the better part of a year since she'd seen them last. She thought about Falgar, always ready with a joke, and Sullivan, who took everything in stride. And Dorian, oh, gods, kind, earnest, determined Dorian. Was he thriving, now that he'd found other dragonauts like himself?

"Tai!"

Tai looked up from peeling carrots to see her mother and Jace quickly approaching. The difference in their bearing could not have been more starkly pronounced. Reora tugged on the cuff of her robes, looking nervous, while Jace bounded forward like the Autumn Festival had come early.

"I've just heard the best news!" Jace said eagerly. "High Councilor Gideon wishes to speak to you!"

"Oh!" Tai screwed up her face into the politest expression she could muster. Jace presented it as if she'd been invited to dine with the queen. Tai knew that High Councilor Gideon held nearly as much sway over the town as her mother the mayor, but Tai had never paid him much attention. Councilors were the religious leaders of the

Path, and Tai had never had much use for a religion that treated the flightless like perpetual children. Tai supposed, however, that they must follow some alternative version of the Path, in a village where everyone was flightless.

"It won't do to meet him in those old rags." Reora's voice shook nervously. "Come. I'll see if I've anything suitable you can borrow."

Twenty minutes later, Tai finished tying the sash around an elegant lavender robe with embroidery of the Second Waypoint on the cuffs and collar.

"But I'm not at the Second Waypoint," Tai pointed out, stating the obvious.

"Your work at an aeronaut puts you at the third or fourth at least, but this robe is the best I can find on such short notice," Reora said. "If Gideon has a problem with it, he can go through me." But she was nervous, Tai could tell.

Tai ran a worried hand across the silk, feeling like an imposter playing dress-up in her mother's robes. Which, she supposed, she was. Reora was nearly a full head taller than Tai, so Tai had to hike the fabric up to avoid tripping on the hems as they made their way across town towards the Council Hall.

"What an ingenious device," Tai said once they at last climbed onto the rope and pulley lift. She thought wistfully back to her own childhood when she dreamed of building machines like this.

"I must confess," Reora said with a pained expression, "that I never took your complaints about all those ladders seriously until I lost the use of my own wings."

They reached the highest level, and Tai drew in a sharp breath of surprise. Even she, who was predisposed to be cynical about the Path, had to admit Lost Hollow's Council Hall was impressive.

The Council Hall back in Everwood had been simple and unvarnished. Old Councilor Vyr used to rail against what he referred to as *aggrandizement.* "It's called the Path, not the Templath," he used to say, meaning they should value the teachings of the Path itself more than the temples where it was taught.

The magnificent Council Hall in Lost Hollow would *never* meet old Vyr's approval. This was *Templath* at its finest. If anything, *aggrandizement* was an understatement.

The entire domed ceiling was resplendent with stylized leaves and branches done up in silver and gold. In the center of the round room was an altar of still-gleaming silverwood, with intricate patterns of filigree and knot work carved on the sides. A faceless gold statue of the Savior glittered in the lanternlight, holding a golden copy of the Book of Prophecy in one hand and a bejeweled winged sword in the other. Tai doubted even the Grand Council Hall in Silverlake could match it for splendor. She found herself thinking she might not have been so bored at Council meetings as a child, if she'd had all this to look at.

Tai caught a gleam of aether blue from the altar, and edged over for a closer look. The book in the Savior's hand, which she'd originally taken to be Rivka Sevarin's Prophecies, was actually carved with a familiar series of Aerish runes. *Communication runes.* The whole statue prickled with magic, starting at the base and traveling up through the golden sword pointed up towards the clouds above. It should have been impossible, and yet here it was, clearly in front of her. *The statue of the Savior is a Void-cursed aether beacon. But how?*

"Savior's blessings be upon you." One of the lesser Councilors, a silver-haired woman perhaps a few years older than Tai's mother, swept over wearing robes of gauzy glowyrm silk. "I am Councilor Temperance. Please, come refresh yourselves while we wait for His Most Holy Magnificence."

Tai cast one last uncertain glance at the beacon statue before following the priestess into a smaller room off the side of the central temple chamber. Reora's face was a carefully neutral mask, while Jace looked faintly punch drunk. She decided neither of them would be much help in navigating the situation.

The chamber they entered was smaller than the first, but no less grandiose. Embroidered silk pillows surrounded a low parquet table, which was currently covered with pages of — *More spell sigils?* Tai gazed at the strange symbols laid out amidst letters and numbers. *Not spell sigils*, she realized. They were mathematical formulae.

"Forgive the mess." Temperance quickly gathered up the papers and replaced them with a gold-filigree teapot and matching cups. Expensive tea, too, if the aroma of jasmine flower and rose petal was any indication. "His Most Holy Magnificence rarely receives visitors. You ought to count yourself fortunate."

Tai wanted to point out that Gideon was the one who summoned *them* here, but she imagined that would probably be inappropriate. Instead, she said, "What's with all the math?" She inwardly cringed. *Oh, good, like* that *wasn't inappropriate.*

To her surprise, Temperance looked slightly flustered. "Engineering calculations. I... have always liked to tinker. Gideon thinks it is a waste of time, of course, but..."

"That lift up here!" Tai perked up. "You designed it, didn't you?"

"Ah, yes, I did." Temperance tugged on the sleeves of her robe, embarrassed.

"It's incredible," Tai said.

Temperance flushed. "You are too kind."

Tai opened her mouth to ask more questions, but before she could, an authoritative, masculine voice reverberated through the Council Hall. "Here she is at last. Our mysterious visitor."

Tai turned towards the sound of the voice, and even she could not prevent her mouth from falling open of its own accord. High Councilor Gideon strode into the chamber, accompanied by a stern-looking border guard, who she seemed to recall was named Kyre.

Gideon himself was tall and classically handsome with salt-and-pepper gray hair and hawk-like amber eyes. He was one of those rare few Orith whose feathers didn't match his hair — his wings, radiant gold, were small and stunted like Tai's, but no less impressive for it.

But all of that seemed rather trivial compared to the fact that he was *glowing.*

Not *glowing* as in someone with uncommonly healthy skin, but Gideon actually radiated silver-white light like the bioluminescent forest surrounding them. Tai blinked, unsure she was seeing him correctly. Surely she would have noticed something like *that* before.

Reora and Jace lowered themselves into steep bows. A fraction of a second too late, Tai followed suit.

"It's an honor, Your Magnificence," Jace choked out, but the High Councilor ignored him. *Rather rude*, Tai thought.

"You may rise," Gideon said in a bored and condescending tone. To Tai, he said, "You have been making quite the stir about town. You and that *creature* of yours."

His voice was carefully neutral, and yet Tai could practically feel the man's reproach.

"Celestian is not my 'creature', he is a companion I'm traveling with." She thumbed her stolen dragonstone guiltily, recalling that yet another day had passed without setting Celestian free.

Reora and Jace both stiffened at her words, and Gideon's mouth narrowed in disapproval. Warmth rising to her face, Tai hastened to add, "It has never been my intention to cause trouble. The people of Lost Hollow have been kind to me, and I only wish to repay that favor."

Jace and Reora both relaxed, but Gideon's expression remained stern, scrutinizing.

"I appreciate your willingness to make yourself useful," Gideon said with barely hidden condescension. "However, I would advise you not to make my people too dependent on your witchcraft."

"Witchcraft?" Tai blurted without thinking. At her side, Reora drew in a sharp breath of dismay.

"Our community has thrived for Cycles without inviting demons into our midst," Gideon said. "I stand firmly against anything that would jeopardize that."

"Celestian isn't a demon," Tai protested. Reora and Jace flinched, but Tai didn't care. To the Void if His Most Holy Magnificence High Councilor Fancy-pants disapproved. Bad enough Celestian was stuck here on her account. She wasn't just going to let this puffed up humanoid lantern call him something he wasn't.

"The line between demon and dragon is very fine indeed," Gideon said. "Anyway, it is by our good graces that we allow you to stay here at all. I ask only that you respect our ways."

Tai ground her teeth, but she lowered her wings in surrender. She supposed this wasn't the time or place to pick a fight, even though at the moment she really, really wanted to. This haughty glowing man set her feathers on edge. "Of course, High Councilor. I understand." But she didn't understand. Not in the slightest.

Gideon swept away without so much as a goodbye.

"That's it?" Tai asked. The meeting couldn't have lasted longer than five minutes.

"Show some respect," said Kyre, the border guard, before he, too, spun around and followed his master like a faithful hound.

"Well." Tai breathed out. "He's pleasant."

"His Most Holy Magnificence is a very busy and important man," the lesser Councilor, Temperance, said. Perhaps it was Tai's imagination, but she thought Temperance sounded exhausted rather than reverent.

"It's not a wise idea to make an enemy of the High Councilor," Reora agreed.

"Nor should you want to," Jace quickly added, and for the first time since she'd arrived, he looked genuinely worried. But he hid it quickly, and said, "He'll come around, though, once you've shown how useful you and Celestian are."

"Here's hoping." Tai was just glad the meeting was over. She'd never had pleasant experiences with Councilors in the past, and Gideon had done little to change her mind. "What's with the glowing, though? He says he disapproves of magic, but that has to be some kind of Illusion spell."

"That's not an illusion!" Jace sounded downright affronted. "Gideon is the Path's own Chosen!"

Tai raised her eyebrows. "Be serious."

"You think I'm not?" Jace asked. "He fits almost line by line with the prophecy. 'He shall fly on stunted wings and reclaim the light of the moon.'"

"The prophecy says he'll fly on *broken* wings, not stunted. He might be Flightless like the rest of us, but those wings of his didn't look broken to me."

"A mistranslation," Jace said. "The Prophetess Rivka Sevarin spoke High Orith, didn't she? The actual word was *tavarash,* which could mean stunted *or* broken. I've suspected for a long time that the Path's Chosen Savior would be Flightless, even before I became Flightless myself. It simply makes sense."

"I suppose so," Tai said, hoping her skepticism wasn't too obvious. Tai didn't believe for a second that there would ever be such a thing as the Path's Chosen Savior, and she certainly didn't think it was that arrogant priest. Rivka Sevarin's famous prophecy was nothing more than a story the Orith told one another to feel better about themselves.

«All religions have a grain of truth,» Celestian said.

Tai blinked. «Don't tell me *you* believe in the Path.»

«Not the Path specifically, no. But certain aspects ring true, just like the Aerish tales of the seven gods. There *are* seven powers that govern this world. Zekador, and Meroneth, and the rest, though we dragons call them by different names among ourselves. We have a prophecy, too, that a mortal who walks between worlds will one day remedy the mistakes of the past. That very well could be the same as your Orith savior.»

"Walks between worlds..." where had she heard that before?

«It probably matters little,» Celestian said. «No prophecy is absolute, and the future is always in flux.»

Tai was just about to get back on the lift, thinking the whole meeting had been a bizarre waste of time, when she heard frantic footsteps behind her.

"Miss Lunstrum!" It was the other Councilor, Temperance, who'd greeted them when they arrived. "Sincerest apologies, but may I have a word? In private?"

Tai glanced at her mother and Jace, but they only shrugged. "We'll meet you back at my dwelling," Reora said, and the two of them climbed on the lift and departed, leaving Tai alone with the Councilor.

"Can I... help you?"

The silver-winged priestess tugged on her kerchief, obviously nervous about something. "This is... a strange request, I know. But do you think you could... teach me to do magic?"

Tai raised her eyebrows. "Unless you're willing to take on a demon, there's not much—"

"I don't need a power source." Temperance waved her hand reassuringly. "I just want to know the basic theory. I... know it wouldn't be the same as practice, but..."

"Does Gideon know about this?"

Temperance cast a glance over her shoulder as if checking for eavesdroppers. "Of course not," she whispered.

Now, that was interesting. Dissension in the Holy Council. Tai had only met Gideon briefly, but she could already tell she didn't like him. And the seven Aerish gods knew she could use something more interesting to do than scrying for mushrooms and peeling carrots.

"All right." Tai flashed a conspiratorial grin. "I'll teach you everything I can."

For the next several weeks, Tai met with Councilor Temperance at her home at the base of the massive Council Tree. Tai had never taught anyone how to use magic before, but she had some experience teaching others, particularly from when Dorian enlisted her help to become a proper aeronaut. Temperance, for her part, proved a willing and receptive student.

Outside the magic lessons, Tai started spending most of her time with Jace Farnham. Jace quickly became the best friend and confidante that Tai could hope for. Jace clearly loved the town of Lost Hollow, and that love shone through in everything he did. He eagerly introduced Tai to everyone in the village, taught her how to catch the best fish in the river, and showed her the best spots for mushroom foraging.

When he finally declared her sufficiently recovered, he even took her riding on his favorite gryphon. Never far from the town, and never very high, but she treasured these moments nonetheless. It almost, almost reminded her of flying with Dorian and Solaris.

Jace also practiced with her daily with swords and staves until she finally felt her old strength returning. With the young border guard's help, she felt like she could truly become a part of the community.

Tai knew she needed to get back to Cloudfire and free Celestian as soon as possible. Yet with every passing day, the world outside Lost Hollow seemed more remote and distant. It was like the rest of Cyrna was some kind of fever dream, and this village was the only thing that was real.

One bright summer morning, Tai and Jace returned from gathering mushrooms to find Celestian in deep conversation with Councilor Temperance. Tai felt a flare of jealousy, which she quickly tamped down. She had no reason to be jealous. Celestian was, of course, free to be friends with whomever he pleased.

«Councilor Temperance has just had the most wonderful idea.» Celestian swished his tail back and forth with more enthusiasm than she'd ever seen from him. *At least he's happy,* she thought.

"What idea is that?"

"Well... I don't have all the details hammered out yet..." Temperance looked slightly flustered.

«Do not be so modest,» Celestian chided. To Tai, he continued, «Temperance thinks we can build a windmill!»

His draconic eyes sparkled with excitement, which Tai was evidently expected to share.

Jace wrinkled his nose. "Why a windmill?"

"To thresh grain?" Tai suggested. The town already had a water-wheel for that, however.

«It is not for grain,» Celestian said. «With the correct sigils, if I infuse the windmill with some of my power, it could itself work as an arcane power source that could last moons, maybe even years.»

"There's no way." Jace looked taken aback.

Temperance grimaced and shook her head. "The plan... certainly has its flaws, I'm afraid."

Tai, however stared at the others in awe. Runes and sigils danced behind her eyelids in new and exciting ways. If the movement of the fan blades distributed the magic in order to charge up an aether crystal... It could work, she realized. Even beneath the clouds, it could work.

"We have the Savior and his miracles," Jace protested. "What in the Depths do we need a windmill for?"

Tai's mind raced as she put the pieces together. "If we could distribute magical energy beneath the clouds, we could stop the blight that's damaging the silverleaves. If the windmill works the way I'm envisioning it, it would stretch the power out, make it last much longer than a blast of dragon magic to the trees directly. We could..." Savior's Wings, the possibilities were endless.

Jace continued to look unconvinced. "We'd still need a dragon to recharge the thing, and I don't imagine your Celestian will want to stick around Orith powering up windmills forever."

«It would not have to be me,» Celestian replied. «Any dragon could come by occasionally to see it done.»

Tai's heart sank. She'd recently gone and *kidnapped* the only dragon who'd ever actively helped the Orith. She was sure Solaris would help if she could, but Lady Sylvia had already made it clear that the Order's precious secrecy trumped everything else.

Temperance, however, looked hopeful. "Perhaps the dragons in Cloudfire..."

"We can expect no help from them," Jace said bitterly.

Tai gaped at them both. Temperance and Jace knew about the dragons in Cloudfire? *How?* Since when?

Temperance dusted her hands on her silk Councilor's robes. "If we make it known how important it is, I'm sure they will—"

Jace shook his head. "We can't depend on them. They've made themselves plenty scarce since the *incident.*"

"Incident?" Temperance and Tai asked at the same time.

He spoke the word with such gravitas, Tai felt certain something must have gone seriously wrong. *Void Eternal.* If her friends had been injured or worse while she was playing magic teacher in this remote village, how would she ever know?

Temperance, for some reason, looked every bit as shaken as Tai felt. "I was not informed of any *incident.* Am I a Councilor or am I not?"

"Forgive me, Councilor Temperance. A grave oversight on my part." Perhaps it was Tai's imagination, but Jace seemed to deliberately avoid meeting either of their eyes. "Anyway, short version is, they'd been sending their 'demon possessed' to help combat tree blight. But it was just more of that witch woman's illusions. They were sending *dragons* instead. And a few weeks back, half of Silverlake finally saw the fraud for what it was."

"They were trying to help." Tai obviously didn't know the whole story, but she still felt the need to come to her friends' defenses. She could do little else to quell the anxiety that rose up within her at this news. It sounded like the Order's secret was out at last. If this many people knew about the dragons in Cloudfire, it was only a matter of time before Emperor Callahan found out, too. If he didn't know already.

"What happened to the dragonauts in Silverlake?" Temperance demanded.

"They got away," Jace said, as though they'd committed some kind of crime. "Been real quiet holed up in their castle ever since, so I've heard. So much for their alleged altruism."

Tai opened her mouth to argue, then closed it again. Perhaps she'd spent too much time as a spy in Kasanarae, but her instincts told her it wasn't a good idea to appear too interested in Cloudfire.

She dusted her hands together and put on an expression of practiced nonchalance. "Well. Regardless. If we had windmills in every town, then they wouldn't need the dragons nearly as frequently."

"Yes, yes, the windmill, of course." Temperance ruffled her one good snowy wing. "It's all just theoretical, anyway. The formulae work at a small scale, but it falls apart the instant you try to power anything as large as a town."

"I could help, if you want," Tai blurted, before she'd really had a chance to think it through.

Temperance looked surprised. "Do you know much about windmills?"

"Not exactly, no," Tai admitted. "But I did make a lot of clockwork toys when I was a kid." She winced, fully aware how pathetic that sounded. "Well, I can help with the magic side of things, at any rate."

Temperance, however, smiled. "By all means. I need all the help I can get."

Between continued magic lessons and the windmill project, Tai found herself even busier than she had been during her earliest days as an aeronaut. The voice in the back of her mind reminding her she needed to set Celestian free was still ever-present, but she found herself becoming better and better at ignoring it. *Just one day more* became her constant refrain, even as weeks turned into moons.

«I must admit,» Celestian said one afternoon while they sanded windmill blades, «This is a truly ingenious device, even without the addition of magic.»

"They use them in some towns to thresh grain," Tai said. "We need to make do with what we can, down here, without magic to aid us."

«Remarkable. We dragons are so consumed with the past, we never think of making anything new. You mortals truly know what it is to learn and grow.»

"Well, Temperance is above and beyond your average mortal," Tai said. Even after years working on skyships, she'd never met anyone with the Councilor's knack for engineering. Maybe, if she'd been allowed to become an artificer... but there was no use thinking about that now. "Gods know I could have used something like the pulley lift, back home in Everwood."

«I am surprised they have not come up with something similar in Aeris,» Celestian said.

"Sometimes I think the Aerish rely on magic so much that they've lost the ability to go without," Tai said. If Janus Callahan got what he wanted, the Aerish people were in for a rude awakening.

«With windmills like these, we dragons could keep the magic flowing for a long time yet,» Celestian mused. «It would not be the same as fully restored magic, of course. But it would be something.»

Tai nodded thoughtfully. She still felt an undeniable sense of loss when she thought about the possibility of Aeris sinking beneath the clouds. Even the windmill seemed like little more than a stopgap. But if this project worked, it could help everyone on Cyrna, not just the Orith.

Unfortunately, that first required that the people of Lost Hollow were willing to share it. As fond as Tai was of the townsfolk, no one could deny that they were frighteningly reclusive.

Nobody ever seemed to come or go from the village, save for the border guards, who regularly donned their traditional masks and capes and made the rounds to keep away wild demons and interlopers. They almost never ventured far, though on occasion, Jace or Kyre or one of the other guards would return to the village with their cape torn and tattered, sometimes covered in blood.

"I'm scared you're going to get yourself killed," Tai confided in

Jace one afternoon. "What on Cyrna are you finding out there that puts you in such danger?"

"You worry too much." Jace smiled and moved a stray lock of Tai's hair behind her ear. Tai's heart did a nervous flip-flop. He stood close to her, so close that she could smell the pine-scented soap he washed with, so close she could reach up and caress the side of his face...

But no, no, this couldn't be right. Dorian... well, she supposed it didn't matter about Dorian, because he was her friend, and they were not romantically involved. But Jace was her friend too. And he was a border guard, a pillar of this community. He deserved so much better than a short-lived fling with someone who was just passing through.

Tai stepped backwards, and tugged on her hair where he'd touched it, suddenly self conscious. It had been so long since she'd cut it, it now fell almost to her shoulders.

"Jace..." She bit her lip. "You know I can't stay here forever..."

"Oy, Jace, are you coming?" Kyre, his fellow border guard, waved him over. "Gideon won't like it if we're late."

Jace jumped as if aether-struck. "Sorry Tai. But the Savior needs me."

He scampered off after Kyre, looking equal parts nervous and excited. Tai shook her head as she watched them depart. She liked Jace very much, but she couldn't for the life of her figure out what he saw in the bloody Void-cursed High Councilor. Gideon was a pompous fraud at best, and downright dangerous at worst. It worried her, slightly, that her friend afforded him such unwavering devotion.

Tai set her worries aside, for now, and found Temperance in their usual meeting spot. She, too, was watching the departing border guards with thin-lipped concern. "Whatever Gideon has planned with those two, I wager my one good wing it's nothing good."

"You're both Councilors," Tai observed, "But I somehow get the impression you and Gideon don't exactly get along."

"It's against the Path to speak ill of the High Councilor," Temperance said with a weary sigh. She paused for a long moment before continuing, "I... had a son, many years ago. He... wasn't like you and I. He had working wings. The most glorious pair of snowy white wings. But... the Flighted are not welcome in our village."

"Not even children?" Tai was aghast.

There were, of course, children who frolicked around the village, but now that Tai thought about, not many were older than twelve or so. Those few older children she saw were all like Tai and the others — Flightless. "What happens to all the Flighted children?" She almost didn't want to know.

"In my boy's case, we had a choice." Temperance's eyes shone with sadness. "We could either ritually amputate his wings, or we could send him away. Most people—" her voice caught. "Most people choose the former option. But I couldn't do that. Not to my baby boy. He had an aunt and uncle in Westfall who were happy to take him in. It... seemed at the time the most prudent option. The best way for him to have a happy life. But oh gods, I miss him every day." She dabbed at the corners of her eyes with her embroidered sleeve.

"Fallen take me," Tai swore.

"It's not all bad." Temperance dusted herself off and assumed an expression of forced cheer. "It's not as if I never get to see him. He helps the village, too, in his own right. Like the border guards, my son acts as a sort of liaison between our town and the outside world, but from the other side. And who knows. Perhaps once Gideon accomplishes all his dreams, then we can all live together in harmony." She didn't sound like she believed her own words.

Hearing Temperance's story made Tai think of her own family. She, too, had left at a young age, because her flight status made her different from the rest of her community. But that was a choice Tai made herself. It wasn't forced on her.

"Did you ever consider going with him?" Tai asked without

thinking, and then cursed herself. "Sorry. I know it's none of my business."

"No," Temperance said, "I mean, I'm not offended. But Lost Hollow is my home. I can't leave." But the Councilor didn't meet Tai's gaze, and Tai felt a chill, like a Kassoria-granted premonition that made her feathers stand on end. Did she mean "can't" as in she shouldn't, or "can't" as in she *couldn't*?

"There you are," Jace said when she returned to her mother's dwelling a few hours later. He'd arrived ahead of her, and had already donned an apron and started chopping carrots. Fallen Depths, did the man ever relax? "I was beginning to worry."

"Just working on the windmill," she said, both flattered and a bit annoyed at his concern. She put on an apron of her own and set about de-veining shrimp. "How was the meeting with Gideon?"

"Oh, it was fine. Are you all right? You look upset."

Tai's wings lowered, and she opened her mouth to dismiss his concerns, but the lie died halfway to her throat. "Is it true? Do they just... mutilate or send away children who *aren't* born flightless?"

"Ah." Jace lowered his remaining wing. "I'm guessing Temperance told you about Dax."

"Dax?" Tai blurted out in surprise.

"Well yeah." Jace wrinkled his nose. "That's the boy's name."

Dax. The Orith dragonaut in Cloudfire was named Dax, wasn't he? Tai suddenly felt a chill that had nothing to do with the early Autumn weather. That *would* explain how Temperance and Jace already knew about the dragonauts.

Jace shook his head. "The removal of wings... it doesn't happen as much as you'd think. Most flighted children have relatives on the outside."

"Even so!" Tai protested.

"Think about it, Tai. Dax would've never fit in here. It was for the best for everyone. However... Once Gideon's formally acknowledged as the Savior, everything will change for the better. With all of

Orithkind united under his banner, we won't need to exclude anyone."

Tai frowned. "What is this secret plan of Gideon's, anyway?"

Before Jace could answer, the door swung open, revealing Tai's harried-looking mother.

"Something smells delicious! You've outdone yourself again, Jace. What Tai or I did to deserve all you do for us, I'll never know."

"Tai helped too," Jace said quickly.

"An Autumntide miracle," Reora said. "Used to be I could never get her to help around the house."

Tai's wings twitched. All these years, and her mother could still get under her skin with a carefully weaponized comment.

"As I used to always tell her," Reora said, "The way to a man's heart is through his stomach. How she ever expects to get married when she can't even cook."

"I can cook fine," Tai grumbled. She wasn't especially interested in romantic advice from her mother, who had one child out of wedlock and then ran away from the man she eventually married. "As it happens, however, the man I fancy is a much better cook than I'll ever be." *Gods,* what she wouldn't give for a slice of Dorian's plum and ginger pie right now.

Jace and Reora exchanged knowing glances, and Jace stirred the pot with renewed vigor.

"Thank you for making dinner, at any rate," Reora said. "Lately I've had no time to cook, and I'd hate to eat at the tavern again. All this paperwork, and with Gideon breathing down my neck and all! That's one man who'll never be reached, through his stomach or otherwise."

"You shouldn't speak that way about the Savior, Lady Mayor," Jace said faintly.

Reora looked like she might argue, but then she lowered the ragged remains of her wings in assent. "Point is, the sooner this windmill project is done with, the happier I'll be."

Tai threw a shrimp shell into the compost bucket, suddenly

feeling sick to her stomach. It was time to broach a topic she'd been dreading.

"I think," she said, "That it's probably time that I leave here, after the windmill is complete."

Jace's face fell. "But you seem so happy here!"

Tai felt her resolve waver, but she shook her head. She'd put this off far too long. "I need to set Celestian free, and get back to the Order."

"Temperance says you've been invaluable on the windmill project," Reora said. "It would be quite irresponsible for you to leave before you even see it in action."

"I'll stay at least until we know if the windmill works or not," she assured them.

But with increasing worry, she wondered if she'd be allowed to leave even then.

CHAPTER TWENTY-EIGHT
AN UNWANTED VISITOR

Dax paced outside the beacon tower, trying to soothe his own irritation. He'd told Valmont that Lunstrum was in the lavatory, but it didn't take a genius to guess where the boy had actually gone. Tanis wasn't supposed to use the beacon tower without permission. However, Dax couldn't summon the correct amount of sternness towards Tanis. How could he blame the boy for wanting to speak to his own mother, with Graigor Beckett's taunting words still echoing discordantly in his mind?

Your own family didn't want you. Dax didn't need to know Dorian's family situation to know that was an awful thing to say to someone. But what he *did* know was that it wasn't always a matter of being wanted. Some families had to send each other away, whether they liked it or not. It wasn't always a choice. And Graigor shouldn't be so flippant about it.

«You are projecting,» Tempest said from his perch in the dragon aerie on the other side of the castle. There was no accusation in his mindvoice, it was simply a statement of fact.

"I know I am." Dax sighed and shook out his feathers before taking several breaths to calm himself. He was just tense, that was all. Jumping at shadows, because Falgar and Sullivan were about to investigate Lost Hollow, might be about to figure out Gideon's secrets and blow the whole thing wide open. Even now, Dax couldn't decide whether that would be a good thing or a bad thing.

Dax shook his head and sighed. No sense ruminating. He ought to join the others at breakfast. He ought to make nice with them all, Graigor included, he ought...

His train of oughts cut off abruptly at the sound of someone's approach.

"Dorian? Is that you?" But Dax had a sinking feeling it wasn't Dorian.

With impossible speed, the cloaked figure in the plague mask closed the distance between them, pinning Dax to the wall and pressing a wicked-sharp daggerpoint against his throat.

"Ky... Kyre?" Dax could hardly speak, lest the blade pierce his throat. What was his old childhood friend doing here? How had he gotten past the security wards?

"Come now, Dax," Kyre purred. "There's no reason it has to come to blows. We were friends, weren't we?"

Dax didn't even dare swallow. His attacker lightened the pressure just slightly, knife still brushing his skin, but at least now Dax could speak.

"It was you, wasn't it?" Dax choked out. "You stabbed Falgar in the village. You chased the other dragonauts out of Silverlake."

"Hardly. I have no need to act so brazenly. My comrades in arms, though, well, they have their own way of going about things. We all want the same thing in the end."

Dax gave the barest twitch of his feathery white wings. "You can't be here. How did you get past the wards?"

Kyre stepped back casually, turning the knife over in his hands, as if deciding that Dax wasn't a threat worth bothering with. "The wards were shut down."

Dax stared, flabbergasted, at the masked assailant. *Shut down?* Who in the Void would do that? Dax swallowed and forced a semblance of calm. "Gideon and I had a deal, *as you well know.* He swore as long as I reported on the political situation in Aeris, he'd leave the Order alone."

"Ah, but you see." His former friend spun the dagger. "Gideon made that deal with *you.* He made no such promise to young Tanis Lunstrum."

Dax felt a chill. "That's... that's impossible. Tanis would never..."

"I'm afraid he's right." Tanis came out of the signal tower, wings lowered, looking dejected, spirit energy streaming out of him into a smug-looking Malachite perched on his shoulder.

"Tanis." Dax twitched his wings with chagrin. "What have you done?"

"I didn't want to." Tanis blinked back tears. "But Gideon wanted... he was going to arrest my mother! He said if I didn't..."

Dax's hands curled into fists. This was a new low even for Gideon. But Tanis... oh, Path preserve him, poor Tanis. Dax realized with dismay that he had always been oblivious where the boy was concerned, because he reminded Dax so keenly of himself. Cut off from the community who raised him, desperate for any sense of home, of family. But it was easy to forget, sometimes, that Tanis was *not* Dax. Dax had spent the past Cycle in a careful balance between his loyalty to the community that birthed him and the organization that took him in. But Tanis didn't owe anything the Order. Why should he?

"I have been a fool." Dax's voice cracked.

"Your little friend here has been immensely helpful, both in shutting down the castle wards and retrieving an artifact of great importance." Kyre's border guard cape fluttered, and for the briefest moment Dax caught a glimpse of a narrow cloth-wrapped bundle strapped to his thigh. "Tanis just finished reporting back to Gideon that his mission was accomplished. His mother should be safe... for now. As for you..."

Tanis looked sick. "I didn't mean to. I swear to all the gods I didn't mean to."

Before Dax could react, the youth took off down the hallway. Dax hesitated for a fraction of a second too long, torn between facing Kyre and chasing after Tanis.

Kyre made the decision for him. Dax sidestepped, barely in time, as Kyre's knife plunged into his shoulder. He was lucky it wasn't his heart.

"Gah!" Dax staggered backwards, hand covering the bleeding hole in his uniform sleeve.

«Dax! What is happening?» Tempest's mindvoice pounded in his brain.

«I might be in trouble.» Dax gritted his teeth and yanked the blood-soaked blade free of his shoulder.

«I will be right there,» said the worried dragon, but he was all the way on the other side of the castle, and they were in a narrow corridor. Dax didn't see any way Tempest could get there in time.

Dax drew his dragonaut's blade, though he knew it was no good. He was more than a match for a border guard on a good day, but this wasn't a good day, and with his fresh injury he felt worse than useless.

Dax's best hope was to lead his opponent out of the cramped hallway and into the courtyard, where Tempest could reach them. Dax desperately edged towards the nearest doorway and staggered outside. As soon as they were clear of the threshold he pumped his snowy wings, desperate to get airborne. This was one advantage he had over flightless Kyre.

But Dax knew it wouldn't be enough. His wounded shoulder made it near impossible to maneuver, and even as Dax wheeled around for another attack, his former friend produced a second knife and threw with impressive force. Dax tried to dodge, but he was slow, too slow. The weapon struck the humerus of his right wing, and Dax's world flashed red with pain.

Dax collapsed to the ground, breathing hard. *Some... dragonaut... you are.* He fought to regain his feet.

Dax couldn't see the guard's face under the bird mask, but he knew, somehow, that Kyre was sneering. "Pathetic. If this is the finest the Order has to offer, then we shall have no problem burning your useless organization to the ground."

"Why... are you doing this?" Dax closed his eyes against the pain. "We have... no quarrel... with Lost Hollow."

"Ah," Kyre said, "But Lost Hollow has plenty of quarrel with you."

"I don't understand," Dax said through gritted teeth.

"You wouldn't, you're too far up that Aerishwoman's arsehole," Kyre spat. "Queen Alyssandre should have never given Rivka Sevarin's castle to foreigners. It's profane."

"You're doing all this," Dax said with disbelief, "Because you want us out of the building?"

"It's the only way." Kyre whistled, and a moment later, a second border guard landed in the courtyard riding a majestic tawny gryphon.

"You got it?" the other guard asked.

Kyre nodded triumphantly. "I got it."

Dax's former friend leapt effortlessly onto the gryphon's back behind his companion. Clearly, Kyre didn't need working wings to fly.

Dax flared his own snowy white wings, but knew he was too badly injured to even attempt taking flight.

"I'd go see a Healer if I were you." The second border guard might have almost sounded concerned. "Though if you wind up Flightless, perhaps Gideon will welcome you back into the fold."

"It'll be a warm day in the halls of Meroneth before I join Gideon," Dax said through gritted teeth.

"Swearing by the Aerish gods." Kyre clicked his tongue and shook his head. "They really have made you into one of them. How disappointing."

And with that, the border guards and their gryphon took off into the cool evening air.

Tempest settled in the courtyard several moments later, radiating frantic concern.

«I got here as soon as I could,» he said. «Though I fear I am too late.»

Dax took several deep breaths, leaning against the green-blue dragon's scales for support. "We're going after him."

«Now? But how will we catch him in such a state? You need the Healer.»

Dax shook his head. "I'll make do with the herbs in my med kit." With the apprentice healer dragonaut Sullivan away on a mission, Healer Estevan had too much on his plate already. It pained Dax to leave without saying goodbye, but the fewer people knew his whereabouts, the better. For their own safety and his.

«And the Lunstrum boy?»

Dax felt like a gryphon's claws were clamped down upon his heart. He ought to find the boy. Get his side of the story. If necessary, warn the others. But Void curse it all, there was *no time.* Stopping Gideon was more important.

Dax's heart clenched further as he thought of Falgar and Sullivan, on their way to Lost Hollow at this very moment. He should have never let them go unprepared! He should have gone with them, defying orders if need be. But perhaps with Tempest, he could get there in time to warn them. Perhaps he could even help.

"I'm going home, Tempest," he told the dragon, patting him affectionately behind the neck ridges. "I'm going to take our town back."

Dorian and Solaris flew in great sweeping loops above the highest castle turrets. Dorian removed the leather cord that held his ponytail in place and reveled in the Autumn breeze running through his copper hair. If they flew too much higher, they'd go beyond the range of Sylvia's Illusion. Dorian knew better than to do that so blatantly. But Ancients help him, it was tempting.

"What if we ran away?" Dorian meant it as a hypothetical, but at the moment, he could imagine nothing better. "Just you and me. Free the rest of your kinfolk on your own."

«Part of me is tempted,» Solaris said. «But I remain reticent to put you in danger. And what of our responsibilities here? To Tanis, at least, if not the rest of the Order.»

Dorian sighed and nodded. Tanis, of course. The Orith boy, still recovering from fugue, was his responsibility, and he knew he could never forgive himself if he shirked it now. Tanis had become something like a younger brother — perhaps he had some family here, after all.

His stomach gave an insistent rumble, reminding him that, yes, really, he needed breakfast, and with a sigh he took Solaris back down to the landing rampart and the depressing reality that awaited him there.

What he hadn't expected, however, was to see Jameson, Hildegard, and Graigor standing there waiting for them, every one of them wearing grim expressions.

"Surely it's not a crime to go flying now." Void, he *hadn't* broken through the Illusion, had he? Dorian dismounted from Solaris and gave everyone an unsteady smile. "Shouldn't you all be at breakfast?"

They met his attempt at levity with stony hostility.

"All right," Dorian said, "What's going on?"

"The attacker returned," Jameson said. "This time, he struck within the palace walls."

Dorian's heart plummeted. "It... it can't be. The Illusion. The wards..."

"The wards were shut down." Hildegard looked graver than he'd ever seen her.

Dorian's mind felt blank. "How... *who*..." his heart fell even further still as he surveyed who was gathered on the rampart. And who *wasn't*. "Where is Dax?"

"Missing," Jameson said. "We think the attacker took him captive. And with him, the moon glass."

"Oh, Void."

"This is all your fault," Graigor all but spat. "Flying about on your little joy ride while this happened under what was *supposed* to be your watch?"

Dorian blanched. He hadn't been assigned lookout duty and forgotten, had he?

"Graigor," Hildegard warned, but the burly dragonaut waved her off.

"To the Void with that. I'm sick to death of this puffball here getting special treatment just because he's—"

"Enough, Graigor," Jameson snapped, and this time, Graigor quieted, at least for now. But the Flight Leader's expression remained stormy, and he fixed Dorian with a glare that could melt stone.

Dorian swallowed. "I, um, would have stopped the attacker if I'd known, of course, but I, ah, wasn't up there more than a quarter of an hour, I'm not sure why—"

Why is everyone acting like I did it?

"The fact is, someone knew enough to shut down the wards. Furthermore, the attacker seemed to know a great deal about our schedules, and secret routes through the castle," Jameson said. "Information that no outsider should have known."

Dorian paled. "You surely can't think *I*—"

"Not you." Hildegard wouldn't meet his eyes. "But someone in your charge."

She moved aside, and from behind her, Tanis stepped forward, his wings lowered, his wrists bound, his expression one of abject guilt and misery.

CHAPTER TWENTY-NINE
THE WINDMILL

"Okay." Tai let out a long nervous breath. "If I put this rune of transference at a forty-five degree angle from this rune of connection, then it should work."

She gestured to Celestian, who breathed a shining stream of blue-white magical energy into the incomplete windmill. Tai gave the windmill a spin, and to her absolute delight, the power swirled around her, charging her aether crystal and allowing her to cast magic without drawing from Celestian further.

"Incredible!" Tai laughed in disbelief and drew a light rune in the just for the joy of it. She sobered immediately however when the dmill stopped spinning and the magic died out. "Yes," she said, ng her lip, "We'll have to work on that. Still. I really didn't expect amplify the magic as well as it did."

«You have reason to be proud,» Celestian said with a chuckle. t let us not get excited too quickly. My energy was only more effi- tly distributed, not amplified.»

ai frowned. "Does it make a difference?"

the day to day lives of these villagers? No. The power will er because of the windimill's distribution. But I believe it is important for arcanists like us to be precise. Magical energy cannot truly be amplified. It simply is what it is.»

Arcanists like us. Tai liked the sound of that. But she bit her lip and narrowed her eyebrows in confusion. "Can't be amplified at all? But what about aether crystal, and the moon glass?"

«Those are in many ways quite the opposite of this windmill,» Celestian said. «While this distributes magical energy to a wider area, aether focuses it to a narrower point, and the moon glass to such a narrow focus that it often becomes... explosive.»

Tai nodded, running her hand along her meticulously-carved woodwork. She had spent much of her life attempting to figure out Aerish magic, but she still felt like she had so much more to learn.

"You know a lot about arcane lore," she commented to the dragon.

«It is something of a hobby of mine.» Celestian modestly declined his neck but she could tell he was proud of himself. «When I was a young dragon living in the Vale, I had hoped that I might one day become my Clan's next Chronicler. The keeper of our kind's collected memories,» he added at Tai's puzzled expression. «Nocturne always seemed puzzled by my love of fictional tales, however. He wondered why I should be so enthralled when reality was so much more interesting. And perhaps he was right, in a way.»

"I remember now," Tai said. "You were reading a book that first time we met."

«*The Voyages of Tanazar Felanthryn*, yes. An old favorite of mine, even though it was written by humans.»

"That doesn't seem like such a bad thing," Tai said. "Lots of useful information in those old tales."

«Perhaps,» Celestian agreed. «But in the end, Solaris was always Nocturne's favorite.» Celestian tried and failed to hide the obvious twinge of jealousy that reverberated through their connection. «She always envied my ability to gather light at the full moon. But I would have given anything to have the Chronicler's respect the way she seemed to.»

Tai smiled ruefully and thought of Dorian, with his proper dragon bond and book of lost Ancient knowledge. "Believe it or not, I think I know exactly how you feel."

Celestian made a motion like shaking raindrops out of his wings, «Well, I may never become Chronicler, but I am pleased to be able to provide whatever arcane knowledge I might have.»

"And it is well appreciated." Tai affectionately scratched the dragon underneath his horns.

«It is funny.» Celestian was suddenly thoughtful. «In my old dragon clan, it was always Nocturne who said that we should help mortalkind, even though the Elders strictly forbade it. If Meteor knew that I was helping distribute magic to villagers beneath the underclouds, there would be no end to his fury.»

Tai ruffled her wings. "Well, thank you," she said, "For taking that risk for us."

«I am taking that risk because it is the right thing,» Celestian said. «We dragons have become so insular, so obsessed with self sufficiency, that we have forgotten that we, too, are part of the world. And that, I think, is a mistake.»

"Part of the world, huh?" Tai looked around, at the busy people going about their seemingly idyllic lives in Lost Hollow. But they didn't really feel like part of the world. If it weren't for the border guards' occasional comings and goings, it might be easy to forget there even *was* a world outside Lost Hollow. Once they finished the windmill and gave the villagers free access to magic, Tai had a sinking feeling the village would only become more insular. "I just hope we're doing the right thing."

Celestian seemed to agree with her line of thinking. «I can sympathize with the villagers' desire to keep isolated. But the outside world needs to know about what we have discovered here.» He twitched his tail back and forth as if fully aware Tai wouldn't like what he was going to say next. «I know you do not agree with them, but Janus Callahan and his people back in Kasanarae have good intentions at heart.»

Tai snorted derisively. He'd been right, she didn't like it. "They *kidnapped you and forced you into bonds.*"

«And that was abhorrent,» Celestian agreed. «But you must understand. It was the only way to make our kind see reason. Meteor and the others would have never let us work alongside humans otherwise.»

Tai shook her head. "The emperor wants to sink Aeris. I don't care if he thinks it's for the greater good or whatever, that's just plain not right."

«They do as they feel they must, as do we all,» Celestian retorted. «I know you do not like my rider Kadmin Crowley. And...» he let out a small stream of sparks, «You might have good reason. But need I remind you that you, too, retain control of my dragonstone, regardless of what I have to say about it?»

Tai staggered backwards as if he had actually struck her. "I—" he was right, Void curse it. She still fully intended to set Celestian free. But if she was really true to her principles, wouldn't she have done so a long time ago? Instead of hanging around in this village tinkering with arcana so that she had an excuse to feel clever and important?

«I do not blame you,» Celestian said, more gently this time. «As I was in Kasanarae, I am happy to be of use for the greater good.»

"But you should have more say in it." Tai massaged her temples, guilt gnawing at her like a rusty saw blade.

«You mortals are complicated, never all good or all bad. We dragons, I think, are not so different. Emperor Callahan only wants to prevent disaster. Flight Leader Vivienne, Guard Captain Corynne, your friends Owain and Lewellyn... they are all decent, reasonable people. And if they had access to arcana like this, perhaps they would not have to sink the lands of Aeris. Perhaps there could be a peaceful solution after all.»

"Perhaps," Tai said, but it was more to avoid further argument than because she actually agreed.

She sat down against the shimmering silver tree trunk and

closed her eyes. *Void take it all.* She needed to set Celestian free soon, or she really *was* no better than Kadmin and the others.

If she caught him by surprise, she could do it right now. Sneak up behind him with a blade and destroy his physical body. It wouldn't kill him, not like it would a mortal being, but it would sever his connection to the dragonstone, like when Dorian decapitated Corynne Beckett's enslaved dragon all those moons ago. But that would leave Celestian in a severely weakened state beneath the cloud layer with no reliable way to get home.

No. She needed the Order's help. They would know what to do. Tai just had to finish the windmill, then she could figure out how to leave Lost Hollow, with or without permission. Then, she could free Celestian, and deliver the now disconnected dragonstone to the Order, and all would be well.

If she told herself enough times, she might almost make herself believe it.

As summer gave way to Autumn, the humid Toreenish air took on a cooler, crisper quality, and the shining leaves faded from silver to faint gold. The windmill was near to completion. After moons of hard work, they'd finally install it on the evening of the Autumn festival.

It was fortunate that Tai was by now finally recovered from her injuries — when she first arrived she wouldn't have had anywhere near the stamina necessary for all these last-minute preparations. Tai worked long hours with Temperance and her team, tweaking magic runes and fitting cogs and sanding and staining and glossing the fine wood. It seemed like almost everyone had something to contribute, even Reora, who painted the fan blades with an ornate gold-leaf wave pattern. The windmill had a practical purpose, but it was a work of art as well.

Reora was already gone by the time Tai came down for breakfast on the morning of the festival. As mayor and officiant of all the festivities, she had to start the day early to get everything ready. Still, Tai couldn't quite suppress a twinge of disappointment that she couldn't wish her mother a happy festival morning.

Even after staying in her dwelling for moons, things were still quietly tense between Tai and her mother. They were polite to each other, of course, but the things left unsaid hung about the dwelling like a miasma. And despite everything, Tai couldn't shake the feeling that Reora was hiding something, too. Maybe something important. This morning wasn't the first time she'd been absent for without explanation.

Tai had only just ladled herself some porridge out of the cook pot when there was a knock on the door. Jace entered, carrying a brown paper bundle under his arm and looking extremely satisfied.

"What's this?" Tai asked, feeling both curious and perplexed.

"Gifts," he said proudly, carrying what she now saw was actually two packages down on the table. "One from me, one from your mother."

Tai felt the heat rise to her face. "But... Autumn festival's not a gift giving festival, is it?" It hadn't been in Everwood, but perhaps they did things differently in Lost Hollow. "I'm sorry. I didn't think—"

"No, no, don't worry about it." Jace waved his hands placatingly. "Think of it as a 'Thanks for help with the windmill' gift, if that makes you feel better."

Tai wasn't entirely sure it did make her feel better, but she smiled gratefully anyway as she pulled on the twine to open the smaller of the two parcels. The paper fell open to reveal a crown of dried silver-leaves, painted in gold leaf to match the Autumn glow of the trees outside.

"I know it's not much," Jace began.

"It's beautiful," she said. And it truly was. But even as she said it her mind rushed with the implications. A crown of leaves like this was a courting gift. Did she *want* Jace to court her? Gods, she would have when she was younger. She used to dream of just this thing. But she wasn't thirteen years old anymore. She liked to think she was far from that awkward teenage girl who fell in the river in a misguided attempt to impress him. So what did she *really* want?

Jace was always friendly to her, and he made her smile, and he was a flightless Orith just like she was. Courting Jace fit, it made sense. And yet, as she beheld the golden crown, for some reason all she could think of was Dorian. Dorian's eyes, Dorian's smile, the way his hair shone like copper in the sunlight. Dorian's kindness and determination. But, as she constantly had to remind herself, she and Dorian were friends and nothing else. Surely, Dorian wanted her to be happy, regardless of who she ended up with romantically. So why did even thinking about accepting Jace's romantic overtures feel like such a foul betrayal?

"It really is beautiful," she repeated. "But you know I have to leave soon."

Jace seemed not to hear her as he lifted the circlet and placed it in Tai's shoulder-length hair. "I like your hair longer," he observed as he settled it into place.

Tai prodded at the crown in discomfort. The leaves and twigs stuck out at odd angles, scratching her scalp and tangling with her too-long hair. Jace may like it longer, but Tai just found it irksome. But Tai left the crown in place, to spare Jace's feelings as well as to avoid making any rash decisions. There'd be plenty of time to discuss the future tonight at the festival.

Jace smiled as he handed her the second parcel. "Can't claim credit for this one, sadly, it's from your mother. She wishes she could give it to you in person, but, you know. Mayor things."

"Mayor things." Still feeling wrong-footed after receiving the leaf crown, Tai nodded and pulled open the second, larger package. Her breath caught in her throat. "This is—"

"The silk came all the way from Silverlake," Jace said proudly, "But Reora did the embroidery."

Tai ran her hand reverently down the smooth, dark silk. The fabric ran through her hands like water. It was a robe of formal Toreenish design, high-necked in the front with the back open to leave room for her wings, embroidered on the sleeves and hems with a golden wave pattern not unlike the one on the windmill. It perfectly matched the gold leaf of her crown, too. Tai wondered if Jace and Reora had plotted this together. Reora must have gotten little sleep these past few weeks if she'd done this on top of all her other duties. Was that the secret she'd been hiding? Tai hoped so. *And yet, and yet...*

"I... I can't accept this," she stammered. "I haven't earned the right... the Path..."

Jace's satisfied expression didn't falter. "The rules of the Path, as written, have always been unfairly limiting in scope. You never achieved your first flight, so what? Nobody in this village has wings that work. Besides, you've told me all about your life in Aeris. If all that time in the Linking doesn't count as flying, then I don't know what does."

Tai clutched the garment close to her chest like it was a child's toy. Words, suddenly, felt hard to reach. An embroidered robe, and a courtship circlet from Jace, all in one day, it was everything thirteen-year-old Tai would have wanted, *and bloody Void-cursed yet!*

"I'll let you get changed in peace," Jace said, still blushing. "But I'll see you after the ritual, yeah?"

"Yeah." Tai sniffed, fighting back tears. Why was she crying all of a sudden? Utterly ridiculous. "Yeah, I'll see you there."

Later that morning, Tai looked around in awe as she rode the lift to the Council Hall. Overnight, the folk of Lost Hollow had transformed the village into something out of a children's tale.

Tiny paper lanterns fluttered about, glowing different colors against the perpetual overcast sky. With its wide windows papered over with semitransparent tissue of vivid red and gold and green, the Council Hall itself looked like a giant lantern.

Tai had never considered herself religious; neither the seven Aerish gods nor the Orith Path ever seemed to offer much more than judgment. But she had to admit that there was something surprisingly *right* about entering the decorated temple, something like coming home.

Tai scanned the Council Hall for Jace, hoping they could stand together for the ritual, but he didn't seem to be there. Missing, too, was his friend, the border guard Kyre. She felt a spike of unease, but a moment later Gideon started talking and she was forced to pay attention to the dais.

High Councilor Gideon was resplendent in robes of red and gold, every inch embroidered with complicated patterns.

"On the day of the Autumn Festival, the light retreats from the sky, but not from our souls," Gideon began, repeating the well-worn words of the Ritual that Tai had known since childhood. "The Light was once far greater, in the times of old, when our land floated in its rightful place above the clouds. And so the Savior shall come and bring the Light again."

Gideon spoke with such conviction that for a moment Tai almost wanted to believe him. She didn't like the man, but she had to admit that he was a fantastic orator. He didn't drone on, like old Councilor Vyr from her hometown. There was no going through the motions here. *He really believes he's the Savior.*

"The Savior's wings shall mark him outcast, and yet he shall rise above the clouds. He will restore Orith to its former glory, and usher in a new golden age for the faithful, for those who do not stray from the Path."

"May we never stray from the Path," the other townspeople intoned, and Tai repeated it too, just a fraction of a second too late.

After the ritual, the townsfolk shuffled out of the Council Hall to go watch the installation of the windmill. Tai made to hurry outside — since she'd had an instrumental role in building the device, she was supposed to be on the dais — but paused when she saw Jace and Kyre moving urgently towards the Councilor.

There you are, she thought.

Both Jace and Kyre still wore their traveling cloaks, Jace's bird mask hanging askew around his neck. Kyre reverently carried a cloth-wrapped bundle under his arm. There was a disheveled air about both of them, but they looked triumphant, too. It couldn't have been more than a couple hours since Jace had given her the courtship crown in her mother's kitchen. What in the Void had he been doing since?

Tai hung back near the periphery of the crowd, trying to eavesdrop without making it obvious.

Gideon's hawk-like eyes lit up as Jace approached. "Did you get it?"

Jace fell to one knee and proffered the bundle. "I did, my Lord Savior. We always suspected it might be in Cloudfire. Now we know for sure."

Tai's feathers stood on end. *Cloudfire?* Jace had been to Cloudfire and back? In the past *two hours?*

Gideon pulled back a corner of the fabric, and Tai saw a flash of blue light. "Our benefectors will be pleased," he said.

"And they'll keep their word?" Jace asked hopefully.

Gideon's hawk-like eyes darted towards the departing crowd. It might have been her imagination, but she thought the High Councilor's gaze fell on her directly. "We'll discuss it later," he said, voice hardly above a whisper. "For now, come. Let us enjoy the festivities."

Tai's wings twitched as she hurried out of the Council Hall. *Cloudfire.* Jace had been to Cloudfire. She forced her way through the crowd, intent on confronting him directly, but her mother found her first. "There you are, don't just stand around gawping," Reora reprimanded her. "You're needed at the windmill installation."

Tai swallowed. "Right! Of course. The windmill."

Tai tried to push her worries aside as she joined Temperance on the dais. This windmill project had been her driving sense of purpose during her long recovery. And if it worked, it could very well change everything. She had every reason to be proud. She just wished she could dismiss her fears so easily.

Above them, in the top branches, Jace and Kyre held up the gorgeous construction. Jace had at least taken off his mask, though he still wore the traveling cloak. *He came here from Cloudfire.* Her heart pounded.

"It is my great pleasure and honor," Temperance said from the podium, "To commemorate the installation of — oh!"

Kyre slipped, dropping his portion of the fan blade. "Councilor Temperance, watch out!" Jace wavered helplessly before dropping the whole thing, which careened end over end towards the dais below. Despite Jace's warning, Temperance stood frozen in the wheeling blades' path, wide eyed, like a mouse facing down a gryphon.

Tai reacted on instinct. In a single fluid motion, she drew her athame from the folds of her sash and drew from Celestian's power to slash out a rapid levitation spell. The fan blades ceased their headlong plunge and spun midair for a few moments before settling. With another wave of her knife, she gently settled the fan blades onto the apparatus.

"There we go!" Tai laughed nervously. "Windmill installed."

For a moment, the crowd sat in stunned silence. Tai couldn't hear anything except for a ringing in her ears. Then, suddenly, the entire town erupted into thunderous applause.

Still looking horrified to have come so close to a grisly death, Temperance dusted herself off and stepped forward to spin the blade. Magical energy shone from the blades and bathed the dais in pale blue light. *It worked!* Tai allowed herself a moment of quiet elation. Celestian and Temperance had really figured out a way to make magic work under the clouds!

«And you as well,» Celestian put in. «Credit where credit is due.»

Tai smiled at the dragon. «Kind of you to say, but this is Temperance's brainchild. I was just an extra pair of hands.»

«You saved Temperance's life just now,» Celestian said. «The crowd's applause is for you as much as it is for the others.»

Tai supposed that was true, but she felt a prickle of unease. Had the stumble and near miss been a simple accident, or a more sinister attempt on the Councilor's life?

Ashen-faced Temperance, wide-eyed Jace, and guilty-looking Kyre were the only ones who showed any sign that Tai's alleged heroics were not a scheduled part of the afternoon's entertainment.

Well. Almost the only ones.

On the far end of the dais, High Councilor Gideon stood, his hawk-like eyes boiling over with unbridled fury.

CHAPTER THIRTY

THE AUTUMN FESTIVAL

"Void." Falgar let out a litany of every swear word he knew while he and Sullivan trounced through the eerie glowing forests of Toreen. "Void Eternal. Zekador's Poorly Fitting Pants. Meroneth's cold and shriveled Balls. Nahiira's slightly inflamed sphincter. *Void.*"

"Why would Nahiira's sphincter be inflamed?" Sullivan raised his eyebrows.

"Not enough fiber," Falgar said. "Or maybe too much."

"If you didn't want to go on the mission," Sullivan said, "You should not have struck Graigor."

"You wound me," Falgar said. "My dear bond would never let me hear the end of it if I simply rolled over and accepted Graigor's insult."

«If you did not want to go on the mission,» Meridian put in, «You should not have struck Graigor.»

"Traitor," Falgar said.

Sullivan's expression softened somewhat as he looked Falgar up and down. "Seriously, though, how are you feeling? Healing magic may work miracles, but it takes a lot out of you."

"Void Eternal, Sul, I got stabbed more than a moon ago. I seem to recall you were back to flying skyships less than a day after getting your broken arm Healed last year. I'm fine." Sullivan's concern *was* endearing, though, Falgar supposed.

It wasn't actually all that far from Cloudfire to Lost Hollow, less than an hour's flight by dragonback. Unfortunately, the strange energy they were looking for wasn't much likely to be visible from the sky. So that meant a ponderous full-day hike through dense undergrowth and uneven terrain. There didn't appear to be any actual *roads* to Lost Hollow either. *Can't make things too easy, can they?*

«I will watch the skies, but you know full well that I am useless on the ground,» Meridian reminded him. «To find what we are looking for, you must keep your eyes open. And your ears. And your nose.»

"I'm not a Void-cursed bloodhound," Falgar grumbled. But he took in a deep whiff of air anyway, noting the loamy scent of moss and fallen leaves, of rainwater and pine needles. In the far distance, he thought he could almost catch the salty breeze wafting through the forest from the nearby undersea.

"Wonder if there are any dryads in this forest?" he wondered idly.

"Those are just stories, and I thought they lived in Pazarae, not Toreen," Sullivan said.

"They're more common in Pazarae, but I'm sure they live all over the place. I hear they appear to mortals as beautiful women. Or men," he added, waggling his eyebrows.

"Plan to be unfaithful to me with a beautiful tree spirit?" Sullivan's tone was more playful than wounded.

"Never." Falgar put his hand on his heart. "But I mean, I don't know if you'd be into, like, you know, with three of us. Beautiful tree spirit men don't come along every day, you know."

Sullivan tugged awkwardly on his collar the way he always did when he was embarrassed. "I'm not... wholly averse to the idea," he admitted, "But it would have to be someone we know and trust, not a mythical—" he cut off, frowning. "Do you hear that?"

Falgar strained his ears. Now that Sullivan mentioned it, he *did* hear something. A rhythmic pulsing. Drum beats? And when he really focused, he thought he could hear someone playing the flute as well. "Music," Falgar said. "Someone's playing music."

Void. It *wasn't* sexy dryads, was it? Falgar had been *joking*. Mostly.

«I doubt it is dryads,» Meridian said dryly. «Most likely, it is the village we seek. But no doubt, there is a strange power up ahead. I have never sensed anything like it.»

«There is not just one power source,» Sullivan's dragon, Northstar, confirmed. «There are three.»

"*Three* dragons?" Falgar felt a rush of excitement mingled with apprehension. The other side only had three dragons left, and one of them was bonded to the Emperor. Surely Callahan *himself* couldn't be here in middle-of-nowhere Toreen.

«Three *power sources*,» Meridian corrected him. And, clearly to forestall him, she added, «*Not dryads*. There *is* a dragon like we thought, but also... some kind of turbine device infused with magic? How strange. And... oh, sweet Zekador, I do not know what that third source is, but it is vile.»

Falgar closed his eyes and tried to sense the magic around him. But no matter how hard he tried, all he could feel was the cool autumn breeze, plus a few remaining droplets from an earlier rainstorm dripping down from the leaves. He straightened the straps on his rucksack and moved in the direction the two dragons indicated. Time to get down to business.

"If it is Kadmin or Vivienne in that village, they're both excellent fighters, so I expect—" Falgar cut off abruptly at the sound of rustling. A spike of anxiety from Meridian alerted him to the fact that something was amiss.

«We are not alone here.»

Now that she mentioned it, Falgar felt their presences all around. Snipers with crossbows perched perfectly hidden in the trees, and beneath them, soldiers with spears, crouched and ready to pounce.

"We mean no harm." Falgar raised his hands to show he held no weapons. "We just want to talk."

"Good." An Orith man materialized out of the foliage. Not a dryad, alas. Falgar had no way of knowing the man's actual age, especially given the possibility of dragon magic, but he supposed the man could be anywhere between forty and seventy. He had a confidently smarmy air, the type Falgar often associated with used-ornithopter merchants. *Also, he glowed.*

"Correct me if I'm wrong," Falgar said, "But people don't usually glow, do they?"

From behind the glowing man, two more figures approached. Falgar couldn't make out either of their faces, because they both wore identical bird-like plague masks.

"Oh, Void," Falgar groaned. "I'm getting *so* tired of these guys."

"I think," Plague Mask Number One said, "You'd better come with us."

The Orith approaching from behind gently butted their spears into Falgar's lower back. Realizing he had no other choice, Falgar followed.

After the eventful installation, the villagers gave Tai pride of place at the celebration. It seemed like everyone wanted to clap her on the back and tell her what a great job she'd done. A guilty part of Tai relished in the attention, but she knew it wasn't right. This was Temperance's project, hers and Celestian's. They deserved the credit, the attention.

The villagers didn't seem to care about that, though, and continued plying Tai with greenwine. Despite her resolution to only drink sparingly, she finished one glass and then another, and started to feel light-headed.

"Our famous, mysterious dragon girl," Gideon said, when it came time for him to offer his own congratulations. "I think it is no secret I disapproved of the windmill project. But I must say, your stunt today was dashing and heroic, even by your lofty standards."

Tai blinked, trying to figure out if the priest was giving her a compliment. "I only did what I had to, My Lord Councilor."

"And it was very impressive indeed," Gideon said. "I could use more clever and resourceful Orith like you in the new world I hope to build."

Tai raised her eyebrows. "So it's true, then? You..." she reeled in her tongue before saying *you think you're the savior.* "You believe you might be the Savior?"

"In fact, I know I am," Gideon said. "'The Savior's wings shall mark Him as an outcast, yet He shall rise above the clouds,' so spoke the prophetess Rivka Sevarin. And what could mark an outcast more, I wonder, than wings that never worked in the first place?"

Tai twitched her own stunted wings. *What indeed?*

"Honestly, High Councilor, don't scare the poor girl," came the stern but welcome voice of her mother. "Tonight is a night for celebrations. Not everything has to be about your brave new world."

Gideon's mouth narrowed, but he simply nodded and said, "Good evening to you, Lady Mayor. I was just speaking of your daughter's heroism." He gripped Tai's shoulder unnecessarily tightly.

Tai and Reora were saved from having to respond when Kyre, the border guard, rushed in, face flushed, though from exertion or from wine, Tai couldn't tell. "My Lord High Councilor," Kyre said. "We need your attention at the border."

"Right away," Gideon replied. He gave Reora and Tai each a terse nod before departing.

Tai grimaced. "What's going on at the border?"

"Oh, something of utmost importance, I have no doubt." Reora shook her head, glowering, as she took a larger-than-necessary swig of greenwine.

Other than the loss of her wings, Reora seemed little changed from the woman Tai remembered. She was perhaps thinner now, the lines on her face more pronounced, but she had the same stately presence she'd always had, and the same stern unwillingness to tolerate nonsense.

"The people of this town put their trust in me when they elected me as mayor, and yet, he seeks to undermine me at every turn." She shook her head. "But no matter. I would never wish to give the impression that I am only here out of lust for power."

Then why are you here? Tai wondered, but didn't say. Reora downed the rest of her greenwine in one gulp and eagerly refilled it from the cask. Tai, to keep her hands busy, refilled hers as well.

"We... should talk." Tai's heart pounded in her chest as she forced herself to have the conversation she'd been putting off for weeks on end.

Reora sighed and lowered the remains of her black-feathered wings. "Yes," she said, "I suppose we'd better."

"I'm sorry," Reora and Tai both let out at the same time.

Tai blinked. "You're what now?" She'd been annoyed at her mother, furious even, first for favoring Tanis and then for leaving him. But an actual apology threw her off kilter.

"I know I drove you away when you were young," she said. "I had this idea about what life was supposed to be, perfect home, perfect family. It was easy to forget, sometimes, that my children are individuals, and not just extensions of myself." She sipped her wine. "I knew as soon as you left it had been a mistake to let you go. I wanted to journey to Cloudfire myself and beg you to come back. But I thought it was best to let you try on your own, too. If my mistake was being too overbearing, then hunting you down across the skies of Aeris would hardly change that impression."

"I—" Tai swallowed, trying to think. *Void.* How much wine had she had? "I... shouldn't have left the way I did. I don't regret going, not exactly. I've really enjoyed my time in the sky." She laughed weakly. "But... I shouldn't have turned away from you, and Tanis, and Roan. I should have come back and visited, at least. I never knew about your fugue, or Roan's leg, or how you—" she trailed off, just barely stopping in time not to start the fight that she'd been dreading.

"How I abandoned Roan and Tanis," Reora finished for her. She gazed out, not at Tai, but at some unseen point in the distance, across the festival grounds, beyond even where Temperance rearranged the bunting and the baker's wife told a joke to a group of laughing hangers on.

"Well, yeah." Tai downed the rest of her wine, resolving her courage. She'd never been good at avoiding conflict, so better just say what she needed to say and be done with it. "Tanis thinks you're dead, Mother. What kind of mother doesn't even let her son know she's still alive?"

Oops. Maybe a little too blunt.

Reora's face took on a pained expression. "As it happens, I *have* been in contact with Tanis."

Tai blinked. "But he told me—"

"It's been recent, only the past couple of moons," she said. "He's in Cloudfire with your friends, if you can believe it. Him and Temperance's son, Dax."

So the dragonaut Dax *was* Temperance's son. She'd guessed as much. But she frowned. "Tanis is in Cloudfire?" Clearly, she'd missed a lot while she'd been in Kasanarae. Then, she remembered the conversation she'd overheard between Jace and Gideon. She opened her mouth to say something about it, then closed it again. Tai's mother *never* opened up like this, and it wouldn't do to interrupt.

"It is as you say," Reora whispered, and Tai could tell it cost her something to do so. "I ran away. I abandoned them. I convinced myself that Tanis and Roan were better off without me. They didn't need a wife and mother who couldn't even keep a single demon under control. I'd already lost you. I thought perhaps I deserved to lose them, too. And for what? Bloody Gideon and his bloody schemes. And now he wants to drag innocent people like Tanis and Jace into it, too."

Tai wasn't sure whether she wanted to laugh or cry, but the anger leaked away faster than the festival wine. "We're the same, aren't we?" Tai asked. "We left because of stubborn pride. Stayed away because we couldn't stand to admit it was a mistake."

Reora sighed and shook her head. "I would return to Everwood if I could. But I am the mayor..." She gazed across the clearing to where Gideon, Jace, and Kyre manhandled a couple of miscreants. "Too much greenwine," Reora tutted. "Anyway, it wouldn't be right, to flutter off and leave all the responsibility to Gideon."

You won't abandon these townsfolk, but you'd abandon your family? Tai wanted to accuse her. But she felt a prickle of unease as she remembered her own suspicions about Lost Hollow.

"Maybe you could just *visit* Everwood," Tai suggested carefully.

"If you hadn't noticed, the people of Lost Hollow are not exactly fond of the outside world."

Tai's heart clenched. It was as she feared. "So... so once we confirm the windmill is working, I..."

"There you are! I'm off duty at last." Jace, plague-mask hung casually around his neck, ambled up to them and filled his greenwine mug from a nearby cask. "And Lady Mayor, too. I was wondering if I could borrow Tai for a dance?"

"Oh!" Tai felt warmth rise to her face, and almost against her will her left hand reached up to adjust the leaf crown on her head. Guiltily, Tai realized she'd practically forgotten about his overtures of courtship. After the chaos of the windmill installation and the fact that he'd apparently gone to Cloudfire, it felt like Cycles had passed since the morning. "Yes, I suppose I could." At the very least, she'd at least be able to get some answers out of him.

Reora responded with a knowing, mischievous smile. "You two have fun."

"You were in Cloudfire this morning," she stated bluntly, as soon as they were out of her mother's earshot.

"Oh, yes, of course, it's not far at all to the base of the mountain, quite a fast ride on gryphon back. I'm sorry, I thought you knew." He said all this very casually, as if he'd simply gone to the market for some turnips.

"What were you doing there?" she asked.

"Keeping Kyre company while he visited Dax," Jace said, as though this were the most obvious thing in the world. "Dax and Kyre were good friends when they were younger. Anyway, never mind that. It's the festival! Let's have fun! We finally get to have that dance." Jace lifted her bodily and spun her around. After so much wine, the motion made her stomach protest.

"Finally?" Tai fought to keep the contents of her stomach down.

"Before you left Everwood. You asked me to dance at the spring festival."

"Oh!" Tai flushed at the resurgence of that long-ago embarrassment. "That's, um, right, I suppose I did."

"Well." He flashed her a smile, which was, to be fair, just as genuine and charming as she remembered it. "This is me saying yes. I'm, ah, sorry it took me eight years to do so."

Tai was not at all prepared to stop grilling him about Cloudfire, but despite herself, she found her annoyance cracking slightly. Void take it, he was still charming, all these years later. Part of her reasoned that this should make him all the more suspicious, but with the greenwine now coursing through her veins, she found it difficult to care. "But... how will we do the aerial dances? Neither of us can fly now."

Jace's eyes lit up. "I forgot! You haven't seen the platform." He took Tai's hand rather forcefully, and she had to scramble to keep up as he dragged her to the edge of the clearing. They finally reached a wide silverleaf tree, where a ladder led up to a platform high in the branches. It reminded Tai of the diving docks she'd seen in Aerish lakes.

Tai watched with fascination as the party-goers took turns leaping from the platform, and attempting airborne maneuvers before landing in the dry Autumn grass.

"Good thing we Orith can take a fall," Tai said.

There was a line to climb up to the platform, but it moved quickly enough. Pretty soon, Tai and Jace stood at the top, gazing down at the festivities below. Tai had never considered herself afraid of heights — besides being Orith, she'd worked on a skyship, for the Ancients' sakes — but she couldn't suppress a wave of vertigo as she looked at the clearing, and instinctively moved back towards the solid trunk.

"It's all right," Jace said. "Come with me."

Jace took Tai's hand, and together, they took a running leap off of the platform.

"Oh!" Tai gasped in combined fear and excitement as they spun and fell together, delighting in the aerial acrobatics. They landed in the soft grass, an ungainly pile of tangled limbs. She laughed and extracted herself from Jace, heart racing.

"What did you think?" Jace asked, with that hopeful puppy expression she found so charming.

To her slight surprise, she'd actually enjoyed that. She doubted she'd done any of the flips or turns at the proper time. She'd mostly just fallen in a pile. But that didn't matter. "It was fun," she said.

"There are advantages to being in a place where everyone is like you."

Where everyone was like her. What a strange and wonderful feeling.

"Come have a drink with me," Jace said.

Tai had already had quite a lot to drink, but she agreed anyway. Jace filled two generous mugs full of wine from the public kegs and led her to a table decorated with a shimmering silverleaf branch in a vase next to a red and gold lantern.

"Tai." Jace cleared his throat. "I just wanted to say it was... very impressive, the way you helped Councilor Temperance this afternoon. I... never should have let the windmill fall like that." He rapidly downed his massive mug of greenwine and hastened to refill it.

Tai shifted uncomfortably. "It was an accident. You did the best you could. And anyway, I acted out of instinct. And it was really Celestian's magic that saved her, not me."

"The point is... you don't realize how impressive you are." He gulped down more greenwine and tugged on his embroidered cuffs. "The people back home in Everwood never appreciated you. And those Aerishmen you hung around with never did either. But me, I see you, I've always seen you."

"Oh," Tai said, and, not knowing how else to respond, she took a sip of her own wine. Ancients help her, but she did *not* look forward to her hangover tomorrow.

"I guess what I'm trying to say is," Jace said, "You don't have to go back to your Order of dragonauts. You could stay here. With people like you. In a place where you belong."

"But... Celestian..."

"I know you have to let the dragon go. But with the windmill, you wouldn't have to give up your magic. And... and *you* could stay here. With me."

For a moment, Tai allowed herself to revel in the possibility. She could stay in Lost Hollow. She was useful here, welcome here. Not like Everwood, where she was pitied and minimized. Not like Kasa-narae, where she was forever an imposter. And not like Cloudfire, with its constant reminders of her own inadequacy. Lost Hollow was the first place she'd ever felt like she could really, truly belong.

Well. Not *quite* the first place. There had also been the *Phoenix*. And that was the problem, wasn't it? For all that it seemed ideal, this place could never be the *Phoenix*. And Jace, for all his many charms, could never be Dorian. It didn't matter if he didn't feel the same way about her; it didn't even matter that he was a dragonaut and she wasn't. All those petty jealousies seemed ludicrously insignificant now. He was her dearest friend, and she would far rather have him as a friend than not have him in her life at all.

If Tai stayed here, she knew deep down that she would never see Dorian again. And not just Dorian. Xander, Falgar, Sullivan, even the puffed up lordling Bradford. The ship might be gone, but they were still crew. They were her people. The family she chose.

She'd gone and done it again, she realized. She'd abandoned the people she loved out of some misplaced sense of shame.

"Jace." She tried to sound as gentle as possible, "These past couple moons been like something out of someone else's life. It's been wonderful, really. But I can't... I'm not..."

Jace set his mug — *empty again?* — down and seemed to wrestle with some fierce internal debate. Then, he lunged across the table, took Tai's face in his hands, and planted a sloppy wet kiss on her mouth.

"Whhhmph?"

Jace's clumsy attempt to swallow her tongue drowned out any hope of protestation. Tai gagged against the smell of sour wine, and it was several long moments before she recovered enough to push herself free.

"Sorry." Tai gasped for breath, "But what in the Depths are you doing?"

Jace's expression flickered several times between hurt and embarrassed and confused. "You... the leaf crown... you accepted..."

Tai let out a deep resigned sigh as she removed the circlet and placed it down on the table. "I'm sorry, Jace. You've been wonderful to me. I just... I'm not sure I'm ready for courtship yet. Perhaps one day... if you're ever in Aeris..."

Jace's brows knit together, and a flash of annoyance breached his wounded expression. "How can you say that after all we've been through together?"

Tai wrinkled her nose. *Been through together?* She liked Jace well enough, and they'd enjoyed a friendly acquaintance for a few moons, but before that, she hadn't seen him since their childhood.

Her confusion must have shown on her face because Jace's hurt expression at last gave way to anger. "Tai, I was at your house every day. I helped you when you were sick. Fallen take it, Tai, I *cooked* for you." He wrinkled his nose as if he could imagine nothing more odious than *cooking*.

"I'm... *grateful* for those things," Tai stammered, "But I'm not... that is... I never asked... I'm not *ready*..."

"I think you owe it to me, after everything I did," he said. He lunged forward to try and kiss her again. Fortunately, he seemed to struggle to hold his liquor, and he'd just downed a massive amount of greenwine. She was drunk, but he was drunker, and he might be a border guard, but she was almost a Void-cursed *dragonaut*. She managed to sidestep him, just barely.

Anger asserted itself beneath her bafflement. "I didn't ask you to do any of those things. I could have recovered just fine on my own. In fact, I would have left weeks ago if left to my own devices. But I stayed because I was *grateful*, because... because we're *friends*..."

"Friends?" Jace spat out the word a full octave higher than his usual register. "You think I would..." Jace's hands curled into fists. "It's that Aerish boy, isn't it? Kadmin or whatever his name was. What in the Void has he got that I don't? I bet he wasn't even nice to you."

"He wasn't," Tai admitted, still feeling confused and wrong-footed. *Void curse all this greenwine!* "But he's not... Kadmin and I aren't... There is someone in Aeris, but he..."

"A *third* man!" Jace's eyes shot open with outrage. "Savior's Wings, Tai, how many men do you have on rotation? To think I did all that for you, not realizing that you were some kind of... some kind of floozy!"

Tai knew it was the wrong reaction, but she burst out laughing. "A *floozy*?"

"You disgust me, Tai Lunstrum," Jace said, and with that, he stormed away, leaving Tai alone with her drunken confusion.

CHAPTER THIRTY-ONE
CONFRONTATIONS

Hildegard had never seen the Dragonmar so furious.

Sylvia paced up and down the length of her office, silk skirts swishing in her wake. Her blue eyes flashed with barely suppressed rage. "Explain."

"Lady Dragonmar." Hildegard swallowed. She was well into her forties, but at this moment, she felt like a twelve-year-old schoolgirl upbraided in the headteacher's office.

I want you to speak to the Dragonmar, Jameson said. *You're the most rational of us,* Jameson said.

She cursed Jameson for lacking the courage to have this conversation himself. She cursed herself for lacking the courage to press the matter.

"Please explain," Sylvia repeated, this time with forced calm, "Why you've locked our Orith guest in the dungeons and confined Dorian Valmont to quarters."

Hildegard drew in a deep breath and let it out. "I didn't want to believe it of them either, but..."

"No 'buts'," Sylvia said.

Hildegard prayed to Nahiira for patience. "If you want me to explain, then let me explain."

Sylvia massaged her temples. "Very well. I apologize. Go on."

Hildegard nodded. "With all due respect, Lady Dragonmar. Tanis Lunstrum admitted to everything himself." She remembered well how bedraggled the poor boy looked, pale and emaciated and still bearing the marks of fugue, as he confessed all that had gone on the past several moons. "He's been in contact with some man called High Councilor Gideon, giving him secret information about the Order, secret entrances to the castle, the dragonauts' comings and goings, and even information about the moon glass. Everything."

Sylvia's posture relaxed slightly, though her expression was still stern. "I understand the need to lock the boy up. But why the dungeons? Confine him to quarters if you must. And why, Ancients help me, is Dorian locked up in *his* apartments? Last I checked, *he* did not betray the Order."

Hildegard sighed. *Curse Jameson to the Void for making her do this!* "Lady Dragonmar. You were the one who said that Tanis's actions should be Dorian's responsibility. We were acting on your orders."

Sylvia waved her hand as if swatting away an irritating insect. "Well, then, I *un-order* it."

Hildegard fiddled with her leather headband. "Lady Dragonmar, you'll forgive me for being frank, but don't you think you might be the slightest bit biased?"

"Is it biased to be *informed*? I have known Mr. Valmont far longer than you have, I *dare say*. Don't you think I would *know* if he was capable of duplicity?"

Hildegard let out a sad, ironic little chuckle. "He might, at that. He might've learned it from you."

Sylvia's eyes flashed, and Hildegard was certain she'd gone too far. But then Sylvia closed her eyes and shook her head. "I suppose I've done a poor job proving myself trustworthy, haven't I?"

"Lady Dragonmar," Hildegard said, more gently this time. "Does he know the truth?"

Sylvia said nothing, which was, itself, an answer.

"You haven't told him."

Sylvia gave the faintest jerk of her head. "That is..."

"You need to tell him."

"I know I do, but the situation..."

"I don't give a fart in the underclouds about the situation. He's been in the castle, what, eight moons? And he still doesn't know?" Hildegard had come here expecting the dragonmar to tell her off, but it appeared it might be the other way around. Still, she had to do what was right.

Sylvia's face was even paler than usual. "I want to tell him. I know I need to, and... I will. I just have to wait until the time is right."

Hildegard ran her hands through her already-rumpled auburn hair. "When the time is right, she says." *Yep, that's me, the rational one. Aren't you glad you sent me to talk to the Dragonmar, Jameson?* "The time will never be right, will it, Lady Dragonmar?"

"Void take it, Hildegard." Sylvia placed her palms on the table. "How do you suppose he's going to react when he finds out I've kept something like this from him? How is he going to feel?"

Hildegard sighed. "And how much worse will it be when he finds out from someone else? Don't think I don't know the *real* reason you sent Xander and Bradford away. Ancients, Sylvia, even you can't keep it secret forever. He's going to find out from someone."

Hildegard knew she was out of line but she didn't care. She spoke not to the high and mighty Dragonmar, but to Sylvia, her childhood friend.

Sylvia gazed at Hildegard over the top of her spectacles, suddenly looking much older than a woman in her forties. "Someone like you?"

"If it comes to it, yes. Someone like me. Kick me out of the Order if you must. But I will not stand by and watch this farce continue."

Sylvia shook her head. She didn't look like she was about to kick Hildegard out of the Order. Instead, she just looked exhausted, and deeply, deeply sad.

"I know," she said. "I know. Very well. I'll tell him."

"Good," Hildegard said. "See that you do."

Tai woke up with the irrefutable knowledge that something was wrong.

Throat dry, she reached for her cup on the nightstand. "Ugh." Her stomach churned, and no amount of water seemed to soothe the wooly dryness in her throat. "We didn't planeshift again, did we, Celestian?" She groaned and tried to piece together her memories of the evening.

There'd been dancing, and wine, far, far too much wine. Not Planeshifting, then. This time, at least, it really *was* just a hangover. She recalled leaping from the platform, her limbs entangled with Jace's, and... Void, she hadn't bedded him, had she? No, no, surely not. She'd remember if she had. Wouldn't she?

«What happened last night?» she reached out for her connection with Celestian, but the dragon was uncharacteristically silent. Probably annoyed about her irresponsible behavior. «I won't drink to excess again, I promise. Now can we stop the silent treatment?»

Still, nothing.

And then, in fits and starts, the rest of the evening came back to her. Jace, drunk, trying to kiss her. Tai's awkward, flabbergasted reaction. He'd stormed away in anger. She'd returned to her mother's home in sadness and confusion. And still, Celestian remained silent.

«Celestian?» She reached beneath her shirt to feel the comforting weight of her stolen dragonstone — and discovered it was gone.

"Void!" Heart pounding, she overturned her pillows and shook out the blanket, then tore through her trunk of neatly folded clothing. Unlike on the day she arrived, it was not simply on the chair waiting for her. Tai became increasingly certain the dragonstone was not in her room at all.

"Void, Void, Void." Heart in her throat, she threw on the first item of clothing she could find and sprinted into the main living area, hoping to see the stone glittering in welcome purple-blue. But it was not there, and nor, apparently, was her mother.

Dread mounting, Tai slipped on her sandals and left the dwelling. The town was eerily quiet; most people were probably sleeping off their own hangovers. But if her mother was anywhere, it was likely to be the Council Hall, so Tai hurriedly hoisted herself up the rope elevator.

The Council Hall was almost empty when she arrived, save for Reora in her green mayoral robes, knelt in prayer.

"Mother." Tai hoped she didn't sound too accusatory.

"Ah, good morning, Tai." Reora rose to her feet. She looked a bit tired from the previous night's festivities, but otherwise in good spirits. "Your friend Jace was by this morning, but there was no stirring you. You might pay him a visit when you get the chance."

"Jace," Tai repeated, blinking several times. "Listen, Mother, my dragonstone, have you seen it?"

Reora looked concerned. "It's not around your neck where it always is?"

Tai lowered her wings. She didn't detect anything duplicitous in her mother's manner, so she had no choice but to take her at face value. Reora really didn't know where the dragonstone had gone.

"Thanks anyway," Tai said, "I'll just—"

"Lady Mayor." Jace burst into the temple, carrying a familiar-looking cloth bundle. "I've just spoken to the prison guard, he said—oh." He saw Tai standing there, and glanced quickly away, looking embarrassed, possibly ashamed.

A nasty thought took root in Tai's stomach like poison bramble-berry and refused to let go. Jace was her friend. His hero-worship of Gideon was a bit obnoxious, and he'd reacted poorly to her rejection of his advances, but at the end of the day, he wouldn't steal from her, would he? Part of her refused to accept the possibility. But she had to know.

"Jace," she said slowly, "*You* haven't seen my dragonstone, have you?"

There was no doubt about it, he definitely looked guilty as he tugged a loose feather and stared at the wooden floor.

"Jace," she prodded again.

"He's the Savior," Jace finally said, "What was I supposed to do, say no to the Savior? And besides. You rejected me. You turned me away. I don't owe you anything."

"Jace." Reora spoke with the reprimanding voice Tai knew so well. "What did you do?"

Jace blanched and refused to look at either Tai or Reora. "His Holiness required the use of an additional dragon's magic. I did as my Lord Savior beseeched me. That's all." He finally looked at them each in turn, his golden-brown eyes hard with defiance, as if daring them to contradict him.

Tai felt a chill. "Additional dragon. So he *has* got one already." She'd suspected as much, given Gideon's so-called "miracles" and the bloody Void-cursed *glowing*. But where was this alleged dragon? And why had no one else in town seen them?

"Several dragons. Speaking of," Jace said, sounding almost bored. "I must see to our new guests."

Jace left without another word. Tai made a hasty farewell to her mother and chased after him, leaping from the platform, not bothering to use the lift. She skidded to a halt on the mossy ground and sprinted after Jace, who made a bee line straight for the town jail.

There wasn't a lot of crime in Lost Hollow, but after a raucous night like yesterday, she saw more than a handful of bleary-eyed townsfolk nursing their hangovers behind bars. Brawling at the festival, no doubt. But they were not who Jace approached.

Councilor Gideon, alongside Councilor Temperance and several border guards, stood outside a cell on the far end of the row. Tai's heart gave a horrified lurch when she saw who was in that final jail cell.

"Falgar," she cried, "Sullivan!"

"Tai?" Falgar looked flabbergasted. "What in the Void are you doing here?"

"I could ask the same of you." She rounded on Gideon. "What is the meaning of this? Let them go!" Tai only came up to about the tall Councilor's shoulder, but she spread her wings as far as they would go and affixed him with her most piercing glare.

"You dare approach the Savior?" Kyre the border guard shoved her roughly with the butt of his spear.

"Now, now," Gideon waved them off. "There's no need for all that." His twisted smile made her stomach sink even lower. "These two fools may have stumbled where they shouldn't have, but their dragons are a gift which will bring us all prosperity." Gideon's blue-gray eyes shone with manic zeal. "With the help of our unlikely allies, and the energy harvested from the windmill and our captive dragons, we shall finally have our vengeance! We shall end the cursed Aerish magic once and for all, and sink their lands to the undersea, just as they did to us all those years ago."

Tai felt like she was going to throw up. *Unlikely allies indeed!* She should have known.

"This ally of yours." Tai's voice shook. "It's Janus Callahan, isn't it?"

It all seemed so obvious now. After all this time, Kadmin hadn't come to get his dragon back, and now Tai knew why. Kadmin already knew precisely where they were, and that the people here were on his side.

"Do you think he cares about Orith at all?" Tai demanded. "Do you think he will share his power?"

"Don't talk to the Savior like that," Jace snapped.

"I realize you are rather emotional," Gideon said. "But I must ask you to please calm down. Your contribution has been valuable. With that windmill of yours, we are now able to drain the power from these dragons all the more efficiently."

"No," Tai gasped. He couldn't mean what she thought he did. Not their windmill. Not the thing that had given her so much hope and purpose these past tumultuous weeks.

"I disapproved of the project at first," Gideon said. "Why sully the Path's own Light with our grubby mortal inventions? But now I see that it can be used for more. So much more."

"You bastard!" Temperance's voice. She stood flanked by border guards, face flushed with fury, as guards valiantly held her back from clawing the alleged Savior's eyes out.

It was a small, cold comfort that at least Temperance wasn't behind whatever Gideon was up to.

"As I said, you have been a useful resource, and I would not squander that," Gideon said. "But it's plain to see that you are too distraught to think logically right now. I think perhaps your constitution is still too fragile. Jace, take her to your home, make sure she gets plenty of rest, and see that she does not... wander."

"She is staying at *my* home." Reora joined them, looking furious, but also terrified.

"Lady mayor." Gideon's voice dripped with bitter condescension. "You have already proven yourself an unfit guardian. Perhaps you are unfit to lead this town as well."

Tai met her mother's eyes, silently begging. *Please. Do not make me go with Jace.* She felt like a small child, waiting for her mother to come swooping in to the rescue. But she had a feeling no rescue was forthcoming. Reora lowered the remains of her wings in surrender and stared at the ground, not meeting either of their eyes.

"Hmph," Gideon said. "As I thought."

"Go straight to the Depths," Tai growled.

"Now, now." Jace tightened his grip around her wrist. "That kind of language isn't very ladylike."

"Take her home, Jace," Gideon commanded. "As for our guests...

Kyre, I want you to move them someplace a bit more secure. The drunk tank, after all, is hardly suitable."

"With pleasure." Kyre jangled his keyring, glowering at Falgar and Sullivan.

"Why are you doing this?" she demanded as Jace frog-marched her back to his dwelling.

Once again, Jace refused to look at her. "Gideon is the Savior, Tai. You'll come to see that he's right eventually."

Tai cast one last look behind her, at Falgar and Sullivan in their jail cell, at Temperance's expression of despair, at her mother's look of grim resignation, at Gideon and Kyre's horrible, unbearable smugness. She'd never in her life been so furious. She'd never in her life felt so powerless.

CHAPTER THIRTY-TWO
VISITORS IN PRISON

«Ninety eight... ninety nine... one hundred.»
Dorian gave an impolite grunt before collapsing in a puddle of his own sweat on the bearskin rug. Probably not good for the rug, but Dorian wasn't feeling especially well-disposed towards the Order's possessions at the moment.

«One hundred push-ups in three minutes,» Solaris said from where she lied curled up next to the fireplace. «Your best yet.»

That was, Dorian noted with a minute flicker of pride, more than even Jameson had managed during their last conditioning test. Surely the flight leader would have to grudgingly admit Dorian was worthy of his dragonstone now. If only it mattered anymore.

Dorian smiled ruefully and tried to take a swig from his canteen. Unfortunately, it was almost empty. He was going to have to ask for more whenever somebody dropped off his evening meal. Assuming they'd stay long enough for him to ask. Hildegard was usually good for a short, apologetic conversation. But Jameson typically plopped the wooden tray on the ground as if Dorian were a dog and then departed without a word.

A petulant part of Dorian almost refused to eat. Let it be on the

Order's conscience if an innocent dragonaut starved to death. But Dorian had never been any good at ignoring his body's hunger signals, so he always finished his supper in the end. *Void curse it all.*

«Your pride,» Solaris would remind him, «Is not worth dying for.»

In his darkest moments he almost, almost thought starving would be preferable to remaining cooped up forever. No matter how he tried to distract himself, his thoughts continued to spiral. He felt like a caged animal, ready to claw at himself in the absence of a more desirable target. But it could be worse. Oh, gods, it could be worse. If things were bad for him, he didn't want to think about how they must be for Tanis.

Dorian felt sick whenever he thought of the young Orith, trapped in the dank and dirty dungeons, still weakened from his demonic fugue, with only Malachite's malicious company. It wasn't right. It wasn't fair. There had to be some sort of misunderstanding. Dorian simply couldn't, wouldn't, believe that his charge had knowingly betrayed them.

But what if he had?

Dorian had taken responsibility for the boy in order to prevent him rotting in the dungeons. Except now, poor Tanis was rotting in the dungeons anyway, and all they had to show for it was a stolen moon glass and a castle on high alert. Dorian's intentions had been good, but what use were good intentions when everyone ended up worse off than when they started?

"Gah," he snarled in frustration. Dorian couldn't shake the feeling that there was something he was missing, a piece of the puzzle dangling just out of reach.

He put his hand on Solaris's ruby scales, his last remaining source of comfort. "If they find me guilty, they'll take my dragonstone," he said. "They'll probably want you to bond with someone else. Someone more worthy. I think... I know I can't tell you what to do. But I think you should bond Tai. When she gets back from Kasanarae I mean." He did not say, *if she gets back.* "She'd... she'd be a good dragonaut. A better dragonaut than me."

Solaris head-butted him gently but firmly, and only long-practiced footwork kept him from falling backwards onto the bearskin rug.

«You are correct about one thing,» she said. «You cannot tell me what to do. I do not wish to bond Tai Lunstrum. I wish to remain bonded to you.»

"But..."

«Perhaps helping Tanis was a mistake,» Solaris said. «I am not convinced of that fact, but let us pretend, for a moment, that it was. Well. So what? I have made many mistakes in my time. Mistakes are universal. But bonding you, my dear human, was never a mistake. Anyone who fails to see that is more the fool.»

"I'm not sure I see it," Dorian admitted.

«Then you are a fool.» Solaris's tone was matter-of-fact.

Dorian laughed weakly. "Suppose I am." To his surprise, this bluntness made him feel better than empty reassurances ever could.

Solaris looked out the leaded-glass window, at the gray skies above and the billowing clouds below. «It is funny,» she said. «The Order puts on these elaborate displays trying to find the ideal dragonaut, and here I found one, entirely by accident.»

Dorian snorted. "Again with the platitudes." If the past two years had taught him anything, it was that he was *far* from the ideal dragonaut.

«I mean it,» she said, and to Dorian's surprise, he thought perhaps she really did. «The dragonauts of old sought the best of humanity. The strongest, the wisest, the greatest magi. But also the kindest, the bravest, the hardest working. More and more, I see you are the former. But you have always been the latter, and that, my dear human, is even more important.»

"I..." Dorian felt a runaway tear travel unbidden down his face. *Stupid tear. Go away.* "I wish I could believe you."

And he wanted to. Oh, gods, he wanted to. Some logical part of him knew he was too hard on himself. Void, if anyone spoke about his friends the way he thought about himself, he'd be hard pressed not to start a fight. And yet, every time the slightest thing went wrong, he felt like he was nine years old again, weak and helpless, desperately trying to dig his father's body out of the rubble of Icereach Citadel. No matter what he tried to tell himself, he felt resigned to shouldering the full blame, all other forces cursed to the Void.

The sound of a key in the lock jarred him out of his self-pity. Hoping it might be Hildegard with the evening meal and, better still, some news, Dorian looked up towards the door — and staggered backwards in surprise.

Lady Sylvia Kane, Dragonmar of Cloudfire, stood outside his door in a somber charcoal-colored gown, her hair tied up in a severe bun, looking graver than he'd ever seen her.

"Hello Dorian," she said. "I think it's time you and I had a talk."

On the fourth day of Tai's imprisonment, help finally arrived.

Any illusion that she was brought to Jace's dwelling "for her own protection" vanished the moment he fitted a set of iron bars around the entrance to her sleeping alcove. Tai was let out three times a day to use the outhouse and get a modicum of exercise, but other than that, she was stuck. At least Jace hadn't tried to kiss her again. Perhaps he had some flicker of decency left in him, or perhaps he'd simply lost interest. She was, after all, a *floozy*.

Tai groaned inwardly when she heard the main outside door slide open. She didn't think she could stomach yet another lecture about how she must repent or face the Frigid Depths. But to her surprise, it wasn't Jace who stepped carefully into the dwelling.

"Dax?" Tai drew back the beaded alcove curtains and peered

through the bars at the white-winged Orith dragonaut. "What are you doing here?"

Dax looked around nervously and swiftly approached the sleeping alcove. Now that Tai saw him, he looked worse for wear. Long gone were his fine embroidered silks, replaced with sturdy woolen traveling clothes. His shoulder was bandaged, and so was part of his wing.

"Jace has gone to the market," Dax said. "I don't have much time."

Dax retrieved a heavy iron keyring from his belt pouch and unlocked her cell door with a loud clank.

"You're letting me out?"

"Only temporarily I'm afraid. If I set you loose now they'll just capture you right away again. But this will make it easier for us to talk," Dax said.

Tai nodded and hopped down, stretching out her cramped legs. The sleeping alcove ceiling was just barely too low for Tai to stand up all the way, so she had a crick in her neck, as well.

"Inhumane, to keep you locked up like that." Dax shook his head. "Anyway. You should know that three days ago, Gideon deposed your mother and took over as mayor of Lost Hollow."

Tai sighed and tilted her head from side to side in an attempt to loosen her tense neck muscles. "Of course he did."

"He arrested your mother for, in Gideon's words, 'sedition against the Savior.'" Dax's hands curled into fists. "After using the threat of it to blackmail your brother, he went ahead and did it anyway once he got what he wanted."

"Wait, what? He blackmailed Tanis? How? Why?" Clearly, Tai was woefully behind on events.

Dax sighed. "It's a long story. But before they hauled your mother off, she asked *my* mother to give you this."

Tai knew a shameful, selfish moment of relief to know that her mother hadn't visited because she was literally imprisoned, and not because she hadn't wanted to. "You're Temperance Vesper's son, aren't you? The one who was sent away because you could fly."

Dax nodded. "I see you're caught up on some of the backstory. Good, that saves us time. My mother wanted to do this herself, but Gideon is watching her every move. Thankfully, Gideon doesn't know I'm here just yet. Our so-called Savior isn't *quite* all knowing." Dax smiled wanly and handed Tai her familiar canvas rucksack.

"My stuff." Tai blinked in confusion. She was glad to have it back, but she wasn't sure what good it would do.

"Open it," Dax urged.

Tai did so, discovering that it was packed for a journey. Mushroom rice balls, wrapped in silver leaves. A canteen of fresh spring water. A magnetic compass. Her athame, ironwood hilt and solid steel blade nestled safely in a leather scabbard. And, wrapped neatly in her mother's usual fashion, her fine silk festival robes. *Not much opportunity to dress up when I'm locked a sleeping alcove,* she thought ruefully.

Tai ran her hand sadly along the silk fabric, thinking about how much simpler life seemed four days ago, when her finger brushed against the sash that kept the garment closed.

"What the—"

It wasn't the plain gray sash she'd worn to the festival. This one was dark midnight blue, bedecked with embroidered stars, with the phases of the moon in the center.

"The night sky? I— but that's impossible."

The moon was emblematic of everything the Orith had lost. The source of all magic, invisible beneath the clouds. The hope of what they may one day regain. The symbol of the Prophetess Rivka Sevarin. The symbol of the Savior.

This was, in short, the type of embroidery only offered to the highest Councilors. She'd never even seen Gideon wear something like this, much less a scrawny flightless girl who spent more than half her life among the Aerish. *One who walks between worlds.*

"I... I can't possibly have this."

"That is between you and the Path," Dax said, not particularly helpfully. He reached into one of his pockets, producing a familiar indigo blue dragonstone. Tai gasped, feeling Celestian's warm, familiar power.

"How did you—"

"Stole it," Dax said. He cast a nervous look out the dwelling window, and Tai could guess what he was thinking. Jace was due back any minute. "I'll try to get through this quickly. Gideon's hosting some kind of fancy ritual in the town square tonight. All his followers are expected to be there, Jace included. He might try and convince you to come along. If you can, feign illness. Then once he's gone, I want you to take these and get as far from here as you can." He pressed the keyring into her hand. "This brass key will unlock your cell. The iron ones will get you into the cellar at the edge of town where your friends and your mother and the dragons are being kept."

Tai stared at the keyring, then back at Dax. "What about you?"

"Sadly, I have more business here. I will rejoin the rest of you as soon as I'm able, but right now, my duty is to this town." His expression softened slightly. "Word is you saved my mother's life. I remain in your debt. Please try to survive so I might repay it."

And then, without another word, he departed.

This was the second time in two years that Xander had wound up in jail. First in Goose Head, and now here, in the Kasani capitol. *What Mother and Father would think of me now*, he thought ruefully. Languishing in his cell beneath the Fountain Palace, he found he had little to do except mull over all the myriad ways his life had gone wrong.

Xander had been such an obedient rule-follower as a youth. If someone went back in time and told him he'd be arrested twice in as many years, he would've been aghast. But he should have known he'd consigned himself to a life of crime when he left the Order and took the moon glass with him. Everything since then had just been logical consequences.

He felt a dull ache in his chest at the thought of Faris's betrayal. Although he knew he should be furious with her, the best he could summon was an exhausted sort of sadness. He couldn't claim he would have done any different, in her situation. They'd used her children for leverage, for the Void's sake. Xander didn't have children, but he had people he valued just as much.

From the adjacent cell, he could hear Bradford singing, slightly off key. "Oh, I've seen troubles. I've seen woes. Got arrested by my father, and... mmmm, don't have any nice clothes."

"Nice clothes? Really?"

"Yes, well, even my extensive education didn't quite include all the finer points of poetry," Bradford said testily. More loudly, he continued, "Fair Lady Vivienne, she broke my heart, now I'm stuck down here, and I have to—"

"Quiet," Xander said. "I think I hear someone coming."

"Can't be meal time yet. It's barely ten bells."

But sure enough, the sound of footsteps against the stone dungeon floor grew louder. More prisoners? Xander hoped not. Bad enough they were stuck down here. He felt a flash of worry for the rest of his friends in the underground.

But it was just a Kasani soldier, and guessing by the crescent moon insignia on her uniform, a mere cadet at that. She was tall and willowy, and had rich brown skin and dark braided hair. Xander didn't recognize her.

"Lords Xander Kane and Bradford Callahan?"

"What's it to you?"

"I'm Judika Lewellyn, Dragonaut Candidate. Over here is Owain Barclay."

A moment later, a second cadet arrived. Even though he knew Tai left moons ago, Xander was oddly disappointed not to see her among them.

"What is this?" Xander sighed. "Are you going to torture us to get all our secrets?"

From the other cell, Bradford made a yelp of dismay.

The girl, Lewellyn rolled her eyes. "Of course we're not going to torture you. We're setting you free, assuming you're not so foggy-headed that you just get arrested again."

"Oh." Xander felt every bit as foggy-headed as she suggested. "That's... that's good. But can I ask why?"

"Does it matter?" Bradford asked with exasperation.

Owain puffed out his chest. "You're Tai's friend, and that's good enough for us."

Lewellyn nodded in agreement, though her expression was much more subdued. "I wasn't sure whether or not I could trust her. But after she left, I realized she was braver than I've ever been." She spread her arms helplessly. "You know the old saying. Never too late to do the right thing."

Lewellyn proceeded to open their cells with a heavy iron skeleton key, then quickly led them towards the spiral staircase. Feeling like a rat or a cockroach, Xander and the others skittered out of the palace through one of the many servant's entrances.

They stole through the cool Autumn night, passing the gates of first the upper city, then the middle, and finally the lower, until they reached the familiar sky-docks, dimly lit with flickering blue aether lamps.

Xander's heart sank as they came to a halt in front of a large group of people, with Duchess Vivienne's distinctive burly form at the forefront. Lewellyn and the others, however, didn't look worried or surprised.

Was this some kind of trap? Why let them out of prison at all, if that were the case? But when Xander scanned the crowd, he realized most of them didn't look like soldiers. Among them, he recognized Faris and her two children, accompanied by an iron-haired Iriya man who had to have been her husband, as well as Donovan, Stokes, Martel, Aldric, and Rona.

"You were all in the dungeons too," Xander stated the obvious.

Owain looked inordinately pleased with himself. "We've been smuggling prisoners out all week. So far their absence hasn't been noted."

"They'll notice after tonight, though," Lewellyn said.

"I'd say so," Xander said. There was quite a crowd on the dock. Even Regnald, the crotchety old dock master, stood waiting for them with the demon Garnet perched on his shoulder. *What in the Void was going on?*

Xander turned to Faris, who looked suitably sheepish.

"This is your doing, I take it?" he asked.

"Not *all* my doing." She tugged at the ends of her graying brown hair. "About what happened..."

Xander glanced from Faris to the iron-haired man and the boy and girl at her side. "Your family is safe," he said. "That's what matters."

Faris looked like she wanted to protest, but then she just nodded stoically.

"Right." Xander ran his hand through his shaggy hair. "Now that's out of the way... seems you've all been busy. I thought the underground was nowhere near trying to free any of the prisoners."

Faris smirked. "Having an ally on the inside moved the timetable up considerably." She gestured to the burly soldier-duchess Vivienne, who had been silent throughout this entire exchange.

"Vivienne?" Bradford said the name like a plea, eyes wide and yearning.

Xander shot him a meaningful glance. *Don't think with your cock, boy.*

Xander crossed his arms and faced the duchess. "You can't possibly expect us to trust you." Faris was one thing, she was protecting her family. But Vivienne's motivations were worryingly opaque.

Vivienne shook her head. "A lot has changed in the past few days, but I'll give you the short version. You remember that powerful Ancient artifact you stole from Emperor Callahan all those years ago?"

"That map thing?" asked Stokes.

"She said years ago, not a few days ago." Martel rolled his eyes.

"She means the moon glass, I think," Xander said. "What about it?"

Vivienne's expression was grave. "Well. He's got it back."

"*What?*"

"Well, some friends of his have it, at any rate, and he'll have it himself soon enough. I don't know all of what he plans to do with it, but he's also found out your dragonaut friends are in Cloudfire, and he's already departed with half the fleet."

Xander looked up in alarm, half expecting to see Callahan's flagship racing overhead. "He's attacking Cloudfire? And he left already?"

"I'm afraid so." Vivienne nodded. "Granted, it will take them a couple weeks to get there with the current wind conditions. You may yet arrive in time to warn your friends, or at the very least provide reinforcements."

"You're coming with us, right?" Bradford sounded entirely too hopeful.

"I'm afraid not," Vivienne said, and to her credit she sounded genuinely apologetic. "I'm far more use to the underground here. Lewellyn and Owain and I will cover for you for as long as we can."

"We, on the other hand, would all love to see Cloudfire," said Donovan.

Bradford, however, had eyes only for the Duchess Vivienne. "Is it true, then? Have you been working against the Emperor all this time?"

Vivienne spread her hands noncommittally. "My loyalty is and always has been, to Kasanarae — not the Emperor, not even the

Empress, but Kasanarae itself. Sometimes that requires making... tough choices."

Bradford looked like he wanted to say more, but Vivienne shook her head. "You need to hurry. Eventually, they'll notice you're gone, and I can't keep them distracted forever."

"If you'll come with me," Dock Master Regnald interjected, "I'll show you to the ship."

"Right," Bradford said. "Ship. We have a ship."

"Didn't think we were going to sprout Orith wings and flap all the way to Cloudfire, did you?" Faris asked.

"I took the liberty of acquiring a vessel for you, yes." Lady Vivienne flashed a grim smile.

They made their way to the docks, and when they got there, Xander was sure there had been a mistake. "What the— *how*?"

"My father was the old queen's brother," Vivienne said. "You'll find I have quite a few strings to pull. Let's just say the Emperor isn't as universally beloved by his nobles as he likes to claim. Now, granted, Emperor Callahan is going to pitch an absolute fit when he sees it's gone, so do *try* to make haste."

They stood before the *Imperial Javelin,* pride of the Kasani Empire, compensation for Callahan's lackluster anatomy. But *Imperial Javelin* was not the name written across the hull in gold leaf. At some point while Xander was in the dungeons, it had been repainted with the name *Phoenix Reborn.*

"Zekador's poorly fitting pants," Xander breathed.

"Father's going to be furious." Bradford sounded both horrified and delighted.

"Most certainly," Vivienne agreed.

Xander swallowed. He still couldn't quite believe all this was real, but he wasn't about to look a gift warship in the mouth. "Right then. Where's the captain? I'd like a quick word."

Regnald looked at him like he'd spouted a second head. "He's right here, obviously."

"You?" Xander blinked.

Regnald rolled his eyes. "Of course not, numb-nuts. I'm not going with you on this fool misadventure, I'm just here to take you to the ship. *You're* the captain."

"*Me?*"

"You have experience in the area, do you not?" Faris asked.

"Well," Xander allowed, "Sort of, but..." Ancients help him, the *Phoenix* had been a fine vessel, but she'd been nowhere near in league with a Void-cursed *warship*.

"I'm acting first mate until you appoint someone else," Faris said. "As such, can I make a suggestion?"

Xander raised his eyebrows. "Go ahead."

"*Fly now, talk later.*"

Xander swallowed, then nodded firmly. "Right. Of course. Let's go. Time to be Void-cursed heroes."

CHAPTER THIRTY-THREE
THE DRAGONS IN THE CELLAR

The next few hours dragged on for what felt like days. Within the confines of her cramped sleeping alcove, Tai had little to do but catastrophize on the myriad ways tonight could go wrong. Jace could come in and notice her rucksack hidden among the pillows. Gideon could catch her trying to free the others. Aeris might sink tonight and land directly on their heads. Some scenarios were farfetched indeed, while others were all too plausible. She dwelled on them all the same.

Finally, the sky darkened, and after another failed attempt to get Tai to repent her wicked ways, Jace departed for the evening ritual. She watched out the tiny alcove window as he wound his way down the narrow path towards the center of town. When she was confident he wouldn't turn back, she retrieved the heavy brass key and awkwardly stuck her hand through the bars to undo the lock. After a few tries, much to her relief, it clicked open.

As Dax had predicted, most of the townsfolk were gathered in the central square. Gideon was ranting about abominations and prophecy and whatever else Gideon always ranted about, and most of the audience's attention was on him, not the scrawny girl on the periphery of the crowd. With her hood up obscuring her features, she could be practically any small-winged villager. It was strange and a bit wonderful, to actually blend in for once. Pity this whole place was run by a delusional cultist.

With the stolen dragonstone safely around her neck, she made her way past the gathered townspeople and followed the pulse of Celestian's life force. Eventually, the pulse led her to a heavy cellar door built into the hillside. She felt a flare of indignation at the thought of dragons, creatures of flame and sky, held against their will in what was no doubt a dank and moist cellar. But there was nothing else for it. Better get down there and rescue her friends before anyone noticed she wasn't at the ritual — or in her cage.

Tai unlocked the heavy iron padlock and pulled the door open with a loud creak. She winced at the sound, but fortunately, something in Gideon's speech merited thunderous applause, so no one in the square heard her. Tai jumped inside and landed about ten feet below in what appeared to be an old mine shaft. Branches of silver-leaf sat arranged in wall sconces like wedding bouquets, dimly lighting the path ahead.

"Hey! Hey, who's there? Aren't you supposed to be at the ritual?" A portly man in his middle years, balding slightly, came running towards her. She might have almost confused him for an Aerishman if not for the tiny wing stumps poking out the back of his jerkin. He had simple leaf embroidery on his cuffs and collar, probably no higher than the Third Waypost.

Tai crouched into a fighting stance and drew her athame. She had no proper weapon, but luckily she had something better: magic.

Zing, zing, zing. With Celestian's unspoken assent, she drew power from him and flung the runes into the air as if they were arrows. *Stasis, immobility, spirit drain.* The guard looked poleaxed for a moment, before collapsing in a pile of snores.

Before moving on, Tai stole the shortsword off of the guard's belt. It looked chipped and slightly flimsy, but fleeing without a weapon was a mistake she wasn't eager to repeat. Thus armed, she hurriedly made her way down the tunnel.

Three cages hung suspended from the cavernous ceiling, respectively containing Falgar, Sullivan, and, to Tai's horror, Reora.

"Tai!" Reora cried out.

"Tai?" Falgar asked.

"Tai," Sullivan observed.

Tai scrambled to reach the cages. "Did Gideon hurt you?"

"Nah," Falgar said, "Mostly I've just been afraid we're gonna die of boredom down here. I mean, they couldn't even let us share a cage?"

"Falgar," Sullivan chided, but he smiled too.

Tai relaxed slightly. If her friends could joke around, they probably weren't too badly off.

Reora snorted from the uppermost cage. "I should think this is hardly the time. What are you doing down here, Tai? Surely Gideon hasn't wrapped you up in this vile scheme of his."

Tai shook her head. "I'm here to rescue you, obviously."

Tai scrambled up on some overturned crates in order to unlock the hanging cages. Reora leapt easily to the ground, while the two Aerishmen had a more awkward time climbing down her makeshift step ladder.

"I believe this is the second time you've rescued us from prison," Sullivan said. "We really ought to return the favor one of these days."

"How did you get out of Jace's dwelling?" Reora wondered. "Last I heard he had the place well secured."

"Dax helped me," Tai began, but her words were lost as everyone began talking at once.

"What was Dax doing here?" "What are *you* doing here?" "Strange magical energy—" "—Gideon's Ritual—" "—Fight with Graigor—" "—Tanis's convalescence—" "Tanis?" "*Convalescence?*"

"Enough, enough!" Sullivan's baritone echoed against the cavern walls. "We can catch up on everything when we're safe. In the meantime, might I suggest finding our dragons and *getting out of here?*"

Tai swallowed and nodded. "Right. Right. Of course. Do you have your dragonstones?"

Sullivan shook his head. "The guard took them."

Back at the entrance chamber, Tai was relieved to see the guard was still sound asleep. As she awkwardly turned him over to get at his belt pouch, he let out a snort and then muttered under his breath, "The demon ate my baby."

Tai rummaged through the man's belongings, revealing a pouch of coins, a set of bone-carved gaming dice, and, thank all the gods and the Savior, two dragonstones, one purple and one gold. She snatched them up and handed them back to her friends. The guard shifted in his sleep as they departed, and said, "Hi, Flightless, I'm Dad."

Fortunately, three large dragons were difficult to hide in a cramped underground space. Further down the tunnel past the cages, the corridor shone blue with aetherlight.

"What in the thrice-cursed Void?" Falgar skidded to a halt just as the tunnel opened into a wide cavern.

"Whoa," Sullivan confirmed.

«Thank the moon and stars you are here,» Celestian said. He was trapped within a glowing stasis circle, with Falgar and Sullivan's dragons next to him in similar straits. She had never felt this much fear from the dragon before, not even when she had persuaded him to try Planeshifting.

The reason was immediately apparent. In the center of the chamber sat a massive cylindrical tank filled with some kind of glowing blue fluid.

"Liquid aether," Tai breathed. The tank looked identical to the drawing she'd briefly seen in Janus Callahan's office. That connection made her feathers stand on end.

Falgar, however, gazed in horror at the thing *inside* the tank. "Is that... a dragon in there?"

«A wild dragon,» his dragon, Meridian, confirmed, «Yes.»

«Or,» Celestian added bitterly, «What is left of him.»

The shape of the unbonded dragon was barely visible in the aetherlight. She could see right through the creature to the textured stone wall behind the tank. She'd seen wild dragons before, of course, but none of them had looked nearly so weak and diminished. It was almost as if he wasn't a dragon at all, but the mere shadow of one.

"Zekador's poorly fitting pants." Tai let out a shallow breath. "What are they doing to him?"

«Draining him of his power,» Meridian said, mindvoice numb with horror. «Of his life force.»

«If you were wondering where Gideon obtained his ability to perform miracles,» Celestian added, «Here it is.»

Silver-white spirit energy drained out of the dragon in a thin shimmering line, rising up towards a spell circle engraved on the stone ceiling. She recognized a few of the circle's archaic runes from her studies of the Planeshifting spell, while others still looked strange and almost alien. Iriya, perhaps?

But she didn't need to understand the runes to know what the circle did.

Someone was draining this dragon's energy against his will, without the "inconvenience" of bonding him first.

"Meroneth's balls," she swore.

Reora raised her hand to her mouth in horror. "The glowing... the miracles... Lost Moon help me, the *aether beacon*... I was so glad to speak to Tanis. I suppose I didn't think *how* Gideon was getting the magic for it." She let out a bitter little laugh. "Some fool part of me wanted to believe he really *was* the Savior. Now I know better."

"My gods. The poor creature." Sullivan shook his head in disgust. "I never thought I'd see something *worse* than what Emperor Callahan is doing." The blue aetherlight gave his dark brown skin a slight pallor, and he looked like he might be sick.

"We've got to get them out of there." Falgar's hands curled into fists.

No one stated the obvious, that freeing yet another prisoner, particularly one so weak and vulnerable, was an added complexity they could little afford. But there was no real choice in the matter. Leaving him in his current state was unconscionable.

"First thing we need to do is shut down that spell that's draining him," Tai mused out loud. "But how in the Void do we turn off a spell we know nothing about?"

How in the Void. Sweet Ancients. How else?

Tai might have almost laughed were she not so terrified. "Right. Okay. I might be about to do something incredibly stupid."

"Normally I'd make some quip about that not being unusual for you," Falgar said, "But that actually *is* pretty unusual for you."

"Falgar," Sullivan sighed.

Tai breathed in and gathered all her focus before unsheathing her athame and carving a sequence of runes into the air.

Tai hoped it would be enough to counter the imprisoned dragon's magic. She hoped it didn't hurt the dragon. She hoped it didn't blow up in all their faces. *She hoped, she hoped, she hoped.* But hoping would do no good unless she tried it.

Tai cast the forbidden spell that Dorian had shown her, in confidence, nearly a year prior.

Tai cast the Void.

She felt as though a vortex opened up in front of her, greedily sucking all magical energy in its wake. Tai wondered where it all went. Back to the spirit realm? Or was it destroyed irrevocably, never to maintain life on Cyrna again? Tai couldn't muse on it for long, because it took all of her concentration to keep the spell under control. *Drain from the circle,* she begged it, forced it, *Coerced* it. *Drain only from the circle.*

The glowing blue aether-light faltered and died. Before the greedy Void could suck down any more energy, Tai made a violent slashing motion with her athame and the spell wonderfully, thankfully, dissipated. Tai staggered backwards, heaving for breath. Like the Planeshifting spell, this one took a lot out of her. But at least this time, she'd been ready.

"The tank." She moved forward to open the tank, but wavered back and forth, feeling punch-drunk.

"I've got it." Sullivan scrambled forward to turn the valve attached to the tank. Glowing aether fluid spilled out, and, almost as if he was made from fluid himself, so did the dragon. The ghostly creature twitched slightly in the cool air of the cavern, but did not regain consciousness.

Sullivan looked nervously over his shoulder. "That guard will be awake any minute."

"What do we do about Ghosty over here?" Falgar gestured at the newly-freed dragon.

«I can move him,» Sullivan's dragon, Northstar, volunteered. He let out a stream of pale gold sparks, and the unconscious dragon drifted down the corridor.

"Will he be all right, do you think?" Sullivan asked.

«It is difficult to say,» Northstar said. «He has been through quite an ordeal. But we will do the best we can for him. We must first get him back above the cloud layer, if we are to have any hope of restoring his strength.» More gravely, he added, «They would have drained us, too, if given the chance.»

"What are they even doing with all that power?" Tai wondered. "Just a small amount from Celestian can power the windmill for moons. That dragon's almost sucked dry. It can't *all* be going towards glowing Illusions and powering the aether beacon."

Falgar frowned as he regarded the now-empty tank, and the pool of pale blue liquid on the dungeon floor. "Didn't Valmont mention some kind of tanks like these at that base in Thlarknia?"

Sullivan nodded in agreement. "Yes, the ones Tanis was guarding. You... you don't suppose there were *wild dragons* in there, were there?"

«Surely... surely not.» Celestian sounded genuinely terrified. «Surely... if they had, I would have known about it.»

Falgar cast him a shrewd glance. "You were Kadmin's dragon,

weren't you? Kadmin recruited Tanis. And Tanis was guarding that building."

Celestian twitched his tail back and forth in obvious agitation. «Even Kadmin would not go as far as that.»

"We may have only seen the beginning of how far Kadmin might go," Tai said.

It was a grim party that made their way back up the winding corridor to the cavern exit. But none of them was grimmer than Celestian, who thrummed with misery and fear.

«If Kadmin was involved with something like this... If the Emperor was doing something like this to wild dragons... Moon and Stars help me, if *Kadmin* was doing this... I did not know. I swear by all the Powers that *I did not know.*»

"I believe you," Tai said. Celestian wouldn't be nearly this distraught if it *hadn't* come as a surprise.

«They are all in danger. If Callahan can do this to one dragon, he could do it to any of us. Nocturne, Thunder... even me, I suppose. But the others do not know. They have not been warned.»

"You didn't care when it was all of Aeris in danger, but now that dragons might be drained, it's suddenly an issue?" Falgar demanded.

"Falgar," Sullivan sighed.

Falgar ran his hand through his sandy hair. "Sorry, sorry. But if it's any consolation, your friends are probably fine. I thought having a dragon was some kind of status symbol to those Imperials."

Celestian lowered his head. «There are always more dragons.»

Tai drew in a deep breath and let it out. She didn't like what she was about to do. She didn't like it one bit. But she'd selfishly used Celestian for her own purposes for far too long. "Then you should go back and warn them. Free them if you can."

«Without my dragonstone, there is little I can...»

Tai shook her head and unclasped the dragonstone from around her neck and lay it down at Celestian's feet. "It's yours. It should have been yours the whole time."

"Tai, what are you doing?" Falgar hissed out of the corner of his mouth. "If he goes back to Kadmin, that's basically putting a weapon in the enemy's hands."

Tai let out a long breath. "Kadmin can't control him unless he holds the dragonstone himself. At least this way, Celestian has a chance to help the others." To Celestian, she said, "This is the best I can do right now, but even with the dragonstone, you're still going to be tied to Kadmin. If you come back with us to Cloudfire, I know we can set you free. Really free. But if you feel it's better to go back and warn Nocturne and the others directly, even knowing that Kadmin could regain control..." She swallowed. "Well. That's your risk to take."

She'd been thinking about it all throughout her interminable imprisonment, and she finally came to the conclusion that there was no other way. She'd kept Celestian here for far too long, and he had almost suffered something unthinkable for it. It would have been *him* in that tank before long. This was about more than her mission, or her personal ambition, or any of her other selfish desires.

«Thank you, Tai,» Celestian said. «I will not soon forget this.»

The dragon, no longer tied to Tai through coercive magic, took the dragonstone his mouth, faded into his ghostly form, and took off through the cavern ceiling. Tai tried not to feel too sad about that. The danger was far from over, after all.

"Didn't that unconscious guard used to be right there?" Falgar asked when they reached the entrance.

"Yes," Tai sighed, "I believe he was."

"Got you!" The guard, now wide awake, brandished an athame of his own, and shot out a barrier spell, freezing the four mortals and three dragons in place.

"What the—"

She'd freed the dragon in the tank. The guard wasn't demon possessed, as far as she could tell. How in the Void did he have access to magic?

"Don't tell me you forgot about the windmill already." Jace strode into the cavern, mouth twisted into a smug smirk, as he turned his own athame over in his hand. *Since when could Jace do magic?*

To Tai's horror, she saw not just the guard, but a whole crowd of people outside the cavern entrance, including a grimly triumphant High Councilor Gideon.

"Oh dear, oh dear." Gideon's tone was almost regretful. "This will not do at all."

"Behold, the traitor among us!" Gideon gestured extravagantly at Tai. "She, who came to us injured and desperate, who we welcomed as one of us, now seeks to divert us from the Path of the Savior! She would undo all we have accomplished! She is, in fact, Anathema!"

Tai strained against the invisible barrier that held her in place, fighting back tears of frustration. *Curse it all*, they were so close!

"Is this all the security your town offers?" a nasal voice cut through the crowd, familiar, though it took Tai a moment to place it. "Miscreants simply walking into your town jail? His Imperial Majesty will not be pleased."

"Jeziah?" Tai gaped open-mouthed at her former fellow Imperial Dragonaut candidate. By his freshly pressed navy blue uniform, the freckle-faced Thlarknian had evidently been promoted. He wore a gray dragonstone pendant around his neck. Tai thought it was inert at first, but from the way it sparkled in the light of the silverleaves, she knew it was connecting to a living dragon. All the posturing and competition between Lewellyn and Owain and the Taggart siblings, and unassuming Jeziah won the prize in the end. What poor dragon had been Coerced into Jeziah's service? And did the dragon know he might yet face a worse fate?

"Hello, Tai." Jeziah's tone was neutral, almost bored. "I'm glad you're having fun, but Kadmin really needs his dragon back."

"That's too bad," Tai said, "Because Celestian's not here."

If Jeziah was surprised by this news, he didn't show it. He turned to Gideon and then said, with cold professionalism, "I trust you will adhere to our agreement."

Gideon sneered. "Callahan will get what he wants." He handed Jeziah the same cloth-wrapped bundle she'd seen him handling before. "Just make sure you keep *your* end of the bargain."

"No problems there." Jeziah lovingly stroked the bundle as if it contained his own child. "With this, Aeris should fall beneath the underclouds by this time next moon."

"And the castle?" Gideon demanded.

"Will be purged of the interlopers, as we agreed," Jeziah confirmed.

"Good," Gideon said. "It never sat right to me, the way the former queen gave the home of Rivka Sevarin over to those *foreigners*." He spat out the word and glared at Tai as he said it, as if it was Tai's personal fault. "Just one of many injustices I, the Savior, will correct."

"You go too far, Gideon." Reora crossed her arms and fixed him with her most Reora-like glare. "I saw that dragon you kept prisoner down there. I know the true source of your power."

"Not a word from you," Gideon spat. "You have already proven yourself unfit for authority."

Reora fumed, fists clenched at her side. Many of Gideon's followers leered at the former mayor, but Tai saw some uncertain faces in the audience, too, and more than one set of eyes gaped at the unconscious wild dragon with a mixture of curiosity and confusion.

Tai cleared her throat and prayed to all seven Aerish gods and even the hypothetical Savior for courage and calm. "People of Lost Hollow," she began, because it seemed like the right thing to say. She'd never actually had to address a crowd before. It felt strange, all their eyes on her like pinpricks. "You took me in when I was at death's door. You gave me a home when I had none. I will always be grateful, and you will always have a place in my heart. But please, you must listen to me. That man, Gideon, is no Savior."

"You would trust the lies of an outsider?" Gideon demanded.

"You might notice," Tai continued, "That he stopped glowing a few minutes ago. That's because we found the source of his power down in that cellar. He's not 'blessed by the path' at all. He was keeping a dragon prisoner!" She gestured at the unconscious wild dragon, still held aloft by Meridian and Northstar's stream of sparks.

"Lies, lies!" Gideon cried. He swiftly brandished his athame to restore his glowing illusion, but surely all the townsfolk would realize it came from the windmill. Surely they wouldn't still fall for his tricks once the High Councilor was unmasked. *Surely*.

But then, heartbreakingly, Jace rose to Gideon's defense. "Does it matter how the Savior got his power? He does what he must for the future of Orith! The Prophetess Rivka herself said that the Savior would create miracles from the mundane."

"We will have our revenge," Kyre, still dressed in his plague mask, chimed in. "Our allies will sink Aeris to the undersea, and at last put the Aerish in their place."

"Our allies will purge the interlopers from Cloudfire Castle, and restore the Fallen Realm to the Orith!" Jace's eyes shone with inhuman zeal.

"The Fallen Realm to the Orith," Falgar choked out. "It was you, wasn't it? You're that border guard bastard who attacked me."

Jace didn't deny it, but continued to stare defiantly in Falgar's direction.

"You *attacked Falgar?*" Tai rounded on Jace, but still trapped in the stasis circle, she couldn't do much.

"He attacked me *twice*," Falgar said blithely.

"And yet," Jace replied through gritted teeth, "You stubbornly refuse to stay down."

"Enough prattle!" Gideon spoke with such force that even Tai was forced to pay attention. "The wingless have flaunted their place in the sky for too long. But no longer. With our new alliance, we shall have our revenge. With our new alliance, we shall purge the interlopers. With our new alliance, the Savior shall rise!"

The crowd cheered, and Tai's heart sank. How could they fail to see Gideon for what he truly was?

"Don't you see?" Tai demanded. "Sinking Aeris will not restore Orith to the sky, and enacting petty revenge will not bring Orith any kind of glory. If you really want to be the Savior, if you really want to lead Orith into the future, then the *future* is what you need to *focus* on, not the past! We should strive to be great in our own time, not just bring others low."

The others all stared at her, and Tai could feel beads of sweat pooling on her forehead.

"What sentimental claptrap," Gideon growled. His golden eyes flashed with an expression Tai found frankly unhinged. "We shall never reclaim the skies by asking nicely! The only way to stop Aerish hegemony is to make sure they'll never sail the skies again!" Flecks of his spittle shone in the wan golden light of the Autumn leaves.

The crowd cheered again, and Tai's wings lowered of their own accord. She'd come to love the people of Lost Hollow, and yet, they were so enamored Gideon that he could strip naked and defecate in front of the whole crowd and they'd probably still find a reason to worship him. But not everyone in the crowd was cheering. Many of them, certainly. Probably more than half. But not all of them, Ancients help her. *Not all of them.*

Tai stood taller and flared her wings to their full span, which wasn't much, but it didn't matter. "I think I can see why you all turn to Gideon. What you've all created here in Lost Hollow is nothing short of miraculous. You have fostered a community where people like us can finally thrive. You've worked miracles with the windmill. Together I believe this town can move mountains. So why wouldn't you want to believe you were home to the Savior of Prophecy Himself? But what I'm trying to tell you is *you don't need that.* You've accomplished so much already, why not use that for good, and not this twisted fantasy of revenge?"

"Use it for good?" Gideon's eyes looked ready to burst out of his head. "I am the Savior of Orith! Everything I do is, by definition, the highest good!"

«You are not the Savior of Orith.» The mindvoice reverberated across the clearing, causing everyone to look upward. For a wild moment Tai thought it was the dragon they'd rescued. But then Celestian landed in a shower of sparks, his purple-blue scales shimmering in the evening light.

"What are you doing, Celestian?" the newly-minted dragonaut Jeziah hissed out of the corner of his mouth. Privately, Tai wondered the same thing.

«The man you see before you is a fraud. He claims the sacred title of the Savior of Orith, the One Who Walks Between Worlds, but I know better. He gained his power through the enslavement of another, and I can think of no greater Anathema to the Path. But worry not! I know who the real Savior of Orith is, and I, Celestian of the Scattered Stars, Dragon of Zekador, proclaim as witness and prophet, that the Savior of Orith is Tai Lunstrum!»

Tai's heart thudded like a battle drum. "What—"

«Just trust me,» the dragon said in a private mindvoice just for Tai. To the rest of the crowd, he continued, «The Chroniclers of Dragonkind tell of a prophecy. The One Who Walks Between Worlds shall rise to fix what is broken. She will be born beneath the clouds, but forged in the sky. She will cross between the two lands, tied to both, yet at home in neither.»

"For though the Savior's feathers cross the heavens," Reora's voice, trembling, quoted the prophecy, "The Savior needs not wings to soar, for the Savior shall traverse the night sky and reclaim the light of the moon."

Tai fought to keep her expression neutral, to hide her utter bafflement. *What in the Void was Celestian doing?* Tai didn't think Gideon was the Savior, but that sure as demons didn't mean *she* was. She didn't even *believe* in prophecy. Kassorian Oracles might have their minor divinations, but even they weren't accurate all the time.

The future was just too much in flux. Tai found it beyond laughable to think that Rivka Sevarin, a woman more than a thousand years dead, could have predicted anything nearly so specific.

Celestian, however, would not be dissuaded. «You all have witnessed what Tai Lunstrum is capable of. From the building of the windmill to the shared knowledge of spellcraft, life in your village has improved elevenfold since she came here.»

Councilor Temperance nodded thoughtfully, and Reora gazed at her daughter with unmistakable awe. Tai, meanwhile, stood frozen with shock and, if she was honest, more than a little confusion. *I am not the bloody Savior. There is no bloody Savior.*

«She *is* the Savior,» Celestian said, «For she knows the secret that will restore the magic of Aeris and Orith alike, who shall even raise the lands of Orith back to the skies. She is the Savior, and she has that power!»

Tai wanted to vomit. She most certainly did *not* have that power.

«What of all you told me on the day you fled from Kasanarae?» Celestian asked her privately. «You claimed you could Planeshift to the moon and restore the magic from there.»

Void take it. Tai supposed she had said that. And if Janus Callahan was right, then Planeshifting to the moon really would restore Orith to the sky. But *Zekador's pants!* That didn't make her any kind of mythical Savior. There was quite a wide gulf between theories and reality.

Celestian chuckled silently. «Your first attempt at Planeshifting might have gone poorly, but I have every confidence that you will figure it out.»

Well. Tai might not be the Savior, but realistically the only way she and her friends were getting out of here was by playing along. With all the false confidence she could muster, Tai drew herself up. "Celestian is right! I know how to restore the magic! So please, follow me! We need not look to the past when we can instead look to the future!"

On a whim, certain she must look and sound ridiculous, she took her stolen shortsword and hoisted it into the air. She wasn't sure what made her do it, just that it seemed like the sort of thing a hero in a tale would do. The sort of thing the *Savior* would do, Ancients help her.

Celestian let out a stream of sparks, and the barrier holding her in place burst apart into crystal shards of magical energy. Tai, newly freed, staggered forward but managed to catch herself before she did anything else too embarrassing.

Then, before her eyes, the chipped and tarnished blade transformed into a full size sword, glimmering white in the light of the silverleaves, with stylized wings at the hilt and a stone of purple and blue on the pommel, the precise shade of Celestian's scales. It didn't have the same style hilt as her friends' weapons, but there was no mistaking it. A *dragonaut sword*. Tai wasn't even his bond, and yet somehow, Celestian had gifted her a *Void-cursed dragonaut sword*.

"You can't give me this," she mouthed, silently, so the crowd wouldn't hear.

«Since when,» he repeated his words from many weeks ago, «Are you the ultimate judge of who gets a sword?»

"That's the sword of the Savior," someone in the crowd said.

And so it was. It was the blade as described in prophecy, the one in the paintings and tapestries. The one held by the statue in the Council Hall that was secretly an aether beacon. *Oh, sweet Ancients, Celestian, what are you doing?*

To Tai's surprise and horror, many in the crowd looked upon her with reverence. Others stood firmly with Gideon and glared at her in contempt.

"Do not listen to this nonsense," Gideon crowed, spittle flying. "I am the Savior, not this foolish upstart girl!"

"Um, Tai, not to be alarmist," Falgar said, "But I think now would be a great time to run while they're distracted."

"Right."

Falgar vaulted easily onto Meridian's back, and since Meridian was nearest, Tai scrambled to follow. Reora looked from Meridian to Northstar, clearly uncertain.

"Are you coming with us, Lady Mayor?" Sullivan asked.

Reora seemed to wrestle with a fierce inner debate before flaring out the remains of her wings. "I will be back to deal with you, Gideon. I have responsibilities to this town, and I do not plan to abandon them. However, I also have responsibilities to my family." With surprising agility, Reora scrambled onto Northstar's back.

Meridian and Northstar launched into the cool Autumn sky, the unconscious wild dragon floating listlessly along in their wake. Tai looked behind her, certain she would find Jeziah and his unknown dragon in pursuit, but so far she saw only empty sky and silverleaves.

«The human Jeziah Morne will not follow.» Celestian's mind briefly brushed against her own, though she didn't see where he went, either. «He has taken the moon glass. He has what he came for. Now he needs only wait for his master to arrive.»

And you? She wanted to ask. *Do you have what you wanted?* But if Celestian could sense her thoughts, he did not answer.

"So," Falgar said, grinning. "Savior of Orith, huh?"

Tai snorted. "I'm not the Savior. Celestian just said that to confuse Gideon's followers so we could get away."

"And what about Celestian?" Falgar wondered. "Are you really going to let him go? What if he gets recaptured? What... what if he goes back to Kadmin willingly?"

"Celestian wouldn't do that." But she didn't know that, not really. Tai sighed. "It's not a matter of letting him. It's his choice."

"Hmm." Falgar frowned. "I know Dorian and Sullivan will disagree, but I've always kind of thought the moral high ground is useless when you're dead."

Tai shook her head. She wasn't sure if it was the right thing to do or not. But it was the only way she could live with herself.

CHAPTER THIRTY-FOUR
REVELATIONS AND REUNIONS

"Ah... come in, Lady Dragonmar," Dorian said, as if he had any say in the matter.

Dorian was keenly aware of his room's disastrous state. He'd never been predisposed towards tidiness in the best of times, and since being confined to quarters, he'd lost any reason to pretend to care.

Dorian awkwardly removed a pile of training clothes from the upholstered reading chair and gestured for Sylvia to sit down.

"No thank you, I will stand." She fiddled with the folds of her skirt, looking everywhere but at Dorian.

Dorian frowned. "Is... everything all right, Lady Dragonmar?"

"As right as it can be, I suppose," Sylvia said. "I don't suppose you have anything stronger than water to drink? No, no, I suppose we wouldn't have given you any." She moved to the sideboard and reached for the water pitcher, only to find that it, too, was empty. "What barbarians we are." She shook her head.

Suddenly, Dorian, too, wished he had something stronger than water. The Dragonmar was normally so unflappable. He hadn't seen her like this since... well, since the first day he'd arrived.

Sylvia took several deep breaths. "I have not been honest with you."

"Oh." Dorian scratched his neck. "Well, that is to say. If you're going to run an underground organization, you're bound to have some secrets, right?"

"Yes, but this is something I have withheld from *you*, specifically, and that is unforgivable."

Perhaps it was because, after days of confinement, he was desperate for any news at all, but Dorian felt more excited than apprehensive. *Finally, some answers.* "We've... met before, haven't we?"

The Dragonmar looked like she might cry. "Oh, indeed we have." She drew in another breath and said, "Very well. Best get right to it. Did you know, Dorian, that I have been the Dragonmar of Cloudfire for less than two years?"

"Oh?" Dorian cocked his head, wondering where she was going with that.

"The old Dragonmar, Tobias Rutherford, named me his successor after Emperor Callahan's rise to the Imperial throne." She let out a long sigh. "*Immediately* after Callahan's rise."

"I see." Dorian felt completely nonplussed, but for some reason, he felt an odd chill.

"Before that, I was a spy," she said. "In Janus Callahan's household."

"You? But... how?" Dorian racked his brain, but try as he might, could not recall seeing Lady Sylvia in Callahan manor. Except... the barest hint of a memory flashed through his mind and then darted away. Something about... *the library?*

Sylvia's knuckles were pale as she clung to her silk skirts. "I'm sure you're aware that I have a penchant for Illusion magic."

"Sure." Dorian's puzzled frown deepened.

Sylvia took out her athame and drew a series of runes and sigils in the air. Dorian recognized some of them from the Illusion spell

Captain Xander sometimes used, but this one seemed a lot more complicated.

A moment later, Sylvia seemed to bathe in blue light, and when the light faded, the woman who stood before him was no longer Sylvia at all.

Dorian was so startled he nearly fell into his laundry pile. Now he felt even more embarrassed about the state of his room, not to mention his own disheveled state. "Stew—Stewardess Tahlia?"

"Hello Dorian." His curly-haired former governess and tutor gave him the same amused-yet-exasperated expression that he knew so well.

"But... but..." his mind reeled as he ran through every memory of every interaction he'd ever had with both Tahlia Weatherbee and Sylvia Kane. Gods above, no wonder her mannerisms were always so familiar. "Is... is this really you, then, and the Dragonmar is the disguise? Or is it the other way around?"

Sylvia-Tahlia's smile faltered, and she looked down at the ground. "I am Sylvia Kane. Tahlia Weatherbee was only one of my many personae. But... after more than a Cycle living every day as Tahlia, she became a part of who I am, too."

Dorian didn't know how to feel. To learn that Tahlia, the woman who had practically raised him, was someone else entirely, should have been even more world-shattering than when he found out Bradford was his brother in truth. But his actual feelings hearkened back to his oldest insecurities.

"So... so me and Bradford..."

"*Bradford and I*," she corrected him in her most Tahlia-like voice.

Dorian almost smiled. "Bradford and I," he amended. "Did you ever care for us at all? Or was that all part of your work as a spy?"

Dorian hated how childish he sounded. But although he already understood on an abstract level that Tahlia had been a household employee and not truly a member of his family, she'd also been the only person in Callahan Manor who'd ever been kind to him. If her name and even her face had been a falsehood, what else might be?

Sylvia-Tahlia took both of Dorian's hands and met his blue eyes with her Illusory green ones. "I care for you more than you know." Her face cracked into a sad smile. "I can't tell you how proud I am, seeing you and Bradford both grow up into such fine young men. Of course, I suppose I can't claim any real credit for that."

"That's not... I mean, you were very good at, uh, governessing..." Dorian grasped for more words, but words failed. Finally, he swallowed, and said, "It's... nice to see you again. I'm ah, sorry about the mess."

Sylvia-Tahlia half laughed, half-cried as she removed a stray strand of copper hair from his face. "My dear boy," she said, "A dragonaut... so brave and so good. I wanted so badly to protect you... to shield you from Janus's cruelty. In that, I fear I failed miserably. But you rose above all that without my help. I wish I'd done better by you. I'm so sorry. And yet, still, I am so, so proud."

Dorian felt a strange warm feeling, simultaneously awkward and comfortable, like a boy trying on his father's overcoat, sleeves dragging along on the floor. "I, ah, take it you *don't* think I'm a traitor to the Order, then?"

Sylvia barked out a bitter laugh and dabbed at the corners of her eyes with her iron-gray dress sleeve. "No, I do not think you are a Void-cursed traitor." She shook her head and sighed. "You should know, I have moved the boy Tanis Lunstrum from the dungeons to an unused apartment of his own. We can't let him free, at least until we've figured all this out, but at least he'll be comfortable. As for you, I intend to let you go as soon as possible, but I... I had to tell you the truth first." Her eyes swum with guilt.

"Well," Dorian said. "Now I know it." He cocked his head slightly to the side, trying to discern why his former-governess-turned-employer was so upset. It was surprising, to be sure, to learn that Tahlia and Sylvia were one and the same, but not enough to justify her obvious distress.

"There's... something else," Sylvia said at length.

Dorian nodded. "I figured as much."

She drew in a sharp breath and let it out. "I'm afraid you're going to be furious with me."

"Wait. *You're* not the traitor, are you?"

"What? Oh, no, of course not." She closed her eyes in an obvious attempt to compose herself. "Before I became a spy for the Order... that is, the reason it was so imperative that I monitor the goings on in House Callahan..." she cut off abruptly once more at the sound of shouting in the hallway. "Oh, what in the Void now?"

The door swung open, and Jameson came bursting in. He looked flushed, as if he'd sprinted from the other side of the castle. "Falgar and Sullivan are back. They brought — well, I think you'll need to see this, Lady Dragonmar. You too, Valmont. You're free from house arrest. Congratulations."

Wondering what more surprising news could possibly be forthcoming, Dorian and Sylvia followed Jameson to the ramparts.

"Good, you're here." Hildegard joined Dorian and Sylvia at the base of the spiral staircase. "Sylvia talked to you, I take it?" For some reason, her tone sounded accusatory.

"She did, yeah."

"Thank Zekador for the small miracles." Hildegard let out a sigh of relief. Sylvia, for some reason, still looked uncomfortable.

Dorian glanced at Hildegard. "You knew, then?"

She grimaced. "Afraid so. I told her she should have told the truth moons ago, but you know how she gets sometimes."

Sylvia snorted, but did not argue the point.

"I just hope... I mean, you're not furious with us?" Hildegard shot Dorian a nervous smile.

"Oh." Dorian scratched his neck. "Ah, no, not really..."

Truth be told, Dorian hadn't fully processed the news. But he didn't *think* he was angry. Sylvia-Tahlia had been a spy, and spies needed their secrets. It wasn't like he could hold it against her. And, a slightly shameful part of him couldn't help glowing with pride at the knowledge that his former governess was *proud of him*. Tahlia had always been good to him, but there'd been an undeniable air of exasperation about her, like she knew Dorian was never living up to his full potential. If Sylvia claimed she was proud of him now, it must mean he was doing *something* right. Though given the mess he'd made of things lately, he thought ruefully, he wasn't quite sure what that might be.

They arrived on the rampart a moment later to find Falgar and Sullivan beside their respective dragons, both looking inordinately pleased with themselves. And they weren't alone. Next to Falgar stood an elegant dark-skinned Orith woman with injured wings, her hair in a tight bun, and on her other side was —

"Tai!" Before he was fully aware of what he was doing, Dorian sprinted across the rampart and swept his friend up into his arms.

"*Dorian.*" Tai leaned into the hug, and by all the Gods, she smelled like citrus and cinnamon, like magic itself. He knew he'd missed her, but he didn't think he'd realized how much until this moment. Being near Tai again felt like coming home.

Then he realized everyone was staring at them, and he let her go and stepped back, blushing deep scarlet. "I'm, ah, glad you're back." Scratching his neck, he turned to his other friends, and elaborated, "I'm glad you're *all* back."

"Yeah, yeah, we know where your priorities are." Falgar winked.

"But... but what are you all doing here together?" Dorian frowned. "I thought Falgar and Sullivan were in Lost Hollow and Tai was in Kasanarae. Where are Xander and Bradford?"

Sullivan cleared his throat and tugged on his collar. "It's a long story and I think there's a great deal of catching up to do on all sides," he said. "But there's something else you all need to see first."

Sullivan gestured at what Dorian initially thought was an empty patch of stone floor. *Except...* Dorian rubbed his eyes, struggling to process what his friend was trying to show him.

"Is that... Sweet Zekador, is that a *dragon?*"

The ghostly creature lying unconscious on the alabaster parapet was so transparent as to almost be invisible. Only the gentle flickering of the aether lamps gave evidence to the faint dragon-shaped presence.

«Moon and Stars,» Solaris's mindvoice was a horrified whisper. «That is Stormwind of the Fallen Rock clan. I did not know him well, but our clan sometimes performed the moon dance with his at midwinter. What in all the skies happened to him?»

«They kept him captive in some kind of strange cylindrical tank,» Northstar said. «He was nearly drained of all his power.»

"Void Eternal." Dorian felt a prickle of unease as he remembered the tanks he'd seen in Thlarknia.

"This is not suitable conversation for the parapet in the middle of the night," Sylvia said. "Northstar, kindly direct the unconscious dragon to Healer Estevan. If anyone can help the poor creature, it is him. The rest of us, let us convene in my study to debrief on what happened in both Kasanarae and Lost Hollow."

Everyone nodded in assent except for the ragged-winged Orith woman, who cleared her throat and dusted her hands off on her richly-embroidered robes. "Before we do any of that, I would know what became of my son. I was told he is here. Where is Tanis?"

Dorian glanced at the woman first in surprise and then in guilt. This must be Tai and Tanis's mother. He could see the resemblance, now. The set of her jaw, the shape of her ears. He squirmed uncomfortably as he recalled what a poor job he'd done looking after her son. "Ah... as to that..."

"Apologies, Madam Lunstrum," Jameson interjected, "But I'm afraid the situation is rather delicate. Perhaps after the debriefing..."

"No," Lady Sylvia said with a sigh, "Madam Lunstrum is right. No mother should have to wait longer than necessary for news of her children. Madam Lunstrum, Miss Lunstrum, you'd best come with me. We will speak to young Master Lunstrum and reconvene in my study at eight bells. The rest of you—" she sniffed particularly in Falgar and Sullivan's direction — "Perhaps a bath is in order. I imagine it has been a rather trying day."

"Valmont." Jameson pulled Dorian aside as soon as Dragonmar Sylvia and the Lunstrums were out of earshot. "I'd like a word."

"Flight Leader?" Dorian fidgeted with his shirt laces. What could he possibly be in trouble for this time?

"Come walk with me."

Dorian's apprehension increased as he followed Jameson down the winding spiral staircase. He looked longingly down the opposite corridor where Tai and her mother had just departed. He wanted to be with her, catching up after so many moons apart, not enduring another lecture from Jameson. But duty called.

Jameson said nothing as he marched purposefully down the hallways, until at last they reached the library.

"What—" Dorian hesitantly began.

Jameson stopped at a shelf, ran his finger across a row of books, and finally selected a volume. "Come sit." He held the book in one hand and gestured to a free study table with the other.

"All... All right." Dorian sat.

"I... wanted to apologize." It looked like it cost something for Jameson to admit it. "I... have been unfair to you."

"I... oh. Um. Thank you?" Dorian found he had no idea how to respond. First Sylvia-Tahlia was proud of him, and now Jameson was apologizing? Why was everyone being so nice to him all of a sudden?

"The truth is, your father and I... never exactly saw eye to eye," Jameson said.

Dorian nodded, not particularly surprised. As a boy, he used to idolize his father. As an adolescent, he despaired ever living up to his legacy. Lately, though, he'd been forced to face the uncomfortable reality that Cyrus Valmont was every bit as flawed and human as the rest of them. "I get the impression," Dorian said at length, "That my father was good at making enemies."

Jameson snorted. "Sometimes. But I don't think he did it on purpose. Cyrus just... liked to jump head first into everything he did. Those of us who prefer to actually think before we act, we were just obstacles between him and his grand vision of glory." He shook his head. "You look so much like your father that these past few moons have almost been like he's back from the dead. But he's not, and you're not him."

Dorian tugged on the ends of his shoulder-length copper hair, the only feature he thought he had in common with Cyrus Valmont. Whatever Jameson and Sylvia might say, he didn't really see the resemblance. But lately he'd started to wonder if being different from his father wasn't such a bad thing.

Jameson sighed. "Ever since you arrived, I've just been waiting for you to swoop in, despite any reasonable qualifications, and take the credit for the things I've been working towards since before you were born. Because that's what Cyrus would've done. But... it was wrong of me to assume that. So I guess what I'm saying is. I'm sorry."

Dorian gazed at the sliver of crescent moon just outside the library window. "I don't intend to take credit for anything," Dorian reassured him. In truth, he struggled to accept credit for the things he actually *did*, much less other people's work. "But... I guess I can't blame you for being concerned. You're right. I *don't* have the same qualifications as the rest of you. I mean." He laughed weakly. "Before last year, I'd, uh, never picked up a sword in my life. Void, I couldn't even climb the single flight of stairs at Callahan Manor without getting winded." Dorian gave an awkward smile, but inside he burned with shame, certain he was confirming every negative thing the flight leader had ever thought about him.

To Dorian's surprise and slight alarm, Jameson burst out laughing. It wasn't an unpleasant sound, light but with a rough edge, like pebbles tumbling down a hillside. Dorian wasn't certain he'd ever heard the Flight Leader laugh before.

"Bloody Valmonts," Jameson chortled. "I don't know which is more infuriating, your father's arrogance or your unfathomable humility."

"I'm... sorry?"

"You have no idea, do you, how Void cursed *impressive* it actually is, to go from never picking up a sword to keeping up with a trained elite fighting force in two years time."

"I'm the worst in the Flight," Dorian said defensively. *Only you,* said his inner voice that sounded like Hematite, *Would be defensive of your own incompetence.*

"Barely," Jameson said. "You're a natural born flier, and in the areas where you lack talent, you make up for it in hard work. I don't think any of the other dragonauts work half as hard as you do. At the rate you're improving, you'll be *best* in the Flight before long."

Dorian's face burned with a combination of pride and embarrassment. "I... um... oh. Thank you." Coming from Jameson, this felt tantamount to being told he was secretly the god Zekador Himself.

Jameson ran his hand through his curly hair and became serious once again. "At any rate. I didn't drag you over here to praise you *or* to insult you. I came to ask for your help."

Dorian had no idea what he could do to help Jameson, but if the Flight Leader seemed inclined to think highly of him for once, he wasn't going to squander it. "Whatever you need."

"Good lad." Jameson smiled and thumbed through the book he'd taken off the shelf, and when he found the page he was looking for, pushed it in Dorian's direction. "Tell me. What do you make of this spell?"

Dorian briefly scanned the runes and sigils, and then his eyes widened in surprise. "This is one of my father's spells." He remembered seeing one just like it in his father's journal, all those long moons ago. Those stolen afternoons with Saedra both felt like yesterday and like a thousand years ago. "We never really figured out what it did," he admitted.

"In point of fact," Jameson said, "It is one of *my* spells."

"Yours!"

"Well, it's some long-dead Ancient mage's spell, I suppose," Jameson corrected himself. "And I fear it is incomplete. But at the time I deciphered it, three Cycles ago, it was... groundbreaking. We thought it would change everything." He straightened slightly, but then shook his head. "Of course, your father, never one for coming in second place, stole my notes and claimed all the credit for himself."

Dorian blanched. "He stole your work?"

Jameson nodded. "At the time, it was a slight I took... badly. But now that I'm older, Ancients help me, a wild gryphon cub could take the credit for all I care, if only we could make the spell actually *work*."

Dorian ran his finger down the page. Even though it depicted more or less the same thing as his father's notes, this one was far more detailed, written down with a great deal more care and understanding. Dorian probably hadn't been able to decipher the spell back in Adenthul because *Cyrus* hadn't really understood how it worked when he wrote it down.

Dorian let out a long breath. "That thing you said earlier about me swooping in and stealing the credit makes a lot more sense now."

"Perhaps." Jameson sighed. "Beyond pathetic, I know, to nurse a grudge twenty years gone. I must say, though, you're taking the news fairly well in stride."

Dorian considered before speaking. "I... want to believe my father was a good man. But the fact that he impregnated another man's wife, then bonded a demon he mistreated so badly that the demon defied his own religion to bond me instead... well... I guess I *wish* all this surprised me."

Jameson patted Dorian on the shoulder in what he clearly hoped was a sympathetic gesture. "I'm... sorry you had to find out this way. But... ah, back to the mater at hand... Can you read the spell? If you had to, could you continue where I started? Could you figure out how to cast it?"

Dorian turned his attention back to the spell circle. It was the most complicated spell he'd ever seen, even more than the one that summoned Solaris. "I could try." He was sure the doubt shone in his voice. But *Void take it*. Perhaps Jameson had a point. Perhaps excessive humility really *was* just as bad as arrogance. He took a deep breath and steeled all the determination he could muster. "Let's see. This sigil represents the moon glass, doesn't it? But the way these lines come together... well, the only way I can see that working is if a bunch of people all cast the spell at the same time."

Jameson nodded ruefully. "Seven. You need seven to properly make use of the moon glass. If I'd followed my own advice, I might not have lost an eyebrow." He gestured at his wispy eyebrow, which still hadn't quite grown back in all the way.

Dorian nodded sympathetically and clenched and unclenched his fist where the moon glass had burnt him when he performed the spell with Hildegard. Two dragonauts had been better than one, but perhaps with seven, he could have avoided injury altogether. "Those Ancient sigils down there look familiar," he said. "This... this is the spell to regulate aether flow, isn't it? It's... it's what the Order's been looking for all this time."

Jameson nodded. "Three Cycles ago, we thought our dream of restoring the magic was in our grasp. Unfortunately, that was right around the time everything went straight to the Void." Jameson smiled ruefully. "So here I am, more than twenty years later, still no closer to figuring it out. And I fear I am very nearly out of time. I must finally admit that I can't do this on my own. I need help. I need the son of Cyrus Valmont."

"Thought you said I wasn't anything like him." Dorian quirked a rueful smile.

"That's—" Jameson spread his arms helplessly. "It's not—"

Dorian became serious once more. "Of course I want to help. But we seem to both agree that I'm not my father, for better or worse. So why me? Surely Hildegard, or Lady Sylvia..."

"If Sylvia or Hildegard could have figured this out by now, they would have," Jameson said. "We need someone new, someone who can come at it from a fresh angle. And frankly, you're the only new recruit I know for sure I can trust. I've been hard on you, I know I have, but I'm also confident you're not a traitor."

Dorian raised his eyebrows. "But... I was responsible for Tanis. You put me under house arrest..."

Jameson shook his head. "My own stubborn pride. I know you're no traitor, and Tanis... well, he did what he thought he had to. Meanwhile we have wasted time locking away people who don't deserve it, and the real traitor is still at large."

Dorian nodded slowly. "You think the attacker will return."

Jameson's mouth narrowed. "I think something far worse than the attacker is coming. That's why it's so important to bring you on board. If I die..."

"You won't die," Dorian said at once.

"Do not patronize me," Jameson snapped. Taking a calming breath, he continued, "If I die, I do not want the knowledge of this spell to die with me."

"Right." Dorian let out a long breath. "No pressure."

He looked out the library window at the quiet evening sky. Dorian estimated he probably had a good half-bell yet until the debriefing with Tai and the others.

Nothing to do now but get to work. He began examining the runes.

Tai covered her mouth against the smell when she and her mother stepped into Tanis's living quarters. The distinct mint-and-sage aroma of demonfire did little to mask the sickly-stale scent of body odor and a chamberpot left to sit far too long.

"My boy!" Reora rushed forward and enfolded him into her arms, regardless of the state he was in. "Oh, sweet Savior Above, what have they done to you?"

"Mother. Sister." Tanis blinked flat and expressionless eyes. He cast a guilty glance at the demon, Malachite, who was nearly the size of his nightstand. Slightly more expression crossed his gaunt and exhausted face, then, as he winced and said, "I *really* didn't want you to see me like this."

When she'd last seen Tanis just shy of a year ago, he'd been thin and gangly in the way of teenagers, but hale and healthy nonetheless. Now, he was nothing short of emaciated, his light brown complexion gray and sallow, with faint blue lines on his hands and around his eyes that might have been early signs of possession sickness. *Void*, he looked like he hadn't eaten or slept in a moon. How could the Order let this happen? How had Dorian let this happen?

Worse by far, though, was the demon, who greedily gulped up Tanis's spirit energy in unpredictable fits and starts. Tanis barely seemed to notice.

"I should have come the moment I knew where you were," Reora said. "We should have never allowed this farce to continue as long as it did."

"Wouldn't have mattered." Tanis winced slightly as Malachite drew a sizable chunk of silver-white energy out of him.

"Stop that," Tai said on instinct, even though the demon had no reason to obey. To Tanis, she said, "Why do you let him do that?"

Tanis barked a bitter laugh. "Feed him spirit energy, and I go into fugue. Restrict him too obsessively, fugue. Fugued if I do and fugued if I don't."

Reora shook him by the shoulders, a touch too roughly for one in such a state. "Did the Order do this to you?"

Tanis seemed to deflate all at once. "The Order... no. The Order didn't do this. Just me and my own fool pride."

Reora ruffled the tattered remains of her wings. "I don't understand."

Tanis sighed and stared at the stone ceiling. "All I wanted was to help Everwood. To help Father." He shot Reora an accusatory glare and Tai had to suppress a smile. There was some fight left in her brother, at least.

Tanis briefly related the story of how he'd joined the Kasani military hoping to learn to control his demon, and how Dorian subsequently found him in Thlarknia.

"So anyway," he concluded, "That smooth-talking bastard Kadmin promised the moon and dumped me in middle of nowhere like yesterday's garbage the first chance he got."

"He does that," Tai said with a sigh.

"Dorian, at least, tried to hep me. He *did* help me. But I was a Depths-sodden fool, I thought I knew better than him. He saved my life, and how do I repay his kindness? By betraying him and everyone he cared about."

He shook his head, clearly disgusted with himself.

"And does this Dorian not help you now?" Reora demanded. She gestured at the disheveled state of both the room around them and Tanis herself, and wrinkled her nose.

Tanis shook his head. "He wants to, I'm sure he does. But ever since... since my arrest, he's not been allowed to visit." Bitterly, he added, "He'd be ashamed of me, I think, to see what a poor job I've done caring for myself in his absence."

"No he wouldn't," Tai said at once. He'd be worried, of that she was certain. But not ashamed. Never ashamed.

Tanis opened his mouth to say something, but Malachite chose that moment to strike. Energy poured out of Tanis, who gazed at the ceiling in combined agony and euphoria, seemingly no longer aware that Tai and Reora were there at all.

"Tanis!"

Tai rushed over to help, but Reora got there first, propping him up and muttering some kind of incantation under her breath. It was strange to see her mother wielding what looked like magic, but then again, she recalled, Reora was also a survivor of demonic fugue. If anyone knew how to help Tanis, it was her.

Tai stood there awkwardly, not sure what to do. Other than a cordial but distant acquaintanceship with Hematite on the *Phoenix*, she had very little experience with demons at all. *So much for my extensive magical aptitude*, she thought ruefully.

"If you want I could—" Tai began hesitantly.

"Leave us," Reora snapped. More gently, she added, "I must concentrate." She went back to her work without looking at Tai.

CHAPTER THIRTY-FIVE
A SPARRING MATCH

"No. No, no, absolutely not." Reora Lunstrum stood with her arms crossed wearing a pinch-faced expression, reminding Dorian of a much more imposing version of the scarecrows they used to keep in the orchards at Callahan Manor.

"Please," Dorian said, even though he knew it would do no good. Tai and Tanis's mother was clearly someone used to being obeyed. "I just want to see him."

"Tanis is ill," Reora said. "He is not accepting visitors at this time, or any time soon for that matter. So please, *leave*." Her nostrils flared.

Through the crack in the door, Dorian heard a slight moan of pain, and saw a flash of what could have only been blue demonfire. Malachite was growing stronger again, and there didn't appear to be a Void-cursed thing Dorian could do about it.

Hematite always used to grow stronger and more powerful during Dorian's darkest periods of despair back in Callahan Manor. He usually urged Dorian to bake a pie or escape into an adventure novel, but on the worst days, the temporary euphoria that came from spirit drain was the only thing that the demon felt like he could offer. *Void*, part of Dorian yearned for a good spirit-draining even now. But Hematite had been Dorian's friend. He never went too far, and he always took great care not to send Dorian into a fugue. The same absolutely could not be said for Malachite.

"If he's struggling with his demon, I can help—" Dorian began.

"I think Tanis has had more than enough of your *help*, thank you." Reora practically spat on his boots.

Dorian knew he was going to get nothing more out of Reora Lunstrum this afternoon. The Orith woman had evidently made up her mind not to like Dorian, and he doubted arguing with her in the hallway would change her mind.

«I thought it was a long-standing tradition for you humans not to get along with their mothers-in-law,» Solaris teased.

Dorian snorted. "She's not my mother-in-law." Though Ancients help him if she ever was.

That would, of course, require that Tai thought about him in that way at all, and since she'd barely spoken to him in nearly two weeks since her return, the odds of that weren't looking especially auspicious. Perhaps she, like Reora, blamed him for Tanis's state. Perhaps he deserved that blame.

Frustrated and despondent in equal measure, Dorian headed to the training grounds. For good or for ill, letting Hematite drain his spirit energy was out of the question, but at least he could take out his woes on the practice dummies.

Dorian fell into the comfortable rhythm of his footwork exercises as he sparred against the enchanted golem. *Swing, block, step. Swing, block, step.*

He'd hoped things would be better, now that his friends were back and he'd been released from house arrest. But lately, he felt more frustrated than ever.

It had been nearly two weeks since Jameson showed him the spell to restore the magic, and Dorian was no closer than when he started to figuring it out. While part of him knew logically that two weeks wasn't nearly enough time to figure out such a complicated spell, it was still Void-cursed *frustrating*. He began to worry if he was any good at magic after all.

«If it were easy,» Solaris reminded him, «Your fellow humans would have cast it by now.»

"Maybe." *Swing, block, step, strike.* "Do you suppose your Chronicler friend Nocturne knew how to do it?"

An undercurrent of fear trickled through their bond. «We had best hope not,» she said, «Or it would be Janus Callahan's knowledge now, too.»

Swing, block, step, strike. That was right. Nocturne was Callahan's dragon. And Dorian was no closer to freeing him than he had been a year ago. Frustrated, he let his form get sloppy, and the enchanted practice dummy hit him with a hard *thwack,* sending him staggering backwards across the sandy floor.

"Ow." Dorian climbed back to his feet, rubbing his sore bottom.

«One thing at a time,» Solaris gently chided him. «Surely you have not exhausted all resources in figuring that spell out.»

No, Dorian thought as he righted himself and faced the practice dummy again. He still hadn't asked Tai.

Tai could help, he was certain of it. Tai was a genius at this kind of thing. But asking Tai required that she actually speak to him, and lately she'd been as elusive as a dryad. She was upset about something, that much was clear from leagues away.

«Perhaps,» Solaris said gently, «You are not the cause of your friend's woes. Why not stop waiting for her to come to you, and go to her?»

Dorian's wooden sword struck the practice dummy, sending it spinning. He dutifully ducked out of the way. "I don't want to be a bother."

«Bother.» Solaris let out a derisive snort. «It is not a bother to help a friend in need. I wonder, what would you wish for Tai to do for you if you found yourself in a similar situation?»

Dorian didn't have to think for long. He knew exactly what Tai would do. He knew what Tai *had* done, last time she caught him acting so despondent.

Dorian smiled ruefully as he examined the practice sword, then tucked it in his belt and fetched another one off the training rack. "It's a big castle," he told Solaris, "But I'm going to find her."

Tai's feathers flared out in consternation as she stormed down the corridors of Cloudfire Castle.

Her Void-cursed mother!

They'd gotten along so well back in Lost Hollow. She'd almost thought they'd be able to repair the rift that kept their family divided these past eight years. But now, without the work of running the town to keep her busy, Reora appeared to have diverted back to her reliable old standby of micromanaging every conceivable aspect of her childrens' lives.

Poor Tanis bore the brunt of it, of course. While Reora was best equipped out of any of them to stop Malachite's relentless attempts to slowly kill him, she really could be overbearing about it. But even Tai was not immune to her mother's constant haranguing.

"You're the Savior of Orith now, you must work on your public image." "The Savior of Orith mustn't dress so slovenly." "Why did you cut your hair? It was growing out so nicely. That bob is not *dignified* for the Savior of Orith!"

It didn't matter how many times she tried to explain to her mother that she *wasn't* the Savior of Orith, that Celestian only said that to keep the villagers distracted long enough for them to escape, or even that she *liked* having short hair. Reora seemed to see Tai's potential Saviorhood as a political opportunity too fortuitous to pass up, and was bound and determined to mold Tai into the most magnificent Savior who ever lived.

It was *exhausting*.

Tai had no intention of dressing the way her mother wanted, or doing her hair the way her mother wanted. But she was willing to humor her mother on just one aspect of this Savior charade. She would at least *try* to figure out how to restore the lands of Orith to the sky. That was what the Savior was *supposed to* do. But like many things, that was easier said than done.

Tai's bad mood followed her all the way to the library. As she slumped down at a study table and prepared to pore through yet another dry old tome, she knew her heart just wasn't in it.

No matter how she turned it over in her head, she always came to the same conclusion. Everything she'd been through this past year had been *pointless*. She'd failed to steal a dragonstone, failed to glean any useful information about the enemy, failed to win over Lewellyn or Owain or even Jace. And now, she'd even failed to make her family get along with each other for *five Void-cursed minutes*.

But worst of all, the frustration she kept coming back to, was her failure to set Celestian free. She didn't know what had happened to him after he returned to Kasanarae. But if he'd succeeded in freeing the others, surely she would have heard about it by now. Surely they would have found their way to Faris Saunderlain in Azure, who would have directed them to Cloudfire. Surely. Instead, all news sources seemed to indicate that Kadmin had Celestian in his custody once more. But had Kadmin captured him, or had the dragon gone willingly?

Despite being back in Cloudfire for almost two weeks, Tai still caught herself reaching out to the dragon, looking for advice or sharing her observations. No doubt, as a would-be Chronicler, he would have been absolutely ecstatic to take a look at what the Order's library had to offer, even if it wasn't *all* fictional adventure tales. But Celestian was gone, and Tai was left with just a hollow emptiness where their connection used to be.

Tai wondered if this was how Dorian felt, after Hematite died. She wondered if she could ask about it without being horribly insensitive. She knew it wasn't the same thing, not really. Ancients help her, at least Celestian was *alive*. But even if she could find a way to word it politely, that required talking to Dorian, something she'd been avoiding far more than she cared to admit.

It wasn't that she wasn't happy to see him again. Quite the opposite, even just seeing his face made her feel like she'd found a part of herself she'd never even known she was missing. But that was the *problem*. She didn't *want* part of herself to be wholly dependent on someone else. Why, Ancients help her, couldn't she just act normal around him? What was so difficult about returning to the uncomplicated friendship they'd enjoyed back on the *Phoenix*?

And then, perhaps inevitably, as if summoned by her thoughts, there he was in the library, the person she both most and least wanted to see at that moment.

"Thought I might find you here." He sat across from her at the study table and flashed that awkward-but-charming half-smile of his. *Gods*, it was unfair, how he somehow managed to become more handsome every time she saw him.

He was clearly fresh from the training grounds, his shoulder-length copper hair glinting in the lantern light, wearing form-fitting breeches and a loosely-laced linen shirt that revealed just the right amount of chest. She also noted he had two practice blades, each clipped to either side of his leather sword belt. Why in all the skies did he need two practice swords?

"Hello Dorian." She carefully looked down at the book she was not reading, anything to avoid his intense, beautiful blue eyes.

"You've been avoiding me." It wasn't a question.

"I—" Tai had no idea what to say, because he was right. She finally forced herself to look at him, and his expressive eyes reflected understanding, but also hurt, and it absolutely killed her inside to think she might have even had a part in causing that.

She thought back to that evening long ago in the galley on the *Phoenix*, when they'd baked a pie together, and he'd looked at her with such crushing sadness that she'd wanted, perhaps naïvely, to banish that sadness from his eyes forever. "I'm sorry," she finally said. It didn't feel like nearly enough.

Dorian smiled sadly and scratched his neck. "I've just been afraid... I mean, I know you probably don't want to talk about it... Like maybe you were mad at me about what happened with Tanis, or..."

Tai gaped at him. "You tried to *save* Tanis. It's not your fault he made his own fool choices."

Dorian remained unconvinced. "Then... maybe about what happened at the Trials..."

Tai blinked. *The Trials?* That felt like such a long time ago it might as well have been another lifetime. It took a moment for her to recall what he even thought she was upset about. The way he'd caught her when her ornithopter malfunctioned... Well, all right, yes, that had been frustrating. But for some reason at this moment all she could seem to recall was how good his arms felt wrapped around her, and how wonderful it was to have someone care enough to dive in after her, even if she hadn't truly been in any real danger.

"No," she said, "No, no, no." She scrunched her eyes closed and shook her head. "I... none of this is your fault."

Dorian's expression softened, and he said, "I know it's been hard lately, with Tanis sick and your mother being, well..."

"My mother," Tai finished for him. She smiled wryly as she tipped her chair backwards and gazed up at the star-painted library ceiling. "It's funny, after all these years, I shouldn't be so desperate for her approval, and yet..."

"And yet you are." Dorian's expression was sympathetic. "Believe me, I get it. I mean, maybe not directly, I don't exactly *remember* my mother, but I sort of just found out that the Dragonmar is my childhood governess, so, ah, I guess what I'm saying is... yeah. I get it."

"The Dragonmar is *what*?"

Dorian scratched his neck, then shook his head. "Never mind. This isn't about me. And I get the feeling it's not *just* about Reora or Tanis, either."

Tai shook her head, and before she could stop herself, Tai spilled out her every insecurity and failure of the past year. Dorian, to his credit, nodded and made sympathetic noises at all the right times. "And I know it's foolish," she concluded. "Just on one hand I've got the Order making me feel like I'm worthless because I'm not a dragonaut, and on the other hand, I've got my mother, who seems to think I should act like some mythic hero of legend, when in reality all I want is—" *to rip that lace-front shirt off you and have my way with you in the middle of the library, and who cares if everyone's watching—* "To be your equal, at your side."

Dorian let out a high pitched noise that might have been a laugh. "My equal? You think... you think we're not..."

Abruptly, he stood up, unclipped one of the practice swords from his belt, and tossed it unceremoniously across the table.

"Eh?" Tai fumbled and caught it, while Dorian seamlessly drew the other one.

"Spar with me."

"Sp... spar with you?"

But Dorian was already bearing down on her, swinging the practice blade down over the table, and Tai had no choice but to scramble to dodge and block him.

"Zekador's poorly fitting pants," swore Hildegard, who was on the other side of the room re-shelving books. "You can't sword fight in the library."

"Right, Flight Second. Sorry, Flight Second." But Dorian did not give up his attack, he simply shifted direction. Dorian drove her into the hallway and out towards the training grounds.

It took all of Tai's concentration to walk and defend herself at the same time. Dorian, meanwhile, had no such trouble. He drove her determinedly down the hallway, forcing her further back with his relentless attack. Tai managed to prevent him hitting her with his wooden blade, but she couldn't do much beyond that. She frantically sidestepped to avoid knocking over a priceless marble bust of some long-dead Ancient dragonaut.

Finally, they crossed into the training grounds, and Tai could at last get her footing. Falgar and Sullivan, who were on the other side of the cavernous chamber taking turns on the squat rack, waved as they came in, but Tai had no chance to say hello, because Dorian's onslaught only increased.

"Don't just react," he complained. "Fight back!" Her blade crossed with his, and she had to duck to avoid his next blow. "You're already my equal, *more* than my equal, Void curse it. Act like it!" There was no sadness in his blue eyes now, only fever-bright determination.

"I'm afraid," she said as she fought to catch her breath, "You've utterly surpassed me at this."

"Then surpass me right back!" His blade crossed hers once more. "You're not a statue." *Thwack, thwack.* "From over here it looks like you're giving up."

"*Giving up?*" Tai demanded in disbelief. Easy for *him* with his fancy dragonstone and his stupid sexy lace-front shirt to talk to her about *giving up.*

She adjusted her footing and crouched into a defensive posture, digging deep within herself to dredge up every single thing she knew about sword fighting, from her earliest lessons with Kadmin on the *Winds of Fortune* to sparring sessions with Lewellyn and Owain in Kasanarae's Imperial Fountain Palace. He moved in for the attack, and she seized the opening, *thwacking* his stupid practice sword out of the way and jabbing him hard in the chest.

"*Ha!*" she shouted in triumph. "I killed you. You're dead."

Dorian smiled and gently brushed her wooden blade aside. "You killed me," he confirmed. "I'm dead."

He did not look particularly upset about it. Instead, his blue eyes shone with warmth and, she thought, pride.

"You let me win," she accused. Except, no. A bead of sweat glistened on his brow, and he was, though far from winded, at least breathing hard.

"I did *not* let you win," he said, and miracle of miracles, she believed him.

"The point is." Dorian cleared his throat and dusted himself off. "Are you feeling better?"

Tai blinked. She *was*, actually. She'd forgotten how cathartic it was to shake out her frustrations with a good sparring session.

"Thank you," she said, "And I'm sorry for wallowing in my misery."

Dorian's understanding smile was almost painful to look at. "Believe it or not, I know a thing or two about wallowing." He gazed out at the rest of the training grounds, at Falgar and Sullivan on the squat rack, and the rows of practice dummies. "You remember the first time we trained together?"

Tai's lips twitched into a smile. "Kind of hard to forget. Hadn't I just finished yelling at you at the galley table and then storming off in a huff?"

"In all fairness," Dorian said, "I *deserved* a good telling-off."

Tai laughed and shook her head. "And I suppose you're going to tell me I deserved you coming after me with a thrice-cursed practice blade?"

"Didn't you?" Dorian cocked his eyebrows.

"I suppose." *Void curse it.*

Dorian gave a wistful smile. "The thing is, Tai, you were angry at me, but you were angry because you *believed* in me, even more than I believed in myself." He let out a laugh that sounded like a hiccup. "Okay, a *lot* more than I believed in myself. It's just... that day, was the first time I ever really felt like I could be more than what I was. That maybe, if I actually pushed forward, actually worked towards something, then..." He shrugged his massive shoulders. "You say I've surpassed you, but Tai, everything I've done these past two years, such as it is, I'm not sure I could have done *any* of it without you. That night on the *Phoenix*..." His blue eyes shone with bright intensity, like miniature aether crystals. "It changed *everything*."

"*Dorian.*" Tai stood close to him, close enough she could almost become intoxicated by his scent of cinnamon and vanilla and linseed oil.

And *Savior help her,* but the last of her resolve chipped away, the last tiny barrier crumbling under the tide of her emotions, and Tai could not stop them even if she wanted to.

"To the bloody Void with it."

Tai pulled Dorian towards her and kissed him. His eyes widened first in surprise, and then in wonder, and a moment later he was kissing her back, passionately, hungrily. Tai had no idea how long they might have kept on like that, were they not interrupted by a whistling noise and the sound of applause.

Right. We're in the middle of the training grounds.

"Void-cursed *finally,*" Falgar said, from over by the squat rack.

Tai broke away, face burning, relieved that her skin was likely dark enough to hide most of her blush. "I'm... sorry," she said. "I... probably should have asked first, if you wanted me to do that."

"Oh." Dorian's voice came out a nervous croak, and the poor man's pale skin did absolutely *nothing* to hide his tomato-red flush. But she dared to hope he looked pleased, too. "I wanted you to," he said. "I definitely, *definitely* wanted you to. Just... are you sure it's what you want?"

Tai fixed him with a flat stare. "Would I have done it if I didn't?" But then she smiled and continued, "The truth is, I've wanted to do that for a long time. A *really* long time. And I'm tired of pretending otherwise, I'm tired of ignoring my feelings, and I'm tired of waiting for some nebulous *someday* when I might theoretically be good enough."

Dorian cupped the edge of her face in his hand, his eyes blazing. "Good enough." He shook his head. "I never want you to feel like you're not good enough. Never, in a hundred million years." His expression twisted into a wry smile. "Though by all means, if you still need reassuring, I can remind you all about how you've been risking your life in Kasanarae, setting yourself up as an Orith hero of prophecy, and uncovering Ancient lost magic while I've been sitting around here playing swords."

"Oh, shut up." Tai lightly swatted him on his muscular bicep. Then her heart jolted as she finally remembered what she'd been doing before Dorian arrived. "Oh, Void. Ancient magic. I left my satchel with all my spell notes back in the library!"

"Oh, right." Dorian flushed and scratched his neck. "Sorry about that, I, uh, got a bit carried away there. We'd better go get it, then."

And so, ignoring their friends' knowing smirks, they departed hand in hand.

CHAPTER THIRTY-SIX
SKETCHES OF THE PAST

"Back so soon?" Hildegard raised her eyebrows when Dorian and Tai arrived back at the library a few minutes later. Her glance strayed toward's Tai's hand in Dorian's, but thankfully, she chose not to comment. Dorian didn't even clearly remember trying to take her hand, it had just sort of happened automatically, because it felt *right*. He felt strangely reluctant to let go, but he did anyway, because it simply wasn't practical to maneuver through the crowded stacks hand in hand like that.

Gods and Ancients. Tai had kissed him. She had actually kissed him! He supposed they would eventually have to have a conversation about what that meant, but at the moment, he felt like soaring head first through the Linking, exhilarated, filled with wonder, and, yes, a bit terrified, but with the wild and desperate hope that maybe, just this once, everything would work out all right.

Tai's satchel, thankfully, was precisely where she left it.

"Thank Zekador for the small miracles," she said. She riffled through the contents, and seemed relieved to find everything was in order. "I don't think I have anything too secret in here, but I can't believe I just left it lying around where anyone could find it."

"Hildegard wouldn't let someone just come in and snatch it," Dorian reassured her.

Tai smiled wistfully as she tapped a stack of loose pages on the table to straighten them before placing them back in her satchel. "Kind of reminds me of old times, the way we used to study magic on the *Phoenix*. Oh, did I tell you? Back in Lost Hollow, I actually had to cast the Void."

Dorian's eyes widened. "You *didn't*." Then, more tentatively, he added, "How was it?"

"Absolutely terrifying," she said. "But it got that dragon Stormwind out of that awful tank thing, and that's the important thing."

Dorian nodded. "I'm glad it worked. I mean. Not glad you had to use it. But glad I taught it in a way that makes sense." He flushed slightly, remembering those long-ago evenings gathered around the Phoenix's galley table.

He'd loved how she was such an active participant in their studies, unlike Saedra, who used to just hover over his shoulder and ask nervously if he'd figured anything out yet. Dorian felt like a scoundrel for comparing the two women, even now, *especially* now. But perhaps it was inevitable. Saedra's affection had always felt like something rare and fragile, a crystal goblet to be placed on a high shelf lest it become broken or tarnished. Tai, on the other hand, was warmth and light and fire. And that was clearly demonstrated in the way she approached the Ancient magic.

As a matter of fact...

"Tai," he said slowly, "Since we're here already, I was wondering if you could take a look at something for me."

"Of course."

Dorian strode over to the now-familiar shelf and fetched Jameson's spellbook. "I'm pretty sure I'm not supposed to show you this," he admitted, "But frankly, if you're the traitor, then I might as well be a traitor too, because I'd side with you over the Order any day."

"You ridiculous man." She squeezed his hand, making it clear she found him ridiculous in an *affectionate* way. "I think I deserve a Void-cursed *medal* for waiting this long to kiss you."

Dorian flushed, then awkwardly explained what he knew of Jameson's spell so far. "He wants me to decipher the rest of it, but I'm afraid I'm, ah, stuck. Extremely stuck."

"I can have a look," she said, taking the tome from him and thumbing to the bookmarked page. Her eyes widened, and she tilted backwards in her chair, nearly falling over.

"What is it?" Dorian instinctively caught the side of the chair lest it tilt further backwards. "Are you all right?"

"Yes, sorry, fine, I just... I've *seen* this spell before."

Dorian straightened at once. "You have? When? Where?"

"In Janus Callahan's study. It was... in your handwriting."

Dorian's heart sank. *Yes,* that made unfortunate sense. "My father stole it, and I copied it down, and Saedra stole it from me, so I guess it's no surprise it ended up in Callahan's hands." Just like the Void-cursed Void spell. What would Callahan do with this information?

"It... wasn't exactly the same, though." Tai scooted her chair closer so she could get a better look. "Callahan had all kinds of annotations. I've got them written down somewhere..." She searched through her satchel and retrieved her notebook, then turned back to Jameson's grimoire. "Looks like Jameson added some new notes to his, too, something about reversing polarities... oh!" She excitedly flipped the notebook open and compared the numbers on the page with the runes in the spell circle. "It's just like the windmill at a greater scale, isn't it?"

"Uhhh..." Dorian knew Tai had worked on some kind of windmill during her time in Lost Hollow, but unfortunately, he was still ignorant on the details.

"Here, I'll show you." She turned the notebook to a blank page and dipped her quill in ink and jotted out some quick sigil calculations. "It's all about power distribution, you see? Take a singular power source and distribute it across a wider network — in this case, all the skies of Cyrna." She drummed her fingers on the table. "But where to find a power source big enough—"

A power source big enough. Dorian stood up abruptly. "Of course!" He paced up and down the library aisle. "*The* power source. The biggest one. The moon." His heart pounded in his chest as he rearranged the runes in his head. "Jameson figured out how to distribute the power but not from where. Callahan knew how to manipulate the energy from the moon, but not what to do with it. You and Temperance got it working on a smaller scale using dragon power, but dragons alone won't be nearly enough for what the spell needs. But it doesn't have to be! It all fits together! The Ancients *Planeshifted to the moon* and cast *this spell*. This is it, Tai! It could work!"

Tai's brown eyes shone with excitement, but then her face fell. "Dorian." She bit her lip. "I know I said I could planeshift, but that spell almost killed me. If we tried to go all the way to the moon…"

Dorian continued pacing, thinking frantically. They were *so close!* There had to be an answer, there just had to be. "The moon glass," he said. "Seven dragonauts working together are supposed to be able to use the moon glass to amplify their spells. That must be how the Ancients did it!" Excitement quickly gave way to frustration. "But Callahan has the moon glass now. *Void on a stick!*"

Tai stood up too, her brown eyes blazing with excitement, and with fragile, desperate hope. "Then we'll *get it back.*"

"We need to report this to the Dragonmar. She might make retrieving the moon glass a priority, if she knows what we can do with it."

"And if she doesn't?" Tai wondered.

Dorian smiled grimly. "Then we get it back without the Order's help."

"I like the way you think!" Tai slung her satchel over her shoulder, and together, they left the library once more, and made their way up the spiral staircase to the dragonmar's study.

Sylvia flounced down in the window seat in her study and poured herself a measure of whiskey. It was just past three bells — Void, she was getting to be as bad as Xander. But after the past few days she'd been having, Ancients knew she needed it.

Almost two weeks had passed since the young dragonauts Falgar and Sullivan had returned with the Orith women and the injured dragon, and things had been such a flurry of activity that Sylvia barely had a moment to think straight.

The dragon, who was evidently named Stormwind, had regained some of his bluish-gray color under Estevan's careful ministrations, but unfortunately, nothing they tried so far had roused him to consciousness. The truth was, none of them, not even the other dragons, knew what to do for a wild dragon who was so badly hurt. This sort of thing simply *did not happen* normally. How could they Heal someone who didn't even have a body?

Ironically, if anyone knew what to do, it would probably be Janus Callahan. He'd always been the best of them at discerning the blurred boundaries between flesh and spirit. But of course, that was impossible. *Hi, Janus, it's me. Long time no talk. Sorry about impersonating your servant. Could you please help me Heal this dragon your friend almost killed?* She might have laughed, were the situation not so dire.

Sylvia had spent countless hours this past week in meetings with the Orith woman Reora Lunstrum. Reora was refreshingly forthcoming, but the more Sylvia learned about their secret operation in Lost Hollow, the more uneasy she felt. Not even Reora could say for sure what Gideon had been planning alongside Janus Callahan, but Sylvia had a sinking feeling something big was about to happen, and soon. She'd known Janus a long time. He *probably* thought he was doing the right thing. But he also most likely didn't care how many innocent people were hurt or killed in the process.

The worst part about being so busy this past week was that Sylvia hadn't had a chance to finish her conversation with Dorian. She'd told him about her past as Tahlia Weatherbee, but that wasn't the whole story, not even close. And now everyone was so busy that she despaired ever getting a moment alone with the boy.

Whiskey in hand, she scanned the shelves in her study, as if any of those books and magical gadgets might contain answers to the questions she didn't know to ask. Her eyes caught the worn leather spine of Xander's old sketchbook, which he'd left in her care before he departed for Kasanarae.

More than Dorian, or Janus Callahan, or anyone else, the person she most wanted to speak to right now was her brother. Alone out of anyone, Xander was the only one who regarded her as an equal. Not an opponent to be beaten, a pawn to be manipulated, an obstacle to be crushed, or a leader to be revered. She'd missed his candor in the Cycles since their falling out. So of course the moment they were reunited she sent him away to Void-cursed Kasanarae. Yet another item on Sylvia's ever-growing list of mistakes.

Sylvia took the sketchbook down from the shelf and thumbed through it with an air of nostalgic melancholy. *Good use of your time, Sylvia,* she chided herself. She should be telling Dorian the rest of the truth, or strategizing with the dragonauts, or meeting with Reora, or seeing to the injured wild dragon. Instead, she was holed up in her study, drinking whiskey far too early, and thumbing through her brother's old drawings.

Impressive drawings they were, too. She'd always been secretly jealous of Xander's skill with pen and charcoal. Sylvia could alter her own appearance with Illusion magic as easily as breathing, but capturing her ideas on paper was another thing altogether.

She smiled as she beheld Dorian and his friends, rendered in confident lines of graphite and charcoal, looking bright-eyed and optimistic and determined. Had there ever been a time when she and her friends were so hopeful for the future, so ready to make their mark on the world? Surely they must have been, but it all felt so very long ago. She thumbed through more pages, admiring her brother's drawings, going back more than twenty years. And then, there they were, herself and Xander and Janus and Cyrus, and *yes*, they really *had* been that young and idealistic, back before everything fell apart. But fallen apart they had. Sylvia's heart ached with not knowing whether or not she could spare Dorian and his friends from a similar fate.

There was a knock on the door, and, embarrassed, Sylvia slammed the sketchbook shut. She pushed the whiskey tumbler awkwardly to the side, certain the room must reek of alcohol. She plucked a sprig of mint from the potted plant on the windowsill and shoved it in her mouth, then smoothed her hair and skirts as best she could manage.

"Enter," she said hollowly.

It was Jameson, and if he noticed her disheveled state, he made no comment. "Forgive the interruption, Lady Dragonmar, but I think you should come to the watch tower right away. Cloud has sensed... well, you'd best see for yourself."

"Of course." Sylvia cast one last wistful glance at her brother's sketchbook and followed Jameson out the door, wondering what in the Void could be going wrong now. Wallowing in nostalgia would have to wait. *Duty calls.*

Dorian took the stairs to Sylvia's office two at a time, Tai only half a step behind him. Heart thudding in his chest, he pounded on the door.

"Lady Dragonmar! Sylvia, are you there? It's important!"

There was no answer, so Dorian tried the doorknob. The door swung open to reveal an unoccupied chamber.

"Void," Tai swore. "Should we go look for her?"

Dorian shook his head. "She could be anywhere. Maybe... maybe give her a few minutes to get back." But his heart surged with worry. He'd never been especially good at waiting.

Sylvia's study looked reasonably tidy, but a few minor details indicated the Dragonmar was under a lot of pressure. Dorian thought he could count on one hand the number of times he'd seen Lady Sylvia so much as drink a glass of wine with dinner, and yet there was an open decanter of whiskey on the desk, near half empty, and a crystal tumbler that showed signs of recent use.

"It's barely past three bells." Tai sniffed the glass, half accusatory. Then she froze as she regarded a leather-bound notebook laying haphazardly on the table.

"What is it?"

"That's Xander's sketchbook," Tai said. "I remember, he was drawing in it when I..." she wrinkled her nose, and she looked, for some reason, guilty. "Anyway, I've seen it before."

"What's Lady Sylvia doing with Xander's sketchbook?"

"Well, he is her brother. Maybe he let her borrow it." Tai flipped it open. "He's great at drawing," she observed as she thumbed through detailed sketches of Bradford, Dax, Hildegard, and the knights Vale and Toric.

"You sure we should look at that?" Dorian frowned.

"Oh, Xander won't mind." She turned the page once more, and said, "Look! There's us!"

Dorian peered over Tai's shoulder at the drawing of the *Phoenix* crew. A grinning Falgar had his arm casually thrown around Sullivan's shoulder, while Tai held a triumphant fist in the air. Dorian, for his part, looked unrealistically heroic, square-jawed and muscular, gazing optimistically towards the sky. Solaris and Hematite both blazed confidently at his side in perfect harmony.

"Took some artistic liberties with me, didn't he?" Dorian smiled wanly.

"I don't know, it looks spot on to me," Tai smirked as she turned the page again, but then her face fell and she snatched her hand away as if aether-stung.

"What's wrong? Are you all right?"

Tai ran a nervous hand through her short, dark hair. "Sorry. It's fine. It's just... This one's us, too."

The date at the bottom of was about a year and a half ago, just a few days after Dorian joined the crew. There was no Solaris in this image, and Hematite looked sullen and peevish. Dorian's own features were softer and rounder, more in line with the way he imagined himself, but much more striking was the difference in his bearing — timid, staring at the ground, hands behind his back, miserable and afraid. At his side, past-Tai crossed her arms and glared, while Falgar wore a petulant sneer. Only Sullivan looked much the same, though his expression seemed wistful, and a bit sad.

"Dorian," Tai whispered, "I'm so sorry."

"Eh? What for?"

"I was awful to you in the beginning. I... the reason I even *recognize* this thrice cursed book is because I went to Xander's stateroom trying to get you kicked off the ship. I was just so angry that he let you on board, with no experience or anything... *Gah*, I've been nothing but a filthy hypocrite."

Dorian's heart surged as he took Tai's hand in his. "But you *didn't* get me kicked off the ship. I mean. You came around quickly enough, didn't you? I seem to recall you were the one who tried to convince me to stay after I wanted to leave the crew back in Thlarknia."

Tai smiled and leaned against him. "That's true. I knew I had feelings for you after Goose Head, but thinking back, I wonder if I didn't fall for you long beforehand."

Dorian flushed bright red, but he smiled, too. He gestured at the despondent crew. "That *was* us. No denying it." But he turned back to the previous page, at the triumphant happy crew who were as close as family. "But *this* is us, too, Tai. *This* is who we are. Well. I mean. Maybe I don't look as impressive as that, but, you know, close enough."

Tai smiled and squeezed his hand. "You absolutely *do* look as impressive as that. And while I may be just a little bit biased, I think you joining up was the best thing that ever happened to the *Phoenix* crew."

Dorian felt a warm happy glow in his heart as they thumbed through pages of past *Phoenix* crews, seeing several faces they recognized, and many they did not. Younger Hildegard, younger Jameson, a stately-looking couple that might have been Xander and Sylvia's parents. It was only when he turned to the last image — the first, chronologically — that his blood ran cold.

"Sweet Ancients," he breathed.

"What?" Tai's amusement gave way to concern. "Surely it's not us looking pathetic again. These drawings have to be Cycles old."

Dorian shook his head, not trusting himself to speak. He dusted himself off and examined the picture again, as if it might show something different this time. But the image remained as it was.

Alongside a much younger Captain Xander, the drawing depicted three people Dorian knew well. Dorian's father, Cyrus Valmont, stood to the right, grinning confidently in a pose oddly reminiscent of Dorian's in the more recent drawing. Perhaps they did look a *little* bit alike.

On the left was Janus Callahan, younger and with a fuller head of hair, but with a subdued expression that perhaps foreshadowed the humorless man he would become. Callahan snaked his arm protectively around the woman in the middle, who Dorian recognized immediately as a younger Lady Sylvia. But even in the drawing, her eyes seemed to gaze only at Cyrus.

Dorian's heart thudded. Sylvia was Stewardess Tahlia, yes, but that wasn't the only reason she was familiar.

This was the woman whose portrait hung in the library at Callahan Manor, whom the servants only spoke about in hushed whispers. Her wide blue eyes were so strikingly familiar because they were just like Bradford's eyes. Just like Dorian's eyes.

"Sylvia Callahan," he whispered. "My mother."

CHAPTER THIRTY-SEVEN
THE ATTACK

Sylvia stood on the parapet, watching the clouds roll in. Clouds above, clouds below. The weather seemed the perfect mirror to the emotions roiling in her heart.

"Are you sure?" She searched Jameson's face, desperate to find some sign that he was mistaken, or even straight up lying. Of course, there was none. He was as serious as he ever was.

"There is a powerful energy signature approaching Cloudfire," he confirmed. "It seems almost identical to what we sensed in Lost Hollow."

"Another captive dragon?" she shuddered. "And you're certain it's Callahan's forces?"

"I can't be certain of anything," Jameson said. "But it all fits together. The masked attacker, the loss of the moon glass, Gideon's alliance with Callahan. They're planning something big. And I think..." he swallowed. "I'm almost certain they're on their way here."

"Meroneth's balls. How long do we have?"

"Impossible to say," Jameson said. "A few days at most, perhaps less if the winds favor them."

Not long at all to prepare, then. *Void on a Stick.* "Makes my own problems seem rather trivial, doesn't it?"

She didn't realize she'd spoken out loud, but Jameson furrowed his brows and said, "Which problems do you mean, Lady Dragonmar?"

Sylvia employed a quick illusion so he wouldn't see her embarrassment. "Trivial things. Nothing you need concern yourself with."

"Try me," Jameson said.

Sylvia opened her mouth to brush him off, but at the last moment, changed her mind. Jameson had long been her friend, after all, and gods knew she had few enough of those these days.

"I tried to tell him the truth." It sounded feeble and pathetic, even to her.

Jameson didn't need to ask which *him* she meant. "But you didn't tell him the whole truth." There was no accusation in his tone, it was merely a statement of fact.

"No," she said. "I ran out of time."

I ran out of time. Forever the flimsiest of excuses.

Her old friend sighed and paced around the parapet, looking out over the edge. His white dragon darted around the turbulent air. Flashes of lightning illuminated the billowing clouds, followed by the rumble of thunder in the distance. Were those the outlines of skyships hidden in those clouds? They still *had* a few more days, didn't they?

"He deserved the truth a long time ago."

She could always count on Jameson to be blunt.

"I know." Sylvia sighed. "I think you and I both know that I have never been a brave woman."

Jameson's expression softened. Gods, he looked so young. It was hard to remember sometimes that he and Sylvia were the same age. He carried just as many scars as she did, Sylvia knew, but his were not so visible on the surface.

"In many ways, you've been braver than most." He straightened, forcing himself to meet her gaze. "I underestimated that boy of yours, you know. Like many, I made the mistake of believing he was Cyrus back from the dead. But he's nothing like Cyrus. He is so much more."

Sylvia let out a long sigh. "Cyrus was a great man. But given the distance of time, I am no longer certain he was a good man. Perhaps the tragedy of youth is to consider goodness and greatness the same."

Jameson shook his head. "Gods know that man was a prick. But he was kind to Xander and Hildegard when the rest of us couldn't be bothered, and I suppose that's something. If all we are defined by is our worst mistakes, then I fear there's not much hope for anyone's legacy."

Sylvia stared wistfully at the horizon. Her mistakes had been grave indeed, first in marrying Janus to begin with, and then in betraying him. And yet, the alternative was a world without Bradford and Dorian in it, and that, she would never countenance. "Perhaps," she whispered, "Even our mistakes have a silver lining sometimes."

Another flash on the horizon, this one blue-tinged. Not lightning, then, but aether-fire. "Jameson, are you certain about your calculations?" Sylvia frowned and focused her gaze on the horizon. It was impossible to see much in the undulating stormclouds.

"As certain as I can be," Jameson said, "Which isn't all that certain at all, really. The truth is, I have... not been wholly honest either."

Sylvia blinked. What could straitlaced, stalwart Jameson possibly lie about? "Go on."

Jameson nervously rubbed the silver-white pommel of his dragonaut sword. "I... I honestly have no idea how to say this. I never, for even a moment, want you to believe that I have ever been anything other than your friend. And even if you hate me, I'll still be your friend, though I suppose that would make it a rather one-sided friendship." He smiled weakly, then shook his head. "This isn't at all coming out right."

"Jameson, you're scaring me," Sylvia said. *Void*, had he been in league with Callahan too? He looked so sincerely guilty, had he perhaps been blackmailed? "Whatever it is, we'll figure it out..."

"I love you." Jameson blurted the words out so suddenly that Sylvia was sure she must've misheard.

"Eh?"

Jameson let out a long ragged breath. "I've been in love with you since we were teenagers. And I know with Cyrus and Janus constantly clamoring after your affections, the last thing you ever needed was me joining the fray. And it's okay if you don't feel the same way. I hope... I hope we can still be friends." He shook his head. "I'm fully aware it's beyond selfish for me to spring this on you now. But the fact is, we could all be dead in a few days. And I would hate it if one of us died without at least telling the truth."

Sylvia stared at Jameson for a long time, utterly tonguetied. Jameson. Jameson Russell. He'd been a fixture in her life all these long Cycles, for as long as she could remember. He was consummately loyal, and handsome in his own way. Far too serious for his own good, but that just made it all the more rewarding when she *could* make him laugh. But romance? Did she feel that way about him? *Could* she?

"Surely you can do better than an old crone like me," she heard herself say.

"We are the same age, Lady Dragonmar."

"But we don't look it."

"You think that *matters*?"

"We could... attempt courtship, I suppose."

Courtship, Ancients help her. Sylvia hadn't had to think about *courtship* in Cycles.

"I... would really like that." Jameson looked patently relieved. "I... thank you for being so understanding. I know that I—"

A sharp twang cut through the evening air, cutting his words off in a strangled gasp. He collapsed to the stone parapet.

"Jameson!" She knelt next to him, horror mounting as she

watched a flower of blood blossom around the arrow protruding from his chest.

"Oh dear." Jameson looked more surprised than anything. *Shock,* a distant part of her thought as she recalled long-ago first aid lessons. *He's in shock.* "Sorry Syl... Looks like I was... wrong about the timing after all." He coughed and a splatter of blood came out of his mouth.

"Oh no you don't." Frantic, terrified, Sylvia ripped the arrow from his chest and pressed down upon the wound as if by will alone she could force his heart to keep beating. But a wound like this one was far beyond her limited skill. She needed a real Healer.

"Help!" she cried out frantically into the night. No one would likely hear them, not way up here, but perhaps one of the dragons... "Someone! I need Estevan! Or Sullivan! Please!" To Jameson, she snarled, "You complete bastard. You can't just say all those things and then Void-cursed *die* on me."

Her brain refused to process what had just happened. It *couldn't* have happened. It didn't make *sense*. One moment Jameson was confessing his feelings to her and now... *this?*

She searched the sky where she'd sworn she'd seen Jameson's dragon just a few moments before. *Please, let someone have heard. Please let one of the dragons send help.* At first, she saw nothing but billowing gray cumulonimbus. But then, a hauntingly familiar chuckle carried through the wind, followed by the sound of wingbeats.

A veritable army of gryphons, ornithopters, and military skyships emerged from the clouds. And at their head, a gaunt, pale-faced man rode on the back of a sepulchral black dragon.

"Hello, Sylvia," he said, dismounting. "Or is that indeed still your name? Would you prefer, instead, I called you Tahlia?"

"I—" Sylvia grasped for words, but words failed her.

"You gave me quite the merry chase, my dear *wife*." Janus Callahan sneered. "But it seems I found you in the end."

Rainfall pelted down on the leaded glass window of the Dragonmar's study, and Dorian thought he heard thunder in the distance. *Convenient.* The weather perfectly matched his mood. His hand trembled as he put the sketchbook back down on the mahogany desk.

Dragonmar Sylvia had been his mother this whole time. *Void Eternal. Tahlia Weatherbee* had been his mother *that* whole time. He understood why she had to lie back then, hiding as an employee in her estranged husband's household. But all those times she'd joined him on the training field or at mealtimes or during chore rotations, why hadn't she thought to mention, "Oh, by the way, Dorian, I'm your mother?"

"Do you think Bradford knows?" But Dorian already knew the answer.

Of *course* Bradford knew. So many of his off-handed comments, arguments with Xander about keeping secrets. Void Eternal, *Xander.* Why hadn't Xander told him? Dorian wasn't sure which stung more, that his captain had seen fit to hide such a crucial piece of information, or that Sylvia would trust Bradford and not him.

Void, it probably wasn't just Bradford and Xander who knew. Jameson, Hildegard, maybe even Dax... At the moment, it wouldn't surprise Dorian if Graigor Bloody Beckett found out the truth before he did. It was like everyone had been laughing at him behind his back. Like everyone was in on some shared joke except for Dorian, because Dorian *was* the joke.

But not Tai. She wasn't laughing. He hand shook slightly as she beheld the image, brown eyes flashing with barely-contained fury.

"How dare she?" Her voice was casual, the sort of carefree tone one might take when watering the hydrangeas. Dorian knew better. Tai only talked like this when she was *livid.* "*How dare she?*" Tai gave a violent twitch of her wings, scattering black feathers across the office. "The dragonmar sits there all sanctimonious, sends me to Kasanarae to do her dirty work — when all the while she — *this*."

Despite everything, Dorian felt his despondence chip away. If Tai was so indignant on his behalf, then it no longer mattered, somehow, what anyone else thought.

Outside the window, he saw a flash of light, followed by a boom of thunder. Dorian's dragonstone thrummed at his chest, and Solaris cried out a terrified «Dorian!»

"Solaris?" Dorian staggered backwards at the surge of fear that came through the bond. "What is it?"

But the dragon did not answer.

"Solaris!"

Another bolt of thunder, louder this time, so loud the window rattled.

Heart pounding, Dorian clutched his dragonstone close to his chest. "I think Solaris is in trouble!"

The next blast rocked the entire tower. A diamond-shaped windowpane fell loose and shattered on the stone floor.

"Zekador's poorly fitting pants," Tai swore.

Dorian swallowed. "That's not a storm. It's a Void-cursed invasion force."

Cloudfire was under attack.

Solaris darted back and forth between the ominous thunderclouds, gazing in horror at the flotilla of approaching skyships. Janus Callahan was here. She knew that with every spark of her being. Janus Callahan was here, and he had brought a sizable army with him, and Solaris honestly did not know if the Order of the Silver Dragon could drive them back. All their training, all their preparation, and Solaris did not think any of them were the slightest bit ready for this moment.

Dorian. She needed to find Dorian. That was the sensible thing to do, the right thing to do.

And yet she remained hovering in midair, paralyzed with indecision. To bring her rider into battle was to bring him into danger. So long as Cloudfire's walls held, he remained safe. And rider or no rider, there was still much Solaris could do. Moon and Stars help her, if Janus Callahan was here, that meant her clan-mates were as well. She would not, could not, surrender her only chance to see them.

Finding Celestian was easy enough. The brash indigo dragon telepathically cried out in horror as that horrible man Kadmin made him rain fire down on Cloudfire's soldiers.

«I did not return for this,» Celestian kept repeating, over and over. «I did not return for this!»

It broke Solaris inside to see her sometimes-rival, sometimes friend reduced to such a state. He had had his head in the clouds, full of adventure tales, smugly entitled to the Chronicler's knowledge, while the rest of the clan valued his moon dancing skills so much more than Solaris's own. But he did not deserve this. Nobody did.

«I will help you if I can,» she promised her former clan-mate. It was nowhere near enough, but for the moment, it was all she could do.

Nocturne, though. She could still help Nocturne.

He, too, proved easy enough to find. There he was, thin and sepulchral, with an exhausted-looking Janus Callahan clinging to his neck ridges, thin brown-gray ponytail flapping behind him like a pennant. Much of a bonded dragon's physical strength came directly from their rider. Janus Callahan, who had sat on a throne for the past two years, was surely no match for her Dorian, who had spent that time training tirelessly to become a warrior. Yet even that could not explain the massive gulf in strength between Nocturne and herself.

Solaris had been weak and spindly during the earliest days of her bond with Dorian, but she was certain even *that* version of herself could easily defeat the frail Nocturne she saw before her. Poor Nocturne seemed to barely hold himself together in the howling winds, every beat of his ragged silver wings reverberating with agony and exhaustion.

Solaris's inner fire stoked with fury at what had been done to him. Nocturne was no ordinary dragon, he was the Chronicler of their clan, the keeper of their ancestral memory. He had once been so idealistic and full of life, brimming with borderline-blasphemous optimism that humans and dragons may one day restore their sacred bond. Well. Look how that had turned out. They may yet restore the bond, but what had been done to Nocturne had been basest abomination.

She hoped that Dorian remained safe in the castle. She hoped that he would forgive her for acting without him. But if she freed the Chronicler got rid of Emperor Callahan in the process, then surely that would be worth any indiscretion.

«I am here, Nocturne,» she reassured him. «I have come to free you.»

«Solaris.» She expected him to be happy to see her, maybe even relieved. But his pale blue eyes reflected only horror at her presence. «You must flee.»

«Flee?» she repeated in disbelief.

Spark's chance in the Void of *that* happening. All these long moons of training with her human partner and playing the Order's ridiculous political games, just so that she might have this one chance, to free her mentor, her clan-mate, her friend. She was most certainly *not* going to flee.

Fangs bared, claws outstretched, flames ready, she dove towards the frail black dragon.

Faster than Solaris thought possible, Nocturne folded his wings and dove out of the way. She let out a frustrated stream of sparks. Weakness or no weakness, the Chronicler had always been nimble in the sky. She had forgotten about that. Perhaps she really ought to have brought Dorian along. She could fly better with her human partner. But no matter. She would not give up so easily.

She wheeled around to strike again, and for the first time, she noticed someone else riding on the black dragon's back behind the Emperor. Solaris pulled up short and barely managed to avoid knocking the poor woman off the saddle. It was Dragonmar Sylvia, the leader of the Order, bound and gagged and looking terrified. *Void Eternal.* Now, if she freed Nocturne and killed Callahan, the dragonmar would most likely also fall to her death. The Order would be none too pleased, if she got their leader killed.

Solaris recalled learning that the Dragonmar was once Dorian's governess, whatever that meant. She did not understand human household structures well, but she knew this woman had some hand in raising Dorian. And... she sensed another connection between the two, something emotionally tangled and fraught. But Dorian cared about this woman greatly. More than simply the Order being upset, her own rider would never forgive her if she caused the Dragonmar's death. But Flames save her, what was she to do? She would not likely find another opportunity like this one.

Solaris's hesitation cost her dearly. In her moment of uncertainty, the stern-faced emperor drew his athame, and flung a hurried-but-deft series of runes into the air. The magic crashed into Solaris like the waves of the undersea breaking on Orith's shores, and Solaris was frozen in place.

May the Ice curse her and her hesitation! Solaris sent out a wordless cry for Dorian, or even for any of the other Order dragonauts, but in the end she knew it was an empty gesture. No one would possibly reach her in time. *Curse it all...* She thought she was stronger than this, she was *supposed* to be stronger than this. But no matter how she flared her wings or thrashed her tail against the invisible bonds of the spell, she remained firmly frozen in place.

Nocturne declined his emaciated neck, looking to all the world impassive and cowed. But his silver-blue eyes whirred with concentration, and when he raised his head again, his black draconic visage was one of grim resignation.

«I, Nocturne of the Moonless Night, bonded dragon to Emperor Janus Everford Callahan Kasani Sanorsk, relinquish my title as Chronicler of the Quiet Mountain, bestowing that mantle instead onto Solaris of the Vibrant Dawn, bonded dragon to Dorian Alric Valmont, passing to her the collected memory and lore of our kind.»

Nocturne breathed a steady stream of magic flames that shimmered in all the colors of the rainbow. In all of her fifty years, Solaris had never seen the like. It was beautiful, but because Solaris knew what it was, it was also terrifying.

«Nocturne, what...» but she could barely even form a coherent sentence as a gushing torrent of information crashed into her mind all at once, so rapidly that she could not possibly hope to process it all.

For a long moment, the rest of the world, the castle and the underclouds and the desperate battle beneath her, faded from view. Solaris was adrift in a realm of stars and galaxies and floating moats of magic. She saw memories of generations past, the sting of the Great Betrayal, the horror and the loss, but also happier memories, too, times when humans and dragons flew as one. For the first time, Solaris understood why the Chronicler always skirted so close to blasphemy. She saw so much all at once that she did not even notice at first when Nocturne rapidly spun towards her.

«I am sorry, Solaris.» To his credit, Nocturne sincerely sounded like he meant it. Then, he raised his whipcord bladed tail and sliced her throat.

At first, Solaris felt nothing but a vague sense of shock as her own head separated from her body. Then, both head and body faded away, and Solaris was whole once more, but insubstantial, ghostly. *Unbonded.* Zekador help her, Nocturne had broken her bond.

«Dorian!» she cried out against the turbulent skies. But she knew he would not hear her.

CHAPTER THIRTY-EIGHT

ON THE PARAPET

Dorian ran up the spiral staircase as fast as his legs would carry him. *Thank the Ancients for those Void-cursed hill sprints.* There was no way he could have done this a year ago.

"Solaris!" He prayed to all seven gods that he wasn't too late.

There was a flash of lightning outside the stairwell's arrow-slit window, and booming thunder so loud the entire castle seemed to rattle. Abruptly Dorian felt a sensation like being punched in the gut, and it was all he could do not to fall backwards and crack his skull on the hard stone stairway.

"Dorian!" Tai reached out to steady him. "Dorian, what happened?"

Dorian clutched his head, reeling, feeling punch-drunk and oddly empty. "Solaris," he barely managed to cough out the word. He'd felt a burst of terror and frustration for her, and then... *nothing.* "Oh, gods, Solaris, she..."

He clutched the dragonstone around his neck, terrified to look at it, because deep down he knew what he would find. In his hand he felt a mere hunk of cold stone, with none of the familiar thrumming warmth of his connection with his dragon.

Tai squeezed his hand. "Solaris will be all right. We'll find her."

Dorian knew this was probably wishful thinking on Tai's part, but her presence calmed him nonetheless, grounded him in the present moment. "Right. We'll... we'll find her."

They reached the top of the tower and staggered outside into the frigid winter air. Although the parapet itself seemed deserted, the skies above were filled with the sights and sounds of battle. Flashes of aetherfire, voices crying out, and the discordant clang of metal against metal pierced the evening sky. Dorian held Tai close to him, as if he might somehow be able to protect her from the maelstrom, even though he felt as vulnerable as a newborn himself.

"Dorian." Tai extracted herself from him and pointed near the crenelated edge of the parapet, her hand shaking. "Look."

Dorian's heart sank further still as he sprinted over to investigate. The watchtower parapet was not so abandoned as he initially thought, for a motionless figure lay collapsed on the ground. From the blood-stained white cloak and golden flight-leader's epaulets, he knew with heart-wrenching certainty that it must be Jameson.

"No." All the chaos around them narrowed to a single nightmare point. "No no no no no."

Jameson couldn't be dead. Not now, not when the two of them were finally starting to get along. He turned the figure over, and to his horror found that the flight leader's entire torso was sticky with blood. Horrible memories flashed before Dorian's eyes, of the ruins of Icereach Citadel, trying desperately and futilely to save his father from the ruble.

Jameson stirred in his arms and let out a sputtering cough.

"Jameson!" *Alive.* Ancients help them, he was alive. "We have to get you to the infirmary."

Ashen-faced, Jameson raised a trembling arm and clung to the folds of Dorian's shirt. "No."

"But—"

Jameson coughed again, and this time blood oozed out of the corner of his mouth. "Too late. For me. You must... help Sylvia. Callahan... took her."

"He kidnapped my mother?" Dorian's eyes widened in alarm.

A look almost like relief crossed his face before giving way to pain again. "So you know about that... good." He coughed again, then, trembling, pressed his dragonstone into Dorian's palm. It thrummed with his connection to Cloud, but even Dorian could tell the connection was a weak one. "Give that... to the Lunstrum girl." He jerked his head slightly in Tai's direction. "If she... summons... Cloud will answer."

"Tai can't summon Cloud because *you're* Cloud's rider and you're *not* going to die." If Dorian had been able to keep Jameson talking this long, that meant there was still a chance, right? *Surely* it had to mean that. "Tai and I just figured out the rest of that spell of yours. You have to be the one to cast it, after all these years. It's *your* spell. You can't die yet."

Jameson coughed again, and there was no denying it sounded like a derisive snort. "You're just... as stubborn... as your father. But a better man... by far." He opened his mouth as if to say more, but the last of his energy seemed to go out of him, and he collapsed, eyes staring lifelessly into the turbulent winter sky.

"Jameson!" Dorian shook Jameson by the shoulders, but there was nothing for it. He was gone.

As if to punctuate that fact, Dorian felt the dragonstone grow cold in his hand. He watched as it faded from pearlescent white to lifeless gray. The same lifeless gray as his own dragonstone no doubt was, though he still hadn't summoned the courage to look at it.

A stray tear fell down Dorian's face. Dorian irritably wiped it away with his shirtsleeve, but more came, a stubborn stream that threatened to become a torrent. Jameson, Solaris, *Sylvia*... it was all so much, so fast. Jameson should not have had to die like this. Jameson should not have had to die at all.

Tai squeezed his hand, her brown eyes warm with concern. She didn't tell him to pull himself together, for which he was grateful, but he knew that he had to anyway. He took several deep breaths and pressed the dragonstone into her hand.

"Jameson wanted you to have this. He said... he said if you cast the Summons, Cloud will answer."

Tai's brow furrowed, perplexed but also curious. "I've never really spoken to Cloud."

"Solaris and I had never spoken before, either." He gave her what he hoped was an encouraging smile, but he was well aware it probably looked like a pained grimace.

Tai closed her eyes, clutched the dragonstone, and nodded. When she opened her eyes again, her jaw was set in grim determination. "Right. I'll do it. Of course." She met his eyes, her gaze grim and level. "Are you going to cast the Summons too?"

She left unspoken what she truly meant, but it hung uncomfortably in the air all the same. *Will you cast the Summons, knowing that Solaris might not be able to answer?*

Dorian forced himself, for the first time, to look at the dragonstone on its heavy gold chain around his neck. It was, as he feared, gray and inert, just like the one Tai now held. He thought back to his last Summons, back in the kitchens of Callahan Manor. Another lifetime. Part of him *was* afraid to cast it again. Afraid to confirm once and for all that Solaris was gone to him forever. Like Hematite. Like Jameson. Like his father.

But none of that mattered right now. If there was a chance he could summon Solaris again, he had to do so. "Let's both cast it at the same time."

Tai nodded in understanding and clutched her own dragonstone, which had so recently belonged to Jameson, who lay dead not two dragon's lengths away. Dorian knew how conflicted she must feel. She wore an expression of grim resolve paired with vulnerability that made her resemblance to her brother all the more pronounced.

Meroneth's balls. Tanis! Dorian leapt to his feet and shoved the dragonstone pendant back under his shirt.

"What is it?" Tai asked.

"Your brother. He's is still under house arrest." Dorian clutched his head and started pacing around the parapet. "Void, did anyone think to let him out of his apartments? Your mother never had a key. Jameson's dead, and the Dragonmar..." *I will not think about the Dragonmar right now.*

Tai's eyes widened. "Then we've got to get down there right away." She glanced regretfully at the dragonstone, then back at Dorian.

Dorian's mind raced as he considered the possibilities. "You... should take cover somewhere safe and cast the Summons. I'll go after Tanis."

"What about Solaris?"

Solaris. Gods. "She's a dragon. She can take care of herself." Gods, he hoped that was true. "Your brother, he's ill. He needs my help. I did take responsibility for him, after all."

Despite everything, he felt suddenly and inexplicably clear-headed. Here was something he *could* do, someone he *could* save. As long as he focused on that, he could keep the rest from overwhelming him.

Tai nodded, fiddled nervously with the dragonstone, then abruptly strode up to him and kissed him. Her cinnamon and citrus scent filled his nostrils and for a brief and wonderful moment he allowed himself to forget all about the grim and messy reality currently crashing down around their heads. He couldn't believe it had been only a few short hours ago she'd first kissed him in the training grounds.

"I love you," he whispered, and then sprinted back down the stairs, hoping against all hope that this kiss would not be their last.

Alone on the parapet, with only Jameson's corpse for company, Tai allowed her tears to flow freely. Jameson, dead. Her friends and family, in trouble. And Dorian...

Dorian, you brave, foolish soul. She'd finally had the courage to kiss him, and now he was off to rescue her brother, and she might never see him again. She tried to be optimistic about his chances; dragon or no dragon, he had trained with the best. But the way the battle seemed to be going, she wondered if any of them would survive the night.

Tai was still alive for now, however, and she still could make a difference. Taking a deep breath, she held her athame in one hand and Jameson's dragonstone in the other, and traced the runes of the summoning.

Unlike Dorian, who'd first cast the spell in ignorant desperation, Tai knew exactly what she was doing. She'd had this circle memorized for almost as long as she'd known Aerish magic existed, and drawing each rune felt as easy as breathing. A tingle of excitement ran down her spine despite the dire circumstances. She'd never really thought this day would come.

With the runes and sigils in place, Tai stepped into the center of the circle and held the dragonstone in front of her. The dull gray stone lit up like a beacon, signaling to all dragonkind that she was ready for a bond. She'd never understood why dragons needed these Ancient artifacts to complete the bonds, whereas demons could take whatever mortals they chose. But right now the stone in her hand felt *right* and *necessary*. She thought she ought to say something profound and impressive, but only one word came out. "*Help.*"

The sounds of battle faded, and for a moment Tai floated in empty space. Motes of light dashed and darted in her peripheral vision. Wild dragons, she realized. Wild dragons, investigating her. Tai felt exposed, her entire soul open for their perusal. Most ignored her, some reacted with open disdain.

"Cloud..." she reached out to Jameson's pale white dragon, feeling forty-nine kinds of fool. "Jameson said you might help me..."

And there, thank the Ancients, he was, ghostly silver eyes alight with grief for his lost rider, but filled also with resignation and duty. Not ideal circumstances to form a powerful bond between souls, she thought, but there was no helping it. He seemed to agree.

«I, Cloud of the—» he began.

Tai heard too late the twang of a bowstring released, and Cloud's ghostly form dissipated into a puff of silver-white spirit energy. Terror surged through her. He wasn't dead, was he? No, surely not. It took more than an arrow to kill a dragon. But while the dragonstone still glowed the bright silver-white of the Summoning spell, her burgeoning connection with Cloud was shattered, and Tai had no chance to reclaim it. She was no longer alone on the parapet.

"Foolish, Tai, leaving yourself exposed like that." Kadmin wore his usual smirk as he set his bow aside and pointed his sword at her neck. A regular sword, not his dragonaut's sword. Had Celestian revoked the privilege? Now *that* was certainly interesting. She felt her own last gift from Celestian reassuringly at her side, but she knew the moment she made a move for it, Kadmin would plunge his mundane-but-deadly blade into her throat.

"We've got to stop meeting like this," she sighed, deadpan. The failed summoning took a lot out of her, and right now all Tai wanted was a nap.

Kadmin shook his head. "You really thought you could steal my dragonstone and get away with it?" He spun the chain of Celestian's achingly familiar stone around the finger of his free hand, grinning arrogantly. "Foolish girl. I've told you already. Celestian is mine."

"He's his own dragon. Besides. If Celestian is so loyal to you, how come you're using that plain sword?" If Tai was going to die anyway, she figured she might as well annoy him first.

"That is no concern of yours." Kadmin's hand wavered just slightly, and, miracle of miracles, Tai saw the opening she needed.

Tai kicked outward at Kadmin's sword hand, and the deadly sharp steel skittered across the parapet. Tai sprung to her feet and drew her own weapon.

Kadmin, however, hadn't become an imperial dragonaut on sheer chance. He reacted quickly, seizing his fallen weapon before settling back into a fighting stance.

"Where did you get that?" Kadmin glared down at her own blade with hatred and, she thought, perhaps fear.

"From a mutual friend."

They circled around each other, predator and prey. She was no rank novice, but Kadmin was an expert. Her chances didn't look good. *Unless...*

Wavering, heart pounding, Tai moved back towards the ledge. *Make him think he has the upper hand.* She didn't need to do much to be convincing. Her terror was all too real. *I hope this works.*

"Foolish, foolish girl," Kadmin mocked her again. "Now you've nowhere left to go."

"See," Tai said with forced confidence, "There's where you're wrong."

"Eh?" Kadmin looked genuinely confused.

"There is somewhere to go," Tai explained. "Down."

Before she could change her mind, Tai grabbed the front of Kadmin's shirt and tilted backwards. Kadmin jabbed frantically with his sword, but the strike went wide, hitting only the gap between feathers. Kadmin desperately windmilled his arms to right himself, but it did no good.

In a tangled mess of wings and limbs, Tai and Kadmin plummeted together off of Cloudfire's highest tower.

CHAPTER THIRTY-NINE

THE BATTLE OF CLOUDFIRE

Tanis pulled the brocade coverlet up to his chest as another volley of cannon fire rocked the building. Some good it did, being moved to nicer quarters. He was still going to die here. The dank dungeons where they'd shoved him initially might have actually been safer.

Savior help me, he thought as guilt and shame cooked a toxic potion in the cauldron of his stomach. *This is all my fault.*

«I can make the pain go away, you know.» Malachite's maliciousness was the lightest brush against his mind.

Although he knew he should not, he let Malachite have his spirit energy. First a trickle, and then a steady stream.

He'd been good, almost impossibly so, ever since his mother and sister returned. He'd done everything Reora instructed, completing the stupid meditation exercises and keeping his spirit barriers up at strategic times while also allowing them to rest. It was Void-cursed *tedious*, and worst of all it didn't even seem to matter. Malachite was as powerful and malignant as ever. At least doing it Dorian's way, he might have stood a chance.

But he hadn't done things Dorian's way. In fact, he'd betrayed Dorian and everything he stood for. And now he was locked in this stupid room with no one but the Depths-sodden demon for company. And as if that wasn't bad enough, the castle was under attack, too. Tanis was fairly certain he was going to die, and he was fairly certain he deserved it. Why not let the sweet euphoria of demonic fugue carry him away into oblivion one last time?

He heard the sound of shouting outside his chambers, and a moment later, the heavy wooden door blew off its hinges in a flurry of splinters. Tanis abruptly cut off the flow of spirit energy with a hastily-woven spirit barrier. He supposed he had enough pride and shame left to want to face death fully conscious after all.

But it was not attacking forces on the other side of the door. It was the bald, muscular dragonaut, Sullivan, alongside Tanis's harried-looking mother, each holding either end of a battering ram.

"Tanis, thank the Savior." Reora set the heavy log down and sprinted forward to embrace him.

Tanis quietly tightened his spirit barrier, fiercely grateful his mother hadn't quite walked in on him going into another fugue. "How did you— that battering ram—"

"The door was locked," Reora said. "We thought this would be the most expedient way to get to you."

"We're evacuating all the civilians," Sullivan elaborated. "However, I and everyone else with Healing skills are needed in the infirmary. We could always use an extra pair of hands, if you're willing."

Tanis would have been happy to never see the infirmary again, but he also saw the opportunity for what it was. Far, far better to make himself useful than to be hauled around like cargo yet again. Sullivan was extending a peace offering, a chance to redeem himself.

He ignored Malachite's disparaging whispers and said, "Of course I'll help."

Tanis had never seen the infirmary so crowded. Healer Estevan, who was usually so composed, had dark circles under his eyes and his wispy white hair stuck out at odd angles. Splatters of blood stained his white Healer's robes. Nearly every bed in the long white hall was occupied, and Tanis was confronted with the metallic scent of blood and a foul scent of rot.

"Fallen take me," he swore in Toreenish.

"Horrible, isn't it?" Sullivan asked.

"On second thought," Tanis said faintly, "Maybe I was better off under house arrest."

"Thank the Ancients you're here." Healer Estevan moved frantically between the sick and the injured, like a bee in a field of grotesque flowers. "We can use all the help we can get."

"Whatever you need," Sullivan said. He was already tracing Healing runes into the air.

Reora, too, quickly got to work, her efficient no-nonsense attitude as effective as ever at sensing what needed doing and seeing that it got done.

Tanis, of course, didn't know how to cast Healing. He didn't know much magic at all, if he was honest. The desire to cast spells to help his family was the whole reason he was in this mess, and yet even after everything he'd been through, his repertoire remained laughable. He decided that if he got out of this alive, he'd make it a priority to do something about that. Unfortunately, that was a pretty big *if*.

For the moment, he made himself useful in whatever way he could, mixing poultices, cutting bandages, and refilling pitchers of fresh cold water while the two Healers performed their life-saving work.

"Bring me a scalpel," Sullivan said.

"I need more echinacea oil!" Estevan cried out.

Tanis could do nothing but scramble. If anything, he was glad to keep himself busy. If he allowed himself to relax, even for a moment, he might never bring himself to do anything ever again.

As he scanned the shelves of medicines looking for echinacea oil, he caught a glint of strange light out of the corner of his eye. What he'd thought was an empty hospital bed was actually occupied by a wild dragon, so pale and ghostly as to be almost invisible.

"Who is that?" Tanis had never seen a dragon like this, neither in Cloudfire nor with the Kasani army.

"That's Stormwind," Reora said sadly as she tied a poultice together. "We found him underground in Lost Hollow. We... believe he was powering the beacon I used to speak to you."

Tanis squirmed guiltily. "And powering the aether beacon did *that* to him?"

"Among other things," Reora said through pursed lips. "I shudder to think what other sinister experiments Gideon performed on the poor creature."

Gideon. And Tanis had helped him, Depths curse it all.

Tanis instinctively put his hand over the spectral form and felt the faint but steady thrum of Stormwind's magical life force. Not so different from a demon, he thought, though he sensed no malice from the creature.

Abruptly, the dragon opened his eyes, which glowed bright and shining blue.

"Wha—"

«The enemy...» a soft mindvoice brushed across Tanis's consciousness like the gentlest gust of wind. «Took my essence... to help summon... a Voidwraith... You are all in danger.»

Tanis's voice came out a full octave higher than normal. "Voidwraith?"

Sullivan looked up in alarm. "Who said anything about Void-wraiths?"

"The dragon—" Tanis began, but when he look back over at the ghostly form, he saw that Stormwind had fallen back unconscious, and he doubted anything he did would rouse him.

"We've no time for children's scare-tales." Healer Estevan said, a touch churlishly. He snatched the echinacea oil out of Tanis's hand. "I thought you agreed to help cut bandages."

"Of course. I'm sorry." But he shuddered, because he knew Void-wraiths were no scare tale.

Tanis reached for a fresh roll of bandages when an explosion rocked the castle. The table full of surgical equipment fell to the floor with a clatter.

"What in the Void?" someone cried out. Tanis wasn't sure who, because the ringing in his ear made it difficult to hear. But it was immediately obvious what caused the commotion.

A cannon blast had hit the infirmary wall directly, knocking out the shelves full of herbs and medicines and leaving only a gaping hole to let in the cool evening air.

"Meroneth's balls," Sullivan whispered.

"They would attack the injured?" Estevan protested. "Do they have no shame?"

"We need to evacuate everyone." Sullivan stood upright, ready for battle, hand on his dragonaut's sword.

"Bloody Void, how, man?" Estevan's frazzled voice held none of its usual composure. "The entire castle's overrun, we'll never get the civilians to safety."

Tanis stared in horror out the new window the enemy had blasted into the castle wall. A dark speck appeared against the setting sun, growing larger by the moment. As it came closer, he saw it was a skyship, one with shimmering white aether sails bearing the crest of the Kasani navy.

Reinforcements for the *enemy?* How was *that* fair when the people of Cloudfire were *already* outnumbered?

This is it, Tanis thought. *This is how I die.* He tried to make peace with it, but mostly he felt indignant. *I'm only sixteen,* he thought. *I want to live.*

Then the oncoming ship fired its cannons, not at the castle, but at one of the other Kasani ships.

What the —

The enemy ship exploded in a hail of fire and debris. Tanis shielded his face and dove away from the opening in the wall.

"That was the most ludicrous thing I've ever seen!" said a welcome and familiar voice. Sullivan's lover, the sandy-haired drago-naut Zachary Falgar, flew up to the opening with his golden dragon Meridian.

"What's going on?" Tanis wasn't sure whether to laugh or cry.

"We're going to have to be gentle, but we're taking the injured and the civilians on board this ship," Falgar said. Behind him on the ship, a stocky middle-aged Iriya woman laid out a gangplank between the ship's deck and the hole in the infirmary wall. "This ship will take you to safety."

Tanis didn't want to be carted off with the civilians, but as there was little he could do here, he nodded. "I don't understand," he said. "That's a Kasani ship."

"Yes," said the captain, who stood triumphant at the bow wearing a ragged blue captain's jacket, "But I am no Kasani."

"Captain!" Sullivan's voice was alight with relief.

"Not a captain anymore, remember?" The grizzled man scratched his neck. "Or wait. Suppose I am. Anyway, it doesn't matter. We'd best get to work."

They were joined by a curly haired man Tanis vaguely recognized as Dorian's brother, Lord Bradford. The captain, then, must be Xander, Dorian's old mentor. Now that Tanis thought about it, he vaguely recalled meeting them both when they accompanied the porter crew up Cloudfire Mountain all those moons ago. But he hadn't had much interest in making friends, back then.

Both men looked a bit like Dorian, Tanis noted, and also a bit like the dragonmar. He filed away this information for later and set about helping the injured across the gangplank on stretchers.

Malachite clawed at his insides, seeping poison into his veins, begging, demanding that he give up his spirit energy. But Tanis erected the best barrier he could muster, knowing it was far too important to keep a clear head while they got the civilians to safety.

"Captain, can I have a word?" Sullivan asked worriedly as they worked.

"Of course," Xander said.

"I have my concerns about what Callahan's forces are doing here."

Xander snorted. "'Concerns' is certainly one way of putting it."

"Of course, Sir." Sullivan smiled faintly, then became serious once more. "I mean... I have reason to suspect he wants the fortress for reasons other than a simple grudge against the Order."

Xander frowned. "Go on."

"Cloudfire's a strategic location," Sullivan said. "Whoever holds it will still be able to cast magic, even if the other continents fall beneath the clouds."

"You're saying he intends to sink Aeris right away?" Xander's eyes widened.

"Hard to say what he plans," Sullivan said. "But a captive we rescued mentioned something about a Voidwraith."

Tanis's head jerked towards Sullivan in surprise. Had Sullivan heard the injured dragon? Did he, unlike Estevan, take his words seriously?

Xander's mouth narrowed into a thin, worried line. "He summoned a Voidstorm against the *Phoenix* two years ago," he said. "Unfortunately, summoning a Void*wraith* is probably also within the bounds of possibility."

"Pity Regnald's not here, we could use his demon," Lord Bradford put in as he and Falgar rushed past carrying the injured Order Knight Toric Verity on a stretcher.

Xander, Sullivan, and Tanis all shot him a sharp look. "What's this about a demon?" Xander asked.

Bradford gently set Toric down on the ship's deck with the rest of the injured civilians and hurried back over to explain. "Back on the docks in Kasanarae, when we got hit by a Voidstorm, his demon Garnet beat it back somehow. It should be the same with wraiths, too, shouldn't it?"

Xander scratched his chin, thoughtful. "Valmont's Hematite got us safely through the underclouds, and those are basically like one giant Voidwraith. You might be onto something. But Regnald stayed behind in Kasanarae, so there's not much we can do about it now."

Tanis stood frozen in place, mind reeling. Regnald, whoever that was, wasn't here. But Tanis was. Tanis had a demon.

He felt Malachite stir within him, blue flames flared, forest-green tail twitching back and forth in anticipation. «You know what this means, do you not?»

Tanis had expected the demon to sound angry, or peevish, or perhaps in the best of cases reluctant or resigned. He did not expect Malachite to sound *eager.*

«You *want* to fight the Voidwriath?»

«It is what I was created for.» Malachite primly examined his claws. «But to pull it off, I need power from you. So much power.» The demon practically vibrated with yearning. «I cannot guarantee your safety.»

Tanis smiled ruefully and shook his head. «You never have.»

Dorian skidded to a halt in the hallway outside Tanis's apartment, only to find the door blown off its hinges, and the chambers empty.

"No," Dorian said. "No no no no no."

"Valmont, there you are, thank the gods."

Dorian spun around at the sound of the voice, for a wild moment hoping to find Tanis, but it was the Order Knight Vale, golden ponytail askew, face splattered in blood.

"Are you all right?"

"I'm alive, which is a start." Vale winced. "Where have you been? Have you seen Flight Leader Jameson?"

"Jameson's dead." Dorian's voice cracked, as if saying it out loud made it real in a way that even watching the man die in his arms could not.

Vale's face fell. "Sweet Ancients. Then things are even worse than I thought. Hildegard's injured, Dax went missing weeks ago, and Sullivan's got his hands full in the infirmary, so it's just Falgar and Graigor guarding the skies."

Dorian's frown deepened. Falgar and Graigor were not his first choice of dragonauts to work together.

"Why aren't you up there?" Vale demanded. "Where in the Void is Solaris?"

"Solaris…" Dorian's heart felt squeezed in a juice press. He shook his head. "I'm looking for Tanis. Have you seen him?"

"He went with Sullivan to the infirmary," Vale said. "But—"

"I'm sorry, Vale," Dorian said. "But I have to go find him."

"All right," Vale said, but he still looked distinctly put out.

Dorian felt bad about leaving Vale standing there, but he desperately needed to make sure his charge was safe, first. Then, gods willing, he'd have the clarity of mind to handle the rest of this nightmare.

He arrived at the infirmary to find it just as much of a mess as the rest of the castle. Someone had blown a hole in the alabaster wall and set up a gangplank to a nearby skyship, to which they were evidently moving the injured civilians. Reora Lunstrum seemed to be in charge, imperiously barking orders while Estevan and Sullivan frantically moved stretchers back and forth. Tanis was there too, helping where he could, though he looked a breath away from winding up on a stretcher himself. But he was alive. Wonderfully alive.

"Thank Nahiira."

"Dorian?" Tanis looked up in surprise. "What are you doing here?"

"Looking for you," Dorian said. "But it seems you had things well in hand."

Tanis twitched his wing. "'Well in hand' is relative." Then, he turned towards the ship, and said, "Oy, Xander, get down here?"

Xander? Dorian jerked his gaze towards the ship, where, sure enough, Xander Kane came barreling across the gangplank to wrap Dorian into a tight bear hug. Despite everything, despite all the death and chaos and confusion and uncertainty, Dorian's heart lifted at the sight of his mentor. A moment later, Bradford joined in, and Dorian, unused to so many people hugging him at once, was momentarily terrified he'd fall out the makeshift window.

"Sorry," Bradford said once they were on solid infirmary floor. "Just, when we got here and saw the state of things, and didn't immediately find you, I was afraid I was too late." He stepped back to examine Dorian as if to make sure he was really still there. "You look good," he observed. "Put on more muscle since I left, I see. Really unfair that you keep doing that."

"Ah, we're in a battle," Dorian said delicately, though he couldn't help smiling just a little. "Is now really the time?"

"No, no, of course not." Bradford awkwardly dusted his hands and got back to work helping the injured. He looked like he'd gotten stronger in their absence as well, though the young lord had always been athletic. He had callouses on his hands, now, and a bronze cast to his pale skin that must have come from spending time outdoors.

They were joined a minute later by a severe-looking Iriya woman with spiral ram's horns and hair tied back in a tight braid. "Ah, so you're Xander's other nephew, are you?"

Xander's eyes widened. "*Faris...*"

Dorian felt like the wind had been knocked out of him. "That's right," he said, as much to himself as to the Iriya woman. "Xander is my uncle."

Xander's brow furrowed with worry and guilt. "So you've found out, have you?"

Apparently I'm the last one on Cyrna to know, but yes.

"Why didn't you tell me?" Dorian's voice cracked embarrassingly. "All those moons on the *Phoenix...*" He shook his head frantically, brushing away the thoughts of hurt and betrayal like irritating gnats. "Never mind. There's no time. The enemy took Sylvia. And Solaris is... missing."

I will not say she's dead. Not without knowing for sure.

Bradford staggered backwards. "Mother— they took our mother? Then we have to go after her!" He put his hand on his side sword and puffed out his chest. "I will borrow an ornithopter and face down my father myself."

Xander sighed. "No one doubts your courage or your sword arm, Brad, but you spent the entire voyage here vomiting into the underclouds. You will most certainly *not* fly an ornithopter through the heat of battle. I suppose I'd better—"

"I'll do it." Once the words were out, Dorian knew it was the right thing to do. Now that he knew Tanis was safe, or as safe as he was likely to get, he needed to be in the sky. "I... can't fly Solaris." More of that heart-in-the-juice-press feeling. "But I can fly an ornithopter. I'll find my mother." *And hopefully get an explanation from her while I'm at it.*

Xander nodded and put his hand on Dorian's shoulder. "If anyone can do it, you can."

"I'll go with you," Tanis said at once. Everyone turned to look at him — Bradford and Xander, confused, Faris, skeptical, and Reora, outraged.

"You most certainly will not." Tanis's mother crossed her arms.

"I know how to fly one of those ornithopters." Tanis probably meant to sound tough and defiant, but his voice came out higher than normal, and Dorian thought he was probably scared, too. "Dorian taught me. I'm even pretty good at it. Please... I can help."

Dorian opened his mouth to tell Tanis not to be ridiculous, until he saw the look on Tanis's face. He seemed determined, yes, but there was also a familiar glint in his brown eyes, half-shrewd, half-excited. *You have a plan, don't you?* But was it a plan to help the Order, or to help the Kasani?

To the Void with it. Tanis was his responsibility. That meant keeping an eye on him, whatever he intended.

"Fine," Dorian said. "Let's go to the hangar."

"But—" Reora protested.

Dorian met her gaze levelly. "I'll do my best to keep your son safe."

He just hoped it was enough. He hoped he wasn't about to get the boy killed. He hoped he hadn't just put everyone in even greater danger.

Reora Lunstrum watched with pursed lips as her son departed with the Aerishman.

Curse it all to the depths! She'd finally been reunited with both her children, and now it was all literally coming down around her head. She looked at the opening in the wall, and shuddered, thinking how close they'd all come to death. How close they still might come.

She did not like or trust this red-haired Aerishman who seemed to have both her children so enthralled. But if he kept her boy safe, she supposed she'd never say another word against him. She supposed.

"That's the last of the injured," the elderly Healer said, crossing the makeshift gangplank. "If you don't mind, Madam Lunstrum, I think you should get on the ship now. It's time to evacuate."

Reora straightened and put on her most haughty expression. "Not without my children."

"I'm sorry, Madam Lunstrum," Estevan said. "But without reinforcements, I fear they'll kill us all. It's not safe to remain much longer."

Without reinforcements. A wild idea began to take shape in Reora's head. "And what if we *had* reinforcements?"

"Not sure where we'll get those at this late hour," Estevan said dismissively.

"Please. Healer Estevan. Can I use the castle's signal beacon one last time?"

"Out of the question!" Estevan huffed.

But the dragonaut, Sullivan, seemed to realize what she planned. "I'll escort her, Healer."

"Very well."

Sullivan and Reora sprinted full tilt down the hallway towards the signal tower.

Please, she thought, *If the Savior is real, let Dax and Temperance have succeeded in taking over the signal beacon!*

Dorian clung white-knuckled to the ornithopter's controls as he and Tanis darted and wove their way through the turbulent sky. He'd taken the best and fastest ornithopter the Order had available for his mission to rescue the Dragonmar, but it still paled in comparison to flying with Solaris.

Despite everything, however, there was a small part of him that delighted in simply being airborne again. Beside him in formation on the other ornithopter, Tanis clearly felt the same way.

"This is incredible!" Tanis's voice came distorted out of the beacon crystal embedded on the ornithopter's central stem. "I mean, we're probably going to die. But still! What a way to go! Incredible."

Dorian's mouth twisted into an involuntary smile. "Glad you're having fun."

Despite his injuries and Malachite's erratic behavior, Tanis proved more than competent with the ornithopter. Dorian thought perhaps he and Tanis were cut from the same cloth in that way. Happier in the sky than on the ground. He just hoped it would be enough to keep them both alive.

A swarm of enemy soldiers engaged, and Dorian drew his drago-naut sword and frantically flung spellfire in their direction. The enemy ornithopters caught ablaze and went careening down towards the clouds below.

Dorian screwed his eyes shut and suppressed the feelings of guilt wriggling about like worms in his stomach. *So much death.* Those soldiers may have been his enemies, but they were still people. They most likely had friends and family who loved them. But those soldiers *had* attacked first, and Dorian's *own* friends and family were in danger.

Family. Ancients help me. It's my mother *we're going after.* Somehow, that fact still didn't quite feel real to him.

A gryphon rider bore down on Tanis, but Tanis swiftly unseated him with a swipe of his sidearm. The gryphon, bereft of his rider, lunged for Tanis, and Tanis deftly spun out of the way.

"Nice one, Tanis!" Dorian shouted, but he triumph was short lived because Tanis now stared in pale-faced shock at the castle receding behind them.

"Tanis?" Dorian pulled up beside the young Orith and looked in the direction he pointed.

Two figures fell down from Cloudfire's highest watchtower. Even from this great distance, he'd recognize Tai's silhouette anywhere.

"*Tai!*"

He swerved the ornithopter back towards the castle. Could he catch her? Perhaps, if he flew at full tilt. But if he did that, he might lose his only chance to reach the flagship. *Void curse it all!* He thought back to the Trials, and the way his heart had done somersaults as he watched her fall from her malfunctioning ornithopter. But she hadn't been in any actual danger, then. *Maybe...*

"She... Orith can take a fall, right? She might survive?" Dorian's voice came out ragged and plaintive, like a small, scared child. Because that was what he felt like, in many ways.

"I don't know." Tanis sounded even more terrified than Dorian felt, and why shouldn't he? That was his sister falling towards her possible doom. "Maybe, but... That's quite a tower. There are falls, and there are *falls*."

Dorian closed his eyes and clenched the ornithopter controls so tightly it would surely leave marks in his palm. "We continue towards the flagship," he said, voice hollow. "Tai wouldn't want us to abandon the mission."

He expected Tanis to argue, maybe even *wanted* Tanis to argue, but the boy only nodded grimly and followed at Dorian's side.

It took everything Dorian had to hold back his tears. But there was no time for tears. Even sick with worry as he was, he had a job to do. So he drew his dragonaut sword and, using it as an athame, hastily erected a barrier spell around himself and Tanis.

The dragon-scale texture on his sword's hilt grounded him with a sense of familiarity. *Still a dragonaut sword, even after the bond was broken.* It would be just his luck if, at the crucial moment, it reverted to the chipped and rusted thing he'd found in the old Phoenix's arms chest.

I'll just add "Get a backup sword" to my to-do list, assuming we don't all die today.

With the most basic of protections in place, Dorian brought his ornithopter to a landing on the flagship's main deck. He dismounted and held his sword at the ready, skin prickling at the sensation of a hundred Kasani arrows trained in his direction. Dorian swallowed his terror and tried to put on a brave expression. His barrier spell now seemed laughably inadequate.

"Stand down," Janus Callahan's cold, familiar voice commanded from the helm of the ship. "This is no way to treat our guests, is it?"

Slowly, the surrounding Kasani soldiers lowered their weapons. But Dorian swore he could still feel the hostility emanating off of them in waves. Heart pounding, Dorian put on his most stoic expression, and turned to face his stepfather.

Callahan stood in front of three cylindrical tanks full of blue liquid, identical to the ones he'd seen in Thlarknia. Were there captive dragons inside, ready to be drained of power? And what, he wondered with a spike of fear, did Janus Callahan possibly intend to drain them *for*?

Callahan himself looked much the same as Dorian remembered. His clothes were perhaps finer now, and his hairline had receded a bit further back on his forehead, but he was still the same cool and imposing man who always used to make Dorian cower. It took all his willpower not to start cowering now.

He stepped forward to confront his enemy and was confronted instead by a wordless cry. Only now did he notice Sylvia, bound and gagged and tied to one of the dragon tanks, her blue eyes awash with pain and fear.

"Mother!" Dorian rushed towards her.

Sylvia thrashed against her bonds and shouted something unintelligible.

"There's no need for all this hostility." Callahan's voice was so hauntingly familiar, it was almost like being back in Frostvale. "A nice little family reunion is overdue, don't you think?"

"Hello, Stepfather." Dorian gripped the sword hilt as if it was the only real thing left in the world.

"My, my, look at you." Janus's pale blue eyes were shrewd as he looked Dorian up and down. "You almost look a proper dragonaut. Though, of course, it seems you have no dragon."

Dorian's heart thudded in his chest. How in the Void was he supposed to respond to that?

"His Imperial Majesty wasn't sure you'd come." Another familiar voice. "But I knew you'd swoop in to the rescue like the fool you are."

"Graigor." Dorian's long-time rival leaned casually against a stack of crates, spinning his emerald dragonstone's chain around his finger. "I ought to have guessed you were the traitor."

"I'm not, actually." Graigor tossed his dragonstone in the air and caught it. "Well. I suppose I am now. But that's a rather new development. I like to be on the winning side, you see. And the Order... well, I don't think the Order is going to win this one."

Dorian sneered and turned away. Graigor was a bastard, but he was also far from Dorian's highest priority right now. "Let my mother go," Dorian demanded of Emperor Callahan with far more confidence than he actually felt.

"So she finally told you who she is," Callahan said. "I'm honestly surprised. Didn't think that woman had an honest bone in her body."

Dorian winced. *No, no she didn't.* Sylvia lowered her head too, in obvious guilt.

Janus burst out laughing. It was a strange and eerie sound. "Ah, I see, so you found out some other way! Typical. So deliciously typical!"

Dorian glared at his stepfather. "You lied to me too, you know." Though why he bothered to say anything, he wasn't sure. He expected, *what*, for Janus to feel bad about it? Lying to Dorian was so far down the list of Janus Callahan's crimes that it was almost laughable.

To his surprise, though, Callahan did look remorseful, at least a little. "I did, that. I suppose I did. But! You are all here now. Just in time to see me make history."

Callahan spread his arms towards the three dragon tanks near the skyship's prow. In the tank on the far left, Dorian saw a black dragon who could have only been Solaris's former mentor Nocturne. He looked thin and sickly, but still solid, still trapped in his unwanted bond with Callahan. But it was the sight of the ghostly red dragon on the right that nearly made Dorian's heart stop.

"Solaris!" He rushed forward and pounded on the glass, desperate to free his companion by any means necessary. If she noticed him there, she gave no indication. Solaris floated suspended and immobile in the glowing blue liquid.

"Now, now, we can't have that." Graigor Beckett grabbed Dorian's arm and roughly pulled him away. Dorian yanked his arm free and reached for his sword. He was more than happy to fight Graigor Bloody Beckett, and after two years' hard training, he thought he might finally stand a chance at winning, too.

Callahan, however, raised his hand to forestall them. "I advise against doing anything foolish," he said. "You wouldn't want to hurt the dragon."

Dorian stepped back as if aether-stung. *No. Of course he didn't.*

"If possible," Callahan continued, "I will not hurt her either. She is simply there as backup. And, since you are here, to ensure *good behavior.*"

Dorian snarled, but there was little else he could do. His stepfather was, unfortunately, correct. Dorian would probably do almost anything Janus asked, if it kept Solaris safe.

"The real prize, anyway, is what's in the middle one," the traitorous Graigor Beckett said, sounding far too pleased with himself. He pointed at the third remaining cylinder and smirked. "Look familiar?"

Dorian turned towards the tank, wondering with mounting horror which dragon he might find there. Cloud? Starfire? Meridian or Northstar?

But it wasn't a dragon at all. At least, he didn't think it was. Graigor was right about one thing, though. It was *definitely* familiar. A spiral figure of living smoke, curling in on itself, seeming somehow both alive and dead. It radiated *wrongness* down to Dorian's very soul. But he still had no idea what it was. Not a dragon. Those creatures in the tanks in Thlarknia hadn't been dragons, either. He was sure of that now. Above the tank, a brightly glowing aether stone fed spirit energy into the tank in a slow trickle.

Tanis stood stock still, staring at the sinister thing with rapt fascination.

"You recognize it?" Dorian asked.

Tanis shook out his black feathered wings. "Stormwind. I don't know how I can tell, but I think that crystal contains Stormwind's life essence."

"Stormwind?" Dorian asked.

"That dragon my sister and the others rescued... he spoke to me... I didn't know what those smoke things were, back in Thlarknia, when I had to guard the things. Depths take me, there were so *many* of them... If I'd known, I'd..."

Tanis was babbling, clearly terrified. But Dorian thought he got the gist of it. "You know what it is, now, though."

The apple at Tanis's throat bobbed as he swallowed and then nodded. When he spoke, the words came out in a cracked whisper. "*Voidwraith.*"

CHAPTER FORTY

DEMON, DRAGON, AND VOIDWRAITH

In all his two hundred years of life, Celestian had never made a mistake graver than returning to Kadmin Crowley.

Arrogant though he knew it was, Celestian always fancied himself some kind of hero in a tale. Was it ideal, to be captured and forced into a bond against his will? No, of course it was not. But it was the beginning of an adventure. And so Celestian had convinced himself that this was all for the greater good, that he and his captor may yet play some pivotal role in saving the world.

But there was nothing great or good about what was happening now.

Tai Lunstrum had captured him too, of course. When she held the dragonstone, he had no choice but to follow her. But she had never *intentionally* tried to control him. She had spent the entire time they were in that Orith village trying to set him free. When he was honest with himself, that too-brief time in Lost Hollow with the Lunstrum girl had been the happiest of Celestian's long life.

So of course he had to ruin it.

He should have accompanied Tai to Cloudfire to secure his freedom once and for all. Then, he might have had a chance to stop what was happening. Instead, he'd tried to warn the others about Callahan's sinister plans. But they knew already. Of course they did. Celestian had not even made it halfway to Kasanarae before his former rider intercepted him, along with the rest of the invasion force. Caught off guard, he put up only the scantest excuse for a fight before he was under his master's thrall once more.

Pathetic.

This horrible attack on Cloudfire Castle was worse than Celestian had ever dared imagine. Celestian would never forgive Kadmin for what was happening here. He did not think he could ever forgive himself.

Kadmin wheeled him down to the castle's tallest parapet and drew his sword. Not his dragonaut sword — Celestian had revoked that straight away. It was one of the few freedoms still left to him.

Kadmin brandished his plain, non-magical sword, and shoved Celestian roughly as he dismounted and stalked angrily towards the lone figure standing on the parapet. Celestian's entire being surged with hope and terror alike when he saw that it was Tai.

He called out for her, but with an angry jerk of his dragonstone, Kadmin silenced Celestian's mindvoice. Celestian burned with hatred for Kadmin, but no matter how hard he tried, he was powerless to break through the compulsion.

"Foolish, Tai, leaving yourself exposed like that."

Not Tai... I cannot let him hurt Tai. But Celestian's hated rider clutched the dragonstone like his life depended on it.

«*You will not interfere.*» Kadmin's mindvoice came out like a snarl, but the words had the force of the gods. Try as he might, Celestian could not move from where he floated immobile in the cold evening air.

Celestian was forced to watch helplessly as Kadmin and Tai circled each other with their swords drawn. Tai was a good fighter, he knew she was. But Kadmin was better. Kadmin was one of the best on Cyrna. It was why Celestian had once put his faith in him. If the long-ago dragonauts of the Ancient times had not confused competence for moral fortitude, perhaps they might have lived, and Orith and Iriya would have never sank below the clouds. But now, centuries later, Celestian had made that same mistake, and he was all the more a fool for it. No wonder Nocturne never saw him as Chronicler material.

Kadmin skillfully maneuvered Tai to the edge of the parapet, and Celestian knew that this was surely the end, that he would be made to witness his rider heartlessly butchering a mortal for whom he had come to care a great deal. But then Tai did something he did not expect. She teetered backwards off the ledge, plummeting downward and taking Kadmin with her.

"Celestian!" Kadmin cried out in frantic horror. "Celestian, you must catch me!" But even as he flailed windmilled his arms, Kadmin could not grasp his dragonstone, and could not complete the Compulsion.

The previous Compulsion held.

«I am sorry, Kadmin,» Celestian said with just the tiniest hint of grim satisfaction. «I have been ordered not to interfere.»

Celestian felt the force of Kadmin hitting the ground like a battering ram to the chest. With the force of a taut rope snapping, Celestian's bond broke, and with it, the Compulsion holding him in place. At last freed, Celestian fluttered down in his ghostly form to the two broken bodies at the base of the tower.

Kadmin Crowley was undeniably dead, neck broken, eyes staring lifeless and glassy at the overcast sky. Celestian was uncertain what he felt about that. He was relieved to be free of the man, and thought perhaps on the whole that Kadmin got what he deserved. But Celestian felt a certain sadness nonetheless. Regret, perhaps, and grief for the man Kadmin could have been, rather than the man he was.

The other one, though. Tai Lunstrum. Towards her, his feelings were clear, and agonizingly painful. It rent him apart to see her there, battered and broken, eyes closed, limbs splayed out at unnatural angles. If he could have shed tears in his ghostly form, he would have done so.

«I am sorry, Tai. Sorry I could not save you. Sorry I returned to Kadmin in the first place. Sorry that any of this happened.» If Celestian had not been so foolish as to return to Kadmin, perhaps the remarkable mortal before him might still be alive.

Except...

Was she still alive?

Celestian looked on with mounting excitement as he watched her chest move slowly up and down. *Orith can take a fall.* She was unconscious and badly injured, with multiple broken bones, but she was, for the moment, alive.

How much longer could she remain that way? Celestian did not know the full extent of her injuries. Even Orith were so terribly fragile. She might wake to find she could no longer walk, could no longer even move. She might never wake up at all.

If she were a dragonaut, he was confident she would make a full recovery. The dragon bond made it possible to heal from injuries swiftly and thoroughly. That was part of why they lived longer on average than their unbonded counterparts. But Tai was not a dragonaut. *Unless...*

Celestian could scarcely believe his good luck. The unconscious girl still clung tightly to a dragonstone, which gently pulsed with the silver-white light of the Summoning. It beckoned to Celestian as it did to all dragonkind.

«I accept,» Celestian declared for all to hear. «I, Celestian of the First Star at Dusk, accept the human Tai Alyste Lunstrum as my bonded rider!»

Voidwraith. Dorian's heart thudded, hoping, praying that he'd heard it wrong, or that Tanis was mistaken. But Tanis didn't look mistaken.

The boy's brown eyes were wide with terror, but his jaw was set in an expression of grim resignation.

"That's... bad," Dorian said. He cleared his throat, and, heart pounding, turned to face his stepfather. "What in the *actual Void* is wrong with you?"

I have to stop him. Oh, gods, even if I die too, I have to stop him.

Dorian drew his blade and stepped forward, gripping the hilt with all his might, praying to all seven gods that Callahan wouldn't notice how badly he was shaking.

He expected Callahan to display anger or contempt or maybe, in his most far-off hopes, fear. He did not expect the way his stepfather looked at him now, however, with something like... *fondness*. It was such a strange expression that Dorian momentarily stalled, taken aback.

"It really is remarkable, Callahan said, "How far you've come in two years."

Off to the side, Dorian's brain vaguely registered Graigor rolling his eyes, but it was hard to care. It was hard to care about much of anything, as the world seemed to narrow into a tiny pin-prick tunnel with Janus Callahan on the other side of it.

"I know I was hard on you as a boy," Callahan continued, with a tone that truly, genuinely sounded like remorse. "But look at you now. So brave and so strong. A true warrior worthy of the Order. Worthy to be a dragonaut."

Dorian could barely hear over the ringing in his ears. Callahan was mocking him, surely. Except... Dorian knew Callahan's mockery. Was used to Callahan's mockery. This did not sound like mockery. Did his stepfather truly at last approve of him, now, after all this time?

"You should have been my son," Callahan said, and his voice was well and truly pained, now. "Gods and Ancients curse me, you should have been!"

Dorian stood frozen in place, his sword arm lowering almost of its own accord. *Strike, you need to strike, curse you. It doesn't matter if he's being weirdly nice. He's going to summon a Voidwraith, for the Ancients' sakes.* But Dorian's traitor body wouldn't move.

This man had killed his father, and made the latter half of Dorian's childhood miserable. And yet, he had also taken Dorian in when he had nowhere else to go, had raised him, even cared for him in his way, despite his own feelings of hurt and betrayal. Dorian's soul felt ragged from all of the hostile strangers he'd been forced to kill in the past two years. What in Meroneth's frozen Void would killing his own stepfather do to him?

"You don't have to do this," Dorian pleaded. "There has to be a better way."

"That's where you're wrong." And with a snap like a spell dissipating, all traces of warmth and fatherly compassion were gone from Callahan's bearing. He gazed down at Dorian with cold fury, once again the hard and uncaring stepfather Dorian remembered. "Seize him."

No fewer than a half dozen armored soldiers surrounded Dorian, grabbing hold of his arms and dragging him backwards while Callahan brandished the moon glass with one hand and his athame with the other and began carving out a spell.

Dorian thrashed and flailed, but it did no good. There was no way he could fight off all of them. Someone roughly twisted his sword arm and his dragonaut sword clattered uselessly to the deck. In the ensuing chaos, it slid out of sight. *Curse it all!* Like a Void-cursed fool, he'd been taken in by his childish yearning for acceptance. And now he'd lost his only chance to stop this abomination.

Dorian could do naught but watch in horror as Janus finished his casting. The spell lit up blinding electric blue. Both the crystal containing Stormwind's essence and the last of Nocturne's life force drained away. Silver-white light traveled out of the tank that imprisoned him and into the one containing the nascent Voidwraith. The only tiny consolation was that Solaris's tank, for now, remained untouched. But Ancients help him, how much longer could that last?

The blue light grew brighter and brighter, painfully bright, until

Callahan staggered backwards and dropped the moonglass, clutching his hand in pain. *That's right,* Dorian thought. *That's what happens when you try and use the moon glass on your own.* But it didn't matter. The spell had run its course.

The Voidwraith tank burst apart, and Dorian did his best, pinned as he was, to shield his eyes against the flying shards of glass and aether liquid. When it finally felt safe to do so, Dorian looked up, but he almost wished he hadn't. The monster of living smoke that rose out of the remains of the central tank was shaped like a twisted, broken dragon, but it was far, far larger than any dragon Dorian had ever seen. *Void,* it was bigger than the Kasani flagship. It might have been bigger than Cloudfire Castle itself.

Void-cursed Void Void Void!

The wraith let out an ear-splitting cry that sent his hair flying backwards as if from a gust of wind. Then, abruptly, the monster took off into the sky, not towards Cloudfire Castle like he expected, but straight upwards. The skyship shuddered in its wake, and Dorian felt a familiar vibration under his feet of an aether engine strained to its absolute limit.

"It's draining the ambient magic somehow," Dorian said. "But where is it going?"

"Aeris." Tanis swallowed, looking even more pale and sickly than he had that morning. "It's heading for the floating lands. It's not the kind of Voidwraith that wrecks cities. It's the kind that brings down *continents.*"

Dorian stared at the creature in horrified fascination. The closest floating landmass was the Northern Reaches. If that Voidwraith was as dangerous as Tanis said, it would take down Thlarknia and Pazarae and Narea all in one go. *Tonight.* Callahan intended to begin his grisly work of sinking Aeris *tonight.* And Dorian couldn't think of a single thing he could do about it.

Dorian's gawping was brought to a halt when the flagship listed dangerously to the side, sending all the soldiers and crewmembers scrambling. Dorian seized the momentary reprieve to break free of his captors, but his sword had disappeared in the fray. *Void curse it. Definitely should have had a backup sword.*

He looked around wildly, both for something to use as a weapon, and to see the cause of the disruption.

A veritable flotilla of gryphon-mounted soldiers dove into the fray, raining flaming arrows down on the Kasani soldiers. Dorian hastily ducked behind a stack of crates to get out of the way. The ship rocked again, this time unmistakably from dragonfire.

«Looks like we are just in time,» the aquamarine dragon, Tempest, said.

"Dax! Tempest! But—"

"It's the villagers from Lost Hollow!" Tanis said. "My mother must have gotten a message through."

Dorian had never met anyone from Lost Hollow other than Reora, so he didn't recognize anyone. But he saw now that every single one of the gryphon riders was Orith, and many of them had stunted wings like Tai, or wings that were obviously injured or amputated. They could fly fine on gryphon back, however, and dispatched the scrambling Kasani soldiers seemingly with ease.

"What in the Void is this?" Janus Callahan rushed into the fray, a crystalline magical barrier protecting him from the worst of the arrow strikes. "The people of that Orith backwater were supposed to be on *my* side."

Tanis flashed a grim smile. "Not all of them."

The ship rocked again, more violently. This time the attack couldn't have come from dragonfire. Only a powerful aether cannon could pack such a powerful punch. A mast rose out of the mist, followed by the rest of the vessel. Dorian caught a glimpse of the words *Phoenix Reborn* written on the side in gold paint.

"Xander!"

The dragons Meridian and Northstar, along with their respective riders, dove towards the Kasani flagship, knocking Kasani soldiers out of the way with their bladed whipcord tails.

"Hurry up and get on." Falgar extended his hand. "This ship is going down, and I don't want you on it when it does."

The ship teetered again, and Dorian felt off-kilter in more ways than one. "Solaris, and my Mother! We have to help them!"

"Your what now?" Falgar raised his eyebrows.

"The Dragonmar. I'll explain later." As if to punctuate his urgency, the ship rocked again.

"Of course. Let's hurry up and cut her free."

Dorian sprinted to where Sylvia was still tied to the now-empty Voidwraith tank, and used the edge of his athame to cut her free of her bonds.

"Dorian..." her eyes swam with a hundred unreadable emotions, but whatever she wanted to say to Dorian, there was simply no time.

"You're with me, Lady Dragonmar," Sullivan said, and he gently lifted her behind him onto Northstar's saddle.

Once he was sure his mother was safe, Dorian spun frantically towards the last remaining tank. He wasn't going anywhere without Solaris. To his horror, however, in all the chaos he'd failed to notice that it, too, was empty, drained of aether liquid, and no longer bathing the deck in their signature blue glow.

"Solaris." His voice came out a strangled gasp. She hadn't been drained of her power too, had she? He swore she hadn't been. Dorian's mind refused to even consider the possibility.

"The ship's on bloody *fire*, we've got to *go*." Falgar grabbed his arm.

Dorian nodded vaguely, still frantically scanning the deck for his dragon. He noted that the deck had, in fact, caught fire, but there was no sign of Solaris. Fighting back tears, he grabbed Tanis by the arm and scrambled onto Meridian's dragon saddle.

The white-gold dragon launched up into the sky, leaving the ruined skyship to fall to the clouds in their wake. Dorian still scanned the skies, desperate to find Solaris. And then, miracle of miracles, he saw her, a bright red spot against a turbulent gray sky.

"Solaris!" Except... something was wrong. She was solid again, even though he hadn't re-cast the Summons. And there was another human riding on her back. Dorian's heart plummeted to the under-clouds. He recognized that human, and knew Solaris would never let him ride her if she had any say in the matter.

Callahan.

At some point in all the chaos, Dorian's stepfather had forced Solaris into a bond to replace his own murdered dragon. Dorian wanted to be sick.

"We have to go after her," Dorian said, but Falgar shook his head.

"Look," Falgar said, and sure enough, an honor guard of Kasani ornithopters and gryphon knights flanked Callahan and Solaris, ensuring a single dragon and his riders couldn't get close.

"Solaris..." Dorian reached for his sword, realized he no longer had it, and lowered his hand, feeling helpless.

Graigor on Borealis flew up on next to them on Borealis, wearing a sullen expression. "They've taken the castle," he announced. "But they took heavy losses to do so. The Order fought harder than I thought they would." His tone was almost grudgingly respectful.

"You'll be going with them, I imagine? Or not so sure, now that your big strong buddies lost their flagship?" Falgar made a rude gesture with his hand.

Graigor looked uncertain for a moment, then his expression darkened, and he wheeled Borealis around and followed after Callahan and his forces.

Falgar sighed and ran his hand through his sandy hair. "All right, all right, I suppose I could have been nicer just then. Maybe I could have convinced him to join our side."

Dorian shook his head, feeling his mouth draw into a grim line. "With friends like him, we have no need for enemies." He swallowed and looked upwards, where the massive monster of smoke and ash still tore its violent way through the sky. "I want to know what we're going to do about *that*."

Falgar grimaced. "Not much we can do, is there? It's a bloody-cursed Voidwraith. Even the Ancient dragons used to fear those things."

"Dragons, maybe," Tanis said from his position on the saddle between Dorian and Falgar. His voice sounded weaker than normal, and he was drenched in clammy sweat. Void take it, Dorian should never have agreed to bring Tanis along into battle. He should have left Tanis on the *Phoenix Reborn* with the other civilians, however much he might have sulked and complained. At least he would have been safe.

Except, if that monster really could take down Aeris, then nowhere would be safe.

"Is there really no way we can stop it?" Dorian asked.

"I think..." Tanis swallowed. "I think there might be one way."

Dorian's heart momentarily lifted, then came crashing down again as he realized what Tanis probably intended. "No... no, you can't."

"I have to," Tanis said.

Before Dorian could stop him, Tanis collapsed in Dorian's arms, silver-white spirit energy pouring out of him in a gushing torrent. Malachite rose out of Tanis's barely-conscious body, a towering creature of verdant green swathed in sapphire flame. It should have been impossible for a demon to grow so rapidly. But few humans released their own life force in such a gushing torrent as Tanis did now.

"Tanis! No!" Trembling, Dorian drew his athame and tried to construct a spirit barrier, but he knew before he even started that it would do no good. This went well beyond an ordinary demonic fugue. Dorian wasn't even sure Estevan could stop it this time, and the Healer was nowhere nearby to try. It was like watching a second Voidwraith come to life.

"Void curse it all." Tears streamed down Dorian's face. "You fool, Tanis, that creature was born from two sacrificed dragons! You could give every ounce of your spirit energy to Malachite and it sill wouldn't be enough to stop it."

«It is what I was made for,» Malachite said. His fiery blue eyes met Dorian's. «I am not your Hematite. This is no senseless self-sacrifice. Should you both survive, I will find you again.»

It was a threat. It was a promise.

Malachite took off like an arrow through the turbulent sky, swiftly catching up with the rampaging Voidwraith. From his place on the back of Meridian's saddle, Dorian could do naught but watch as the demon darted back and forth, ripping and tearing at the monster of ash and smoke.

Brilliant iridescent light burst forth from Malachite and the wraith. Even as horrified as he was, Dorian had to admit it was a breathtaking sight.

Malachite was enormous, the largest demon Dorian had ever seen. But the gargantuan Voidwraith dwarfed even him. "Malachite can't win," Dorian said, feeling sick to his stomach. The wraith was going to kill Malachite, and then it was going to make its way to Aeris anyway, and then Tanis's sacrifice would have been for nothing.

"No," Falgar said. "Look."

Dorian looked where Falgar was pointing, and, miracle of miracles, it seemed like the wraith was falling apart at the seams.

"Saedra wanted to restore Aeris's demon population," Dorian recalled. "Because they can stop the Void." He'd thought she just intended to use them as imperfect power sources, the way Tanis and Reora had tried to do. But he now realized that this was what his former lover had meant.

The light from the wraith's body was almost blinding as its ashen form sloughed off and dissipated away. And then, with one last defiant cry, both demon and wraith collapsed into the billowing underclouds.

The chaos above the clouds, however, was far from over. Broken ships and ornithopters littered the skies around Cloudfire City, flames and heaps of splinters raining down on the city below. Dorian could only pray that the civilians made it to shelter in time.

The Order, or what was left of it, had no choice but to flee.

Like the Dragon's Fangs all over again, Dorian thought numbly as Meridian made her frantic way back towards the *Phoenix Reborn*. He was becoming so, so tired of running away.

They skidded to a rough landing on the deck of Xander's new ship. Sullivan rushed over and swept Falgar up into his arms, while Dorian gingerly lowered the immobile Tanis down to the deck with the other injured.

Ancients help him, there were a lot of injured. The Order Knight Toric lay unconscious on a pallet on the deck, next to Hildegard, who was awake but heavily bandaged. And there, on Hildegard's other side, was Tai.

Dorian rushed towards her, tears pricking the corners of his eyes. She was unconscious, but her chest moved slowly up and down. *Alive.* Thank all the gods and Ancients, she was alive. And clutched in her hand was the dragonstone Jameson had given her, not inert gray like when he'd seen it last, and not Cloud's pearly white, either, but a rich dark indigo blue. She'd bonded a dragon after all. One good thing to come out of all this misery.

Dorian wiped aside stray tears and examined Tai's younger brother. His chest did not move, or if it did, it was such a small and shallow movement that it was imperceptible against the thrum of the *Phoenix Reborn's* aether engine.

"Please don't be dead." Dorian's tears flowed freely now. First his father, and then Hematite, and now Tanis. Why did so many have to keep dying for him? But when he put his hand on the side of Tanis's neck, he thought he caught the faintest trace of a pulse.

Hope kindled anew inside Dorian as he softened his gaze and did a thorough scan of the boy's spirit energy. At first Dorian saw nothing but bleak emptiness where the boy's life force used to be. But there, in the center of his chest, right where his heart was, the faintest silver-white light pulsed.

Dorian started crying anew, but this time they were tears of joy and relief. For he saw now that the tiny ember didn't remain by mere coincidence. Tanis had protected it intentionally, surrounding it by a perfectly-woven spirit barrier, just like Dorian had taught him, all those moons ago.

CHAPTER FORTY-ONE
THE PHOENIX REBORN

T ai woke up to the familiar thrum of an aether engine and
the sensation of moving through the sky. For a moment,
she thought she was in her cabin on the *Phoenix*, but no,
that wasn't right. She blinked, gazing up from yet another unfamiliar
bunk at yet another unfamiliar ceiling.

She was getting awfully tired of doing that.

The room was small but well-appointed, not unlike the officers'
quarters on the *Winds of Fortune,* though seemingly in much better
repair. She was on a skyship, no doubt about it. But which skyship,
and why? How had she gotten here?

She racked her brain for the last thing she could remember. She'd
fought with Kadmin on the parapet, hadn't she? Hadn't she fallen off
the highest tower? Sure, she was Orith and meant to handle a fall,
but from a plummet like that she should have at least broken some
bones.

Tai did not know how long she'd been out. Someone had kindly
gone to the trouble of giving her at least a sponge bath, and dressing
her in a silk Orith dressing gown that, from the lavender smell of it,
might have been her mother's. She found the clothes she'd worn to

fight Kadmin folded on a nearby chair, though too dirty and torn to consider putting back on. She also found, to her great relief, Celestian's dragonstone.

Just like Lost Hollow all over again, she thought. *Can't go losing that again.* She slung the silver chain around her neck.

Then she blinked. *Why* did she have Celestian's dragonstone?

«That is not the dragonstone you stole from Kadmin,» Celestian's mindvoice rang clearly in her head. «That is the one given to you by the dead dragonaut Jameson Russell.»

Tai was so startled she almost dropped the dragonstone. Guilt and grief welled up in her as the memories came rushing back. *Jameson's dead.* She hadn't known the man well, but no one deserved to die like he had.

"Kadmin's dead too," she realized. "I killed him."

But then... why was Celestian here?

In her mind, the indigo dragon chuckled. «You cast the Summons. I answered.»

"You — but how?"

Briefly, Celestian relayed the events that transpired in the brief moments after she and Kadmin fell from the tower.

"So... this isn't a Kasani ship, then."

«It was,» Celestian said, «But now it belongs to your Captain Xander.»

Tai massaged her temples. "Right..."

«I know I do not deserve your forgiveness for allowing myself to be recaptured,» Celestian said, «But know that I am glad to find you safe.»

Tai blinked several times, feeling disoriented. "Forgiveness. Right. Right. Only... you bonded me? Of your own free will?"

«I did.»

Tai gave a weak laugh and flopped back against the pillow. Celestian was her bond in truth. She felt... relieved, but too exhausted for much more than that. It didn't seem real yet. "What about everyone else? Falgar and Sullivan, and... Dorian." Her breath caught in her throat as she remembered the kiss they shared.

«Dorian is right here,» Celestian said. A moment later, the wooden door slid open, revealing her dearest friend.

"*Tai.*" His blue eyes were awash with worry and relief. "Thank the gods you're awake."

«The human Dorian Valmont has scarcely left your side in three days.»

"*Dorian.*" She smiled and reached for his hand. "Are you all right?"

"I'm just glad that *you* are," he said, which, she noted, was not an answer. "You were in quite a state after the battle. Sullivan Healed you, but you were still unconscious for days. I was..." his voice caught. "I thought you'd never wake up."

Tai frowned and beheld her friend more closely. His wore a rumpled shirt and trousers, his ponytail askew, and there were prominent dark circles under his eyes. He seemed to have lost even more weight, too, giving his cheeks a slightly hollow appearance.

"How long has it been since you've eaten or slept?"

"Awhile," he admitted. There was a haunted expression in Dorian's blue eyes, pain he failed to hide with a forced smile.

"Dorian." She bit her lip. "What happened?"

Dorian sighed and slumped his broad shoulders. "Your brother, Tanis, he... he gave almost all of himself to stop that wraith. He almost died. He didn't, but... he still hasn't woken up."

"Oh, gods." Guiltily, Tai realized she'd scarcely thought about her brother at all. "Will... will he be okay?"

"Estevan thinks so," Dorian said, "But it's his second fugue in as many moons. It's... going to be a long recovery."

Tai sighed ruefully, thinking back to her earliest days in Lost Hollow. "I imagine he's going to hate convalescence as much as I did." But Dorian still looked morose, so Tai frowned and said, "There's something else, too, isn't there."

Dorian sighed and thumbed his dragonstone, which still hung

gray and lifeless around his neck. "Callahan... took Solaris. For himself. To be his own bond."

"Oh." Tai let out a puff of air like exhaust from an aether engine. "Oh, Dorian."

His eyes found the indigo-blue dragonstone around her neck. She awkwardly tucked it into her shirt, feeling embarrassed, as if she were bragging about a feast to a starving man.

"I'm glad you bonded Celestian," Dorian said. To his credit, her poor dear friend, he really did sound like he meant it. "I mean. It's great. No one deserves it more than you. I— why are you crying?"

"I'm not crying," Tai said. And yet, sure enough, she was.

Before she knew it, she was sobbing openly, and couldn't seem to stop. Soon, tears streamed down Dorian's face as well.

"Sorry..." she hiccupped. "Didn't... mean to make you cry too."

Wordlessly, Dorian took her in his arms, and they held each other and cried into each other's shoulders, as the magnitude of everything that happened washed over them like a Voidstorm.

When they finally broke apart, Dorian's tear-stained face was still somber, but his eyes no longer swam with that awful despair. He squeezed her hand and said, "For what it's worth, I'm really, really glad you bonded Celestian. You'll love being a dragonaut. Really, it's..." he cut off, looked down at the floor, scratched his neck, and tried again. "We should, ah, get you to the mess hall. You're probably starving. And, ah, so am I." He grimaced, and as if to punctuate that statement, his stomach audibly grumbled.

Tai chuckled. "Probably could go for some food. So long as it's not cheese again. That stuff makes me sick."

"Can fall off the highest parapet without dying, but can't eat cheese. That's quite a trade off." Dorian smiled ruefully and climbed deftly down from the bunk. Tai followed, feeling a bit stiff after being unconscious for so long, but she thought she felt pretty good, all things considered.

«Falling off of Cloudfire Castle is apparently less taxing on your

Orith body than Planeshifting,» Celestian observed. «You will need to keep that in mind for when we try it again.»

"Try again?"

«Planeshifting, that is. Not falling off buildings.»

After the disastrous consequences last time, Tai had thought the dragon would never want to Planeshift again. But in her mind's eye, Celestian shook his head. «We have to. Especially given... well, you will see. For the moment, by the gods, eat your breakfast. I feel as though I am about to waste away and I do not even eat human food.»

This new skyship, whatever it was, was evidently larger than the *Phoenix* or even the *Winds of Fortune*. While Tai was used to only a small dining area, this ship boasted a mess hall that took up the better part of the upper decks, with row after row of neat wooden tables and bench seating. Aether-lanterns glittered in red glass sconces, giving the place a cozier ambiance than what one might expect from such a large open area.

"Thank goodness, you're awake." Although Tai's mother couldn't fly on her own anymore, she still gave the impression of swooping down as she brandished a bowl of porridge in Tai's face. "You need to eat. Saving the world is hungry work."

"Not that again," Tai said, but she took the bowl gratefully anyway. The porridge was a bit bland, but not unpleasant, and Tai had a feeling bland was about the most she could handle at the moment. "How's Tanis?"

"As well as can be expected. He has not yet woken, but Healer Estevan says his spirit energy is increasing steadily." Reora turned her gaze sharply towards Dorian. "Estevan also tells me I have you to thank for that."

"Oh, well, I um..." Dorian flushed scarlet and scratched his neck.

"Woven like a fishing net," Roan agreed, joining them. "You taught him how to utilize his own strengths. I must say, I did not much approve of the last Aerishman Tai brought home, but you... you I like."

"*Roan.*" Tai groaned and covered her face with her hand. Then she blinked. "Wait a minute. Why are you here?"

"Dax and his dragon came for me," Roan said. "Hardly seemed right that my entire family should fly off without me." His face suddenly became stern. "Speaking of, young hellion, I thought you said you wouldn't go so long again without writing."

Tai squirmed in discomfort. She *had* said that, hadn't she?

"Oh, leave her be." Reora affectionately squeezed his shoulder. "It's not like she could've sent a missive from the Kasani fountain palace. And once she got to Lost Hollow, there was no way she could send a message to Everwood." She grimaced. "Believe me, I tried." More quietly, she added, "I still can't believe you forgive me for that."

"I'm just glad to have you back again," Roan said, and he kissed Reora on the mouth.

"Ugh, I did not need to see that," Tai said. But she supposed things could be worse. Her parents could be in the same position as Dorian's mother and stepfather.

"A great number of people wish to speak with you," Reora said. "Your captain Xander, of course, and the refugees from Lost Hollow. And the other dragonauts, I suppose." Tai couldn't suppress a tiny jolt of thrill at the phrase *other* dragonauts. "But you'll need to eat first. And for the Savior's sake — for your sake, I suppose — try to put on something decent. If you're going to be the heroine of prophecy, you must at least try to look the part."

Tai coughed and sputtered, hurriedly covering her mouth with a cloth napkin. "For the last time. I am *not* a hero from prophecy."

"The people are afraid," Reora said. "They need you to be their beacon of hope."

"Will Callahan go back on his word to leave Orith alone?"

"It's not about Callahan," Reora said. "It's about averting disaster." Tai's confusion must have shown on her face, because Reora swore under her breath and said, "You don't know, do you?"

"Pretend she's been unconscious for three days," Dorian interjected.

Reora swallowed, her iron-clad composure cracking. "Tanis did a very brave thing in stopping the wraith. But even just by existing for as long as it did, it destabilized the ambient magic. Badly. He may have prevented the Northern Reaches from falling then and there, but unless something is done, all the lands of Aeris will crash catastrophically before next year is out."

"Callahan's surely got to be growing more of those Voidwraiths too," Dorian said gravely. "He destroyed the ones we saw in Thlark-nia, but who knows how many others he has?"

Tai pushed her bowl aside, no longer feeling quite so hungry.

"The people want to hear from you," Reora said. "As Savior, they believe you might have the power to fix it."

"No pressure." She gave a high-pitched squeak of a laugh. Tai knew she wasn't the Savior, not really. But that didn't stop the world from needing saving. *Somebody has to do it.*

About an hour later, dressed in her fine silver-gray festival robes with the ornately embroidered moon sash, Tai stepped up on deck into the glaring winter sunlight.

Gods, that was an enormous crowd. How large was this ship, anyway? She scanned the crowd for faces she recognized. She saw Vale and Toric from the Order. Bradford and Captain Xander stood next to a family of Iriya. A girl of about five squirmed on her father's shoulders, while an older boy, perhaps eight years old, looked on with solemn curiosity.

There, too, on the deck were those residents of Lost Hollow who'd sided with Reora instead of Gideon, who'd come when her mother made that last call for help. No sign of Jace, she noted, with mingled feelings of disappointment and relief. But Temperance was there, reunited at last with her son Dax. Reora and Roan stood near them, also reunited. Then Tai's gaze found Dorian and Falgar and Sullivan and Hildegard, the ragged remains of her chosen Aerish family, and she realized they were her people, too. And they were all in danger together.

And somehow, *somehow*, these people had it in their heads that she was going to fix it all. She wanted to laugh at how ridiculous it was. The world was ending, and she, a scrawny flightless runaway who couldn't even steal a dragonstone, was supposed to put things right? How in the *Void* was she going to do that?

Except... she *knew* how. She'd known for a long time, hadn't she? What else had all this been for?

"I think we can save the magic," she said, projecting her voice with confidence she didn't feel. *Fake it until you make it.* That's what she'd done in Kasanarae, and it was what she had to do here. "No. Scratch that. I *know* how to save the magic. And if we do this right, we can even bring Orith back to the sky."

Speaking the words out loud, she allowed herself for the first time to consider what restoring Orith might even mean. Was it truly what the people wanted? Their lives would undergo a complete upheaval. But things would change for the worse anyway if she *didn't* act.

"We have a year before disaster strikes," Tai said. "And there's a lot of work to be done between then and now. But we will do what needs to be done. All of us, together, we're going to save the magic. We're going to save Orith and Aeris, and probably Iriya. The demons and the dragons and the gryphons and the squirrels, we'll save them too. We're going to save the world."

Dorian clapped and cheered with the rest as Tai finished her speech. *Gods and Ancients*, but she was magnificent. He himself suddenly felt dirty and grubby and wholly unworthy. She was the Savior of Orith, and who was he? Nobody, that was who.

Stop it. Tempting as it was, now was not the time to feel sorry for himself. They had a year to save the world, and surely, *surely* there must be some way he could make himself useful. He might not be a dragonaut anymore, but he could still fly as an aeronaut. He could use a sword. Perhaps when Tanis woke up, there would be more he could learn from Dorian. If nothing else, Dorian could bake thrice-cursed pies for the cause. As Reora Lunstrum said, world saving was hungry work.

Anything was better than doing nothing. Anything was better than staying still. Anything, *anything* was better than sitting back and allowing himself to think, to process all that had happened these past few days.

"Always move forward," he whispered to himself. "That's what you taught me, Solaris."

But of course, Solaris did not answer.

No one did.

Dorian tried to repress the sting of jealousy as Tai joined the other dragonauts for a private meeting. His important friends, doing important work. Without him. Perhaps there was a practice dummy in need of a good mauling. Perhaps there was more pie that needed baking. Perhaps he could drown himself in a head-sized mug of strong Toreenish greenwine. *Perhaps.*

Still undecided, he moved towards the railing, where he found Sylvia gazing morosely out over the billowing underclouds. It was nearly dusk, and the clouds were lit up in shades of warm pink and yellow.

"Aren't you going to the meeting?" he asked. "You're the Dragon-mar, after all."

Sylvia jumped as if aether-stung, and then flushed and turned away, obvious guilt and shame reflected in her wide blue eyes. She had been like this, ever since their harrowing escape from Callahan's flagship.

"I think you and I can both agree that I have no skills at leadership." Her voice came out rough and strained, as if she had recently been crying.

Dorian drummed the polished oak railing, feeling as distraught as she looked. "Ancients, Mother. What did Callahan do to you?"

Sylvia almost smiled, but it didn't reach her miserable blue eyes. "Callahan? Nothing." She let out a long breath. "No, I fear that, as ever, all my problems are my own doing."

"I'm a bit of an expert on causing my own problems, so if you ever need any advice..." Dorian forced a smile, trying to lighten the mood, but Sylvia did not return it.

If anything, she looked even more miserable than before. "You are not to blame for any of this," she said, "And I never, ever wish for you to believe that you are."

Dorian blamed himself for a great deal of things, not the least of which were Solaris's disappearance, Tanis's sickness, and the summoning of the Voidwraith. But no good would come out of pointing that out. He just wished he knew what he could say to Sylvia instead.

He wasn't sure what he thought, or how he felt. He wasn't even sure if he was angry with his mother or not. He wished she'd told him the truth sooner, of course, but to be angry at Sylvia Kane for lying was like being angry at the wind for blowing.

No. If Dorian was upset with anyone, it was his uncle, Captain Xander. Xander, who took Dorian in when no one else would, who protected him, who taught him the sword. Why, during all those moons together on the Phoenix, had he never found it necessary to mention that he was Dorian's uncle? That Dorian's mother was *still alive*? Xander hated lying and politicking, he always said so, that was why he'd left the Order behind to begin with. That he'd lied to Dorian about something so important hurt far more than anything Lady Sylvia had or hadn't done.

But Xander was not there with them at the moment. He'd been too busy running the ship to give any of them the time of day lately. Bradford, too, had been avoiding Dorian. Perhaps he was ashamed of keeping secrets, but for some reason, Dorian couldn't find it in himself to be too mad at his brother. Like Sylvia, Bradford was a born politician. Xander, though...

Dorian ran a frustrated hand through his hair. He'd always

wanted a proper family, Void curse it. So why, now that he had one, couldn't he figure out how to talk to them?

Perhaps, he thought, this was how Sylvia had felt, all those countless times she'd tried and failed to tell him the truth. And at that thought, his hurt and anger cracked apart, just a little.

"Oy." Falgar's voice cut through the mother and son's pensive brooding. "Aren't you coming to the meeting?"

"She says she doesn't want to," Dorian said with a shrug.

"Not her. You." Falgar hooked his thumb in Dorian's direction. "Get your arse over there or we'll both be late."

Dorian shook his head. "It's a meeting for dragonauts. I'm not a dragonaut."

"That," Falgar said, "Is the stupidest thing I have ever heard in my life."

The rest of dragonauts joined them on the deck. "You have as much a right to claim the title as the rest of us," Hildegard said.

"More than many," Sullivan agreed.

"So get your attractive bottom back over here," Tai concluded.

Face burning, he said, "If you all could stop discussing my posterior in front of my mother, that'd be great."

He cast a glance at Sylvia, who looked momentarily amused, but hid it quickly. "Go," she said. "The others are right. You and Solaris have suffered a... setback, but you're as much a dragonaut as they are."

Dorian shrugged. It wasn't worth arguing, and anyway, attending the meeting was probably a better use of his time than standing around sulking.

The dragonauts climbed belowdecks and took seats around the oblong table in the war room. Ancients help him, the *Phoenix Reborn* had an actual *war room*. This certainly wasn't like any other ship he'd been on before.

Despite everything, Dorian was glad to be in the sky again. He knew he'd missed the original *Phoenix*, all those moons cooped up in

Cloudfire Castle. Up here, with the deck under his feet, and the Linking just a heartbeat away, was where he belonged.

"Right then." Hildegard dusted her hands off and poured everyone some Kasani wine out of a bottle she'd found in the galley stores. "With Jameson... gone, I am the senior-most dragonaut. So that makes me, regrettably, Flight Leader. Sylvia most likely intends to resign as dragonmar, and we don't have a replacement lined up, so I suppose I'm in charge for now." She sounded less than thrilled at the prospect.

"Surely Tai should be Dragonmar, as she is Savior of Orith," Dax said.

Tai scowled. "I wish people would stop spreading that around."

"A useful myth," Hildegard said, "Has its own way of becoming truth."

"What about Xander?" Tai asked. "He's captain of the ship, and he's got a history with the Order. He should probably be in charge."

Hildegard ran a frustrated hand through her hair. "Curse Jameson to the Void for dying on me! This leadership nonsense is like herding gryphlets. Believe me, I intend to defer to Tai or Xander or whoever else as soon as possible. But for the moment, let's stay on topic? The question is, how do we stop Aeris from crashing." She unrolled a large scroll of blank parchment and laid it out on the oblong table. On the top, in her neat scholar's hand, she wrote STEPS TO SAVE CYRNA.

Falgar looked mildly amused. "A to-do list?"

Hildegard shrugged. "It helps to organize my thoughts."

"Suppose the first thing we ought to do is retake Cloudfire," Sullivan began, but Hildegard was already shaking her head.

"Our welcome there was already worn thin three Cycles ago. If we'd listened to the people of Toreen to begin with, we wouldn't be in this mess. No more poking around where we aren't welcome. We'll deal with Callahan one way or another, but when we do, the castle should remain where it always belonged — in the hands of the Toreenish."

Dax nodded. "No doubt he intends to set up shop there once Aeris has fallen, but for the moment, our spies say the Emperor kept his word to his new allies. Gideon was left in charge of Cloudfire, while Callahan and his forces have returned to Kasanarae."

Tai pursed her lips, clearly unhappy with the thought of leaving Cloudfire in the cult leader's hands. But if she had any objections, she didn't voice them.

Hildegard dusted her hands. "Either way, we have a year to stop disaster. Tai, you say you know how to do that. Is that correct?"

Tai straightened her feathers and nodded. "I may not be some mythical Savior, but I'll save Aeris if I can. We just need seven dragonauts and the moon glass." With a weak laugh, she added, "No pressure. We have six dragonauts now, so we'll need to recruit one more, and find a dragonstone somehow."

Hildegard dutifully wrote NEW DRAGONAUT, DRAGONSTONE, and MOON GLASS on the parchment.

Dorian awkwardly raised his hand. "Um, I hate to be the one to point this out, but we only have five dragonauts."

"Six," Tai said, giving him a pointed stare. "Which brings us to what I think the next line item should be."

Hildegard nodded, and, seeming to guess what Tai was thinking, wrote "RESCUE SOLARIS" in her neat and efficient hand. Dorian felt a rush of warmth and affection for them both.

"Sounds to me," Hildegard said, "Like all these lead us to the same place."

Tai nodded. "The Kasani Fountain Palace. Good news is, I know my way around there now. Bad news is, it'll be risky. Extremely risky."

"Risky?" Falgar snorted. "Let me tell you about risky. In the past two years, I've been attacked by assassins, beaten up by town guards, and thrown in prison twice. Twice!"

Dorian flushed. "I'm sorry..."

"Don't be!" Falgar spread his arms. "Most fun I've had in my life.

But the point is, I am sick to bloody death of being rescued. This time, I want to do the rescuing."

The others all nodded in agreement.

"So, that's the agenda," Tai said. "Free the dragon, steal the moon glass, save the world. Easy."

"A cake walk down strudel lane," confirmed Falgar.

Dorian scratched his neck. "Now you're making me hungry." But his levity was short lived. He felt better knowing they had a plan, but with that plan in place, he could no longer hide from what he knew he needed to do. What he'd always known he'd need to do, if he was honest with himself. "There's... one more thing."

"Go ahead," Hildegard said.

Dorian downed the rest of his wine, thinking that if there was any time he needed some liquid courage, it was now. "My whole life I've been too afraid to act." He sat up straighter, hands curled into fists. "You say you're tired of being rescued, Falgar? Well. I'm tired of the people I care about *needing* to be rescued. I'm tired of people getting hurt because of me. My father, Solaris, Hematite, Tanis, you. But you're all not *just* being hurt because of me. I see that now. It's because of *him*, too. The threat against Aeris, the capture of those dragons, it *all* comes down to him. And that's why..." He drew in a sharp breath and let it out. "I know what I have to do now. I failed on the flagship, but I *won't* fail again."

The others exchanged worried glances, but then, one by one, they nodded, united and resolute.

Hildegard picked up the quill pen and added one last line item to the parchment.

ASSASSINATE JANUS CALLAHAN.

ACKNOWLEDGMENTS

This book took three years to write, an eternity in the world of indie publishing. During that time I learned a ton about the writing process, and I probably learned more writing this book than I did over the years of false starts and abandoned rough drafts I spent writing book 1. I am so privileged to finally be able to release Dorian and Tai's story into the world. Obviously, I could have done none of this alone.

Thanks always and especially to Matt for supporting me through some difficult times, last-minute beta reading, listening to my whining, and pushing me to get the darn thing out into the world, already.

And thanks again to the Fireside Writers, Elizabeth Mitchell and Elise Baldwin, for always being there to bounce ideas off of, helping me fix my sticky plot holes, and making poor Tanis's entire character arc make sense.

I suppose I also owe apologies to Dr. Frances Bagenal from the University of Colorado, whose extremely well-taught lessons in planetary science I completely ignored, along with many of the laws of physics, when building the world of Cyrna.

Thanks again to Keylin Rivers for the excellent cover art and Nathan Hansen for the beautiful interior art.

Lastly thanks to you, the reader, for making it all the way to the end of book 2! It sincerely means a lot to me, and I hope that you will stick around for the end of Dorian and Tai's journeys in book 3.

ABOUT THE AUTHOR

Morgan lives in Washington State with their husband, child, and an enthusiastic corgi. When not writing, Morgan enjoys lifting weights, making digital art, running, and dabbling in game development. Morgan has worked as a software engineer, science lab assistant, and cashier at a haunted tourist destination, but their first love has always been bringing fictional worlds and characters to life.

 bsky.app/profile/morgankbell.bsky.social

 facebook.com/morgankbell

 instagram.com/dragonmorganbell